TREASURE FOREST

Treasure Forest

BOOK ONE OF
THE FOREST INSIDE TRILOGY

Cat Bordhi

ACE BOOKS, NEW YORK

THE BERKLEY PUBLISHING GROUP
Published by the Penguin Group
Penguin Group (USA) Inc.
375 Hudson Street, New York, New York 10014, USA
Penguin Group (Canada), 90 Eglinton Avenue East, Suite 700, Toronto, Ontario M4P 2Y3, Canada
(a division of Pearson Penguin Canada Inc.)
Penguin Books Ltd., 80 Strand, London WC2R 0RL, England
Penguin Group Ireland, 25 St. Stephen's Green, Dublin 2, Ireland (a division of Penguin Books Ltd.)
Penguin Group (Australia), 250 Camberwell Road, Camberwell, Victoria 3124, Australia
(a division of Pearson Australia Group Pty. Ltd.)
Penguin Books India Pvt. Ltd., 11 Community Centre, Panchsheel Park, New Delhi—110 017, India
Penguin Group (NZ), Cnr. Airborne and Rosedale Roads, Albany, Auckland 1310, New Zealand
(a division of Pearson New Zealand Ltd.)
Penguin Books (South Africa) (Pty.) Ltd., 24 Sturdee Avenue, Rosebank, Johannesburg 2196, South Africa

Penguin Books Ltd., Registered Offices: 80 Strand, London WC2R 0RL, England

TREASURE FOREST

PRINTING HISTORY
Namaste Publishing hardcover edition / December 2003
Ace trade paperback edition / April 2006

Ace trade paperback ISBN: 0-441-01369-4

Library of Congress: Control Number 2005 055 874

PRINTED IN THE UNITED STATES OF AMERICA

10 9 8 7 6 5 4 3 2 1

To you, the reader:
May you discover the ever-present grace of The Forest Inside

Contents

1. Down the Drain   1

2. A Will, and the Dearest Freshness Deep Down Things   4

3. Home Sweet Home, Daggett-Style   10

4. A Forest in the City   13

5. A Pond and Its Mystery   21

6. Raccoon Ruffians and Experiments   32

7. Terror and an Invitation   39

8. Another Mysterious Visitor, and a Funeral   43

9. Footprints and a Private Eye   46

10. The Forest and the Basket   54

11. The Garden Beneath   61

12. Living Like Scaredy-Cats   70

13. The Deal   77

14. Kaleidoscope Eyes   79

15. Through the Pickle Jar   92

16. Trading Places   96

17. Falling into a Trap   105

18. The Booklet of Betrayal   111

19. Raven-Boy   118

20. A Willing Captive   126

21. *You Could Die Trying*   133

22. *The Light of Home*   140

23. *Struggle and Surrender*   143

24. *Skunk Cabbage*   148

25. *The Lie Takes Root*   153

26. *The Search Begins*   157

27. *The First Lesson*   163

28. *A Treasure Found and Lost*   166

29. *Organized Chaos, and Comfort*   170

30. *Daggett's Maze Is Discovered*   176

31. *Loyalty and Lies*   182

32. *The Coyotes*   188

33. *A Tree in the Sea*   193

34. *Aloft*   200

35. *Dragonflies, Mountain Goats, and Cow Magnets*   208

36. *The Golden Thread*   215

37. *Grandpa Henry's House of Marvels*   223

38. *Rupert Fox, the Trickster*   228

39. *The Homing Device*   232

40. *Knitting a Tree House*   238

41. *Namasté*   247

42. *The Tree of Many Apples*   251

43. *The Yellow Socks*   259

44. *Silver to Gold*   268

45. *A Riddle Unraveled*   280

Acknowledgments   287

About the Author   289

Down the Drain

Through his wet eyes, Ben's unfinished map looked as blurry as his future. He paced back and forth in his small bedroom, clenching the hand-made drawing. How could Grandma Daphne be dead when he could almost hear the whisper of her voice, and sniff the freshly baked ginger cookies in her kitchen? And that breeze that filled her white curtains until they danced like ghosts now seemed to be billowing through his room, lifting the hairs on the back of his neck. Suddenly an ambulance screamed past his house with a merciless howl, shattering his reverie and leaving him shaking. There had been no ambulance to save his grandmother. Not in the forest. If only it had happened when she was visiting them here in the city, she might still be alive.

During the long months of seventh grade, Ben had dreamed of the forest by spending hours painstakingly filling one half of a large white sheet of paper with familiar details: the steep cliffs and springs of Mount Portal, winding pathways, creeks, the cedar throne, disappearing deer trails, the giant boulder that had split in two so you could walk through it, the pond, and the towering fir tree he'd climbed last year to watch ravens playing in the sky and to see beyond his grandmother's side of the forest. Down the middle of the paper he'd drawn the ravine and swamp that divided the forest into his grandmother's side, where he and his younger sister, Sara, spent summers exploring; and the far side, forbidden and dangerous. Until now he had kept his promise to his grandmother and never set foot in it.

At the sound of a knock, Ben folded the map and hid it inside a book.

"Ben?" Sara, wrapped in a blanket, her freckled face puffy and her eyes red and swollen, appeared in the open door. "I can't sleep," she sniffled. "Can I come in?"

"I guess."

Sara pushed the door closed with her long toes and curled into a ball on the floor. Her white rabbit, Bijou, poked his head out of the blanket to sniff the air. Then he squeezed out one paw with a black mark on it that looked like a single clover leaf with a stem, and squirmed free, revealing another black mark, this one on his left hip, that resembled three clover leaves, without a stem.

"What's going to happen?" Sara's voice came out in a squeak. "Who'll take us to the forest now? Mom hates it there."

"Maybe Dad," replied Ben. "I'd rather go alone anyway."

"How could she have died?" cried Sara.

"Heart attacks just happen," Ben muttered, pushing his dark hair out of his eyes. "You'd better go back to bed now."

"How will we spend the summer at Grandma Daphne's without her?"

"I have no idea. In case you haven't noticed, I can't sleep either."

"I miss her!" sobbed Sara.

During the week after her death, Grandma Daphne's empty house in the forest received special visitors. Right now there were two. One was hiding at the edge of the meadow, watching the other visitor, who was just leaving.

Archie stepped out onto the front porch, wiping his eyes on his sleeve. Daggett waited until the white-haired man set down his tattered briefcase and began to shuffle through his keys, then threw back his head and let loose with a string of piercing coyote howls. From the far side of the forest his pack responded with a lunatic symphony of yips, shrieks, and screams. Archie froze, and the keys dangling from his motionless hand ceased moving as if they too were stunned. The sun slid behind a dark cloud, abandoning the man to clammy coldness, and a menacing growl rumbled across the meadow. Seizing his briefcase, which caught on a nail and gave way with a ripping sound, Archie lurched towards his car and fled, having quite forgotten to lock the house.

Once the engine's sound faded, Daggett trotted out of hiding, padding over the spring grasses that were just beginning to shoot up. As he passed beneath the apple tree, two pink petals fell on his gray, straggly hair. Another crept beneath his collar.

This was too easy. He pulled the door open and left it swinging, creaking on its rusty hinges, and began to prowl through the two-story wooden house. In the dim hallway he stared at a fading black and white photograph on the wall. For a moment the sinister expression on his face dissolved, and his eyes softened around the memory they held. Then a tremor of anger rushed through him. His breath quickened, and he moved on. He searched the bookcase in the living room and removed a small volume, tucking it inside his patched jacket, ignoring the basket beside Daphne's spinning wheel. Behind his back, something rotated slowly beneath its green cloth.

In the kitchen he turned the faucet on full blast and grinned at the sight of the clear water swirling down the drain, back into the earth. The well would run dry. With luck, the pump would burn out as well. He studied Daphne's shelf of homemade preserves, dropped a jar in each pocket, and stepped out the back door, leaving it swinging. A black fly buzzed inside as Daggett slipped out, and a moment later, the lanky man vanished into the forest, back across the swamp to his home.

A Will, and the Dearest Freshness
Deep Down Things

"Fill her up and check under the hood, will you, Roy? I'm going inside for coffee."

"Sure thing, Archie," the attendant replied.

The café door swung shut with a bang, and the waitress looked up. "Morning, Archie. Breakfast?"

"Just coffee today, Sylvia. I'm driving up to the city." Archie nodded at a deputy sitting at the counter. "Morning, Joe."

"Hey, Archie."

"Say, Joe, do me a favor, would you? Keep an eye on Daphne's house if you're out that way? I've got an uneasy feeling about it."

Joe gave a short laugh. "Sure. But what could happen? Nothing ever happens around here."

"So why wasn't Daphne's daughter at the memorial service?" asked Sylvia, handing Archie his coffee. "Went all through school with her, would've been nice to see her again."

"Lily didn't much like it here," murmured Archie. "Real uncomfortable. Guess they had a private service for Daphne in the city."

"Lily always was a little spooked," said Sylvia. "High-tailed it out of here the minute she graduated, like she couldn't wait to escape Cedarwood."

Archie sighed. "I remember. Not sure what's going to happen now." He started for the door. "You'll check on the house?" he asked Joe again.

"Yup. Don't worry about a thing," replied the deputy.

·   ·   ·

"Ben, Sara," Lily Maclennon explained, "this is Grandma's lawyer, Archie Greenwalt. He's come all the way from Cedarwood."

"Weren't you one of my grandma's friends?" asked Ben.

"We've heard stories about you," said Sara, looking curiously at the stranger. She pushed her apricot-colored hair behind her slender ears.

Archie smiled. "Your Grandma Daphne and I were friends ever since childhood. I helped her with legal matters as well." He put a warm hand on Ben's shoulder. "You were just a little guy, maybe two years old, when I moved away eleven years ago." Ben shuffled his feet in embarrassment and shoved his oversized hands in his pockets.

Turning to Sara, Archie added, "And you—you were just taking your first steps. My, but you look just like your grandmother did at your age. You must be what, twelve?" Sara nodded. "Looking at you brings back memories." He stared at Sara until tears came into his eyes. "Ever since I returned last fall, I watched Daphne counting the days until your summer visit." His face drooped and his voice grew hoarse. "She didn't quite make it. I am so, so sorry."

"Could we maybe live with you this summer?" asked Sara. "We *have* to spend our summers there."

"Sara, really!" cried Lily. "Go on, you two. Go find something else to do."

"Actually," Archie said. "Ben and Sara are named in the will, so they need to stay."

"I see. Shall we sit down?" Lily wiped her eyes and nodded to her husband, Peter, who pulled out a chair for their guest.

"Tea?" Lily asked, her deceased mother's china teapot poised above a mismatched set of cups. A bead of water began to swell at the bottom of a hairline fracture on the porcelain pot, and fell to form a tiny damp circle on the tablecloth.

"Yes, please." The quiet that followed was embroidered with the tinkle of the last cup being filled. "A fine woman she was," Archie murmured. His fingers twitched, and at the sound of crinkling paper, everyone's eyes darted from his face to the will in his hands.

Archie took a sip. "Daphne insisted on writing her last will and testament in her own words."

To my daughter, Lily, I leave the home you grew up in. Please consider living there with Sara, Ben, and Peter for a year or two, before deciding what to do with it.

Lily gasped. Ben and Sara threw her an eager look, and when Sara began to speak, Ben kicked her under the table. Archie looked up at Lily, his eyes scanning her face as if searching for clues in the pages of a book he'd read a long, long time ago. He sighed, and turned back to the will.

It's not that far from the city, so Peter can travel back and forth as needed for conducting his business. There should be enough money left in my bank account so that you can take a few years off from teaching if you like. Sara and Ben could attend the same small school in the village as you did, or you could teach them yourself for a year if that suits you better.

I promised the grandchildren I'd try to fix things so they could always be here. They love the forest and Mount Portal like I do, and like their Grandpa Henry, who they never knew, also did. You could say it's a family tradition. Now that I am gone, I hope you'll keep my promise alive, and that the house and land will always stay in the family. Since I am leaving the property in your hands, it is now up to you.

Lily, we are all safe here. You knew that when you were a little girl, and then you changed. If you will just watch your children and learn from them, you can rediscover what you knew once. It is my final wish for you.

Lily stared at her children as if they had suddenly been replaced by alien doubles.

To Sara and Ben I leave the enclosed envelopes.

Archie hoisted his elbow to point at two bulging, oversized white envelopes beside his cup.

They are to be allowed to open them privately, without being asked to share what is inside. I also leave each of my grandchildren the sum of $100, which they may spend without comment or interference from anyone. Children, as always, I trust you to honor the boundaries in the forest and not go beyond them.

To Peter I leave my collection of poetry books. Some may need rebinding; I know you will take care of them with your wonderful talent for reviving what the poet Gerard Manley Hopkins called "the dearest freshness deep down things."

Lily, it is that heavenly dearest freshness deep down in things that Ben and Sara know so well from their summers here in the forest, and that you must find and trust once again. I am not blind to your terror. I know our house and the forest bring back memories. But I beg you to take the risk of facing your nightmares so your children can continue to grow here in their heaven. Ben and Sara are on the threshold of discovering the forest's deepest treasure within themselves, so that they can be with it anywhere. But unless they have more time here, I fear they may lose their way, and have to go through much suffering to earn this knowledge again. Do not let Ben and Sara suffer as you have, my dear. Let them flower here in their heaven while you discover that your nightmares are imaginary.

To Archie Greenwalt, I leave the bag of steel jacks we used to play with when we were young. You can't get good jacks like that anymore. You'll have to buy a new red rubber ball yourself. Thank you for your friendship and help all these years.

"Not the jacks!" cried Lily. "I need those. They—they're the last thing I had before—"

Archie looked at her with surprise, then slowly nodded his head. "Oh, yes, of course," he said, "I don't need the jacks. I want you to have them." He exhaled and stared into his cup. "The paperwork will take a few more weeks, but you could move in anytime you like. Well, once school is out." He looked up. "That is, if you decide to." The echoes of coyote cries were creeping through him and biting at the spaces between his heartbeats. He tried to shake them away.

"We'll go, won't we?" begged Sara.

Lily collected the cups and carried them to the sink. Peter threw a troubled glance in his wife's direction, and stuffed his hands in his pockets. "We'll think it over. There's quite a bit to consider," he said and shook Archie's hand. "Thank you for coming. And for letting my wife have the jacks."

Archie smiled. "It's quite a game. Daphne could play for round after round, picking off twosies and threesies, never bumping the others, like magic. It was a spectator sport, playing with her, it was. I hardly ever got a turn, because she never missed."

"Will you play jacks with us when we move to Grandma Daphne's house?" Sara asked Archie.

"I hope we can do that," he replied. "You and your brother may just have some of her magic in you." He smiled awkwardly at Lily, who had wrapped her arms tightly around herself, tears dropping from her haunted eyes. "I'll be in touch," Archie assured her. "It's a long drive back, so I'd best be on my way. Please let me know if there's anything at all I can do. If you decide to move, we'll be just a few miles apart, and I hope you'll think of me as a nearby friend."

"Call me when you're ready to play jacks, eh?" He winked at the children and let Peter usher him out of the room.

The two men stopped to talk behind the closed door of Peter's workroom. Ben tiptoed into the adjacent bathroom and locked the door. So he could hear better, he took the toilet paper roll and laid it flat against the wall, and then pressed his ear over the hole. Through the small round chamber he could clearly hear Archie speaking.

"Don't you worry about that old hermit. Daggett stays in his part of the forest," Archie said. There were muttered words from Peter, and then Archie spoke again. "I know. No one's ever been able to get Lily to talk about it." Archie's voice dropped, and Ben couldn't make out what he said next. But he could hear them opening the workroom door, so he switched his toilet paper spying device over to the other wall.

"Are these old family pictures?" Archie was asking. He must be looking at Ben's dad's collection of sepia portraits in the entry.

"Some of them," said Peter. "It's what I do for a living. Resurrect lost images in old photographs, restore antique books and old letters, manuscripts, that kind of thing."

"Daphne hung on to a lot of memorabilia," commented Archie. "Attic's full of it. Photos, letters, newspaper clippings, and more. From way back."

"I've seen a bit of it," said Peter. "Thanks for coming, Archie. I'll be in touch."

Home Sweet Home, Daggett-Style

Only the scritch-scratch of his jacket catching on the crooked branches revealed Daggett's movement beneath the underbrush, and there was no one to hear it, as usual. But the sneaky habits he had adopted over fifty years ago, when he had first hidden away from all mankind in this forest, had become ingrained.

And so Daggett crawled like a four-legged animal through the maze of tunnels hidden beneath thickets of sword ferns and prickly salmonberry bushes. The maze finally led, if the correct turns were chosen, to a passageway descending into the earth mound that buried his home near the base of Mount Portal's steep cliffs. A jungle of greenery had long ago disguised the mound. Unless an invader managed to discover one of the entrances, there was no way to know the forest floor hid a cozy home.

The passageway opened into a large round chamber. Daylight streamed through the dozens of huge upside-down pickle jars Daggett had embedded like skylights in the roof. Decades ago he'd collected the jars from behind the Cedarwood general store in the middle of the night, taking just one every few months, careful as always not to around suspicion. The last thing he wanted was for townspeople to come looking for their pickle jars or other missing belongings in his woods.

A shelf holding jars of dried herbs curved around the wall, and snares and traps crafted of wood and sinew hung from roots that grew through the ceiling. The cleverly built devices were designed, it seemed, to catch rabbits, squirrels, and deer that populated the forest. But Daggett made sure his human scent coated the snares and traps before he set them out, so the wildlife he shared his forest with would avoid them. It was people the traps and snares were designed for, not to capture them, but to make them retreat for fear of being stabbed by razor-sharp carved spears or strangled by spring-loaded nooses. For years, this strategy and certain others had kept invaders out.

Next he reached under his jacket for the book he'd taken from Daphne's shelf, and slowly turned a few pages beneath the light filtering through a pickle jar skylight. Daggett stopped when he reached the page with the poem. There it was. All those years ago he and Daphne had memorized it together. He'd forgotten everything but the one line that streamed through him like his own blood: "There lives the dearest freshness deep down things." To his surprise, the long-lost lines of the poem crowded awkwardly around the familiar words, as if they no longer belonged together. He trembled and closed the book to shut them out, then added the volume to his collection of stolen books in a fruit crate.

His boots and pants were still damp and stank of swamp slime from the trip home. As he built a small fire in the pit in the center of the room, steam began to rise from his legs, and the fetid smell began to bother him. Until his ravens had alerted him to Daphne's death one week ago, he hadn't crossed the swamp in years. Adding wood to the fire, his mind replayed for the hundredth time the events of that day.

He'd climbed the mountain to spend a few days high on the rocky summit where he could watch the spiral-horned mountain goats, creatures he admired because they survived on so little and did not trust him. From the edge of the towering cliffs he had a view of his territory as well as Daphne's home, her forest, and the village of Cedarwood. It had been early morning and he was crouching behind a scrubby tree, watching a newborn kid bleat and scramble after its mother as she grazed along the thousand-foot drop at the edge of the ancient cliffs.

After they trotted out of sight, a movement in Daphne's meadow caught his eye. A tiny spot of yellow was leaving her house, and he knew it had to be her. She disappeared in the trees and reappeared in the clearing where there was a cedar stump carved like a chair, and sat down. But she hadn't moved from the chair all day, even when the sun began to sink. When Friend and Wife, Daggett's ravens, began to soar in circles above her, giving their sharp alarm cries, he knew something was wrong. He'd started down the mountain at once, but it had taken him all night and half of the following day to reach her.

And just as he was finally near the edge of the clearing, he'd heard weeping, and spotted Archie, bending over Daphne's limp form. Instantly Daggett had retreated behind a tree, his heart frozen. When Archie hurried back towards the house, Daggett had crept up to Daphne. It was eleven years since they had last spoken, and that had not gone well. Flooded with confusing memories, he stood beside her until he heard footsteps, then vanished behind the trees. Archie and two strangers had carefully loaded her on a stretcher, covering her with a sheet, and carried her out of the forest forever.

Dancing flames licked at the old man's hands and awakened him from his trance. Soon he had a pot of barley bubbling on the hearth, and another of bracken fern tips, and the swamp smell was replaced by a nutty fragrance. He broke an egg into the pot of greens and watched the transparent gel turn white. Fern tips were one of his favorite spring delicacies, lasting only a week or two. But he ate good porridge every day all year round. He did his grocery shopping in the dark of the night by slipping into barns on the edge of Cedarwood, collecting a few eggs, and filling a bag with grain. A few missing handfuls from a fifty-pound sack of feed for the horses or cows would never be noticed. Nor would the quart of milk he took from a sleepy cow.

After supper, Daggett washed his dishes in the hollowed cedar log that carried a stream of water from the mountainside through his home and then dropped down to disappear into the talus beneath his floor, deep with centuries of broken rocks fallen from Mount Portal's cliffs. The talus swallowed every drop of water that entered it, and kept his house dry. He took his drinking and cooking water from the top of the log, and washed at the bottom, and always had clean running water.

He pictured the faucet he'd left running in the house on the other side of the forest, and smiled. His water was running non-stop too, but it always had, courtesy of nature. Daphne's system was limited, and would self-destruct. If he could not have her, he would at least take possession of the forest she had loved, and make sure her home rotted, dissolving into the earth from which it came.

A Forest in the City

After saying good-bye to Archie, Peter returned with a somber face. "You two head upstairs," he ordered Ben and Sara. "Your mom and I need to talk."

"Can we have pizza for dinner tonight?" asked Sara.

"Out!" demanded her father, and shut the door after them.

"Mom's going to ruin everything!" groaned Ben as his sister followed him down the hall.

"She can't keep us from moving there," insisted Sara.

"She will, though. Wait and see." Ben slugged the banister. "She wouldn't even let us stay with Grandma Daphne until a few years ago. Like the forest was *dan-ger-ous*. Made her promise to stick close to us the whole time." He shut the door at the top of the stairs behind them. "I would've gone crazy if I hadn't snuck out at night." He grinned at his surprised sister.

"You snuck out? How?"

"It was easy. Nothing wakes you up, and Grandma's hearing wasn't so good."

"Where'd you go?"

"The forest, of course." He raised his eyebrows. "I know things you don't know."

"Like what?"

"Why would I tell you?"

"You don't know anything." Sara glared at her brother and then looked away. "I'd sure like to know why Mom acts like there's a monster out there."

"That's exactly what I've been investigating," said Ben. "Like all those Daggett stories no one wants to talk about."

Sara rolled her eyes. "Grandma Daphne always told us they were mostly rumors."

"I'm serious. You know how Dad and Grandma used to stay up late talking when she was here?"

"How would I know? I sleep at night."

"Well, I like to know what's going on," replied Ben. "And you can get out of my room now, because I'm going to open my envelope." He opened his door. "Out!"

Sara shook her head. "Wait," she said.

✳ Downstairs, Peter shut the kitchen door and set water to boil for more tea. "Come on, honey," he begged his wife. "Relax."

"I can't!" Lily hissed. "How could Mom ask me to move there! Of all people, she knew best why I can't! I won't!" She laid her head in her arms and began to sob. A slow whistle rose from the teakettle.

"It's the same old thing, isn't it?" asked Peter.

Lily lifted her head and stared at her husband with wild eyes. "You promised not to bring it up!"

"I'd like to have a year out there," said Peter, "and it's obvious the kids—"

"Traitor!" cried Lily. "I can't, I just can't."

"You could get over it," suggested Peter, handing her a steaming cup. "We could help you."

✳ Sara hugged her envelope to her chest, and planted her feet in her brother's doorway. "I'm not going to open my letter until we're at Grandma's so I can read it in the forest."

"That's stupid." Ben grabbed his envelope and sank onto a floor cushion. "Could be weeks before we go, or even longer. Could be never." He glared at Sara. "Go on, get out!"

"Wait!" Sara stopped him, her light blue eyes pleading. "Let's go there inside ourselves, at least. You know how Grandma made us promise to practice that. It'll only take a minute. Just let me go get Bijou."

While Sara was out of the room, Ben took his map out of its hiding place in *Tom Brown's Field Guide to Wilderness Survival*, which Grandma Daphne had given him for his thirteenth birthday, and stared at his drawing of the swamp and ravine that separated the two sides of the forest. Until his grandmother had suddenly died, he and Sara had been going to spend the summer with her again, and he'd been planning to fill in all the missing details of his map. Last summer he'd snuck out one moonlit night with a rope to lower himself down the steep ravine to Daggett's side, and had almost experienced the exhilaration of stepping into uncharted, deliciously forbidden territory, until he'd discovered his rope wasn't quite long enough to safely reach the bottom. To fulfill his dream of finding Daggett's lair, spying on him, and discovering first hand who and what he really was, Ben needed to explore in full daylight, and to do that, they had to move there.

I'm young, and Daggett's an old man now, he reassured himself whenever fear crept up his spine. He could always outrun the hermit if he had to, like a wily fox escaping an elderly grizzly bear. Every day after school, Ben practiced the thrilling chase, racing the two blocks home from the bus stop, his backpack slamming against his shoulder blades, imagining Daggett trying to catch him. And all winter long Ben had been practicing the "silent fox walk" described in the survival book, rolling each foot from the outside to the inside as it touched the ground, slowly pouring his weight down each leg like sand into a container, his alertness flowing forward like water. Why, if he never made a sound, he'd be practically invisible. And so Ben would finally learn the truth about this man that everyone feared. Besides, Grandma Daphne had always taught Ben and Sara, "Don't believe the things you hear. Believe your own experience." He couldn't agree with her more.

Sara returned with Bijou, so Ben hid the map, picked up his letter, and sat down, folding his legs beneath him.

Sara settled her rabbit in her lap and sat facing her brother. "Now," she began, "close your eyes and feel the Forest Inside." Their eyelids dropped, and their breathing gradually slowed until it sounded almost like they were asleep. "Are you there?" Sara whispered after a few minutes.

"Mmm-hmm," Ben mumbled. His face, like his sister's, had become peaceful, and the hint of a smile lifted the corners of his mouth. Their slow breathing washed the air like waves lapping the shore of a lake. The muffled whine of their mother's voice burrowing up through the floor did not distract them.

Ben's envelope rested in the tingling warmth of his relaxed fingers. In fact, his entire body tingled with alertness. When Grandma Daphne had first taught him and Sara to enter this wondrous place, they'd been outside on a sunny day, and the sun's fireworks behind his closed eyelids had filled his entire body with vibrating light. In the weeks that followed she'd guided them inside again and again, and Ben had been astonished that such an intensity of sunlight existed in his body even in the blackest night. Now, as he and Sara sat, his hunger to know what was inside his letter quieted. The envelope gently rose and fell with his hand, as if it too were breathing.

Footsteps clumped up the stairs. Ben opened his eyes, tightened his body, and fervently wished the interruption away. "I *was* in the forest," he muttered. The envelope lay lifeless in his clenched hand.

Their father opened the door, his head sagging. "Your mom's having a rough time," he told them. "Come on down and set the table." He turned and left.

"Don't move," Sara whispered when Ben started to get up. "Sink back down into the warm pool at the bottom of your breath."

It was that warm well of darkness that Ben knew so well, identical to the shimmering sun-stream although it seemed the opposite.

His sister spoke again. "Leave Grandma's letter here on the forest floor, on the moss, the leaves, and the ferns."

Ben put the envelope down, and it did seem to settle onto a soft surface, as if the hardwood floor were matted with foliage. He and Sara rose, brushed the leaves and dirt from their pants, and walked across the smooth floor to join their parents.

Ben slid the last slice of pizza onto his plate, stretching a glob of cheese until it snapped free, and dangled it into his upturned mouth. "Mom," he ventured, "Sara and I wouldn't mind if you were our teacher for a year. I bet it'd be a lot easier than a whole classroom of kids like you've got now."

Lily smiled weakly at her hopeful son. "Probably."

"We'd practically teach ourselves!" added Sara.

"You deserve a vacation," insisted Ben.

Lily pushed her plate away, choked on a sob, and rushed from the room.

Peter began clearing the table. "Don't worry," he reassured his stunned children. "This is, uh, normal behavior for someone who's just lost their mother. Try not to push her."

Back upstairs, Ben and Sara sat down without speaking and let their breath deliver them again and again to the place deep in their chests where a velvet space as still and moist as the air suspended inside a flower awaited them. *Home*, Grandma Daphne had called this, or the *Forest Inside*. Ben felt a river of air flow up through his chest, wobble at the top of his throat, then release to slide down into the deep silent pool of Home again, where he could bathe for what seemed like timeless moments, before rising with his breath for the next cycle. The powerful flow reminded him of his silent fox walk.

Ben opened his letter without asking his sister to leave. A carved wooden acorn fell out, and he caught it before it hit the floor. A cap etched with tiny scales topped the silken smooth shell, which had two small holes. He stared at it, forgetting the letter that remained.

"Can I see it?" Sara asked finally. Ben hesitated, then handed it to her. "So are these supposed to be bug holes?" she asked, peering into a tiny opening while holding it up to the light, and handed it back.

Ben tried blowing into one hole. Only a *fftttt* sounded. But when he tried the other hole, the room bristled with raven cries that continued long after he had stopped blowing. Both he and Sara searched the room for the bird, who was not there.

Ben blew again, and a symphony of bird songs rose and spiraled through the room. Luminous green treetops swayed to and fro against the blue sky behind Ben's closed eyelids, and he breathed in the familiar warm scent of the forest.

"We have the forest here," whispered Sara, staring at her arms as if they were clothed in feathers. "Even if we don't move to Grandma Daphne's, we *are* there."

Ben looked down at the acorn bird-flute in his hands. "You've got to open your envelope and find out if you have one too."

"Uh-uh," refused Sara. "I don't need an acorn to be in the forest."

Ben stared at her for a moment, then nodded.

In the waning light of the skylight above, stars began pulsing their tiny spikes of yellow-white light, and they sat for a long time, the letter forgotten. Quiet footsteps approached, and the dark room suddenly flooded with amber light.

"I came to say good night." Lily seemed puzzled by her children's peaceful faces. "Oh, you're reading your letters." She bent down and mournfully caressed her mother's familiar handwriting on Sara's envelope. "In the dark?"

"It's dark?" asked Sara.

"We could go to Grandma Daphne's for just a weekend, Mom, to see how you feel," Ben suggested, skipping over his mother's confusion. "I could even miss my baseball game."

"Maybe," sighed Lily. "And maybe not."

The forest's radiance was still pulsing through Ben. He placed one hand on his chest, on his Home spot. "Oh, Mom," he said, "trees comfort you if you let them. They practically purr."

Tears ran down Lily's face. "I don't know what you're talking about."

"You could learn, Mom," whispered Ben. "I'll help you."

Sara stood up and wrapped her arms around her mother. "I think that was Grandma Daphne's plan, Mom, for us to teach you. There's nothing to be afraid of."

"Home-schooling," said Ben. "The ultimate lesson."

In the forest, the molten gold of the sun had drained through the trees to disappear for another night, but the sky was clear and bright, and a dozen pale pickle jar circles of moonlight began their ghostly orbit across Daggett's floor. He lit a second beeswax candle and stretched out on his bed with his ragged copy of *Ishi, Last of His Tribe*. A brittle page fell out and fluttered to the floor. Daggett checked the page number and carefully put it back in place. He had never forgotten the awe he'd felt as a boy, holding Ishi's bow and arrow in the museum in San Francisco, and how kind the curator had been. The elderly man had actually known Ishi, a Native American who had survived alone in the foothills of Mount Lassen for several years after his tiny family had been hunted down by white settlers. The curator had answered Daggett's endless questions about this Stone Age survivor who had actually spent his final years living in the museum in the city. The curator had unlocked glass cases so the boy could touch the spearheads, snares, and bone tools that Ishi had made. When Daggett had run his fingertips over Ishi's death mask, he'd felt as if the mysterious man lay just beneath the thin material. The museum and the curator became Daggett's refuge from the home he shared with his violent uncle and bitter mother. And Ishi became his hero, the man he dreamed of being.

When the fourteen-year-old Daggett finally ran away the night his uncle held a switchblade to his throat, he'd hopped a freight train north to become another Ishi, to live free in the wilderness. But the city boy hadn't realized what would happen when he appeared alone in the small town of Cedarwood, hundreds of miles away. Everyone eyed him suspiciously, insisting on knowing his name and where his parents were. No one believed his story that he was an eighteen-year-old orphan, so he was placed in a foster home and sent to school. He started fistfights with his new classmates, threatened his foster parents, and ran away again. Daggett was caught and placed in a second foster family, who had a son his age, named Henry. At first Henry and his constant companions, Archie and Daphne, had tried to include Daggett in their activities, and the four had even begun to build an elaborate tree house in Henry's yard, with Daggett as the architect. But before the last floorboard was nailed down, Daphne had fallen for Daggett. She was smitten with the black-haired, defiant youth with the gleaming dark eyes of a raven. Daphne let him know, and he began to respond. Horrified, Henry and Archie realized that they were about to lose their devoted friend, so one morning before school Henry and Archie threatened to beat up Daggett if he didn't stay away from their Daphne. At recess Daggett attacked Henry. Blood was streaming down Henry's face when Daphne burst between them, screaming at the bewildered Daggett that she hated him and always would. He'd been put in the town jail overnight because Henry's family refused to take him back, and the townspeople soon concluded he was a savage beast. In the morning the sheriff led him to the station and shoved him on the next train, warning him never to show his face again. Daggett lowered himself out a window on the other side, hid in the forest, and became Ishi, following his original plan.

Daggett's mattress of cedar boughs and thick moss squeaked beneath him as he shifted to ease his aching bones. He blew out the candles, pulled his fur blanket around himself, and curled up like a lonely animal.

5

A Pond and Its Mystery

❉ Ben settled on his bed to read the pages of his grandmother's old-fashioned script.

If you are reading this, dear Ben, then I am on the other side, watching you. Hallo down there!

Now, I have a surprise for you. You know I love stories, and here's one I've been saving your entire life. On the day of your birth, there was a very old woman in the hospital waiting room with your Grandpa Henry and me. During those suspenseful hours she asked us if we'd like to hear a story about the forest. Of course we said yes. It turned out to be a kind of fairy tale, full of mystery and promise, and your grandfather decided it was a gift meant for you, for when you grew up a bit. So he asked a nurse for paper and wrote the story down on the very pages that you are now holding.

Grandpa Henry! He'd died while Ben was still a baby. Ben's heart was beating so hard he could feel it pounding in his ears. At the top of the first page of his grandfather's unfamiliar handwriting, he'd written, *"For my grandson, Ben."*

I was working at being born while he was writing this down! Ben gasped, ran a trembling finger over the word *grandson* and began to read the story.

A century ago, there was just one farm here in the valley. A man and his wife lived there with their three sons. They raised goats and made cheeses, which the farmer took to the village on the other side of the mountain to trade. The sons worked hard, milking the goats, taking them out to pasture, feeding the chickens and collecting their eggs, and cleaning out the barn. Their father built fences and helped birth the baby goats, grew corn and wheat and rye to feed the family and the animals, and taught his boys to carve pretty things to sell in the village. Their mother made cheeses from the milk her sons carried to her, and laid them in the root cellar to age.

Once a month the father left the farm to sell the carvings and cheese, walking most of the day alongside a small wooden cart pulled by Hansel, their donkey. He was always gone for two days, sometimes three, on these journeys, and was glad he could trust his wife and three sons to take care of the farm while he was absent.

One day the farmer returned with three puppies in his cart, and gave one to each boy. To the youngest boy he gave the largest pup, to the eldest boy he gave the runt, and to the middle boy he gave the liveliest of them all. The little dogs followed their young masters everywhere.

Because the wife and sons never went to market, and travelers rarely ventured as far as their farm, only the farmer himself was accustomed to meeting strangers and talking with them. Most of what the wife and sons knew about the rest of the world came from the tales he told them of his journeys. Nobody else lived within a half-day's travel of the family, and the little road that led to their farm stopped there, with nothing beyond but thick, dark forest and a tall mountain. At that time bears and wolves still roamed the deep forest and it was a fearsome place. So it was quite a surprise when one morning, about an hour after the farmer had set off, that a young woman with long dark braids walked out of the trees. She was alone, a basket swinging on her arm, and her feet were bare.

Strangely, the dogs did not bark. The eldest son's dog, the runt, went running through the open gate to the girl and sat, looking up at her eagerly. She kneeled before the dog to caress his face. Then she and the dog walked side by side towards the farmhouse, where the mother and three sons stood inside the garden fence, staring at her in bewilderment. The other two dogs waited until the girl came through the garden gate. Then they took positions beside her, as if presenting a noble guest to the family. When the girl set her basket down, the middle son noticed that it contained a folded green cloth, and it reminded him of something, although he knew not what. His dog picked up the basket in its mouth and carried it through the open door.

"Why, hello, miss," the farmer's wife finally managed to say, "however did you come here"—and she pointed to the forest—"from there?"

The girl looked at the farmer's wife the way a mother gazes tenderly upon a babe in her arms. Her eyes were like still pools of blue water. She did not speak, and the farmer's wife could not look away, nor did she want to. "Oh," the farmer's wife finally said, "oh."

All three dogs were sitting at the girl's feet now, looking up at her adoringly, and two barn cats were purring and winding in and out of her legs.

The youngest son spoke first. "Who are you?"

Her head turned towards him, and he felt the power of her eyes, and the tenderness of their silence. "Oh," he said, and sighed and said no more.

"My dog seemed to—know you," spoke the eldest son. There was eagerness in his voice, as if he hoped for something. The girl turned to face him, and he felt suspended in a radiance like the warmth of the sun as it melts like butter on the horizon at the end of a day. "Oh," he finally said, "oh."

The middle son wanted to speak, but before he could think of what to say, the girl turned to him and reached for his hands. The warmth and peace of a curled up, sleeping cat seemed to purr from her fingers into his, and the sensation rushed through him, filling his whole body. When she pulled her fingers away, he could not speak, not even to say, "Oh," and the shimmering feeling swam through his body like a school of fish.

When the girl walked through the back door of the farmhouse and sat at the table as if waiting for a meal, everyone followed her. The farmer's wife cut thick slices of bread and cheese for their guest, sliced a pear the eldest son brought from the orchard, and brewed her a cup of tea from the kettle of water on the woodstove. When the girl had finished eating, no one questioned her when she climbed the ladder to the loft where the family slept, wrapped herself in a quilt, and fell fast asleep.

"We'll let her rest, poor thing," said the boys' mother, although she felt foolish calling the lost girl a poor thing. She felt herself more of a poor thing than the girl seemed to be. "I hope she can speak. We'll find out after she wakes. Go," she ordered, and shooed her sons outside, "and get your chores done."

The girl slept all through the day and into the night. When the boys and their mother got up in the morning, she was gone. One by one they went outside to look for her. The barn cats purred and rubbed against the boys' legs as they searched the haystacks, the goats' stalls, and the tool shed, all in vain.

That evening the farmer returned. His cart was full of goods, and he was weary from walking all day long. His family gathered around him, but instead of begging him to share tales of his travels, they told him about the mysterious visitor.

"She didn't say a word," his wife told him, shaking her head. "Poor thing!"

"She had bare feet, but her clothes were beautiful," added the middle son.

"Our dogs didn't bark at her," marveled the eldest. "My dog ran to her when she came out of the forest, and seemed to know her."

The youngest son described how she had sat at their table and eaten bread and cheese and a pear, and drank a cup of tea, then climbed up the ladder as if she were familiar with the house, curled up in a quilt, and slept the rest of the day and into the night.

"And then," mused the farmer's wife, "when we awoke, she was gone."

"And we haven't found a trace of her anywhere!" complained the eldest son. "Do you think she'll return?"

The farmer couldn't make sense of the story, and asked for supper, so he could end his long day and go to sleep. "Maybe you imagined her," he said, shaking his head.

"We didn't," his three sons insisted, their mother nodding agreement.

The sons unloaded the cart while their mother put supper on the table.

After supper the farmer climbed the ladder and went to bed. His sons lingered outside until the moon rose, hoping the girl would return. Their mother stood and gazed out the window towards the forest. Finally the moon passed across the top of the sky and began to fall into the trees, but still there was no sign of the mysterious visitor.

The next day, and the next, there was no sign of the girl, and their father complained if they spoke of her. He believed his sons and wife had lost interest in him, and that the mysterious maiden had them under a spell. In the evenings he watched as his sons paused to stare at the rabbits, acorns, and coyotes they were carving, as if listening to the girl tell them where to cut next.

Weeks passed, and when there were enough cheeses and carvings to take to the market, he asked his wife to accompany him, hoping to win back her devoted attention. "Our sons are old enough to take care of the farm themselves," he told her. "And your customers want to meet you." And so it was that the next morning the farmer and his wife set out for the village, leaving their three sons behind.

The boys did chores near the forest, hoping their visitor would reappear. Late that afternoon, the middle son was sitting *on a log at the edge of the forest, sharpening his axe, when the girl suddenly glided from between the trees beside him, without even looking at him. She passed through the garden gate and climbed the steps to the back door, and disappeared inside. The boy flung his axe and sharpening tools aside and ran after her. She was not in the kitchen, nor in the big room where they sat at night. He slowly climbed the ladder to the loft, and there she was, fast asleep already, wrapped in a quilt like before. The toes of one foot stuck out, and he tucked the quilt over her toes and went back downstairs.*

When his two brothers came inside to eat the supper their mother had left for them, the boy was sitting as if in a trance. "She's upstairs," he whispered, "don't disturb her."

It was decided that the three brothers would stand guard, so that the maiden could not leave without their knowledge. Two would sleep on the floor while the third stood awake by the door, and when the guard grew weary, he would wake the next in line.

The moon began to cross the sky, and the brothers took their turns by the door. The eldest brother prayed she would awaken, and come down, so he could try to speak to her, but she did not. He could hear the steady whisper of her breathing from the loft above.

When the youngest son stood guard, he too longed for the girl to rise and climb down the ladder. He remembered her tender eyes, and closed his own to picture hers better. She seemed to appear before him then, and he felt himself grow dizzy, and suddenly shook himself awake. Had she left while he slept? He crept up the ladder to peer at her in the darkness. There she was, still wrapped in the quilt, sound asleep. Good.

Not wanting to risk falling asleep again while on guard, the youngest brother awakened the middle brother to take his place, and curled up on the floor beside the eldest brother to sleep.

This was what the middle brother had been waiting for. He patiently watched until he was certain his two brothers were fast asleep. Then he put on his boots and crept up the ladder. The maiden slept, or appeared to, as he gently wrapped the quilt around her and lifted her in his arms. He backed down the ladder, unlatched the door, and slipped out into the night. His dog did not awaken.

When the farmer and his wife returned that evening, the goats had not yet had either their morning or evening milking, and their udders were so swollen they were bleating and moaning. The boys were nowhere to be found. Cursing, the farmer and his wife began milking. The farmer's wife ignored her husband's anger, and looked dreamily towards the forest.

"It's that girl, isn't it?" snapped the farmer. "That girl came and lured them away!" His wife shrugged her shoulders and leaned down to pull the last drops of milk from her goat, and poured the bucket into the big jug.

They ate supper alone, but neither climbed the ladder to sleep.

In the middle of the night the eldest son returned. "I'm sorry," he said, hanging his head, standing limply before his parents. "I can't believe I forgot to milk."

"Where were you?" shouted his father.

"The girl came after you and Mother left," he answered. "Out of the forest again. She went upstairs to sleep like before, but ate nothing. We stood guard, one by one, but when I awoke, the girl and my middle brother had vanished, with the quilt."

His mother smiled, but his father cursed. He ordered his son upstairs.

An hour later the youngest son returned. When he told the same story, his father cursed and bitterly ordered him away as well.

The middle son did not return. His mother and father fell asleep by the fire, which had gone out.

In the morning the farmer forbid his sons to speak of the girl or their missing brother. "Milk the goats," he demanded, "and repair the fence. The buck will break through soon if you don't." After lunch he gave them more chores to do, until the day was done.

His wife spent the day in her vegetable garden, looking longingly at the thick trees and dreaming of what they hid. That night a bear lumbered out of the forest and carried off a newborn goat. The dogs had not barked.

Two days passed, and three. When five days had passed, the middle son returned. He walked slowly out of the forest, carrying the quilt, his eyes shining with a certainty that his brothers had seen in the eyes of red-tailed hawks.

Like the girl, he walked silently into the house and sat at the table. His mother cut the heel from a loaf of warm bread, added a wedge of cheese, and placed the food before her son. He ate without a word, then climbed the ladder, still carrying the quilt, wrapped himself in it, and fell into a deep sleep.

No one disturbed him that day, or that night, not even his father. In the morning the boy awoke and helped his brothers with the milking, but spoke not a word. He collected the eggs and shoveled manure out of the barn, then came in for breakfast. His father sat at the head of the table and watched his silent son, and felt afraid. The other brothers watched too, and waited.

That afternoon, the boy took a shovel and began to dig a hole in the meadow near the forest. He carefully cut clods of earth and piled them to the side. Soon he had dug a bowl the width of a man, nearly a perfect circle. Deeper and deeper he dug until the sun had almost vanished behind the trees. Finally he sat in the bottom, and then went to help his brothers finish the evening milking.

Still he did not speak, and the rest of the family began to speak less and less, as they watched him and waited. That night thunder struck the valley, lightening blazed through the blackness, and rain pounded the earth. In the morning the family rose and saw that little rivulets of water ran everywhere.

The sun shone brilliantly on the freshly washed world, and by evening the flowing water had soaked into the earth. The *hole the boy had dug was full to the brim, and the tiny pond, now undisturbed, became smooth. The blue sky reflected in its mirror-like surface and the pond became a blue jewel in the green meadow.*

At supper that evening, the boy began to talk. "I took the girl into the forest," he said. "Wrapped in the quilt, fast asleep. It was night. She awoke, and stood up. I wrapped the quilt around her to keep her warm, and took her hand in mine. Together we walked, the moon lighting our way. I did not know where we were going, but the forest seemed to belong to her, and so I just held her hand and walked with her. When we heard coyotes howling, she sang to them and they answered her.

"We came to a pond. She motioned me to sit down beside her, and I did. She gave me part of the quilt to wrap around myself, and we sat there together, huddled in its warmth. Neither of us said a word.

"I must have fallen asleep. When I awoke, she was standing like a statue in the moonlight in the shallows of the pond. Then she spoke.

"'I'm looking for what is at the bottom of the pond,' she said, 'I cannot rest until I get it back.'

"When she dove straight into the middle of the pond, I could not move. It was as if my body was not mine. After a few moments bubbles began rising from beneath the surface, and she surfaced, her braids black and streaming, her eyes silver in the moonlight.

"'I found it,' she said, but did not look pleased. 'It's of no use to me this way,' she added, throwing something to the ground.

"I went to see what she had dropped. It was just a dark rock. I picked it up and studied it in the moonlight, searching for something unusual in it, when she plucked it out of my hand and threw it back into the pond.

"'It's your turn now,' she said softly. 'At the bottom of the pond lies a treasure. It is useless, like that rock, if you disturb the water to bring it up. No one knows how to go down

there without disturbing the water. If you can do it, I will marry you.'"

The boy sighed, and his eyes rolled within to sink into memory. "That's why I'd carried her off into the forest. I wanted her to be mine." He released a long breath.

"'Now you know,' she told me. 'Now you know what you must accomplish.'

"In the morning she bade me go home. I refused. I had to at least try to find the treasure. I tried wading slowly into the pond, but that disturbed the water. I watched the fish swimming, and saw that they disturbed the water. I tried standing up to my neck in the water without moving, until the water became still again, but then I had no way of reaching the bottom without disturbing the water. She watched me trying and failing, again and again, and laughed and laughed. She wasn't making fun of me. It just made her laugh, until tears fell from her eyes, and her laughter made me love her more.

"Finally she spoke again. 'It is said that all effort is useless. A raven will bring me a message if you succeed, and if you do, I will return to you.' Before I could reach out, she began to glide backwards, her eyes on mine, warning me not to follow. I watched until I could no longer tell her from the trees. I stayed by the pond for three more nights, trying to come up with a way to search the bottom of the pond without disturbing the water. I failed completely. Why, I had no idea, even, what I was searching for! I remembered then what she had told me, to go home, and so I am here. I dug the little pond in our meadow to practice in."

The boy looked up at his family. His older brother seemed to be thinking very hard about something. The younger brother smiled at him, and responded, "I hope you succeed. I'll help you if I can." His mother seemed startled, and his father confused.

The story ends here, Ben. It is not a story with a finish, like most. Is there a way to retrieve a treasure underwater without disturbing the water? If you can do that, will it change your

*life? You will have to find out for yourself. This is your story,
Ben, and that is all I know.*

    Our love always.

    Your Grandpa Henry and Grandma Daphne

It was very late when Ben heard a soft knock on his door. Sara appeared, her eyes darting from her brother's face to the letter still in his hands. "So, can I—"

"No! It—it's personal."

"Oh. Well, whatever." There was envy in Sara's voice, and she added, "You look like you're in the forest."

6

Raccoon Ruffians and Experiments

Dawn was still breaking as Daggett prowled through the ruins of Daphne's kitchen. Crackers, cereal, rice, beans, noodles, everything in Daphne's pantry that hadn't been canned or bottled, was now strewn across the room. And the water was still swirling down the drain. He turned the faucet off, because he'd hiked over here to try one hot bath, a pleasure he only faintly remembered. Afterwards the well could run dry for good.

A shredded bag of flour lay on the bathroom floor, and the toilet bowl was full of what looked like lumpy pancake batter. Had the raccoons actually tried to wash the flour in the toilet?

Floating in the steaming bath was such a shocking pleasure that Daggett had to force himself to turn the kitchen tap back on afterwards by reminding himself to put step two of his plan into action. A rotten rat in the heating system would make the house unbearable.

He had just begun to poke around the inner workings of the basement furnace when the sound of tires crunching onto gravel made him jump. He bounded up the stairs and out the open back door, dashed into the woods, then crept between the trees until he had a view of the driveway, where he recognized a patrol car. He'd observed this particular deputy late at night, lazily cruising the empty streets, singing along to the country music on his radio. The vehicle idled while the man gazed at the house, and then he gunned the engine, and drove off.

Daggett carried the rotten rat down to the basement. The repulsive thing fit nicely behind the furnace's burner assembly, with just the end of his tail sticking out. Its stink would reach the keen noses of the vultures that patrolled the skies, and perhaps they would help the raccoons vandalize the house. A few minutes later Daggett walked out the back door again, leaving it ajar, looked around his new territory with satisfaction, and headed home.

Ben burst into the kitchen where his dad was buttering toast and his mom was slicing oranges. "We *have* to move to Grandma's!" he cried.

"What are you talking about?" Peter asked.

Ben waved the letter at his parents. "It's all here! Grandpa Henry and Grandma Daphne left me a task, and it can only be done in the forest. It's educational. I've been thinking about it all night long."

"Your Grandpa Henry? He couldn't have written that! Let me see," said his mother, and reached for the letter. Ben yanked it away.

"You can't read it!" he shouted. "It said so in Grandma's will! And we have to go live there or I can't do what they want me to do."

Lily turned to Peter. "He's probably making it up," she told her husband.

Peter looked sternly at his desperate son. "We can't read your letter," he said. "But you know, your grandma had no way of knowing if we'd really move there or not. I don't think she would have set you a task that was impossible, now, would she?"

A tear rolled down Ben's cheek. "Dad, please."

"We'll get there for a few weekends at least," Peter promised.

"No! I have to *live* there. I have to! It's my birthright," Ben cried. "And you can't stop me! If you won't move, then I'll—I'll live with Archie!"

"Go get your math book off the top of the TV, Benjamin," Lily shouted after him as he stomped out. "Put it in your backpack and then get in here and eat breakfast as soon as you calm down."

Ben was still not speaking to either of his parents after school and baseball practice. He got a soda from the refrigerator, pretending that his mother, who was correcting social studies tests, was invisible, even though she twice said hello to him.

Sara rushed in, cupping something in both hands. "Look!" she cried.

Ben glanced over out of the corner of his eyes and stomped upstairs, pulling his damp hand along the banister to make the squealing
noise that drove his mother crazy.

Lily peered at the small blue egg cradled in her daughter's palms,
her eyes lingering on the crack that zigzagged around one side.

"Can we save it, Mom?"

"It's a robin's egg, isn't it?" asked Lily, bending over her daughter's
treasure. She stiffened. "The mother won't accept it now that it's been
touched."

"What if I keep it warm in my hands?" pleaded Sara. "I'll hold it
until the baby bird is born. I'll be its mother."

Lily's face stiffened. "You can't save it," she declared. "Put it back
under the tree before you get too attached to it." And she turned back
to her papers. "I've got work to do."

In Ben's science class that day, they'd begun studying surface ten-
sion and had done an experiment of lowering a small paper clip flat
onto a saucer of water, so that it had miraculously floated on the invisible skin of the water's surface. And then they'd used eyedroppers to
mound water on the surface of pennies, so that the tiny ponds bulged,
until they finally burst through their invisible skins. Ben had been sure
this mysterious information about water would somehow help him
solve his secret riddle. But then he realized that he had to disturb the
invisible skin to even get into the pond.

Angry and impatient, he decided to ignore what he'd learned, and
do some independent experimenting. He walked past his mom, who
was conveniently ignoring *him* now, and dug a glass bowl out of the
cupboard, and filled his empty soda can with water. Back upstairs, feeling suddenly like the middle brother in the story, he lowered a stone on
a string right through the invisible skin. The water seemed to scarcely
move, even when he slowly pulled the string up and down a few times.
How was he supposed to see the water better? He ran downstairs and
was just slipping a bottle of blue food coloring in his pocket when his
mother said, "You making cookies up there?"

"I'm doing my homework," he answered sullenly. "That should
make you happy."

The thick blue drop went straight through the invisible skin as if it wasn't even there, and instantly branched into loopy tendrils winding around the string and stone, like a fantastic octopus with way too many legs. When he pulled the stone treasure up, the tendrils swayed gently as if synchronizing their movement to allow the treasure to pass through undisturbed. Could it be this simple? Mesmerized, Ben lowered and raised the treasure again and again until finally all the accumulated movement dissolved the strands of blue. And as they dissolved, Ben's excitement collapsed too. He wasn't supposed to disturb the water, period. And, whatever the treasure was, it sure wasn't going to have a string attached.

The sun-stream sensation of the Forest Inside was tingling in his arms, his hands, his whole self, so that his frustration mingled with hope. Grandma Daphne had always said that when you needed a really creative solution, you had to go inside to the silence of this sun-stream sensation, away from thinking. Let the solution rise out of the silence if and when it wanted to, not forcing it with your thinking mind. But Ben couldn't stop thinking. He obviously needed a real pond, like Grandma Daphne's, or better, the one he'd glimpsed last summer deep in Daggett's side of the forest, from his perch high in the tall fir tree. Could Sara have a riddle to solve in her letter, he suddenly wondered? She just had to open it now, because if she also had a riddle to solve in the forest, then their parents would absolutely have to give up and move.

That evening Sara ate her dinner with one hand, and refused to do the dishes because she had to keep holding her egg. At bedtime her father stretched a big sock over her hands to keep them safely together while she was asleep. Then he helped her climb into bed in between the rows of pillows she had arranged so she wouldn't roll over.

Ben knocked on Sara's door after their dad had gone downstairs. "Sara, you've got to read your letter *now*."

"Why?" Sara was gazing adoringly at her sock-covered hands.

"Because if your letter has a riddle like mine—"

"You have a riddle?" She looked up eagerly. "What kind of riddle?"

"It's basically an impossible task I have to figure out," he said. "I don't think I'm supposed to tell anyone. But you've got to read your letter and find out what your task is so we can convince Mom and Dad we have to move!"

Sara looked away from her hands. "You mean the task has something to do with being at Grandma Daphne's?"

"Definitely. It's impossible to do anywhere else. I already tried here and it was a complete failure. And," Ben figured this would be the clincher, "it was actually Grandpa Henry that wrote most of my letter. Don't you want to find out if he wrote yours too?"

"You are so lucky," cried Sara. "But he couldn't have written *me* a letter. I didn't even exist then."

Ben look discouraged, then brightened up. "I still think you should find out. Maybe he wrote something just in case there was a second grandchild."

"I doubt it," murmured Sara, and smiled blissfully. "My hands are pregnant."

"You're out of your mind," said Ben.

In the morning Sara still refused to open her letter, and flat-out refused to go to school either. "It's a matter of life and death, so I'm not going," she proclaimed, and lay on the couch reading, while the egg kept warm tucked under her armpit. "*I* am a good mother."

After wolfing down his lunch so he could play basketball with his friends, Ben sat like a lump in his history class where the teacher was lecturing about the uniformity of clay bricks in the ancient Indus River Valley. Ben was doodling in the margins of his notebook, drawing cutaway views of small ponds with a diamond in the bottom. Suddenly it was obvious: you had to come up from below!

Imagining he was the boy tunneling under the pond, Ben pictured the mysterious girl watching him vanish into the ground. She was totally paralyzed with admiration of his astounding genius. In a moment he would hand her the diamond! Obviously, she would be madly in love with him after that. She probably looked like—uh—like Rosa Tamaya, the dark-haired beauty who sat on the other side of the room and usually ignored him.

He drew a tunnel and connected it to the underside of the pond, right beneath the treasure, and suddenly stopped. The second he broke through, water would flood into the tunnel and drown him. In despair, he slumped down on his desk and buried his head in his arms.

"Ben? Ben?" When his teacher's voice broke through, he heard giggling and realized he'd been hearing her voice for a while. "Everything okay in dreamland?"

"Sorry," he said, and sat up, holding his pen as if ready to take notes. The teacher continued droning on about two ancient cities and how they kept flooding and getting rebuilt. Ben blinked his eyes and stared at the teacher. Flooding?

Then it hit him. Dry ice! If he tunneled down under the pond and brought dry ice with him, and pressed it up through the bottom of the pond, he could freeze the water so it wouldn't flood through, and then he'd get a blowtorch and melt the water *just* around the treasure—

The roar of the blowtorch became a ringing bell, and everyone stood up to go to their next class. Ben stumbled out, the blowtorch still blazing against the dry ice in his mind, and realized how pathetic his idea was. Freezing water and then melting it would disturb it. Duh!

"I'm worried about my baby bird," Sara whimpered as she came into the kitchen where Lily was leveling a cup of sugar for the brownies she was baking for dessert. "My egg smells funny." Sara sniffed at the egg in her trembling hand.

Lily quickly pushed a pile of broken eggshells out of sight behind the box of cocoa powder. Then she bent down to sniff Sara's egg, and straightened up with a sigh. "I was afraid this would happen," she murmured. "Your bird is dead, sweetheart. First he fell, and then his shell cracked—he was doomed from the start."

Sara burst into tears. "You're wrong! I'm going to wash my egg in nice warm water, and you'll see! My baby will live!" And she rushed from the room, almost colliding with her brother in the hall.

"I'll hold the egg for you for a while if you want, Sara," offered Ben, hoping to get on her good side so she'd open her letter. He rubbed his hands together to warm them.

"Go away!" sobbed Sara, and kicked the bathroom door shut.

.   .   .

Ben spent another restless night struggling with his riddle. He could glue metal to the treasure and use a powerful magnet to pull it up; or siphon all the water out of the pond until only the treasure was left; or he could train a big fat frog to bring it back for him like the golden ball in that fairy tale. At one in the morning he came up with his best idea yet. He'd get one of those inflatable arm-float things little kids wore when they were learning to swim, and put it around the treasure and then attach a tube and pump air into it until the treasure slowly floated to the surface of the water. Finally he had to admit that every single one of his brilliant ideas would disturb the water and that the whole thing was hopeless. Unless they moved to the forest, where all things seemed possible. And as he finally dozed off, he had one last idea: he'd just wait until the water was asleep.

7

Terror and an Invitation

The far-off yipping and barking of the coyotes awoke Daggett, and he stood beneath his smoke hole to listen. They were broadcasting news of a kill.

Quickly pulling on his boots, he crawled through his passageway into the starry night. When he slipped through the ferns, there was a sudden flurry of wings, and an owl hooted angrily and rose like an inky blur into the sky. As it soared past the moon, its clenched talons and the struggling mouse they held flashed in sharp silhouette. And then a howl pierced the darkness, and Daggett moved towards the sound as if it were a compass.

A ten-minute jog from Daggett's home the coyotes had brought down a doe. The biggest male stood with his front paws on the body and ripped at the flesh, while the others paced back and forth, waiting. When Daggett appeared, the male backed away from the carcass, then sat on his haunches, and finally crouched down, whimpering.

There was enough undamaged hide left to be useful, so Daggett skinned the warm animal. The loin, the choicest part of the deer, was untouched, so he sliced it out and wrapped it in the bloody hide. Then he leaned against a cedar trunk with his bundle in his lap, and watched his pack resume feeding. When morning came, his ravens would feast on the scraps, and add to their food caches. There was plenty for everyone.

It was still dark out when Ben awoke. He often rose before anyone else in the household, and liked it that way. In the stillness nothing moved except the thoughts that swam through his mind. He took a long swig of milk from the carton in the refrigerator door, tossed an apple in his backpack, and slipped out the front door without a sound. The streetlights were still glowing amber in the early dawn. Ben began to jog the ten blocks to a decrepit brick building slated for demolition. For days now, he'd been sneaking out early in the morning to explore it, determined to find any treasures it held before it was too late.

In the alleyway Ben had worked a board loose so it pivoted open and closed. He slipped through and climbed to the second floor. Behind a heap of water-stained papers, he'd hidden two crystal doorknobs, a heavy, old-fashioned black dial telephone with a fraying fabric cord, a marble paperweight, and an elegant fountain pen crusty with black ink.

Today he'd try the third floor. He crept up the stairs that spiraled around a central opening, so that he could look down to the very bottom floor as well as all the way to the highest. At the top, he spit into the opening and watched the glob drop to the marble floor far below, setting off a little dust storm.

The third floor had the same layout as the second, and Ben spotted another crystal doorknob. He reached for his screwdriver and began loosening it. The knob on the other side clattered to the floor, and he pulled out the knob on his side. Then he heard a noise. A scritchy-scratchy sound raced and paused, then raced and paused again across the floor on the other side of the door. Was it a rat, or a mouse? Ben reached through the round hole in the door where the knobs had been, to pull the door open and find out. Instantly something on the other side of the door seized his fingers and pulled his hand through the opening, and yanked the door shut. Ben screamed, "Let me go!" and struggled desperately to pull his hand free, but it was held tight. Held tight, by another hand! He wrenched his arm as hard as he could, kicked madly at the door, and shoved himself against it with all his might, but the hand on the other side didn't budge, and the more he struggled, the more deeply the sharp edges of the hole cut into his wrist. His opponent had the grip of a gorilla.

Somehow Ben stopped screaming, battling, and twisting. He tried to slow the stampede of his heartbeat and to stop gasping for breath. As he did, the hand on the other side of the door miraculously eased its grip just a little. With everything he could muster, Ben forced himself to relax his hand, and as he did so, his opponent's hand relaxed too.

Then the unseen hand actually let go. Wiggling his hand back through the narrow hole, Ben instinctively moved to the left so his enemy couldn't see him through the opening. He kept one foot wedged against the door, his body pressing it shut, and the other foot poised to escape, while his mind raced. The moment he moved, his pursuer would come through the door. He'd have to be fast, faster than him. Silently he counted, *one, two, three,* and turned and raced for the stairs.

Footsteps thundered behind him as he flew down the spiral staircase, and wrenched at the boarded window—but it was stuck. The man's breath was thick and hot on Ben's neck as he dashed down the long hall that led to the alley. Rubble blocked the alley door, so he raced up the narrow back stairs, taking three at a time, the crazed man panting behind him. Ben grabbed the crystal doorknob of the first door he came to, threw himself through, and slammed it behind him. There was an old-fashioned lock and he turned it frantically, then braced himself against the door. No sound came from the other side. His own breathing was harsh and loud, and his rapid heartbeat boomed like thunder. He struggled to quiet himself so he could listen. A small light in the gloom of the darkened room caught his attention. Eyes—red eyes! Two powerful hands seized his, and he fell backward.

Breathing as hard as if he had sprinted a mile, his heart heaving, Ben stared around himself in the dark. He was—in his bed—had it been a nightmare? Fumbling for his lamp, he flicked it on and stared blankly at the acorn lying in the circle of amber light on his bedside table. It seemed to glow in a comforting manner, so he reached for it, and switched the light off.

He fell back to sleep, and felt himself moving swiftly down a long passageway, as if pulled forward by a conveyor belt. At the end of the tunnel it became lighter, and opened into a bright clearing where a few people were moving about in what appeared to be cloud-like meadows. Out of nowhere he heard Grandma Daphne's voice.

"Sweetheart, you're letting your imagination hunt you down," she told him. Ben looked around but couldn't see her. Her voice continued.

"Rest in the deep presence of the Forest Inside. Your imagination won't bully you there."

"Grandma Daphne," Ben called out, "where are you?"

She emerged from one of the cloud-like meadows, striding towards him with a power he'd never known her to have before. "It's just a dream, Ben. Remember, when something terrifies you, and you cannot escape, return to your true Home inside, and with the eyes of Home turn and look into the eyes of whatever you fear. It will transform then, revealing its true essence behind the monster you imagine. But you'll have to discover this for yourself."

The ground, if that was what it was, suddenly fell out from beneath Ben's feet. He plummeted downward, drifting into forgetfulness, and came to lying in the alleyway behind the old brick building. Staring up at the sky, he felt the stars twinkling inside his body and shining through his eyes, as if he were the ocean reflecting the night's beauty, as if there were nothing in the world to do but be Home. Then a distant voice called his name, and up out of the silent shining sea there rose a pale image of the thirteen-year-old boy he was so familiar with, the one who played shortstop, detested asparagus, and had a geography test today. Ben the ocean was radiating warmth upon Ben the boy when suddenly the boy leaped to life and the sea faded and—

"Ben! Get up! It's nearly seven-thirty!" his mom was yelling. He sat up in bed, startled. A car alarm was blaring in the distance, and the jumpy brown scent of coffee tickled his nose. What *had* he been dreaming about? Grandma Daphne felt so near that he whirled around to see if she was behind him. She'd been telling him something important. Something about the ocean?

"Ben! School!" His dad's voice crashed, a huge wave thundering through the rest of Ben's fragile memory. Ben the boy groaned, tugged on his clothes, grabbed his heavy backpack, and bounded down the stairs to breakfast.

8

Another Mysterious Visitor, and a Funeral

Black flies were buzzing along jagged paths of air in the late afternoon sunlight above Grandma Daphne's tulips when a faded sedan swayed up the driveway and lurched to a stop. Two skinny legs swung out, then a cane poked into the gravel, and finally a grasshopper of a man straightened himself out as best as he could, and stared at the wooden house. He stood six feet tall, and his wispy gray hair stuck out in all directions. He scuffled around the side of the house, scowling, muttering to himself the whole time. When he reached the open back door his eyes grew bright.

On the top step he almost lost his balance when the stench of ripe rat hit him. Pinching his nostrils, he hobbled into the kitchen and gaped at the mess, then stuck a bony finger in a jam paw print and tasted it. "She always was a good cook," he said. Then he turned down the dimly lit hall.

At the foot of the stairs he looked up, but made no attempt to climb. Down the hall he went, to the hall closet near the front entry. He had to let go of his nose to open the door. Pushing the coats and jackets out of the way, he reached for the doorknob they concealed.

Sara buried her egg beneath the tree it had fallen from. "Oh, Mama Robin," she wept, searching the leafy foliage above, "your poor baby is gone." She held up the egg in case the mother was watching, then wrapped it in a sock. Meanwhile Ben held the shovel for her, taking shallow breaths to avoid smelling the egg.

He thought his sister was going way overboard, but he was determined to maintain a worshipful appearance no matter what. Then she'd owe him, and have to read her letter like he wanted her to. "I think I heard a chirp up there," he said hopefully.

"Grandma Daphne will take care of you now," intoned Sara. "Fly to her, little one." She laid the little bundle in the hole and wiped her face with her sleeve, then fell to her knees and sobbed. Ben rolled his eyes and handed her the shovel.

"You didn't come to the funeral," Sara accused her mother when she and Ben went inside. "Don't you even care?"

"Of course I care, honey," protested Lily. "I just didn't want to see you get hurt."

"So I wasn't even supposed to try to save the egg?"

"I knew it wouldn't survive. I guess you had to find out the hard way."

"It almost lived! You don't understand anything!"

"Sara's right, Mom," said Ben. "The bird had a chance of surviving. She did the right thing."

Sara looked at her brother with amazement and gratitude. *Score!* thought Ben.

"Well, we'll never know, will we?" snapped Lily, and resumed folding laundry. "And you are definitely going to school tomorrow, young lady!"

"Sara?" Ben had waited until evening to try his sister again. He heard sniffling behind her closed door, knocked, and opened it. "You okay?"

"No," she moaned.

"I just thought you might want to read your letter. It might make you feel better, you know, like Grandma Daphne's here or something? I'll bet you would've phoned her today if she was still alive."

Sara sat up. "Yeah." But then she lay back down and pulled the covers almost over her head. "No, I'm going to wait."

"Just go to the Forest Inside, and read it there. It's practically the same thing."

"No thanks."

"Sara!" Ben lost his patience. "You're going to mess everything up! Don't you even want to go?"

"Don't be a moron!" cried Sara, sitting up and switching on her lamp. "I'm not going to open my letter here, so don't ask me. But if that's what it takes to convince Mom, I'll tell her I did."

Ben smiled. "Fine. Do it your way."

· 9 ·

Footprints and a Private Eye

Archie noticed the light on his answering machine was blinking, and hit the play button.

"You'd better check on your friend Daphne's house," warned a muffled voice. "It don't smell too good or look too good."

Archie replayed the strange message. What in tarnation was going on?

Everything looked okay as Archie parked in Daphne's driveway, but when he tried the front door, it was already unlocked.

The hallway was covered in white footprints, and the house stunk like road kill. Archie covered his nose and froze, listening. Nothing. He crept down the hall, and as he passed the open bathroom door he was so surprised he let go of his nose. White goop was everywhere, except for the bathtub, which had a dark ring of scum around the surface. Archie studied the prints of a man-sized hiking boot, and realized that they were on top of earlier layers of raccoon prints and some kind of huge bird prints. So the house had been invaded first by raccoon hoodlums and hawks and then by a man? Archie gaped at the toilet bowl and the shredded flour sack beside it. Had a mad pancake thief in hiking boots attacked the bathroom? Am I going crazy? Archie groaned. Or dreaming?

When he glanced in the living room, he breathed a sigh of relief. The lunatics hadn't gotten this far, apparently. But the food splattered around the kitchen was enough to make him collapse on the threadbare sofa beside the refrigerator, the very spot he had spent many peaceful afternoons, watching Daphne putter around her tidy kitchen while they visited. He stared blankly through the open back door at the woodshed and wild forest beyond it.

So that was how the raccoons had gotten in. And the hawks, or whatever they were. But had one died and gone rotten to make this awful smell? Wait! He spotted a second shoe print, this one smooth-soled.

The shrill ring of the black dial phone on the wall jolted Archie out of his dismal thoughts. "Hello?" he said. "Hello?" There was a long hollow silence on the other end, which was abruptly broken by a wild laugh that echoed as if it were bouncing out of the far end of a long tunnel. "Who is this?" shouted Archie. He waited through a minute of silence, and then growled, "I know who you are. I recognize your laugh," and slammed the phone down. If only his words had been true.

It rang again.

"Archie? Is that you?" asked a familiar voice. "I tried you at home and then it occurred to me you might be out at the house."

"Who is this?" demanded Archie.

"Peter. Sorry about that. Just wanted to let you know we're planning on spending the weekend at the house. Lily isn't sure if she's coming yet. But the kids have been hounding me to go ever since you were here. We're hoping you can come have supper with us Saturday night."

Archie's heart sank. "Uh, sure. I'd like that. Let's see, today's—"

"Wednesday," said Peter. "We'll leave first thing Saturday morning. How about if we give you a call when we get there?"

"Great," replied Archie, closing his eyes to shut out the disaster before him. "I'll look forward to seeing you." The phone stuck to his hand when he tried to put it back in place. He pulled his hand away and stared at the smear of jam. He was supposed to get this place cleaned up by Saturday?

In this small town, gossip spread faster than spilled milk. If something interesting happened in the morning, it was supper table conversation in every home that evening. If word of this invasion got back to Lily, it would be all she needed to turn tail and run, if she ever even arrived to begin with. So he couldn't risk asking anyone to come help him clean up. There was only one person he could dare talk to, and that was Rupert.

Rupert, a private eye with a passion for bloodhounds, lived alone down the street from Archie. He'd give him a call now and ask if he could stop by on his way to get cleaning supplies.

But first Archie had to find the stinking carcass and get rid of it, or he'd probably have a heart attack, too. The stench seemed strongest near the heating vents. In the basement stairwell the smell was over-powering. The latch to the metal access door of the rusty old furnace was open and rattling. Archie peered down to look at the ring of flames inside the round metal burner. A thick wire was hanging out on one side. It didn't belong there, so Archie pulled on it. And then he screamed.

It was not a wire at all, but the stiffened tail of a roasted rotten ro-dent that had gotten itself wedged in the furnace. Its fur was singed off and its belly had burst open, so that the putrid insides spilled out. Why oh why hadn't he turned the heat off last time he was here? Archie kicked the nauseating creature into an old box, and fled up the stairs and out the door holding the container at arm's length. He galloped through the meadow and into the forest and flung the whole thing into the trees.

When he squatted by the garden faucet to wash his shaking hands, the tap choked, a few drops of water sputtered out, then nothing. No! Archie cursed as he made his way to the pump house, where he in-stantly recognized the telltale smell of smoldering electrical wires. The pump must have sucked the well dry, and be about to burn itself up. Archie slammed the off switch with his fist and collapsed against the door like a beaten man.

When Rupert appeared in his doorway in response to Archie's knock an hour later, the sinking sun's beams lit up the bristly hairs poking out of his nostrils. He motioned Archie inside, where a mourn-ful howl rose from behind a closed door. "That's Matthias," explained Rupert. "We'll have an easier time talking if he stays out of the way." And he gestured for Archie to follow him into the dim living room.

"So, talk," Rupert ordered when they sat down.

Archie explained everything to him in one hurried narrative, start-ing with the request in Daphne's will, Lily's reluctance to move, the hopeless mess of the house, the drained water system and the stinking rat, the strange phone message, the phone call with the crazy laughter, the two sets of footprints, and finally, that with Daphne's family arriving Saturday he figured he had no choice but to clean it all by himself to protect what little peace of mind Lily had.

Rupert listened without interrupting except for a few chuckles. "I'll try to get out there tomorrow and poke around," he said. "Save a couple of those footprints for me to take a look at. Now you mighta left the door open yourself, but it's not likely. But let's say you left it not quite latched and the wind blew it open. That explains the raccoons and the vultures. I'm surprised there weren't more'n two sets of footprints. You'd be surprised how many folks get curious after someone dies and go snooping through their stuff, especially if there's no neighbors nearby. May be some stuff missing. The message on your machine—that must've been a snoop. And rats, they squeeze into odd places all the time. Bet Daphne hadn't been servicing that furnace too regularly. But the caller with the evil laugh, well now, that's a stumper. Sounds like you've got an enemy. And more coincidences than could be coincidences."

"Do you think I should call the police?" asked Archie.

Rupert gave him a serious look. "If you do, you might as well hire somebody to help you clean up, 'cause the whole town'll know about it. On the other hand, if you don't call the police, you may regret it later."

Archie groaned and looked at his watch. "I've got to protect Lily from all this. Daphne had her heart set on getting her to move here with Peter and the kids. So I'll leave the police out of it. Thanks." He stood up. "Guess I'd better get started."

"Mom, Bijou needs more food. Will you take me to the pet store before they close at seven?" Sara started to put her rabbit down on the ironing board.

"Don't!" cautioned Lily, putting her hands beneath Bijou. "It's hot." She scratched him between his ears and smiled. "Your homework done?" Sara nodded. "Okay. Let me finish this skirt, and we'll go."

Lily slowed at the yellow light and watched it turn red. As cars hurried across the intersection, she glanced at her daughter. "I can't believe you're practically a seventh grader."

"Only two more weeks of school!" Bijou was squirming in Sara's lap. "They should make seat belts for rabbits, Mom."

"Maybe you'll invent them," laughed Lily. "And get rich."

"Mom? Can I ask you something?"

The light turned green and Lily moved forward. "What?"

"Is it Daggett that scares you so much?"

"Daggett?" Her hands clenched on the steering wheel. "That man scares *everyone*."

"But did you ever actually see him?"

Lily could feel Sara's eyes on her. If only you knew, she thought. "No," she lied.

"I'd like to see him just once," said Sara. "He's so mysterious. But I never will, will I?" She touched her mother's arm. "You lived there all those years and never saw him. Mom," she hesitated, "were Grandma Daphne and Daggett ever friends? Because, well, they *were* neighbors."

"What a ridiculous idea!" exclaimed Lily. "Of course not!" She laughed nervously. "After Grandpa Henry died, I worried myself sick thinking of Mom living out there all alone, nobody to protect her if something happened."

"You were worried about Daggett?" Sara probed.

"Partly. It's a lot more complicated than you think. Well, here we are," she said, and pulled into a parking space. "Let's hurry."

Sara tucked Bijou inside her jacket. "Grandma made us promise to absolutely stay away from Daggett's side. We're not stupid! We'd never ever break that promise, Mom. And we wouldn't be living out there all alone like Grandma did. You, and me, and Dad and Ben would all be there. You've just got to do what your own mother asked in her will! Don't you think she knew best? It was her dying wish, Mom! Please, oh please won't you at least come with us this weekend?"

"Maybe," replied Lily.

Hoping nothing new had happened while he was gone, Archie drove top speed through the waning daylight to Daphne's.

The house was dark, and the front door remained locked. Good. Archie stepped through the door, switched on the light, and nearly fainted. Scarcely breathing, he took small footsteps down the hall, his mouth gaping.

He looked in the bathroom and moaned.

And turned the corner into the kitchen. Someone had left a basket on the table. Archie lifted the green cloth to uncover the round shape inside. To his astonishment, nothing at all was there. Was that possible? He dropped the cloth into the basket and watched it fall into folds on the bottom, and then collapsed once more on the couch, gasping for air.

The house was spick-and-span. Cleaner, in fact, than Daphne kept it. He'd been gone less than two hours.

It was obvious: He was dreaming, or certifiably insane. With fingers shaking so hard his knuckles chattered, he dialed Rupert's number. "Rupert? Archie again. You're not going to believe this. Yes, I'm at Daphne's. Someone's been here and the place is totally clean. What? No, I'm not pulling your leg. I don't know, I haven't checked. I'll phone you back."

The tap was still dry. In the pump house he found the switch still off as he'd left it. Why couldn't the leprechauns who cleaned up the mess have fixed the water too? Archie's head pounded.

"Rupert, it's me again. No, the taps are still dry. And I forgot to tell you about the bask—" He stared at the sparkling kitchen table. *Where was it?*

"—the-the basket. It was here and now it's gone. It was full but it was empty. I'm going crazy. Rupert, could you come out? Oh. No, I understand. Night vision. Wouldn't want you to have an accident. I've got to go, Rupert."

✳ The sound of the ringing phone jolted Lily, and it took her a moment to remember she was home alone, since Peter and the kids had gone bowling without her.

"Hello?"

"Mrs. Maclennon?"

"Who is this? Are you a telemarketer?"

"No, Ma'am. I'm calling from the Cedarwood Real Estate office, Ma'am. My name's Al Reinhart."

"And why are you phoning me?"

"My family wants to offer our condolences for the loss of your mother."

"Thank you."

"And like I said, I sell real estate here in Cedarwood. May I assume that you are the heir to your mother's estate? Good. In that case, I must inform you that I received a phone call from an interested buyer, someone who's wanted the place for a long time, as a matter of fact. Have you thought of selling?"

"Well, actually, yes, I have."

"Good," said Mr. Reinhart. "I ought to have an offer for you in the next few days." He mentioned the buyer's name.

"Him?" Lily sounded surprised. She wrote down the agent's phone number, and after hanging up, stared into the distance for nearly an hour. Finally she stood up and stretched, then phoned the real estate agent back.

"Mr. Reinhart, tell your buyer that I'll be ready to sell in one year," she informed him. "But you must contact only me, and not my husband, about this, when the time comes. Is that absolutely clear?" Lily studied her face in her bedroom mirror, ignoring Mr. Reinhart's small voice in the receiver while he tried to convince her not to wait so long. "No. I've made my decision. I'll sell one year from now. My family will be occupying the house until then," she declared, and the sight of herself in the mirror, saying those words so decisively, astonished her. "Good night, Mr. Reinhart."

She started a bubble bath, and while it was filling went to phone Archie. The lilting tone of the message she left him sent shivers up her back.

At eight o'clock Archie stretched his aching limbs out on Daphne's living room couch and pulled an afghan over himself. Maybe when he woke up, things would make some sense. But when the phone jangled beside his ear, he jerked out of his troubled sleep with a fright. "Hello?"

"Archie? It's Peter again. Say, have you moved in or something?" he chuckled.

Archie rubbed his eyes and tried to clear his throat. "Actually, I was working on the furnace and thought it might be a good idea to just stay here so the house isn't left alone too much. I've heard of people sneaking into houses after people die, making mischief. Don't want that to happen here."

"Oh, you don't have to do that, Archie. Thanks, though. I just realized we don't have a key. Will you leave us one outside?"

Archie sat up straight. "Uh, how about if I just meet you here? The water pump's been acting up too, so there's plenty to keep me busy."

"Don't trouble yourself, Archie. Call a repairman."

"No, I'm happy to be useful, really. By the way, just so you know, a few days ago some raccoons got in and had a little fun. I think I got everything back in shape, but just in case I missed something, you might want to let the kids know, so they don't say anything to their mother. I figure it's best if Lily doesn't know about it."

"Good thinking," replied Peter. "Sounds like you're doing a lot. We'll make it up to you somehow."

Cricket music scratched through the night's black silence as Daggett rummaged through the second-hand clothes box in the shed at the back of the church. He pulled a musty-smelling sweater over his head, and one of his fingers popped through a moth hole in the sleeve, trapping his bent arm. Socks were what he really needed, but there weren't any in the box big enough for his long feet.

The Mercantile, where he liked to shop in the darkness, had recently put in a burglar alarm, so he didn't dare pick their lock again. So Daggett darted from shadow to shadow along the streets of the sleeping town until he came to a small house with a fenced back yard. Noiselessly opening the metal gate, he glided towards a large box built on to the wall. It had been a coal bin once, back when houses were heated with coal, and Daggett pried open the cover of the tin-lined compartment to see if there was anything inside. A paper bag, folded at the top, sat in one corner.

A light suddenly came on in the window above the coal bin. Daggett stood still as the window creaked up and a head stuck out. "That you?" a voice whispered.

10

The Forest and the Basket

An eighteen-wheeler thundered past the Maclennons' car, spitting gravel at their windshield as Peter slowed for the exit. Beside him, Lily clutched her seat and bit her lip.

"Wow! That sounded practically like a machine gun, Dad!" yelled Ben from the back seat, as his father pulled into a lonely gas station to check for dings and fill the tank.

"You kids need to use the restroom?" Peter asked.

"Can't we stop at the fruit stand later on like we always do?" begged Sara. "They have *huge* ice cream cones."

"Yeah!" agreed Ben. "Can we?"

"Grandma Daphne always got peach," said Sara. "That's what I want."

"Okay," said Lily. "Peter, let's just go on."

As they crossed the overpass above the busy highway, Lily gazed back in the direction of their city home. When she looked forward again they were driving down a two-lane road through fields of lettuce and broccoli.

"Look!" shouted Ben, leaning out his window towards a massive heap of rotting lumber. "That old barn finally collapsed!"

"Strawberries!" cried Sara, her hair flying behind her as endless rows of green dotted with red swept by.

"Roll up your windows," ordered Lily. "It's unsafe to stick your heads out like that."

Ben and Sara rolled their windows up an inch, turned to grin at each other, and then leaned back into the drafts of delicious air. "Just smell the fresh air, Mom," Sara said.

"It smells just like city air to me," sniffed her mother. "Nothing special."

As the car wound through the evergreen trees, a pair of ravens gliding high above in lazy loops began to tighten their turns. First one, then the other bird dropped out of the sky to plummet towards the vehicle. Twenty feet above the trespassers, they screamed, banked, and zoomed back up. Their alarm cries pierced the stillness as they rowed powerfully towards Daggett's side of the forest, where they vanished into the trees and were heard no more.

"I get the bathroom first!" shouted Sara, running up Daphne's porch steps ahead of Ben. The front door opened before they reached it, but instead of their soft grandmother with her dancing eyes and welcoming arms, there was only a white-haired man. Sara braked so suddenly that Ben collided with her.

"Welcome back," said Archie. He helped the kids untangle themselves and went to greet their parents.

Sara locked the bathroom door, and looked around. Her grandmother's toothbrush still stood in the same small glass, and Sara picked it up and held it like a sacred relic. She searched the floor for a strand or two of her grandmother's long white hair. But the bathroom was spotless. Horribly spotless. Close to tears, she unlocked the door and followed voices into the kitchen.

Grandma Daphne's collection of creek stones still sat in their bowl on the table, but their pool of water had dried up. Sara carried the bowl to the sink to refill it, and instantly the stones sprang to life, glistening with vibrant colors. "We call them 'river eyes'," she murmured sadly to no one in particular.

Ben leaned against the kitchen sink and looked out the window at Mount Portal's steep face towering nearly a thousand feet above the forest. "Remember Grandma Daphne's loaves of bread?" he asked his sister, and when he lifted the window a little and blew through the opening, tears began to stream down Sara's face.

According to their grandmother, the end of Mount Portal must have been sliced off, like the heel from a loaf of bread, and carried away. Where the heel had once been, was her home and the forest. Every time she took loaves of bread from the oven, she set them on a rack in the open kitchen window to cool, and blew their delicious fragrance towards the mountain. "Whatever happened to the rest of Mount Portal, I'll never know," she'd repeat to Ben and Sara each time. "But the dearest freshness deep down in things is never lost. So I bake bread for us to eat, and for the mountain to know it's still whole."

"Mom?" Sara wiped her eyes. "Can we bake bread?"

Lily was in the pantry. "I don't see any flour. Besides, we're just here for the weekend."

Ben jabbed Sara and gestured towards the drawer where their grandmother always kept a bag of peppermints for them. It was empty except for a beat-up spatula and some jar lids. Ben whispered, "The raccoons got them!"

Lily opened the refrigerator door and was surprised to see a platter of sandwiches. "I figured you'd be hungry when you got here," Archie explained shyly. "There's soup, too."

"Why, thank you," answered Lily. "How kind of you."

Ben opened the ceramic cookie jar he'd made in art class for his grandmother, and found it full of store-bought peanut butter cookies. He sniffed at them sadly.

"What's this?" Lily asked suspiciously, pulling out the ice cube tray from on top of a roll of bubble wrap tied with string.

"Our icicles!" cried Sara, opening it. "Grandma promised to save them. We never get to see any because we're never here in winter."

"But maybe we will this winter, huh?" asked Ben hopefully. "It would be very educational."

"Go get the bag of groceries from the car, will you, son?" his dad asked, and Ben grabbed a couple of icicles and headed outside, where he held them up to the edge of the roof to see what they'd looked like, and then bit the end off one.

Sara stepped into the stillness of her grandmother's bedroom at the end of the hall. When she raised the window, a puff of forest-scented air lifted the white curtains and they floated down around her like a blessing, as if her grandmother were welcoming her home.

"Was that window open?" Her father's voice surprised her.

Sara whirled around. "I opened it," she answered. "Grandma likes windows open."

"Whew," sighed Peter. "Let's make sure we close everything up good when we leave."

Lily had put the soup on the stove and begun to rummage through the hall cupboards where her mother kept knitting and spinning supplies. She pulled out squashed bags of yarn that smelled like her mother, a mixture of sheep's lanolin and cedar.

"Mom?" Sara tugged at her mother's sleeve. "Dad and I set the table, and the soup's hot."

"I'll be there in a minute," Lily told her. "Call Ben." Suddenly her own mother's presence blossomed behind her, like the warmth of a summer day, and the sensation was so familiar that Lily turned around. But there was no one there.

"Mom! We're eating!" hollered Sara from the kitchen.

Ben refused to try the pea soup, but took a cookie. "Grandma Daphne's were at least a million times better," he mumbled, his mouth full.

"They were, weren't they?" murmured Archie sadly. "By the way, be careful about using too much water this weekend. The power to the pump must have flipped off last week, so the tank's low. I've had it refilling since yesterday."

Lily sighed. "I don't know how my mom ever managed all that on her own. Well, I want to pick up a few things in town for dinner. You'll stay and eat with us tonight, won't you?"

Archie nodded.

Lily drove very slowly down a street beneath arching maple trees, and parked in front of a house with a scruffy front lawn. After staring at the house and gnawing on her fingernails for a few minutes, she drove away.

"Please, Dad!" begged Ben. "Just for one hour?"

"I'll take the kids out if you want," offered Archie. "I know the forest pretty well."

Peter looked at his watch. "I guess that'd be fine. Thanks, Archie."
He gave Ben and Sara a very serious look. "Don't be too long, though.
We don't want your mother worrying. It's two o'clock now—if you're
back by, say, three-thirty, it ought to be okay."

Sara darted upstairs to get her grandmother's letter. In the pantry
she grabbed a clean canning jar, and wrapped it inside her sweatshirt.

Peter watched out the kitchen window as Sara skipped through the
meadow beside Archie, a garden trowel stuck in her back pocket and
her bulging sweatshirt tied around her waist, talking and gesturing,
while Ben galloped ahead and vanished into the trees. "It's a start," he
sighed. Then he hurried upstairs and through a narrow passageway to
the attic storeroom.

Lily drove once again through the canopy of maple trees, a bag of
groceries on the seat beside her, and parked. There was no sign of life
behind the faded green curtains. She bit one last shred off her thumb-
nail and turned off the ignition. Clutching her handbag against the
butterflies in her stomach, she walked up the pebbled cement walkway
to the front door and gave a timid knock.

"Wait for us in the clearing!" Archie hollered ahead to Ben, and
smiled at Sara.

"I'm going to open my letter today," Sara told him.

Archie wiped a tear from his eye. "You are truly your grandmother's child," he said. "Waiting all that time for something precious."

Ben was impatiently dancing from foot to foot beside his grandmother's cedar throne when they arrived. "If you two want, you can
go on without me," Archie told the kids. "I figure you could use some
time to be with your grandmother here in the forest, and you don't
need me around for that."

"Hey, thanks," said Ben gratefully. Sara nodded.

"Just stay on the trail, be back in an hour, and stay together,"
Archie warned them.

"We will," they promised, and set off, while Archie settled himself
in the carved chair where Daphne had died, and began to talk to her.

·　　·　　·

The main trail meandered through the forest up a gentle slope to the base of the mountain cliffs, about two miles away. Just before the cliffs, a deer trail turned to the right, and followed the winding curve of the rock walls, staying about thirty feet away, as if the deer were held back by some invisible power. Grandma Daphne wasn't held back by any invisible power, though, and she'd once led them off the deer trail to a spot in the rock wall where water stored inside the mountain came trickling out of a crack, streamed down the side, and then disappeared underground. Her eyes had traveled up the long cliffs, as if searching for something, and Ben and Sara's eyes had followed. "There's a cave way up there, and at the end of one passageway there's a waterfall. It fills a pool that drains right down through the mountain. It might be here," she'd said, cupping her palms so they filled with the spring water, "that it finally comes out." But she would never explain to them how she knew about the cave, or how to get there.

Ben and Sara left the main trail before they were even halfway to the base of the mountain, turned to the right into the forest, and began to greet one familiar tree after another as they made their way towards the pond. There was no trail to get to the pond, and apparently never had been. And no trail was needed, because Grandma Daphne had introduced them to each tree along the way and taught them to feel each tree's presence by pausing to lay their palms flat against each trunk.

Ben abruptly stopped. "I want to go on by myself."

"But we're supposed to stay together," protested Sara.

"What could happen? Archie'll never know. I'll meet you where we left the main trail in about forty-five minutes, okay?"

"All right," agreed Sara. "I'm going out to the split boulder, just so you know."

Sara came to a creek, splashed water on her face and arms, then climbed over a fallen tree to the other side, and continued through the woods, past the oak tree she and Ben had named Watchful One, because two knot holes halfway up its trunk resembled eyes. Gazing up through the branches, her eyes filled with such brightness that when she looked back down, she was momentarily blinded. Her foot knocked against something, and she bent down to see what it was.

A willow basket lay on its side, and a green cloth spilled out. Sara was brushing bits of dirt from the soft fabric when a raven's sharp "Quork!" shattered the silence. She couldn't see the bird through Watchful One's leaves, but heard the breathy whoosh of his wings and called, "Quork! Quork!" back to him.

Sara had almost forgotten about her letter and how little time she had. She set the basket in the curve of a branch and hurried towards the boulder.

"I can't guarantee you anything," the person on the other side of the chipped table told Lily. "He's unpredictable."

"I'm just asking that you sincerely make the offer," explained Lily. "It would give me comfort to know that he might make everything better." She gulped. "Somehow."

"And if you change your mind at the end of the year?"

"I won't, believe me!" snapped Lily. "There's no way."

The imitation raven cry had come from Daphne's side of the forest. There was a haunting quality about it that Daggett could not place, although it had made his heart quicken in an odd way. But this was certain: the imitator was an invader who must be stopped. Daphne's territory was now Daggett's, so he deftly darted across the unsteady logs floating in the swamp and leaped onto his raft.

"I'd forgotten how small the grocery store is here. Where is everyone?" Lily asked Peter as she handed him a bundle of asparagus and a quart of half-melted vanilla ice cream. Her shoulders tightened when he told her the kids had gone for a walk in the forest with Archie.

"He'll stay right with them, won't he?"

"I'm sure he will," muttered Peter. "He knows everything, doesn't he?"

"I suppose," murmured Lily. "But did you make him promise to stay with them?"

"No," replied Peter. "Relax, would you?"

11

The Garden Beneath

Sara quickened her pace, following a deer trail through a thorny thicket and then through a massive boulder, which had split in half eons ago. A deer or a person could walk right through the tall, narrow cleft. Grandma Daphne had loved this spot, and claimed that you could sleep right in the cleft of the boulder, and stay cozy all night long because of the heat the rock absorbed during a summer day. Out the other side was a grassy hillside, where Sara began to dig a hole to fit the jar she'd brought.

She took the envelope out of her pocket and stopped. "Being in the forest is a beautiful experience," Grandma Daphne had often told her, "but if the forest is only outside of you, you are missing it almost completely." So Sara sat still, her eyes unfocused, her hands motionless, feeling the forest wash through her, filling her with its magic. And now the sensation of Grandma Daphne's shimmering presence arose, as real as the cry of the ravens overhead.

When she tore the envelope open, a wrapped object fell to the ground. She stared at it for a while, then turned away to read the papers in her hand.

Sara, the first page began, *there is so much I have not told you, that I could not. And alas, I cannot tell you now, either. Instead, I am passing you on to my friend Esther. You have not met her. Let me explain.*

I was born in the city, and spent my early childhood there before we moved to Cedarwood. My mother's Aunt Eva lived close to where my home is now, near our forest, and she was my mother's favorite aunt. She was already an old woman when I was born, but hale and hearty. Her husband had died years earlier, and her children had all long ago married and moved away. But, she had managed to live alone, keeping a small farm going all by herself, with a little help from neighbors. Summers, Mother and I and my younger brothers and sisters would go spend a few weeks with Aunt Eva, helping her and enjoying country life, while my father stayed behind to supervise his office. It was on one of our summer visits, when I was about eight years old, that Aunt Eva took me aside.

"Come with me, child," she said, and led me down into the root cellar. I thought she wanted help bringing up some pickles. But to my great surprise, she lifted three planks from the floor and revealed a trap-door set into the underfloor. There was a tarnished flat metal ring hinged to one side, lying in a small carved space. The door, the ring, and the space were caked with grime, and thick with dust and dirt, as if they had not been used in a very long time. While I looked on with big eyes, Aunt Eva reached down and pried the ring up, her farmer's fingers strong and wiry. The door began to creak, and she tugged and struggled, until it suddenly snapped open, and she nearly fell backwards.

"Grab it before it falls!" she cried, and I seized the dark wood with both hands, steadying it while Aunt Eva regained her balance. "There," she stated, as if now I understood what was going on, and propped the door open with a crate of carrots. "There," she repeated, nodding her head, as if the first "there" had just been confirmed.

I had no idea what was going on. I peered down into the darkness and could see nothing but the rungs of a dusty ladder reaching down into the gloom. I thought of rats, and spiders, and shivered.

"It's not like that," murmured Aunt Eva, as if she could read my mind. "Nothing to be afeared of." She reached into her apron pocket and pulled out a candle and a few matches. When the candle burned brightly, she stepped onto the ladder

and descended, holding the candle high in one hand and steadying herself with the other. As she lowered herself and the candle into the ground, I bent down and began to make out the shape of a room. The walls appeared to be made of packed earth, with wooden beams every few feet. "Come down, carefully," Aunt Eva called up, and I gingerly eased myself down the ladder after her.

When my feet finally stood side by side on the packed earth floor, I saw that indeed this was a room, about the size of the root cellar above, and that the beams held up a wooden ceiling, with the door cut out. I suddenly wondered if this was such a secret place that no one else ought to know about it, and what would happen if one of my brothers or sisters peered down into the root cellar, or if my mother saw it. At that moment, Aunt Eva poked a long pole with a claw at the end through the hole and hooked the metal ring and pulled the door shut. The candle sputtered and flickered as the air adjusted itself, and before I could say a word, Aunt Eva turned and headed down a passageway I had not noticed before. She turned and smiled at me, and I followed her, thinking of spiders and rats in spite of her promise that there was nothing to be afeared of.

We continued traveling down the narrow passageway, which seemed to slope slightly downward, for several minutes. Beams were spaced along the walls just like in the room we had left behind, and the wooden ceiling kept the dirt from caving in on us, I supposed. I wondered if this was a diamond mine, and had just begun to imagine a treasure chest full of family jewels when Aunt Eva blew out the candle.

"Don't be afraid, Daphne," she spoke softly, and groped in the dark for my hand. I held onto her bony, rough hand like it was the diamonds I had dreamed of, for fear danced in my head like a devil. It was blacker black than I had ever seen in my life. Here I was, with my Aunt Eva, deep under the earth. I felt something tickle my leg inside my pants and I screamed.

"Shh," Aunt Eva hushed me. "You'll wake them. This part we have to move in the dark." And she tugged at my frightened *little hand and of course I followed her as she moved slowly forward, down the tunnel into what seemed the very heart of the earth.*

She said not a word, and after a while I realized that whatever had tickled my leg had gone. I wanted to reach down to stuff my pants into my socks, so nothing could crawl in there, but couldn't because Aunt Eva did not stop. We continued for I know not how long. My heart was hammering in my chest and against my throat like it wanted to get out. Still we continued.

We must have traveled a quarter of a mile underground when Aunt Eva shook my hand away from hers, for I hated to let it go, and then she struck a match, filling the air with a sulfur smell. Then, she lit the candle again. I have never been so happy to see another face. Her lined, sun-burnished skin glowed in the red flicker of the candle, and her deep green eyes shone with excitement. "We're nearly there," she promised me, suddenly looking oddly childlike. With a renewed sense of hope, I grasped her free hand and we continued down the passageway, which I saw had changed from before. The walls were still earthen, with beams and a wooden ceiling, but roots of plants wiggled through the walls, making me smile, I knew not why. I thought I saw a green tendril several times, which puzzled me, for I knew that without light a plant is white, like the grass that tries to grow out from under a rock. And I believed that the only light here was our candle.

That is where I was wrong. The passageway suddenly took a sharp turn, a curve that reminded me of a tendril's little spiral tip, and then another and another, and soon I realized that the light around us could not all be coming from the candle alone. I could not detect any windows or holes between us and the world above, but even so, the passageway was growing warmer, the air softer, and the flickering shadows thrown off by the candle had vanished. We were surrounded by the kind of light you see in the minutes before the sun begins to flatten its bottom against the horizon. Aunt Eva slowed her pace, and suddenly sat down with her back against the earthen wall, her knees pulled up beneath her chin, and I noticed that the candle had gone out. She spit on her fingers and pinched the charred wick clean, then stuffed the candle back in her apron pocket. Patting the ground beside her skirts, she motioned me to sit too.

I gladly dropped to the ground, out of breath. I leaned my head against her warm bulk, and she put one arm around me.

"Where are we?" I asked.

"Just wait," she whispered, and hugged me closer to her. I must have closed my eyes, snug in her warmth, and drifted into sleep, for the next thing I remember is a hullabaloo. Elves in pointed red hats were scampering about, waving flaming twigs, and I was clutching my hair, trying to keep from being burnt. Aunt Eva shook me and whispered, "Shh," and my dream faded, but not entirely. "Keep your eyes open and you'll see," she promised me. I strained my eyes to their full width until they hurt, and stared about me, still huddled beneath Aunt Eva's strong arm.

I thought I could see the elves, but I wasn't sure. Something was moving faintly about, but it was green, not red, and then I realized. Leaves were growing everywhere, so fast that it was like one of those speeded up nature movies you and I have watched together. But back then there was no such thing as a movie. It was real.

The leaves were not bright and clear like we are used to, rather they were like fairy leaves, there but not there. Roots grew too, shooting their thin white selves in and out of the soil, and pale silky hair sprouted thickly along the fast-growing tips. Unlike the leaves, the roots were bright and clear as day. I turned to look at Aunt Eva and frantically leaped up and stared all around me. She was nowhere! "Aunt Eva!" I screamed.

"Here I am, child," she answered, stepping out from a tunnel that branched off the one I had been sitting in. I saw that she held a small trowel in her hand and a packet of seeds. I ran to her, and she led me down the new tunnel to a garden. It was different than the gardens you are used to, for it was a garden from underneath. Roots and silky little root hairs flowed *through the soil like a million tiny rivers finding their way through the ground. Lush green foliage waved and expanded above it, but transparently, as if it were not quite here. I suddenly recognized that I had been hearing a humming sound for some time, and that it was now quite a bit louder. It was like the sound of a whole meadow full of crickets, but without the rhythmic rise and fall of their song. It sounded like a million crickets all melted together, filling the air with a vibrancy and intensity that made every cell in my body tingle.*

I do not remember what happened after that, dear Sara. I know you will want to know, but I do not have an answer to give you, dear girl, who I am watching from above as you read this. At some point I shook myself awake, and saw that I was riding behind Aunt Eva on her old mare, Brunhilde. My arms were around my great-aunt (for that is what she was, being my mother's aunt, that would make her my great-aunt, but we never called her that, as it was too big a mouthful), and Brunhilde was ambling along the fence line, which Aunt Eva checked for breaks every afternoon so her cattle and sheep wouldn't escape.

"Were we just underground?" I asked my great-aunt, and I could feel her belly shift as she turned around to look at me.

"Yes," she answered, and turned back to study the fence.

"How?" I asked again.

"Don't you pay that any mind," she answered, and pulled up on the reins. Brunhilde stopped her plodding and Aunt Eva leaned down to examine the barbed wire, tipping me with her, for my arms were locked around her waist. Then she righted herself and me, and Brunhilde resumed her walk. "Some things are better left unsaid," she murmured.

"Was it real?" I pleaded.

"I don't know," she answered after a long time. "Tell me," she suddenly swung around to gaze down at me, and Brunhilde snorted. "What was the most important thing you saw down there?"

I looked up at her and shrugged my shoulders. She gave me a look that said I'd better come up with an answer, so I pressed my face against her back and felt her softness and Brunhilde's wide warm rump beneath me, and as we swayed along the grassy path beside the fence I pondered her question.

"What I liked best is how the roots grow white and then somehow they turn to green leaves," I suddenly blurted out.

"That's good enough," Aunt Eva said softly. "That's very good."

That night before supper, Aunt Eva sent me down to the root cellar to bring up a jar of dilly beans. There was a twinkle in her eyes as I looked back at her, and when I reached the root cellar, I found the three floor planks still propped against the wall where Aunt Eva had left them. The hidden door was plain to see, and when I bent down to examine it, I noticed that the dust and grime and dirt were as thick as before. Sure there would be fingerprints, I studied it like a detective. Nothing! The flat metal ring was buried in grime and dirt and no matter how I screwed up my eyes to have a better look, it showed no sign of ever having been pulled free. I'd given up, and was just about to lay the last plank back down when a voice came from the top of the stairs. "Daphne, may I come down?"

It was my small brother, Jack. He wasn't allowed to go up or down stairs without permission, because he was only three. I climbed up to him, and led him down the stairs.

"What's down there?" he asked, pointing to the space where the last plank would go. He poked one finger into the grime around the ring and held his hand up, admiring the crown of dirt on his fingertip.

"Don't," I complained, and studied the ring in the door. His tiny finger had left a clear mark. I felt more confused than ever. "Watch out," I told Jack, and eased the last plank down over the hole.

We left for the city the next day, before I could find a private moment to ask Aunt Eva more questions. That winter she was in a train climbing towards a pass in the Rocky Mountains, on her way to visit her son in the East, when an avalanche came roaring down a mountain, right into the train. A string of cars bounced off the track, dragging other cars with them, and over a hundred passengers died before help arrived. Aunt Eva was one of them. Her farm was sold before summer came, and we never went there again.

I suppose you're wondering about Esther, who I mentioned way back in the beginning of this long letter to you. She'll most likely show up in the forest. She is a funny one, full of tricks, but every trick is meant to teach you something. Trust her.

I wish I could tell you more. I can't! I want to tell you that Esther will carry on for me, like another grandmother for you, but she is more than that.

There will come a time when you and Ben can read one another's letters, and you will find a strange correspondence between them that cannot yet be seen. I hope you haven't already read each other's letters, but if you have, not to worry. The amazing thing is that the most obvious truths remain hidden until you are ready to recognize them.

Above all, trust the forest, the mountains, and the water, and the way their goodness rises in you.

And now I will say goodbye, dear child. You know you are a daughter of my heart, a grand daughter indeed. I shall always be loving you from above.

Your Grandma Daphne

The sun had moved across the sky while Sara sat, and warm air had begun to undulate and dance above the boulder's surface. "Thank you," Sara whispered, "thank you. I have no idea what your story means," she added, "and then I do, do I ever!" She was shaking her head slowly, and it would have seemed to an ordinary onlooker that she was far more puzzled than anything else.

But this was not what the onlooker who had padded silently through the trees was thinking. Daggett peeked around the side of the boulder, holding a leafy branch in front of his face as camouflage if the girl should look his way. Who was she? His eyes weren't what they used to be, so he had to creep closer to see her better. He silently moved into the cleft of the boulder, and peered out at the girl, who was now in profile. Were his eyes deceiving him? It was the Daphne he'd met and fallen in love with when he was a boy of fourteen. She had the same face, the same apricot blond hair, and she was humming to herself, so she had to be real. Daggett suddenly felt himself a boy, daring, feisty, and afraid. Afraid of his fierce loneliness, afraid of not surviving, afraid of being captured. Without realizing what he was doing, he crept closer to the Daphne-girl, forgetting his camouflage. With a dreamy look in her eyes, the girl turned her face in his direction. Daggett froze. Somehow she didn't notice him but turned her face up to the sky and gazed at it for a long time. Daggett glided backwards into the cleft.

Now that he'd seen her face straight on, he realized that of course she wasn't Daphne. Being alone all these years must have made him wacky. He shivered as he reminded himself that Daphne was not only old like him, but dead, too. But the girl was so much like her, so alive, that he just had to creep closer again, to drink in the feeling and sight of Daphne, and feel himself again as a youth. It was impossible not to go closer. The fourteen-year-old boy in him was blundering forward, desperate, unwilling to think, unwilling to lose this last chance.

And the seventy-year-old Daggett was following him.

"You're still here with me, aren't you?" Sara suddenly called up to the sky. Daggett's knees went weak and he drew back into the cleft once again.

Sara picked up the wrapped object that had fallen from her letter and squeezed it, sniffed it, and shrugged her shoulders. She dropped it in the jar, kissed the folded letter before pushing it inside, and tightened the lid. After burying it and tamping the grass back down, she emptied her water bottle over it and ran her fingers through the grass. "Grow," she whispered, "grow, white roots and green leaves." Daggett scarcely had time to dash backwards through the cleft into the camouflage of the trees before she skipped right towards him on her way to go meet her brother.

12

Living Like Scaredy-Cats

Daggett's earthen walls, floor, and ceiling were carpeted with thick wool felt he'd made with sheep's wool he'd collected from barbed wire fences. During the long, dark winters in his underground home, he rubbed the wet, soapy wool over a corrugated washboard until it matted to become dense and strong. It was monotonous work, but the steady rhythm and slowly thickening fabric soothed him.

The felt surfaces were constantly being invaded by pale root hairs that grew and waved their slender fingers in Daggett's space, until the heat of his fire conquered them. But where the floor met the walls it was cooler, and here the little moon-colored hairs teased him, stretching and searching for food like tiny blind snakes that wanted his territory.

He opened the letter he'd dug up, and began to read. When he finished the last page, he looked up in wonder at the root hairs reaching through his walls, and the cricket music sawing through his smoke hole expanded inside him like pulsing light. His eyes filled with tears of gratitude. Daphne was back! Like a miracle, he heard her voice once again. The words she'd written called forth a magic still alive after five decades, enchanting the deepest part of him. She shared his soul; she was his Ishi-woman. Yet somehow she had chosen Henry over him, and had rejected him even when Henry finally died. But now, by some miracle, there was hope again.

Suddenly Daggett noticed that he was holding his bootlaces, and remembered that a few minutes ago his coyotes had called to him. He must go meet his pack, to murmur in Coyotese with them, the animals who were his family, his friends. He would tell them and his ravens about Daphne's return! It was time for celebration.

Ben awoke sometime in the middle of the night in his upstairs bedroom at Grandma Daphne's. When he remembered where he was, joy overcame him and he crept out of bed and leaned out his open window into the forest's sweet breath. Moist layers of warm and cold air slid over each other and around his face, giving him a shiver. Outside his window, the maple tree's leaves, the size of dinner plates, quaked in the moonlight, and he could feel the distant bass croaking of a chorus of frogs vibrating in his body. The forest was singing to him, calling him to enter its embrace *now*. He pulled on his jeans and sweatshirt and crept out the door without a sound.

The trunk of the huge maple divided in three very close to the ground. Ben climbed as high as he could up the trunk that leaned towards the forest and curled himself around a strong branch, like a forest animal. He had no idea how long he'd been there when a movement caught his eye. A shadowy figure glided silently towards the house and then paused at each window, stretching to peer inside. The glow of the nightlights Lily had installed in every room illuminated the man's bony nose. Ben clung to his branch and trembled.

When the man disappeared around the side of the house, Ben began to shimmy down the trunk. But suddenly he froze. What if he didn't make it inside before the burglar came back?

Before he could decide which way to go, the man reappeared, and Ben clung to his leafy hideout, wishing he'd stayed up higher. Suddenly the intruder stepped into the center of the three trunks and began to climb one that leaned towards his bedroom window.

In the silence that followed, Ben's heart beat so sharply that he feared it would shake the tree and alert the intruder. But after one or two minutes the man slithered down to the ground and stared at the house for a long time, then moved silently into the darkness of the meadow. There was no sound of a car leaving.

Ben practically jumped out of the tree and rushed to the safety of his bed, his heart thumping, hoping that no one had seen him, and feeling at the moment more afraid than his mother. And then it struck him like a primal fist in his belly: that had been Daggett.

※ "Move your things and set the table," Lily told Sara, who was playing jacks by herself on the kitchen table while her parents fried bacon and toasted English muffins. "And then go wake up your brother."

"But Mom, I have to finish this set," protested Sara. "Archie says I have Grandma Daphne's gift for jacks," she added proudly. "I beat him and Ben last night."

Peter waited until she threw the small red ball in the air, and while she deftly scooped up three jacks, he caught the ball. "Why don't you play it in your room from now on," he told her, handing the ball back. "Now go get your brother."

※ Ben was reaching for a third muffin when his mother spoke. "I've made a decision," she announced. "I'm willing to live here for a year, if that's what you all really want," she began.

"We do!" cried Sara.

Ben's heart began thudding against his ribs, as last night's fear flooded into his chest. Should he say something about the intruder? Absolutely not.

"But with certain conditions," continued Lily. "If anything happens that makes me feel we aren't safe here, we go home, and that's it. In fact, if I decide we aren't safe here, I'm going to sell the house."

Her husband and children stared at her, stunned into silence.

"But Mom," whispered Sara, "that's not fair. You already don't feel safe here."

"True. But I'm willing to give it a chance. I'm not talking about someone scraping their knee, or getting stung by a bee."

"Mom," began Sara, poking at her eggs with her fork, "maybe you ought to explain the things that are worrying you, so we can make sure they don't happen."

"I'm going to," said Lily. She looked at Peter for support and began. "I don't want you getting lost." She swept her arm towards the window. "We're surrounded by wilderness and wild animals. Coyotes, snakes, spiders. God knows what else." Ben started to interrupt, but

Sara kicked him. "You may *never* go anywhere alone, except in sight of the house." She paused, and then went on. "There are paths in the forest, right?"

Ben and Sara nodded.

"Stay on them, all the time. Don't drink out of the streams, because they could make you sick."

"So Ben and I have to be together when we go into the forest?" asked Sara.

"Actually," replied Lily, "if you want to go more than a very short way, you'll need to take your father." She looked at Peter, who sighed. "Basically, you're going to have to do most of your exploring or whatever it is that you do right along the edge of the forest where I can see you. Unless an adult is with you."

Ben crushed the muffin in his hand.

"I can't ignore my mother's final wish for us to spend a year here," continued Lily. "And so I am sure that you'll understand when I remind you of *her* rule about the forest. No one is to *ever, ever* go anywhere near the other side of the forest." She looked ominously into Ben and Sara's eyes. "Daggett lives there. It's his territory, always has been, even if he doesn't own it legally. You've heard enough stories about him to know he's dangerous. The swamp and ravine mark his boundaries. Stay far, far away from there. Got it?"

Ben and Sara nodded miserably.

"Remember, if anything makes me feel our family is in danger here, we're leaving, for good. So don't argue."

"I'm not," whimpered Sara.

Lily looked at Peter. "What else?"

"Well," he began. "Archie can take them into the forest as well. And maybe sometimes you might—"

"Don't be silly," snapped Lily. "I am *not* going into those trees."

"So if I want to go outside alone, I have to basically stay around the house, is that what you're saying?" asked Ben.

"Yes." Lily brushed some crumbs from the tablecloth into her open hand and closed it.

"Great!" Ben muttered through a clenched jaw. "Maybe you've forgotten, but in the city we have a lot more freedom than this."

"That's different," said Lily, looking at him sternly. "We're all alone here and there's no one to help if you get hurt or something. There's no safety net here." She shuddered.

"So if something goes wrong you'd really sell Grandma Daphne's home, just like that?" asked Sara.

"Just like that," said Lily, and she snapped her fingers. "It's mine now, and I can do what I want. But it's up to you, isn't it, to stay safe?"

"Since when have I wanted to be in danger?" asked Sara, rolling her eyes. Lily gave her a warning look.

"Do you really think this is what Grandma Daphne wanted?" asked Ben. "For us to live like scaredy-cats?"

"Your wilderness guide is gone," said Lily. "This is the best I can do, and if you don't like it, well then, I'll just phone the real estate office right now."

Ben spent the rest of the morning digging a hole in the meadow, ferociously jumping on the shovel, determined to make the hole deep enough to escape the sight of his mother's face, which appeared frequently in the window. Sara meandered behind Bijou like a mournful shepherd as the rabbit hopped about.

"Why are you digging a hole?" she asked Ben after a while.

He ignored her and kept flinging up shovelfuls of dirt. Suddenly he stopped. "Hey, Sara," he called to his sister, who had wandered away. "Come here! I've got an idea!"

Sara looked at him doubtfully.

"We could let Mom and Dad think this is an underground fort, but what if I dig a secret passageway into the forest? I'm serious."

"You sound like a prisoner trying to dig his way out of jail," laughed Sara, then looked glum. "Besides, it might collapse and that really *would* be dangerous. I'm counting on the usual thing to happen, myself."

"What's that?" asked Ben.

"Mom always starts out so strict it seems hopeless, but once she thinks she's got you under control she lets down her guard. She's not going to spend a whole year looking out that window." Sara glanced back at the house and waved to her mom with a cheery smile.

"What else will she do here? I'm going to dig my tunnel," Ben replied, and leaped on the shovel again. "And you can't use it."

"She won't be in charge for long," said Sara, and galloped to catch up with Bijou.

Daggett's breath left a trail of white clouds in the chilly air as he pedaled through the night. The racing bike he'd stolen wasn't a bit like the primitive clunker he'd ridden as a kid. Instead of plump tires and upright handlebars, this bike had wheels as slender as his little finger, and handlebars so low he felt like his nose might scrape the pavement. A barn owl suddenly swooped across the road in front of him and he pedaled backwards to avoid it. In the midst of his astonishment that there were no brakes, one of the owl's great wings whapped him in the neck so hard he almost choked. Then headlights appeared from around a curve and he had no choice but to crash like a madman into the muddy roadside ditch and hide until the vehicle was gone.

When he climbed back out to continue towards Daphne's house, he pedaled cautiously, testing the different levers until he located the brakes, and discovered that the awful racket of metal grinding against metal meant he was changing gears, but not very skillfully. If he could learn to operate this new-fangled contraption, he'd be able to travel back and forth to Daphne's house under cover of darkness whenever he wanted, without losing a night's sleep. He felt like one of his ravens, a sleek dark form flying through the night, the air whistling past his ears, and water leaking from the corners of his eyes in the wind. He was fourteen again, tearing through the night on an adventure. Twice more he had to hide in the ditch when a car passed by. But finally he reached Daphne's home, and was relieved to see the car still in the driveway. The girl had not appeared in the forest all day, and he longed to see her again.

A faint glow shone through the windows. Creeping around the house, Daggett peered in every window, studied Peter and Lily's sleeping forms, and then climbed the maple tree for a look upstairs. In the bed that had been empty last night a boy lay tangled in blankets, his face vacant in the glow of the nightlight on his wall. A second upstairs window shone dimly on the side of the house. That had to be his

Daphne-girl. Daggett found a ladder in the tool shed, but it clattered when he lifted it, so he reluctantly set it back down.

Daggett stood patiently rooted to the ground, unmoving. Then a thought rose up and told him what to do. He could climb the tall fir trees that grew behind the shed, and from there he could see inside the Daphne-girl's window with binoculars. He'd bring them tomorrow night, and look all he wanted. But for now he would ride that crazy bike back to the outskirts of town, stash it in the bushes, and go home to sleep.

"I'll keep an eye on the place for you," promised Archie as the Maclennons piled into their car to drive home after lunch. "Two weeks will go by in a flash," he promised Ben and Sara, "and then you'll have a whole year here!"

13

The Deal

The orchard that backed up to the edge of the forest on the far side of Cedarwood had been planted a century ago, and no one could remember if it belonged to anyone anymore. Every year when the fruit ripened, a few townspeople climbed over the sagging barbed wire fence and helped themselves, always careful to avoid the cluster of beehives in the center of the orchard for fear of being stung.

At the moment, the sweet fragrance of apple blossoms was clouded by the smoke rising from the tin bucket that a solitary man was waving in slow circles around a beehive. Finally he set down his smoker, reached into the hive, and pulled out a frame furred with sleepy bees and sticky wax, and slid it gently back.

An elderly man leaned against a gnarled pear tree, watching. He waited for the beekeeper to secure the lid and begin swinging his smoker around the next beehive, then crept up to tap his shoulder. The beekeeper whirled around, his defiant eyes fierce and hard in his bony face. Then his tight expression relaxed, he grunted in greeting, and set the smoker down.

"Someone wants your services," the elderly man said.

Daggett's face tightened again, and he snorted derisively. But by the end of his visitor's long explanation, he had begun to look pleased.

"So in return for patrolling the forest, and keeping her family safe while they live there, you'll get the diaries and ten thousand dollars after the property is sold to me," finished the elderly man.

"One question," said Daggett. "Why me?" He gave a sinister laugh. "What's there to fear in the forest besides me?"

The elderly man looked amused. "Apparently she thinks there's something else, and that you're the only one who can battle it."

"Meet me here tomorrow," said Daggett, turning away. "I will think."

❋ Ben slammed his history book shut. "Last test of the year," he sighed. "I'm ready."

"Go get the mail, would you please?" asked his mother.

Ben dumped the bundle on the kitchen table and disappeared upstairs. Lily flipped through the letters, tossing junk mail into the recycling bin. That left only one envelope, hand-lettered and addressed to Mrs. Maclennon with no return address.

Inside was a smudged half-sheet of paper, folded small, containing two sentences, but in different handwriting than the envelope, and without a signature:

> *Give me a sample of the diaries you claim*
> *to have. Then I will give you my decision.*

Lily swallowed and stood up, staring at Daggett's thickly penciled printing in her shaking hands. She sniffed the paper, and then looked around herself wild-eyed. Her stomach cramped and her heart stampeded. If this were a student's work, she could've explained her onslaught of fear by pointing to the way the pencil had dug dark furrows into the paper, and how pain cried out from the sharp corners of letters, like "s" and "c," which normally had no corners. But it was not from a student, rather, it was exactly what she had hoped for. She had gone fishing for the biggest fish of all, and she had a bite.

In her bedroom she unlocked her top dresser drawer, and took out a book with a faded green cloth binding, its title, *What Never Happened*, printed in black letters along its spine. The first few pages fluttered by to reveal a cut-out compartment holding a small diary. Her mother's name was written in careful cursive inside the cover. Daggett would just have to accept a photocopy of a page or two, until he earned the whole thing. Lily was in the driver's seat this time.

·14·

Kaleidoscope Eyes

Another half-sheet of paper arrived in the mail seven days later.

Send me another page of the diary.
It is evil to cage a living creature.
Trust nature and set your children free.
Otherwise I won't lift a finger
to protect any of you.

Lily's eyes narrowed and she laid the letter down, staring into the distance. Already the living room was stacked with boxes, and Peter's cousin had agreed to house sit for one year. *I have no choice*, she told herself, and reached for a pen.

Daggett:
Give me a week or two to loosen the reins on my children. I will allow them go to the forest "uncaged." But obviously, they are forbidden to go anywhere near your territory.
I shall not give you any more of my mother's diary until the year is up. For your information, it covers the dates from May 1, 1947 to February 25, 1948. Just keep my family safe, and the entire original diary will be yours, along with ten thousand dollars after the sale of the property.
I have a letter she wrote, but never sent to you, dated December 12, 1947. I will give it to you at the end as a bonus for a job well done. It includes the words "my Raven-Boy."
Sincerely, Lily Maclennon

She copied a Cedarwood address on the envelope and dropped it in her purse to mail first thing in the morning.

The silent house at the edge of the forest was silent no longer. Ben and Sara helped their dad unload the car while their mom put groceries away, and then clattered up and down the wooden stairs, carrying their things up to their new bedrooms.

Ben finished putting his clothes away and slid down the banister, landing with a thump on the floor. His parents were talking in low voices in the small pantry off the kitchen, arranging groceries on the shelves. "Flatten those empty boxes, Ben, okay?" Peter told him. "Then stack them in the woodshed. We'll need them at the end of the year when we move back."

"*You* can move back," replied Ben, and he kicked three cardboard boxes out the back door in the general direction of the woodshed. "*I'm* staying."

"My room's all done!" Sara skipped into the kitchen. "Can I build a fire? Grandma always made a fire our first night here."

"It's not night," said Peter. "I'll make the fire. It's a safety issue." He glanced at his wife.

"Go find your brother," Lily told Sara. "I have something for each of you."

When Ben appeared, Lily pulled two plastic whistles out of her pocket and handed one to each of her children. "They're marine whistles, made for boating emergencies. Not in here!" she shouted, clapping her hands over her ears, when Ben lifted the whistle to his lips. "They're so loud you can hear them a mile away. I want you to always carry one when you go out."

Ben and Sara watched their mother curiously. "Mom," ventured Ben, "you know, if Sara and I were in the forest and you wanted to check on us, maybe we could just whistle back and forth. Then you wouldn't have to worry." Sara nodded eagerly.

"That's what I was thinking," said Lily, and she began wiping and alphabetizing a rack of spice jars above the stove. She set a third whistle on the kitchen windowsill. "If Dad or I whistle out the window, you ought to be able to hear us. But there's a limit to how far the whistle can be heard," she cautioned. "Why don't you go experiment and find out? Ben, you may walk up the road, and Sara, you stay in the yard and listen for his whistle."

"How come Ben gets to go?" complained Sara, scrambling to catch up with her brother, who had already gone out the door.

"Don't look so eager," Ben whispered to his sister as she shoved ahead of him down the porch steps. "If we look like we're being thoughtful and careful Mom might relax."

Sara stuck her tongue out. "At least now I know that Mom loves me more than you! She's sending you up the road as a sacrifice to her big bad forest monsters!"

"Fine by me, but shut up, or they'll hear you," warned Ben, and then he blew two short blasts on his whistle. "Whistle back the same way when you hear me, real loud. If I can't hear you, I'll know I've gone too far, and come back." And he jogged out of sight.

Sara poked at the marshmallows in her cocoa so that they dipped and bobbed, and licked the foam off her finger. The fireplace sizzled as Ben fed the flames with the cedar branches he'd collected on his earlier jaunt up the road. Every time a hot spark burst out and landed on the hearth, he pressed it out, and then examined the soot on his thumb.

"You're going to burn yourself, Ben! Stop that!" cried his mother.

"Those whistles worked great," said Peter. "Two miles is a long way."

"But the road winds around," Sara pointed out. "And sound travels straight. So it wasn't really two miles."

"I suppose," he nodded thoughtfully, glancing at his wife, who was bent over Daphne's old spinning wheel in the corner, polishing the wood with a rag and adding drops of oil to the moving parts.

"I know how we could measure it better," Sara suddenly said. "If we had a really long string." Lily looked up.

"I could hold one end and walk into the forest and keep going until you couldn't hear my whistle anymore. And then we could measure the string." Sara left her mug on the hearth and walked to her mother, touching the edge of the spinning wheel so it began to rotate slowly. "You could spin a really long string for us to use, Mom," she said softly. "A magical string of safety."

"I'm going to have to learn how to spin all over again as it is," said Lily. "It's been years. But I like your idea. I could always pull you back, too, couldn't I?" she laughed.

※ "I finally opened my letter from Grandma Daphne when we were here for the weekend," Sara told her mom as they drove to Cedarwood together to buy string. "Do you want to know what it said?"

Lily glanced over at her daughter questioningly. "Sure. Of course."

"There was a story about Great-Aunt Eva."

Lily raised her eyebrows and waited.

"Was her farm around here?" asked Sara.

"Yes," nodded Lily. "I used to know where. It's all built over now."

"And there was a prediction, sort of, about something I'll learn in the forest."

Lily waited for more details. "Well?" she finally said.

"I don't think I'm supposed to tell you more, Mom, not now anyway. But there's something I want to tell you. Kind of a promise, almost."

Lily caught her breath. "I'm listening."

"Someday, when you notice *the dearest freshness deep down in things* again, and aren't afraid anymore, I'll let you read my letter and then everything will make sense to you."

Lily didn't reply, but drove on through the tall evergreens, safe within the protective shell of the car.

※ "I'll wait for you here," insisted Lily, settling on the warped wooden bench that loosely circled the trunk of the lone apple tree in the meadow. "Your Grandpa Henry built it when I was five," she said. "It's always been my place. He made the bench big so the tree could always grow."

"That was a good idea," said Sara, handing her mom a ball of string. "Just hold it in your hand and let it unravel while I walk. Anytime you want, give a tug and I'll tug back."

"It was my idea," Sara said to Ben, who stood watching them, bouncing from foot to foot. "You can't come."

"It won't even work," said Ben, sneering. "The string's going to get snagged on bushes and trees. You're not going to get very far." He laughed.

"It's going to slide right along," insisted Sara. "Wait and see." She turned away. "When I come to the end of the string can I sit for a while before coming back?" Sara asked her mother.

"I guess so. But when you hear me whistle, come right home, okay?"

Sara nodded, and tied the string to her belt loop. It hung like a long clothesline between her mother and herself as she headed through the soft morning sun. She could almost taste the tingling green fragrances, and began to skip. Grandma Daphne must be waiting for her in the clearing, basking in the sunshine in her cedar throne, and when Sara stepped into the opening her grandmother's soft face would turn and welcome her back with such peace and bliss.

There was a tug on the string and Sara tugged back. Hah! Ben's wrong, she told herself proudly, as she and the string bounced towards the bright clearing in the woods.

Someone did await her; indeed, someone was sitting right in her grandmother's throne. The woman leaned on a knobby wooden cane and stared with delight at Sara, as if the girl was stepping onto the stage in the opening scene of a wonderful drama about to begin. Sara rushed towards her grandmother, tears springing to her eyes, her feet flying across the ground, then came to a sudden halt.

"You're—not—my Grandma Daphne," she whispered. "Who are you?"

"Look closely," smiled the woman.

Sara stepped a little closer to peer at the stranger's eyes. It was like looking into Grandma Daphne's bowl of wet colored pebbles. There was a tug on the string at her waist, and although she felt slightly disoriented, she remembered to tug back.

Avoiding the woman's eyes, Sara looked at her white hair, long and soft and caught up in a bun at the back of her head. She wore an ivory wool shawl over a flowered cotton dress, and held a basket in her lap. Hadn't her grandmother been knitting a shawl like that last year? And then the basket. She stared at it. It was the same basket she'd found beneath Watchful One weeks ago when she'd gone through the forest to the boulder to open her letter. She'd propped it in one of Watchful One's branches, and now here it was again.

"Do you remember now?" inquired the woman, her ancient voice ringing like a child's. She turned her face up towards Sara, who could not look away from the twirling kaleidoscope in her eyes. Inside those eyes, or that forest, she knew not which, Sara fell. And fell. "You know me," the stranger's voice echoed around her, as she spiraled down, or up, or was it sideways? "Do you remember now?"

The insistent tug of the string pulled her back. She was sitting in her grandmother's throne, a little dizzy, with a basket in her lap. The sunlight shone on a tuft of unspun wool as it floated and landed on her hand. Sara closed her hand around the trembling corkscrew fibers, then stared at the basket. A sensation of falling into the woman's eyes flooded her once more.

There was another tug on the string, but Sara hardly noticed it, because something was swelling up beneath the basket's green cloth, like rising dough. And a fragrance—of honey, flowers, and sun-baked tree sap—swirled around her. Then there was a second tug, and a whistle screamed through the trees. Sara pulled on the string but couldn't bear to whistle back, as if the ferocious sound might shatter everything. Cupping her hands over the basket's swollen shape, she felt how warm and alive it was, like the languid belly of some upside-down creature dozing in the sun after a satisfying meal. There was another yank on her string and she yanked back. She left the basket on her grandmother's cedar throne, and headed back to her mother.

Ten minutes later, Lily held up a rewound ball of string flecked with moss and sticky sap. "You didn't whistle back," she complained. "Didn't you hear me?"

"I couldn't make noise," Sara murmured. "The forest is so beautiful." She looked into the frightened surface of her mother's eyes.

"Mom," Sara whispered, "you have no idea how much there is nothing to be afraid of."

Ben tapped his feet impatiently beneath the breakfast table. "Tie me to a string if you have to!" he argued. "I don't care! But I have to get started on the task my grandparents left me." He looked ominously at his parents. "I *have* to go to the forest alone." They stared back at him. "It's educational." Peter raised one eyebrow. "It involves a biological nature study through the cycle of all four seasons, and I've already lost two days of summer!" he cried. Sara held her toast up to hide the amusement on her face.

"Maybe you should tell us about it," suggested his father.

"I've already told you more than I want to. My letter is private and you know it!" Ben stomped his feet. Then he let his shoulders sag. "Okay. Part of the task involves sitting very still in the same spot, camouflaged, day after day, so that the wildlife gets used to me and ignores me and that way I can watch what they really do when no one's disturbing them." His parents sat up a little straighter and looked suddenly interested. "I have to rub myself with stuff like skunk cabbage to mask my human scent." His mother wrinkled her nose. "And I hope it's obvious I can't be blowing a whistle or bringing company along." He eyed Sara darkly. "I have to be able to go alone, and the truth is I need to be able to go day and night to get all the data I need."

"You're not going out at night," said Peter sternly. "There's no better way to get lost."

"What if a dangerous animal shows up?" asked Lily.

"Like what, Mom?" laughed Ben. "That's the whole point. Everything in the forest is afraid of people, so I have to be like a statue or they won't even come near me. One move, and off they go fast as their little paws can carry them."

"Did you have a spot in mind?" asked Peter.

"You haven't given me a chance to find one yet," replied Ben hopefully.

"Well then, I'll go with you today," said Peter. "I'll help you pick out a spot, so we'll know where it is." He glanced at Lily for confirmation. She nodded uneasily.

Ben groaned as if his father were a fool needing to have everything explained again and again. "You can't go with me, Dad! It's bad enough that some of my scent will linger there, but both of us—it could ruin everything. This is a one-man project."

Lily leaned forward on her elbows. "Listen to me!" she said sharply. "I'm trying to make this work. I bought you whistles and sent you two miles up the road, through the trees, all *alone*." She stared at Ben, then turned her dark eyes on Sara. "And I sent you out with nothing but a little string tied to your pants, right into the forest, all by yourself, just the way you like. We've been here what, two days so far? Quit pushing me!"

No one spoke.

"I was thinking of maybe going just a little ways into the forest," said Lily quietly. "It would help me to know more about it, I think."

Still no one spoke.

"I thought maybe the four of us might go for a walk," she said, standing up and looking out the window towards the woods. "Well?"

"Want to go now?" Ben replied.

Lily nodded. "There's insect repellent in the bathroom drawer, if anyone wants it."

"It smells bad," said Sara.

"I am not fond of bugs," replied her mother primly.

Sara and Ben waited on the porch steps for their parents. "Now, we have to be careful nothing worries them," Ben warned.

"Right," agreed Sara. "I'm not sure what would."

"Just think before you do or say anything. We don't want them thinking there are wild animals to eat us, or poisonous snakes, or that an avalanche is going to come down to bury us alive. That kind of stuff."

"Or that we'd get lost," said Sara solemnly.

Peter joined Ben in the front, and Lily and Sara followed behind. A pair of binoculars hung from Peter's neck, and he lengthened his stride and pace until he was ahead of Ben. "Wait, Dad," Ben cried. "Don't you want us to show you around?"

"Can't keep up with me, can you, eh?" grinned Peter. "Well then,

I'll slow down a bit." He looked towards his wife, who glanced anxiously at him.

"Ben," she called in a thin voice, "Ben, is there a path to the pond? There never was when I was young."

Ben didn't turn around or answer right away. Sara scuffled her feet and bent down to pick up a pinecone. "That little pond?" he asked when he finally turned around. He gestured vaguely into the trees.

"I can't remember where it was," Lily answered. "You mean Grandma Daphne never took you there?"

"Oh, we've been there," Sara suddenly piped in, "But there's no trail. Grandma Daphne somehow knew the way."

Peter stopped abruptly, and Ben nearly ran into him. "Well, then," he said in an authoritative voice, "don't try to find it. You could get lost. And if you found it—why—you could drown. Understand?"

"Okay, Dad," said Ben, "we won't try to find it if you feel that way." I don't have to try to find it, he thought to himself, picturing the chain of familiar trees Grandma Daphne had taught them to recognize so they could easily find their way. Neither he nor Sara had to *try* to find their way.

"Sara?" her father asked, looking at her.

"Okay by me," Sara agreed.

"Good," stated Peter, pleased with his children's cooperation.

They had reached the clearing where the sun, now high in the sky, shone down and lit up the forest floor. "Is that some kind of chair?" asked Lily.

"It's Grandma Daphne's throne," explained Ben. "She used to sit there while we played. It's kind of like our home base in the forest."

"Come see this," called Sara. She gently turned a small fern frond upside down on its black wiry stem to reveal clumps of orange powder crowding the underside of the little leaflets. Her parents bent down to look. "These are called spores. They're like little seeds for ferns. Watch." She pressed the spore side of the frond onto the top of her hand, and slapped it quickly. When she lowered her hand, a perfect orange copy of the fern's shape was printed neatly on her hand. "Grandma Daphne called it Transfer Fern," she explained.

"*Pityrogramma Triangularis*," announced Ben from behind them. "That's its Latin name."

Lily touched her daughter's hand as if it were a precious piece of art. "Can I try?" she asked. Sara steadied her mother's hand beneath another frond, and a moment later they stood up to hold their matching hands side by side, admiring them.

"Did Grandma Daphne teach you the Latin, too?" asked Peter.

Ben shrugged. "No. I read it in one of her plant books."

"Shall we continue?" Peter asked Lily. A breeze was blowing puffs of orange powder off her hand and she was staring at the nearly invisible particles as they floated through the rolling waves of air. "Lily?" he asked.

"Sara, look!" she whispered, ignoring him.

"Earth to Lily!" complained Peter.

"Shh, Dad!" whispered Ben.

"I think your mother's forgotten she's scared of this place," muttered Peter. Lily looked up at him suddenly, confused. "Let's get going."

He continued down the path in the direction of the mountain. As they left the sunny clearing, he reached out to trail his hand along a tall plant with serrated leaves. "Ouch!" he shouted, rubbing his fingers. "That thing stung me!"

"It's a nettle, Dad," Sara explained. "You can't touch them when they're green, only when they're dead or dried up, or they sting you."

Peter was examining his fingers, looking for stingers to pull out. "Here, Dad," said Ben, and handed him a magnifying glass. "You won't find stingers, though. They're still in the leaves, along the edges. Want to see something?" He plucked a nettle leaf by pinching the center, then folded it up into a little bundle and popped it in his mouth and began chewing. "They're very nutritious," he said. His parents looked at him like he was crazy. "Taste like spinach. Full of vitamins. I folded all the stingers to the inside where they can't hurt me."

"Where's Sara?" Lily suddenly cried. "Sara!"

"Just a minute," Sara called from a distance. "I'm getting something for Dad's finger!" A moment later she emerged from the trees, carrying a large fern frond. "This is Sword Fern," she announced.

"*Polystichum munitum*," echoed Ben.

"Here," said Sara, "wad it up and twist until some juice comes out, then smear it on your stings. They'll go away." She handed the fern to her dad, who began rubbing it on his fingers.

"Wow," marveled Peter. "It works."

"Grandma Daphne always says that nature balances every problem with a solution," said Sara quietly. "Like this fern fixes the nettle's sting."

Ben chuckled. "Warriors used to whip themselves with bundles of nettles to get all riled up for battle, and to keep themselves awake."

"Really. Why don't you go ahead of me for now," Peter said to his son.

"Don't you like it out here, Mom?" Sara asked.

"I like that fern," Lily said, admiring her hand, "and being with you. But there are so many unknowns out here, and so many bugs— get away from me!" She began swatting at a bee that was circling her.

"Stop that, Mom," ordered Sara. "You're just making it angry. Here, roll down your sleeves," and she tugged at her mom's sleeves. She stopped to sniff at her mom's neck. "You put perfume on this morning, didn't you?"

"Well, yes," answered Lily. "And bug repellent, which doesn't seem to be working very well."

"Bees are attracted to perfume," Sara told her. "You're giving the bee a mixed message."

"Oh," responded Lily meekly. "I've had all I can take. Let's go home," she announced. "Peter! Ben!" she shouted. "Come back!"

"Mom!" protested Sara. "You've been doing great!"

"I don't want to get stung by a bee," replied Lily in a weak voice. "It's bad enough that your dad got stung by nettles."

When they got to the meadow, Sara picked a handful of leaves. Turning to her mom, she said, "This is plantain. You can eat it as a salad, or chew it up and smear the pulp on a bee sting and it will stop hurting. You didn't have to be so scared back there."

"The forest is pretty from the house," answered Lily, her voice rigid. "And I'm not scared."

"*Plantago lanceolata*," said Ben.

"Nature balances every problem with a solution," added Sara. "And Bijou can have plantain for lunch. He loves it."

·   ·   ·

Ben dried while Sara washed the breakfast dishes, even though they were usually just responsible for the dinner dishes. Both kids felt like bouncing up and down, but without exchanging a word, knew it would be wise to hide their excitement. Their mom was in the bathroom, washing her hands, as if being in the forest had unnerved her, and she wanted her house self back. Their dad had gone down to his workshop in the basement, where he had several long-term projects underway.

Lily was sitting at the spinning wheel in the living room, watching as the strand of fluff she fed it was pulled from her hand and twisted into a tight little rope. Ben and Sara peered in at her and slunk silently back out and went through the hall closet down to the basement.

Peter's gloved hands were submerged in a large shallow bath of special solution that he used to clean old documents. He was lifting the edges of a screen that held the papers in the solution, to judge their progress. His children came and stood beside him, watching his slow, careful movements, smelling the familiar smells they had grown up with, and they too studied the scratched sepia photograph as the pungent liquid dripped from it. It was a portrait of a woman from long ago, maybe from when cameras were first invented. It was torn and ragged, badly faded in spots, but Ben and Sara had seen the magic their dad was capable of and knew that he'd make the photo look as good as new again.

Ben glanced up at his father's face and felt a deep peace. Sara looked at her father too, and felt small again, transported back to all those times she had stood beside him just as she and Ben were now, watching, smelling, enchanted by the transformations taking place.

"Hi," their dad finally intoned, his voice as slow and mellifluous as the alchemical broth he was working with.

"Hi, Dad," they chorused softly, continuing to watch. The photograph was almost all the way out of the solution now, supported smoothly on a flat screen, and Peter tipped it this way and that to see if it was clean enough. He blew on it softly, then lowered it into a second shallow bath to rinse it, and went to wash his hands at the sink.

"You two may know a lot about the forest, but I know a lot about this," he said, waving his arm around the basement. "Come on," he said, "let's go find your mom and talk."

✳ Lily looked up from the spinning wheel, and stopped treadling. "My hands remember what I don't," she said happily.

"Your mom and I are pretty impressed with you kids," Peter began. "All those Latin words, and remedies for stings. We didn't realize that Grandma Daphne had taught you so many practical things."

"Safety was her first priority," said Ben solemnly.

"So your mom and I have agreed to modify the rules a little," Peter continued. "We've decided you don't have to have an adult with you."

"Thank you," whispered Sara.

"One," said Peter. "Always let us know where you're going and what time we can expect you back. We want to know where in the forest we can find you if we need you. Two. Nothing dangerous. No swimming, no tree-climbing, no fires. Three. Stay together as much as possible, so if one of you gets hurt, the other can go for help."

Sara stopped him. "So I can go off alone some of the time?"

Peter looked at his wife. "We'd like you to do as much together as possible so you're safer."

"Okay," said Sara. "And you forgot the fourth rule."

"What's that?" asked Lily.

"To stay away from the ravine and the swamp, so we don't end up in Daggett's territory by mistake!"

"Good girl!" nodded her mother.

"I wouldn't go there if you paid me!" cried Ben. "So, can Sara and I go out together after lunch?"

"Yes," said Lily. "But don't any of you forget," she added, "that if something happens to make me believe we're not safe here, back to the city we go."

"That will not happen," said Sara.

"We promise," added Ben, and grinned at his sister, unable to hide his excitement. Except for a few key points, he could actually follow his parents' rules.

15

Through the Pickle Jar

❋ "I want to be alone," Sara told her brother as they entered the clearing.

"So do I. Don't forget we promised to be back by four," Ben reminded her. "Meet me here ten minutes early so we can return together." And with a whoop of joy he ran past the cedar throne and galloped down the path.

Sara wanted to find that woman again, the woman she believed must be Esther, as described in her grandmother's letter. Maybe there had been clues she'd overlooked when she read the letter the first time. So off she went to dig it up and read it once more.

❋ Ben stood at the edge of the ravine and looked down the steep rock wall while he got out his rope. Two hours to spend on the other side, and in full daylight! Somewhere in the wild forest before him lay Daggett's hidden home. Fear skittered up Ben's spine as he studied the dark shadows between the trees. It was just a forest, after all, with familiar plants and animals and weather, nothing to fear. He was trying to decide which madrona tree to anchor his rope to, trying not to think about how, if he fell, no one would ever find him except maybe Daggett, when a powerful whoosh of wing beats exploded over his head.

A huge black bird suddenly flew directly at him. Refusing to be its prey, Ben threw his arms up to make himself fierce. He dared not scream because Daggett might hear him. The raven veered away, shrieking out a series of quorks.

A second raven joined the first, and the two birds dove at the boy while shrieking rattling noises. Ben beat at the air with his fists until a distant raven called, and the birds suddenly rose and began circling high above him, while he tried to catch his breath. They know I'm trespassing, he admitted to himself. Are they warning Daggett that I'm here? That's stupid, he thought, they're wild birds and this is their territory. They probably scream like that when a deer comes through, or a fox. They just want me out. He secured his rope to a strong branch, let himself down across Daggett's cold stone threshold, and began his quest, quietly creeping into enemy territory along the base of Mount Portal.

Daggett scowled when he heard his birds broadcasting news of a trespasser. Whatever it was, it was upsetting them more than the usual wandering dog. But he wasn't willing to turn back today. All night long he'd dreamed of his Daphne-girl, and now he'd paddled his raft across the swamp to look for her. His sixth sense promised him she was here somewhere. Although he had searched the area near the boulder, he had not yet found her. He screamed in Ravenese to his birds to be quiet, and they were.

He entered the cleft of the boulder and sat down, closed his eyes and descended to the place inside himself that was as still and alive as the deep water of his pond. Thousands of times Daggett had sat on its shore, until his eyes closed of their own accord and the water reappeared inside him, flooding the interior space of his body so it expanded like an ocean, liquid and silent, pulsing. Here he could simply rest, or if he wished, drop a question like a fishing line into the water, and wait without movement or desire, for a bite. And so he went to his inner ocean now, and baited his fishing line with the request: "Help me find my Daphne-girl." At the sound of gentle footsteps he opened his eyes and silently glided out of the boulder and into the trees.

Grandma Daphne had told Ben and Sara that the first year after Daggett became a hermit, a few foolish hunters from town had followed deer into his territory, been caught in his well-camouflaged traps, and limped back with arrowheads piercing their calves and sides. The arrowheads couldn't be pulled out because of barbs carved into their edges, and a doctor had to be called to cut them out. After that, she'd said, no one had ever invaded Daggett's territory again, and rumors about him began to run rife.

But all that had happened even before Ben's mom was born, and by now Daggett would be an old man, and must have stopped patrolling and setting so many traps. Plus, Ben thought proudly to himself, he wasn't entering the obvious way, from town, as the hunters had, but from the heart of the forest, where Daggett probably felt safe.

Daggett's forest seemed darker than his grandmother's side. All the better, Ben thought, it'll give me a little camouflage. Through the trees came the murmur of running water, and he instinctively moved towards it. He crept around a jutting finger of the mountain and came upon a frozen avalanche of enormous rocks. They looked like they had spilled out of a giant's toy box, ready for building. Small waterfalls gushed from the rock face and over trees that had toppled and lodged against the cliff.

Ben stared up the side of the mountain and then at the avalanche. He knew that talus, the accumulation of rock-falls, could be very unstable, and that if he could find sections where soil had accumulated and small plants had taken root, it would be safer. But there was no soil, and when he stepped on a large rock, it wobbled. He decided to work his way over to one of the fallen trees that had become jammed against the cliff and see if it would hold him. Then he could straddle the tree, scoot himself over the talus, and get a good look around.

The first tree he tried rocked when he put his weight on it. The second one was rotten and looked like it wouldn't last the winter. The third tree, a cedar, made him curious. There was some kind of channel running down the top, which carried a stream from the cliff right into the ground.

Ben put his hand into the icy water to feel the bottom of the channel. It was rough and soft. When he pulled his hand out, it was blackened. The edges of the trough were charred. Could a lightning strike have hit it? Or? He started breathing rapidly. This was how Native Americans had hollowed out cedar canoes and bowls! If Daggett had used hot coals to burn out the inside of the log, could it mean his home was nearby? Ben watched the water rushing into the ground and shook his head. Daggett couldn't possibly live down there. He wasn't a fish or a gopher, he was a man. But Daggett must have burned out the trough in this cedar log. Ben shivered and checked his watch.

In twenty minutes he'd have to go back. And he didn't really want to go farther, because he had the tingly feeling that he was close to something. He stared at the disappearing water again. Of course, he thought, the talus probably goes underneath this mound of earth I'm standing on. And the water would drain through the loose rocks right back into the earth. But why would Daggett have hollowed out this log?

Since he couldn't safely walk out on the talus, Ben began to explore the ground nearby. It was almost spongy, thick with ferns and tall, spindly cedar and hemlock trees reaching for what little light there was. Sunbeams were just beginning to shoot over the top of the mountain and were angling closer and closer to Ben's location. Like searchlights sent to help him, they slowly skimmed the forest floor. One beam lit a strand of spider silk. Then it passed on, and hovered over something round, the size of a dinner plate. What could that be? Ben tiptoed closer and saw a circle of glass. He bent over the mysterious object just as the beam moved directly above it and shone right through the pickle jar, revealing Daggett's home.

16

Trading Places

"You're late!" complained Ben when Sara finally stepped into the clearing. "Come on, we've got to go!"

"Someone stole my letter," said Sara. She wiped a tear from her eye, leaving a streak of dirt on her face.

"What're you talking about?"

"I buried it, and it's gone."

"You forgot where you buried it," scoffed her brother.

"No I didn't," said Sara angrily, "I know exactly where it was. The empty jar is still there."

Ben looked up in surprise. "Really?"

"Really. Someone's watching us." Sara eyed Ben. "We're not alone."

"Oh, Archie," Lily was saying into the phone when Ben and Sara walked into the kitchen. She glanced at them and kept talking. "That's terrible! Should I send Ben to help you with the dog?"

"What dog?" asked Ben.

"Oh. I see. Well, be careful you don't break your hip too. Thanks for letting us know." Lily put down the phone and looked at her watch. "Thank goodness you're back. Did you have a nice time out there?"

"What happened to Archie?" asked Sara.

"His neighbor, Rupert, fell and broke his hip and is in the hospital. Archie has to look after Rupert's dog until his niece can come."

"Am I helping with the dog?" asked Ben.

"No," Lily shook her head. "It's a great big bloodhound that weighs as much as you and is about twice as strong."

"Yeah, right," muttered Ben. "Show me a dog I can't beat." He sprang into a karate stance.

"Well, Archie said no." Lily studied their faces. "Ben, you look like you just won a prize, and Sara looks miserable. What's going on?"

"Nothing," said Sara, and left the room.

"She misses Grandma Daphne," Ben quickly explained. "That's all."

From his own nest one limb below the ravens' nest in a towering fir tree, Daggett watched the gray world gathering light and color. He often joined Friend and Wife at dawn, trading sweet throaty whispers, the raven version of purring.

He'd climbed the tree this morning with unusual vigor, fueled by a relentless flow of youthful life-force as he pictured his prey: Daphne, alive again, and by some miracle not white-haired and wrinkled, but a girl of thirteen, the girl who had once blushed and smiled when he appeared in the schoolyard. And this time he would have her. This time there was no Henry.

Archie, Daphne's other friend, was still around, in spite of the tricks Daggett had played to discourage the old geezer from returning to Daphne's house. But the fool was no match for Daggett, who had remained strong and agile by swimming in his pond, climbing the mountain, cutting wood, and gliding silently and gracefully through the forest for miles every day. He was as vigorous as a man half his age. And now—well, now he was beginning to feel the surge of power he remembered from the days when his hair had still been as black as his eyes, when he was a teenage boy smitten with Daphne.

Friend and Wife had already gone winging off to scout the forest, as they did every morning when the sky grew light, and Daggett knew they would call to him if the girl appeared. He'd trained his raven companions long ago to let him know if they spotted an invasion. Usually it was a town dog or a fox. He had taught them not to disturb the coyotes, who, along with the ravens, he considered family. There had not been a human invader in so many years that he had almost ceased to believe it could happen.

For many years now, Daggett had thought mostly in Ravenese, and dreamed in it. The sound of English had become strange to him, signifying the presence of an enemy. He scarcely thought anymore in words, except when he thought about the past. In the present moments that made up his life, he thought in the language of the forest: in the throaty warble of Ravenese, in the wild symphony of coyote songs, in the squeaks of raccoons and deer, in the rising and falling emotions of the wind. They were his tribe. And their voices drew him into an intimacy with nature that surpassed everything he remembered of human society. The language of nature was fresh, a song of truth. It was Home.

Daphne, like him, had chosen to live in the forest, and since Henry's death eleven years ago, had been alone. Daggett suspected she too had learned to understand Ravenese and the songs of the coyotes. And now he had another chance to join with her, to have what Friend and Wife had together, but with the young, perfect Daphne. Soon he would be welcoming her into his cozy underground home, the home he had always intended to share with her.

❈ "Will you stay with me today?" Sara asked her brother as they approached the clearing. She shot nervous glances behind herself and looked anxiously at the morning sun shifting in the shadows of trees.

"Why?" replied Ben impatiently. "I've got stuff to do."

"But someone took my letter!" cried Sara. "I don't want to be alone!"

"Then why don't you just sit here and wait?" Ben indicated the cedar throne. "You've got your whistle, don't you?"

Sara nodded unhappily.

"Blow it if you need me."

"You're not going too far from here then?"

"No," lied Ben.

❈ Friend and Wife's cries interrupted Daggett's daydream and he sat up in his nest to listen and watch the birds soaring and dipping above Daphne's side of the forest. Someone was out and about. He called back to tell them to keep watching whoever was moving towards Daphne's pond, then slithered down the rough trunk, dropped silently to the ground, and began padding towards the swamp. The forest's creatures had taught him to think of his feet as paws, and to use them like an animal, softly and silently. Now it was the only way he knew to move.

Standing on the spongy bank of the swamp, Daggett paused to acknowledge the power that lay beneath the water, the power he'd discovered through a nearly fatal accident in his first year here. He'd waded eagerly into the marshy water, expecting to cross and claim the other side of the forest as well. But a short way from shore the greedy, living mud beneath his feet had sucked him under with astonishing force. When he'd struggled, the quicksand monster hidden beneath churning brown water had swallowed his legs and begun reaching for his chest. He'd screamed and beat the monster with his fists, but only hit it once, for on contact his arms were seized as well. Then one of Daggett's feet had struck something solid in the belly of the beast just as the water splashed under his chin, and he'd gasped for air, staring wide-eyed at the sun as if he might never see it again. Overwhelmed by exhaustion, he fell still. Time stopped and the savage grip of the mud softened and became peaceful. Daggett opened one hand very, very slowly, and the quicksand did not react. Then he panicked, and it instantly seized him again.

And so he experimented, forcing himself to calmly solve the riddle of how to extract himself without enraging the beast below. He relaxed enough to free both arms and began to stroke in slow motion, until finally his limp legs also drifted free and he floated forward like a swan. It was an extraordinary sensation, serenity after so much struggle.

After his first lesson with the quicksand, the young Daggett had returned many times to play with it. He played at struggling, and was held fast. He played at surrendering, and was set free. He played this game until winter closed in and the water was coated in ice, and then in the warmth of the spring he played again. The cycle of struggle and surrender permeated his dreams and began to guide his way of living in nature.

Eventually Daggett had built himself a sturdy raft, which he now untied from a tree and paddled across the swamp to reach Daphne's side. Friend and Wife called to him again, announcing that someone was at her pond. He secured the raft to a tree on Daphne's side and climbed the hill. If the Daphne-girl struggled, he would hold her firmly, just like quicksand. He hoped she would surrender. Either way, she would soon be his.

※ "How do you get from one place to the other so fast?" Sara stared at Esther. "I've been looking for you, and suddenly here you are."

"I'm never anywhere but here," chuckled Esther. "Tell me, can you be *there*?" She pointed to the other shore of the pond.

"Sure," replied Sara. "All I have to do is walk."

"And when you get there, where will you be, there or here?" asked Esther.

Sara grinned. "It would be called 'here' I suppose, but it's still there."

"Let me tell you a little secret," chuckled Esther. "You are always *here*. People are always trying to get *there*, but it's impossible. They cause themselves endless trouble for nothing."

Sara stared at her, puzzled.

"Tell you what," said Esther. "Let's go for a little stroll together, and you tell me when we're not *here*."

Sara burst into laughter. "Okay." They left the pond and started towards the boulder together. "We're still *here*," smiled Sara, and then began to tell Esther all about her missing letter.

Esther listened without commenting, and then reminded her, "We're always here, but as you've noticed, what 'here' looks like changes." She followed Sara through the boulder and out the other side. "Carry my basket for me, will you?"

Sara took it and hurried through the grass to the spot where her jar was buried. She set the basket down and seized a handful of grass to lift off the circle of dirt covering the jar. But the grass was firmly rooted. "It's grown back so fast!" she cried.

"Look here," suggested Esther, standing ten feet away from where Sara was looking.

Sara walked over suspiciously. "That isn't where I buried it."

"Here." Esther pointed to a cluster of silken yellow buttercups.

Sara crouched down and yanked at the grass. A circle of soil came loose. But she let go. This wasn't where she'd dug her hole.

"Go get my basket please," Esther suggested, "and take a look under the green cloth."

Sara returned with the basket, lifted the cloth, and gaped at what she saw.

"Touch it," said Esther.

Sara gingerly stretched one hand into the dark space. Her entire arm disappeared into the basket. "It's so warm!" she whispered.

"Can you reach it?" asked Esther.

Sara shook her head.

"I'll get it for you," the old woman said. Down, down her arm went, until it too had disappeared. "Here it is," she said with satisfaction, and pulled out something wrapped in the cloth. "Now," she cautioned Sara, "don't open it just yet. Lift the top off that hole in the grass first."

Sara lifted the circle of flowers and grass, and saw the lid of her jar. Esther smiled at her surprised face. "It's empty!" Sara cried when she held it up. "See?"

"Just drop the green cloth in the jar and then take it out," Esther told her. Sara did so. And there it was: her grandmother's envelope, with Sara's name in her grandmother's familiar cursive, bulging around the wrapped object that Sara had never opened. Her eyes darted side to side as she searched for some explanation. "But this envelope is sealed," she whispered, staring at it in her hands. "I tore mine open."

"What you lose can never be found again," said Esther. "It's best to see what is here now." She folded the green cloth in half and patted it into the bottom of her basket. "Well, are you going to open the letter?"

Ben was one hundred percent certain he had tied his rope to this very limb of the madrona tree at the edge of the ravine. He peered down the cliff to see if it had somehow come untied and fallen. But there was no rope in sight. Someone had to have untied it and taken it.

How was he supposed to get down there now? Ben tightened his grip on the smooth limb and exhaled sharply. Could those ravens have done it? He'd read enough about them in Grandma Daphne's bird books to know that ravens' beaks and talons were strong enough, plus they were smart enough too. But the rope had been pretty heavy. How could they have flown off with it? No, it couldn't have been the ravens.

There was only one other likely explanation and that was Daggett himself. Could he have seen Ben yesterday and followed him through the ravine? Sara had said they were being watched. The thought was both terrifying and delicious. Last night Ben had added Daggett's underground home to the blank side of his map, not quite believing that he had discovered the ultimate prize so quickly.

But right now, just in case Daggett had spotted him, he'd better stay away for a day or two. Reluctantly, he left and headed for the swamp, where he could get started building a raft.

"This isn't the same letter!" whispered Sara.

"How could it be?" replied Esther.

"But it's Grandma Daphne's handwriting!" Sara trembled.

"Things change," said Esther. "The dearest freshness that lives deep down inside things doesn't change." And she vanished.

Sara gasped and clung to the envelope. She stuffed the wrapped object in her pocket, buried the empty jar, and hurried through the boulder back to the pond.

Daggett crept cautiously through the trees, silently padding, becoming still, padding some more, then listening, and always looking around. He paused behind the cleft boulder on the slope below the pond, and grew alert. Someone was humming a little melody.

Ben neared the edge of the swamp and stopped to gaze out over the swamp grass that grew in thick clumps like spiky hair dotting the wet land. A flock of red-winged blackbirds in the cattails stopped chattering to stare at the intruder, then rose suddenly in a whir of red and black. What's that row of logs poking out of the reeds? Ben wondered. He went to take a closer look, his foot caught on the rope that ran from the log to a nearby tree, and he tripped and tumbled onto the mossy surface of the raft he'd dreamed of building.

Sara wandered along the shore of the pond, trying to step on as few living things as possible, then sat down. She, Ben, and Grandma Daphne had often sat here for long periods in stillness, waiting for nature to resume its life around them so they could watch it move. This time Sara sat in the hope that her grandmother would join her, and soon felt Daphne's presence blossom beside her.

A robin landed a few feet away and began poking at the damp ground. A frog's head popped out of the pond's glassy surface, spied the bird, and sank from sight. The familiar sensation of everything all aglitter, all adazzle, pulsated and swelled in every cell of Sara's body and filled the air around her.

In her stillness Sara had become invisible, or at least insignificant, to the creatures of nature, to all but one. And that one was silently padding closer and closer on two feet, watching her and nothing else, his shiny black eyes alert with desire.

Ben clambered off the raft on Daggett's side of the swamp and sank a few inches in the mud. It sucked at his shoes as he struggled towards dry land. He'd have to rinse them off in the pond later, so his mother wouldn't freak out.

The ravens suddenly appeared overhead and began screaming at him. They're just birds, he told himself. He wanted to find the traps and snares, walk the secret trails, discover the way to Daggett's pond, and learn every detail of how the mysterious man survived all alone out here, master of the forest.

The sky erupted with two raven voices excitedly complaining about something. The robin, who now had a fat worm in its beak, looked up for a moment, then anchored its victim with one foot and snipped off a beak full. Sara watched, as her grandmother had taught her, without reacting.

Daggett had stopped observing her and was staring up at the sky. The angry squawking continued. His face tightened with rage. Just a few more minutes, and then he'd leave to defend his land. Just a few more minutes of watching the girl, and he'd go.

Sara stared at the sealed envelope in her hand. Was this a second letter from her grandmother? Where had it come from? And what had happened to the first one? The robin swallowed the last of the worm, tugged a beetle by one leg from beneath a leaf, and chugged it down.

※ Ben was a few minutes into the forest when he suddenly realized that if the raft was on Daphne's side of the swamp, then Daggett probably was too. How could he not have thought of that before? And when Daggett found his raft missing—it was too scary to think of. He retraced his steps back and paddled frantically across the swamp. He'd almost blown it.

He tied the raft to the tree, realizing in increasing despair that since he hadn't paid attention to the knot before untying it, he couldn't tie the same one again. Daggett would know someone had been tampering with his raft. His heart sinking, Ben struck out through the bushes and trees, not knowing where he was going, just away from the swamp. He paused to catch his breath beside a fir tree, resting with one hand on a low limb. Unlike most firs deep in the forest, this one had limbs growing low enough to climb. He'd be safer up in a tree, in case Daggett really was on this side. Fear for his sister crossed his mind as he straddled a thick branch halfway up the tree and clung to the trunk. The ravens who'd been screaming at him earlier flew above him now, circling and studying him with tilted heads, but silently. In the safety of the tree, Ben couldn't help himself. He blasted out his best imitation of their earlier cries, and then muffled his laughter as the birds soared away.

※ Daggett froze when he heard the crude imitation. Was it the boy?

Sara watched the robin abruptly fly off. She sighed, and stood up and stretched.

Daggett slid noiselessly backwards, desperate to conceal himself before the girl saw him.

"Come back!" Sara cried to the robin.

For a split second Daggett's face shone brightly with hope. Then he swiftly turned and fled.

17

Falling into a Trap

Ben had just begun to lower himself to the next limb of the fir tree when he noticed something moving down below. It was a man, and he moved through the forest like a movie with the sound turned off. Ben stopped breathing.

The man vanished in the direction of the swamp. It had to be Daggett, and in a few minutes he was going to find out someone had been fooling with his raft. Ben shimmied down the trunk and rushed towards the clearing to find Sara and get out of the forest.

Daggett stared at the clumsy knot holding his raft to the tree. The boy had been here. Had he also been to the other side? Daggett yanked at the rope, cursing himself. What a fool he had been to ignore Friend and Wife when they tried to warn him the first time!

The robin who had flown away so suddenly did not respond to Sara's cry to return. A water strider skittered across the pond, its pin-point feet scarcely denting the silken surface. Sara sat back down, to await the flood of her grandmother's presence, so that she could open the letter in her hand.

Ben was watching the ground before his feet as he rushed through the trees, and so he nearly went right past Esther, who was propped comfortably on a low branch of Watchful One. The bright colors of her skirt, unnatural in the forest, suddenly registered in Ben's mind and he skidded to a halt and whirled around.

"Well, here you are," the old woman said, waving her walking stick at Ben.

"Who are you?" cried Ben, panting for breath. "This is private property! And it's not safe!"

"Really." Esther looked skeptical. "I'm here to talk to you."

Ben's nostrils flared and he looked nervously behind himself. "You don't even know me."

"Ah Ben, but I do," she said. "We're old friends. My name's Esther. Let me give you a bit of advice, my boy, before you continue fleeing."

"How do you know my name?" Ben hunched his eyebrows and glared at her.

"Watch out for your own mind," said the woman. "It can be your worst enemy."

Ben rolled his eyes. "Yeah, right," he muttered. Hadn't Grandma Daphne once said something like that to him? Or had she? There was something about this stranger's eyes that twinkled like his grandmother's—but no, that was just his imagination. He puffed out his chest and stood tall. "I don't know where you came from, but you'd better stay out of our forest. We own it. If I find you here again I'm going to have my parents call the cops."

Esther sighed. "That's what's coming next. Can't be helped. Now give me a hand, will you?" she asked Ben. "Just hold my basket for me," she said, and he reluctantly took the willow basket. Inside, a green cloth twitched.

He turned away and gave the basket a sharp rap, so that whatever was under the cloth would jump out. Instead the cloth now lay limp.

Behind him he heard a low laugh and then Esther spoke. "Force doesn't work. If you disturb my basket, its treasure remains hidden."

"I didn't—" began Ben, whirling around to defend himself. But the old woman was nowhere in sight, which was impossible, and when he looked down at the basket, it was gone too. A blustery wind erupted above, and two ravens chased each other out of the upper reaches of a tree. Something dropped from one of the birds' feet, and floated down to Ben. It was a nubby cotton thread, the very green of the cloth in the basket that he must have imagined. Bewildered, Ben suddenly remembered that Daggett could be after him, and turned and ran.

Sara was not in the clearing. Ben fumbled for his whistle and then realized he'd left it in his jacket. Where was she? Had she whistled for him when he was too far away to hear? Had she run home? What was he supposed to do now?

The air behind Sara flowered with her grandmother's familiar warmth, so she leaned back, feeling their spines meet. So often they had sat together this way, free of words and wishes.

The envelope rested in her hand like a small peaceful animal. She peeled back the flap and took out the single sheet. It was blank. Her grandmother's warmth nestled around her, and a rose-like fragrance spiraled around them like a cocoon. Then an image appeared, hovering before her, a dream-like version of one of the metal jacks from the game her grandmother had left Archie in her will. The image faded, and Sara opened her eyes. The letter was gone, and she was sitting alone in a meadow of buttercups and thick damp grass.

She stood on her toes and stretched her hands to the sky, curved back into a soft arch, then bent to retie one shoe, and hiked back to the clearing.

"I thought you were scared to be alone," muttered Ben as they hurried up the path homeward. "Where were you, anyway?"

"I'm not scared," replied Sara dreamily. "Or alone."

"I think we ought to stay together for a few days," said Ben.

"Aren't you working on your secret observatory?" asked Sara. "Or was that totally made up for Mom and Dad?"

Ben looked rattled. "No, I've got a place picked out. But I need to get some supplies."

"Well, I don't see what you're so scared of," teased Sara.

"I'm not scared!" shouted Ben.

"Shut up," cautioned Sara. "They'll hear us!" She gestured up the trail, where the meadow and the house were already visible. "And you are too scared!" She took off running, with Ben chasing behind, glancing around his shoulders in case Daggett was after him.

⁂ By supper the sky had clouded over and it had begun to rain. "The radio said we're in for a few days of this," Peter announced. "You kids will have to find something to do inside."

Lily put the ice cream back in the freezer and returned to the spinning wheel in the living room, where she had begun filling a second bobbin with yellow yarn. "Sara, when you and Ben finish cleaning up, come here," she called. "I'm almost ready to knit you a pair of socks and I want you to pick out a design." Peter stretched out on the couch with a book and a mug of coffee.

The rain was drumming on the roof and the dripping eaves plunked steadily. Water music filled the air.

"What scared you?" Sara whispered to Ben. "Seriously. Did something happen?"

Ben sloshed a bowl through the suds and heaved a sigh. "It was always just us and Grandma Daphne," he finally said. "Now I'm not so sure. I think there might be someone else, watching us. I mean, your letter did get stolen."

"What do you mean?" Sara asked. "Did you see someone?"

Ben shivered uncomfortably. "Brrr," he said. "It's chilly. No, I didn't see anyone. But I know something's wrong."

"Wrong?" cried Sara.

"Shh!" hissed Ben. "Weird, wrong, I can't put my finger on it. I just think we should hang together for a few days."

⁂ "The book of patterns is in my bedroom," Lily told Sara when she came in. Sara went to find it and returned carrying the book and an empty suitcase.

"Don't you think it's about time to put this away, Mom?" asked Sara, indicating the suitcase. "You're not going to be needing it for at least a year. I'll go put it in the storeroom for you."

"Thanks, honey," said Lily, as she began plying the threads from two bobbins together to make a stronger yarn. "You're right."

·   ·   ·

Sara hauled the suitcase up the stairs to the storage space under the eaves. It ran the length of the house, and was crowded with boxes and shelves stacked with old books and papers. Sara trailed her hand along the worn spines of the old cloth-bound books, and paused to read the curious titles. There was *Madame Crowl's Ghost and Other Mysteries*, *The Romance of a Tenderfoot in the Days of Custer*, and *Journey to the Center of the Earth*. She'd heard of that one before. Maybe it would make good bedtime reading. Sara pulled it out, blew off the dust, and opened it.

The first page was kind of boring, so she flipped to the middle to see if it got any better. Where the middle of the book should have been was a carved out space, like the inside of a box, and inside the hollow a small booklet lay concealed. *My Life with Henry*, it was titled. Sara trembled and took it out. It was simply fashioned: just a dozen sheets of paper folded and sewn through with yellow yarn that was tied in a small bow at the spine. She glanced past the first page, which was dated, "October 1948." The remaining pages were covered with uneven cursive, as if the writer had been tossed about by emotion. Sara kept turning pages, and suddenly the handwriting turned upside down. In fact, the rest of the writing was all upside down. Eagerly Sara turned the book over and there, staring at her from the back cover was another title: *My Life with Daggett*. She took a deep breath. Her life with *Daggett*? Had Grandma Daphne led a secret life she didn't know about? Sara replaced the booklet inside the carved-out book and carried it into her bedroom, where she hid it under her pillow, and went back downstairs in a daze.

"Did you pick out a pattern?" Lily asked her.

"For what?" asked Sara.

"For your socks!" exclaimed Lily. "What's wrong with you?"

"Nothing," replied Sara. She picked up the pattern book and turned a few pages, but couldn't focus.

"Well?" said Lily.

"How about trees, Mom?" said Sara. "Just put trees on them for me, okay?" She yawned and stretched. "I think I'll go to bed early."

· · ·

Daggett set off through the dripping rain on his stolen bicycle to spy on the family he was supposed to be protecting. He had to find some way of stopping the boy, if it had been him, and it had to have been, because who else could it have been? And he wanted to watch his Daphne-girl by climbing the tree that let him see into her window with binoculars.

Lights blazed in every room in the house except for the boy's. Daggett peered into the living room window first. There was the woman, bent over the spinning wheel, her dark hair hiding her face. The man lay sprawled on the couch, reading. The boy sat cross-legged on the floor beside the woodstove, a book open in front of him, looking from the book to his hands. Daggett went around the corner for a better view. The kid was tying knots, working from drawings in the book. Hah! So it had been him. In that instant Daggett knew he would lay a trap beside the raft, catch the brat and scare him so badly that he would never have to worry about him again. He observed his trespasser-soon-to-be-victim a while longer, then looked through the rest of the downstairs windows for his Daphne-girl. She wasn't downstairs, which meant she must be up in her room, where a light shone through the window. He considered for a moment if the rain was loud enough to mask the sound of the ladder, so he could get really close.

He crept into the woodshed, took down the aluminum ladder, and extended it to its full length. A minute later he was perched below Sara's window, his nose an inch from her window pane, only a few feet from his prey.

His Daphne-girl was lying in bed against a stack of pillows, with a white rabbit in her lap, and a small booklet propped on her knees. She was reading it with a shocked expression. Every so often her eyes would dart around the room, as if she were looking for an escape from the words. Once she whispered something to the rabbit, and wiped a tear from her eye.

Soon she would be his, with no Henry in his way, and her tears would be gone.

18

The Booklet of Betrayal

Sara fell asleep with her light still on, while the rain pounded down on the roof above her head. Bijou struggled out of her arms and jumped off the bed to hop back to the security of his cage. An hour later, when Sara's mother came up to check on her and turn off her light, she had no inkling that less than a minute earlier a man had been standing beside her daughter, watching her sleep.

At the first sound of someone on the stairs, Daggett had deftly lifted the booklet from his Daphne-girl's hand, slipped out the window, and nearly finished closing it before the door opened, Lily appeared, and he had to freeze in place.

The windowsill was dripping, and Daggett had left a puddle between the window and Sara's bed. Lily saw it and groaned, shaking her head at her careless daughter, and shoved the window down, catching the hem of Daggett's shirt as she turned the latch. She closed Bijou's cage, and went to say goodnight to her son.

Daggett waited for her footfalls to die away, then tugged his shirt out of the window and crept down the ladder.

"Here's the grocery list, and these are for Archie," said Lily, handing Peter a bag of freshly baked oatmeal cookies. "And that neighbor he's taking care of. Archie's done so much for us that it's time we did something for him."

"We'll drop them off. Come on, Ben," said Peter, and they headed out the door.

"I brought some of the money Grandma Daphne left me," Ben told his dad as the car splashed through the last pothole at the end of the dirt road and they started up the highway towards Cedarwood. "Can we stop at the hardware store? I need some things to build my blind for observing wildlife."

"So you're making progress with your project, are you?" asked Peter.

"Sure, Dad," Ben smiled at his father. "I'm learning a lot already."

✳ "Are you coming down with something?" Lily asked Sara when she finally dragged herself down the stairs after Ben and Peter had gone. She felt her daughter's forehead.

"No," answered Sara, brushing her mother's hand away. "The rain is depressing." She studied her mother carefully. "Did you come in to say goodnight last night?"

"Of course, sweetheart."

"Because I had a little book when I fell asleep and now it's gone." She studied her mother's face suspiciously.

"Did you check under the bed?" asked Lily.

"I've looked everywhere!" Sara glowered.

"What was the book?' asked Lily.

"Just a little book," muttered Sara. "Nothing really."

"By the way, I closed your window for you. Rain was blowing right in. It's not a good idea to leave a window open in the rain!" Lily scolded.

Sara looked at her mother quizzically. "I didn't open my window."

"Well, it was open, dear. Now take this towel and go wipe up your floor. It's probably still wet."

"Whatever," muttered Sara. "I'm going to go look for something to read in the storeroom. Mom," she paused, "what year was Grandma Daphne born?"

"1936. Why?"

"Just wondering."

✳ While his father checked out the riding lawnmowers, Ben found a shelf display of nylon rope. He picked out two sizes and bought several packages of each. While falling asleep he'd come up with a design for a climbing rope that would get him up and down the ravine as well as up trees without low branches, which was most of the trees in the forest. Best of all, his design would allow him to attach the rope to a tree at the top of the ravine even while he was on the bottom of the ravine, so he could take it with him and not have it stolen again.

They went to the grocery store next, and then Archie's. Nobody answered. "He's probably at the neighbor's," suggested Ben, eager to get home and start working on his invention. "Mom said it's a green house three doors down. Probably that one there."

They knocked on the door of the green house and Archie came to the door. "What good luck to see you!" he exclaimed in a weary voice. "The visiting nurse has the flu and they haven't been able to get a replacement. Any chance I could borrow you for the day to run some errands for me, Ben?"

Ben groaned, but silently. "Uh, I guess," he said. "How will I get home?"

"I'll pick you up later. Just call me," said Peter, handing Archie the sack of cookies. "Lily sent these with her thanks for all you've done for us."

Ben sprinted back to the car for his bag of rope, and then followed Archie down the hallway. Maybe this would be a good place to work on it, where no one would ask too many questions. "Where's the bloodhound?" he asked.

"Left him in the city with Rupert's niece when I went to pick him up from the hospital. She'll be coming out to take care of Rupert in a few days."

"Well, who do we have here?" A gravelly voice came through a dim doorway. Archie steered Ben through the door into the front room, where a bony old man sat in a wheelchair, a black cat curled up on his lap and one leg propped straight out on a footrest. The cat lifted her head to take a look and went back to sleep.

"This is Daphne's grandson, Ben," explained Archie, his hands on Ben's shoulders. "Ben, meet Rupert Fox, my neighbor."

Ben and Rupert stared at each other. "What's he doing here?" growled Rupert, winking at Ben.

"He'll be running a few errands for me and such," replied Archie.

"Humph!" snorted Rupert. "Tell you what. Why don't you run those errands yourself and leave the boy here with me." Archie hesitated.

"Go on, get out!" cried Rupert. He winked at Ben again. "I've seen your ugly face way too much the past few days." He wheeled his chair backwards in a tight curve and darted directly at Archie, threatening to run him over.

Archie dodged Rupert and called to Ben, "Think you can handle him for an hour or so?"

Rupert grinned at Ben, nodding his head furiously.

"Uh, sure," Ben replied, bewildered and entranced.

"Scoot!" shouted Rupert, and took aim at Archie again, chasing him into the hall and cackling.

The cat looked up again and went back to sleep. "So," said Rupert, "you're Daphne's and Henry's grandson."

"Yeah," said Ben.

"What do you have in that bag?" he asked.

"Um, just rope," said Ben.

"Rope," repeated Rupert. "Now there's one of the most useful items mankind has come up with. You can do most anything with rope." And he wheeled himself to Ben's side and looked in the bag. "What have you got in mind?"

Ben squared his shoulders and studied the old man. "I wasn't going to tell anyone."

"Good!" said Rupert. "Smart!" He eyed Ben carefully. "I spent my working years as a private investigator, and one of the first things I learned was to keep mum. Learned to listen. If I talked, I gave nothing away. Set a trap with my words, like a rope around a neck. People'd step right into my noose. You just have to know how to let 'em. They do it all theirselves."

Ben's shoulders relaxed as curiosity overtook him. "But—you're talking to me," he said. "And I'm listening. Are you setting a trap?"

Rupert smiled broadly. "I always set a trap, can't help it, it's been my way for too long. But it's what I do *after* I catch you that counts. You I like. You speak your mind. You're not afraid. That's good. Gives me a hankering to help you."

"Is that why you have a bloodhound?" asked Ben. "For being a private investigator?"

"No." Rupert stroked the cat and it began to purr. "Although all

my dogs have been search and rescue trained. I got my first bloodhound pup when I was younger'n you. My parents bought it for me
after one saved my life. They're the best dogs in the world. More
brains in a bloodhound's nose than in a hundred people combined.
And," he sighed, "they move more beautiful than any creature on
earth."

"Is that how you broke your leg?" asked Ben. "Archie told my
mom I wasn't big enough to handle a bloodhound."

"My hip you mean? No. That stupid Mabel who cleans for me left
my floor wet and I slipped. Matthias carried the phone over so I could
call for help. You'll meet him when he gets back with my niece Thea."

"I've never met a bloodhound before," said Ben, and looked
thoughtful. "If I tell you about my rope, would you keep it a secret?"

"Secrets are my business," said Rupert.

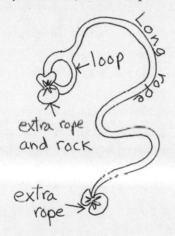

Ben drew a diagram of his design and explained it to the old man.
"See, there's a big loop at the top end of the main rope. You throw the
loop up and over a branch, so it dangles down, and then you thread
the other end through the loop and pull it tight. I'm going to attach a
little drawstring sack at the top of the loop, and put a rock in it for bal-
last so the loop end falls down low enough for me to reach it, plus
there's an extra smaller rope stored inside the bag until I need it. When
I want to climb down the big rope, I pull out the extra rope and let it
hang, so once I'm down I can just pull it to haul the loop back down
and undo the whole thing."

Rupert was listening with his mouth open. "And what's in here?" He pointed to a bag Ben had drawn at the other end of the main rope.

"Same thing, basically," replied Ben. "It's a drawstring bag with a small rope stored inside. You use it if the lowest limb of the tree is too high. You just undo it before throwing the loop up. It gives you more length to work with but hardly any extra weight or bulk to carry. Because, see, I want to keep my rope with me so no one steals it, and also so no one knows where I've been."

"It's a fine use of rope, boy," declared Rupert. "Clever as can be. It's the very sort of thing I would've thought of in my prime. You got a special purpose for your invention?'

"Maybe," replied Ben.

"That's okay, boy. You're wise not to tell. You don't know me. Follow your instincts."

Ben nodded.

"But I may be able to show you a few things about working with rope."

"Great!" said Ben, and began unwrapping the first coil.

Sara opened every single dusty book in the storeroom, but no secret diaries fell out of their pages. Discouraged, she searched her room again, tearing her bedding off, looking inside her pillowcase, even under her mattress. *Journey to the Center of the Earth* still stood beside her bed, its hollow space empty.

The words she had read were haunting her. Her grandmother had called Daggett "Raven-Boy." Until he came along, she had been in love with both of her best friends, Archie and Henry, and planned to marry Henry. But the man who would become Sara's grandfather seemed boring compared to the "sly, clever, handsome, and mysterious" Daggett, and her grandmother had made this little book to try to convince herself of one man over the other. Daphne had even mentioned the names she and Henry had already chosen for their children: Michael and Lily. But there never had been a Michael.

One section Sara had read over and over: "I have always loved my two boys, Henry and Archie. I always will. But my heart beats only steady with them. With Daggett my heart leaps and dances like a startled fawn." How could she have betrayed Sara's grandfather that way?

What if her grandmother had married Henry, but been in love with Daggett? But she had written, "I know I cannot have both Henry and Daggett." So she *must* have given him up, in her heart as well, to marry Sara's grandfather. Her grandmother could not have had a divided heart, not the grandmother Sara had loved without question, until now.

The rain had stopped, and sun broke through the clouds. Sara lifted Bijou out of his cage to take him outside for some exercise and fresh greens.

By the time Archie returned an hour and a half later, Ben had learned how to plait the strands into a loop that wove back into the main rope and held fast. He was sitting beside Rupert, working, while Rupert watched. "Hide it under that blanket!" hissed Rupert when he heard the front door open.

"I was just telling Ben a story about you when you interrupted us," Rupert told Archie. "You got back too soon."

Sara checked all the books in the living room as well, but there were no more secret booklets anywhere.

"Are you looking for something?" asked Lily.

"No," said Sara.

19

Raven–Boy

The sky dawned clear the following morning, with a warm mist above the meadow. For the second morning in a row Sara awoke feeling as if something inside her were hopelessly tangled and knotted, and now she was bitterly certain one of her parents must have taken the booklet out of her sleeping hands. If only she'd closed *Journey to the Center of the Earth* before its secret permanently poisoned her belief that her grandparents had always been perfect sweethearts! Maybe her grandfather had never guessed that his wife loved someone else as well. To think that one or both of her parents had probably read the same horrible pages made Sara squirm. If they tried to corner her for one of their little talks, she would run and hide. But the worst thing was that now Sara doubted she had ever really known her grandmother. She felt betrayed, and very, very alone.

There was an old framed black and white photo in the hallway that Sara and Ben had always loved, and she stopped to study it now. In a huge maple, a tree house was in progress. High in the fork of two limbs a dark-haired boy bent over a platform, hammering. Below was a larger platform, where thirteen-year-old Grandma Daphne and fourteen-year-old Grandpa Henry were kneeling, hammering away. Did Grandma Daphne go home the night this photo was taken and write the booklet? Sara wondered indignantly. The booklet had told how Henry and Archie wanted to kick Daggett out of the tree house they were all building together, even though Daggett was the mastermind. But Grandma Daphne hadn't mentioned *why*.

Near the ground, a young Archie was climbing a rope ladder, carrying something in a sack over his back. Grandma Daphne had claimed that the dark-haired boy at the top of the tree had moved to Cedarwood and soon moved away, and that she'd forgotten his name. Her grandmother had lied to them! In the booklet of betrayal, she'd also written that if she married Daggett, they would build a real house up in the trees, and live there. It was awful. Her mother was right: being here was dangerous.

Ben was already gone, off helping Archie take care of some old man like he had yesterday, which didn't make much sense to Sara, except that it proved he really *was* scared of something in the forest like she'd said. After all, the rain had stopped and that meant they were free to go out again. But with her brother gone, she might have trouble convincing her parents to let her go out alone, and so she was angry already, hungry for a fight.

"Bijou and I are leaving now," she announced to her mom and marched right past her towards the front door. She'd hung the safety whistle around her neck, hoping that would help.

"Not without your brother," warned Lily, without even looking up.

"Bijou has to have fresh air and exercise!" cried Sara. "Don't you even care about him? And I want to try out the leash I made him." She held out a handful of string. Her mother looked doubtful. "Thanks a lot for the vote of confidence," Sara muttered sarcastically.

"Just for a little while," Lily gave in, keeping the promise she'd made to Daggett to set her children free in the forest in exchange for protecting them. "I really don't like you out there all alone."

Sara rolled her eyes. "Don't worry so much," she groaned, and hurried outside, yanking the porch door shut with a satisfying bang.

Ben had spent the night tossing and turning, struggling against a strange impulse to tell Rupert everything. Being a private investigator who'd lived here practically forever, the quirky old man might even know some of Daggett's secrets. After all, who could be more interesting to investigate than Daggett? But Rupert had said himself that he always laid a trap, so Ben would be a fool to think Rupert wasn't laying one for him. Had he already fallen into it?

Then a word from out of nowhere popped into Ben's mind: *vicarious*. It was one of the vocabulary words his English teacher had made them learn. Now the word was singing its name to him like a radio commercial that wouldn't go away. He ignored it and continued thinking about Rupert.

Yesterday when Ben was describing his climbing rope and how it would make it possible for him to climb almost any tree, Rupert had listened and stared into his eyes so intensely, that it had felt like the old man was plunging through Ben's eyes and taking up residence in his private world, as if he were a magician instead of an old man stuck in a wheelchair. *That* was why the word *vicarious* was looping through his head. It fit. The word meant that you got an experience by watching it in someone else instead of doing it yourself. And that was why Rupert liked him so much. Ben had legs, and youth, and freedom. And daring. Rupert couldn't even get out of his wheelchair by himself. He wanted to live vicariously through Ben.

If that were true, then wouldn't the old man also want to keep the secrets Ben might tell him so the shared adventure could continue? You bet he would. It made so much sense that a minute later Ben fell into an untroubled sleep, and when he awoke in the morning his mind was clear: he would confide in Rupert, in exchange for information about Daggett.

Archie responded to Ben's phone call gratefully. "I've got a lot to catch up with in my own home," he told him, "and I'm getting tired of being beat at chess. I'm only three houses away if you need anything, and Thea ought to arrive sometime tonight, and then we'll both be off the hook."

A gray plume of smoke rose from the green mound at the base of Mount Portal, and the heat hissed through the splatter of water that fell from the dripping trees. Rain had pooled in the tops of the pickle jar skylights, and falling drops made circles on the surface of the tiny ponds.

Daggett was curled up on his bed beneath the pickle jars, regathering his energy. He hadn't realized how chilled he'd become in the downpour two nights ago when he'd had to suddenly pop back out through his Daphne-girl's window at the sound of footsteps on the stairs. That woman's anxious face had come within inches of his as she shut the window he'd only managed to partially pull down after himself, and then she'd turned around and seen the wet floor and put her hands on her hips and made a face. Daggett had suddenly heard the clack-clack of his teeth and forced his jaws together to silence them, and almost failed, suddenly weak and cold to the bone. It had been a miracle that he was able to put the ladder away without rattling it to death. In the night he'd awoken with a severe sore throat and a cough, and since then had been doctoring himself by sleeping and sipping a brew of his dried wild herbs. He would not allow himself to roam until he got better, because it was impossible to sneak silently through the forest with a cough, or the possibility of a sudden sneeze.

This was his second day at home, and he was beginning to improve. Friend and Wife had hopped through the tunnel to see him several times, bringing him an offering of fresh worms. When the birds left, Daggett carried the small clammy creatures outside and tucked them under wet leaves.

His Daphne-girl's little diary had been sodden by the time he got home, and when it had dried, the pages were crisp and stuck together. Although the ink had smeared, most of it was legible. He had not known she thought of him as her Raven-Boy, and rather liked it. He touched the now ragged scarf around his neck, and time blurred. Daphne had knit it for Henry, but given it to Daggett instead on that fateful winter day when they had secretly met, months after he had disappeared into the forest. The final bittersweet words she had whispered to him as she handed him the gift had burned themselves in his consciousness. Now, finally, the sweet would be freed, and the bitter thrown away.

While he waited for a pot of water to boil, he tightened the snare he'd built for catching the boy next time he tried snooping around the raft, and then broke open several dozen dried seed pods and let the tiny black balls fall into a clean jar. He mashed the seeds with a spoon, added hot water and a little honey, then screwed on the top. It would be ready when he needed it.

Ben had decided to be direct. "So, do you know anything about Daggett?" he asked Rupert once Archie had left.

"I figured you'd be interested in that varmint," replied the old man, rubbing his bristly chin with a bony hand. "Do *you* know anything about Daggett?"

"I asked you first," countered Ben.

Rupert laughed. "Let me put it this way: I know more than you do. Shall we say that I've kept an eye on that fellow for many years." He looked wistful and began counting on his fingers and chanting words that made no sense to Ben.

"What're you doing?"

Rupert looked up with damp eyes. "I always recollect time by my bloodhounds," he said. "Matthias, Portia, Limbo, Gossamer, Dylan, Thunder, Barsheen, Madara—It was in the time of my Madara when that pipsqueak Daggett first showed up in these parts."

"That's a lot of dogs," exclaimed Ben. "Pipsqueak?"

"It's been a lot of years."

"I know where Daggett lives," Ben blurted out.

"Everyone knows where he lives," muttered Rupert. "In his forest."

"No, I mean I know exactly where he lives. I've even seen the inside of—" Rupert's eyes suddenly bored into Ben's and silenced him.

Rupert released his hold on Ben's eyes, glanced away, then suddenly locked eyes with him again. In that brief moment of assumed privacy, Ben's eyes had revealed something that Rupert now held captive. "Don't jump to conclusions so fast, boy. And don't think out loud." His gravelly voice was very serious.

The black cat slunk out from behind the couch, peered around cautiously, and sprang up on Rupert's lap, stretched out lazily, and began to purr.

Ben watched the cat to avoid Rupert's eyes. Was he a mind reader? Did he know everything already? Then Ben remembered the acorn bird-flute, and pulled it out of his pocket. This would surprise him. "I don't know if you'll be able to hear this," he began, "it doesn't always work."

Rupert straightened up in his wheelchair, wincing at the pain of moving, and wheeled closer to Ben. He plucked the acorn out of the boy's hand, and rolled it around his palm, examining the sides. "So you have one too," he said, and handed it back to Ben.

Ben stared at him, speechless.

Rupert smiled. "No doubt in my mind they both came from the same carver. I'll bet you think only one hole does anything, right?"

"Um, yeah," admitted Ben.

"Well, you're wrong. Keep that acorn with you, boy. It holds the answer to a question, hidden for now. What else have you got in your pockets?" asked Rupert.

Ben gaped at the old man and then stared at the acorn, trying to remember which hole had made the birds sing. What question? Was Rupert talking about the riddle of the treasure in the pond? Sighing, he reached for his grandmother's letter. "I—I'm not sure this is supposed to be read by anyone else. It's from my Grandma Daphne, but my Grandpa Henry wrote most of it when I was being born."

"Hmm," muttered Rupert, and turned his attention to the cat in his lap.

"I don't know if I should show it to you," Ben said hopefully.

"Let's finish up your climbing rope, boy," interrupted Rupert. "You may decide you need it tomorrow. I'll show you how to make those bags for the ends."

"Stop that, Bijou," cried Sara, adjusting her hold on the struggling rabbit, "let's go find Esther." If Esther was her grandmother's friend, she might know her grandmother's secrets. Sara had to know if she could still love her grandmother or not. And she had to know if her grandmother had forgotten about Daggett and married her grandfather and lived as happily as Sara had always believed. Maybe when her grandmother had looked at that photo in the hallway, she'd seen only herself and Henry and Archie, and really had forgotten about Daggett. Maybe she'd forgotten she had ever written the booklet and it was just Sara's bad luck to find it.

Sara was doing her best to remember every single thing her grandmother had ever said about Daggett. Never had she given even the slightest clue that he was of any interest to her, only warned the kids to stay away from his territory. When they'd begged her to tell Daggett stories, Daphne would usually reply, "Rumors are rarely true. You just need to know that he's a man determined to be left alone, and it's best for everyone that his wishes be respected." She, who knew everything, had told them almost nothing.

How was Sara to find Esther? Everything was disappearing: her grandmother's letter, the booklet—what if Esther disappeared too? How could she have been so stupid as to bury her precious letter? Had Ben dug it up? Anger flooded her as she imagined the possibility, and the rage blinded her to everything but itself, so she didn't notice the raven land on a nearby tree. It tilted its head side to side, studying the trembling girl and the rabbit squirming in her arms. But Bijou spotted the bird and froze. The raven broke into song. Sara looked up. The melody seemed to ripple the blue sky into puzzle pieces that immediately blended back together as if nothing had happened. Then the bird warbled down to Sara, and the lovely sound fell around her like flower petals, erasing her anger and troubles. When the raven spread its wings, Sara caught a glimpse of an oblong space where a feather was missing, and it glided in a lazy curve to land on the ground about ten feet in front of her.

Sara knew to be still. Grandma Daphne had showed them that a wild animal can sense a person's energy and intentions, and encouraged them to just *be*, rather than *do* anything, when a creature approached them. The raven poked about in the forest duff a bit and swallowed a large black ant, checking on his audience every few seconds. He suddenly hopped towards Sara and Bijou.

"Cr-r-ruk! Cr-r-ruk!" the raven cried. It peered at the silent girl, continuing to caw. The bird hopped closer. "Cr-r-ruk! Pr-r-ruk!" it demanded. Sara bent her knees so slowly that her body scarcely seemed to be moving, until she was squatting with one arm reaching towards the raven. The bird continued studying Sara and Bijou, cocking its head towards one, and then the other. It hopped to within a few inches of Sara's hand, and stretched out one splayed foot. Dry black skin was pulled taut over its bony legs, and the talons curved like mighty claws. The raven took a step towards her, its plump body swaying, placed a talon on the edge of her hand, and ran its beak over her skin as if searching for something on her palm. Then it nipped lightly at her skin as if tasting it for information. Sara still did not move. The raven peered at her face with one round black eye, then the other, croaked, stretched its wings, and lifted into the air almost as if pulled by a string.

Bijou twitched as the bird flew away, but Sara remained still. When another raven's cry rang out from a great distance, she saw her bird circle, and then fly off towards the cry, the long empty space in its wing sparkling with sunlight. At first she could hear air whoosh each time the raven pumped his wings downward, like a giant heartbeat in the sky, and then the sound and bird were gone.

Sara sniffed at her hand to see if she could smell the raven, and examined the little pink spot where the bird had tasted her skin. I have a raven now, she thought, with a magic wand of light in his wing. Bijou kicked fiercely at her with his hind legs, so she attached his leash, set her pet down, and began to follow him dreamily through the woods.

Daggett paddled his raft to Daphne's side of the swamp, soothing himself with slow deep breaths every time he felt a tickle in his throat threatening to become a cough, and taking sips from the bottle of herbal brew he'd brought with him. He tied the raft to a madrona tree, then hoisted himself up into its smooth strong branches and secured the snare where it blended with the leaves. He didn't set the trigger line, because he wasn't going to leave the raft here today. But tomorrow, or the next day, when he felt better, he would bait his trap for the boy, and once the noose tightened around whatever body part it fell on, the boy would struggle, and his thrashing about would tighten the sinew. The sound of his terror would be music to Daggett's ears. The knots, once tightened, were impossible to undo without a pointed fire-hardened stick, sharp teeth, or a knife. One way or the other, the boy would be scared to death, and realize he was in over his head trying to fool with the master of the forest.

A Willing Captive

When Ben came out of the bathroom after breakfast, his sister was waiting for him. "Come here," she said, and led him down the hall to the photo of the tree house, where she pointed to the dark-haired boy on the upper platform. "Do you think this could be Daggett?"

Ben stared at the boy and then at his sister. "What makes you think so?" he asked.

"I just have a hunch," muttered Sara. "More than a hunch."

"Tell me!" hissed Ben.

"No," replied Sara.

"I know how to find out," said Ben. "And when I do, I won't be telling you."

"You don't have a clue!" cried Sara. "Not a clue."

Lily walked past them with an armload of laundry. "Quit that arguing, and open the door for me, will you please?" she asked. Ben reached for the door. "Bring me all your dirty clothes before you head outside," she added, "and don't forget that we're doing yard work this afternoon."

"Um, we're going to pack a lunch today," said Sara. "What time do you want us back?"

"No later than two," replied Lily, "now go get me your laundry. Oh, and Sara, I want you to try on your sock before leaving. I have to check the length."

"Sure, Mom," said Sara. "I'll go do it now."

Ben and Sara didn't speak to each other until they separated in the clearing, and then it was only to agree to meet back there a little before two. Ben took off up the trail, towards the base of the mountain, his new climbing rope hidden in his backpack. Sara waited until he was gone, and then began to weave her way through the woods towards the boulder, and skipped through its narrow passageway to her buttercup-filled hillside above the swamp.

Daggett felt much better today, and had spent dawn in his cozy perch beneath Friend and Wife's nest, watching the pale radiance behind Mount Portal swelling to become a golden halo. There were not enough sounds in Ravenese to express what he wanted to share with his friends this morning. He could warble about capture, and victory, but how could he communicate the knowledge that his lifelong quest was about to be rewarded? The birds, like all the woodland creatures he knew, lived and responded to what was happening in each moment, and had no language to express time. And so Daggett gurgled his joy, and warbled an image of a glorious cache of food with a pair of birds enjoying it, the closest translation in Ravenese he could manage to represent what his Daphne-girl meant to him. Friend and Wife listened curiously, their eyes gleaming at the image of the food cache. When Daggett had finished chattering, the ravens stretched their great black wings and flew off to search for the treasure he was describing.

Daggett watched his birds until they became small black ciphers in the sky, and then went home to prepare for his day.

At the edge of the ravine Ben looked around once more in case his old rope had reappeared, but it hadn't. He wouldn't have used it anyway, now that he had his deluxe don't-leave-a-trace climbing rope. He and Rupert had tested it yesterday on the big oak tree in his backyard, and it had worked perfectly.

A few minutes later Ben was at the bottom of the ravine, his rope secure in his backpack, and on his way to look for Daggett's pond, which might have a treasure that Daphne's pond didn't. The thrill of being here in forbidden territory was a treasure in itself.

Sara settled herself at the edge of the meadow, leaning against the sunny side of the big boulder. "Okay, Bijou," she told him. "Go eat grass." Checking that his leash was secure, she tied the end to her shoelaces and stretched out, letting her eyes close so the sun spun a geometric design beneath her eyelids. Bijou's leash pulled her foot this way and that, reassuring her that he was nearby. With luck, when she opened her eyes, either her new raven friend or Esther, or both, would be there with her. Instead, a sensation of her grandmother flitted by, and paused, as if to check to see if Sara would still accept her. Sara held her breath and waited for her grandmother to move on, but she did not. Instead, Grandma Daphne's warm presence settled beside her so that they now lay side by side on the grass beside the boulder. Then another presence approached them, and Sara turned her face away from her grandmother who had betrayed her, and towards the visitor instead.

Daggett watched his Daphne-girl basking in the sun, a grazing rabbit tied to one shoe. The same rabbit he'd seen in her bed. He didn't recall Daphne having a rabbit before, but maybe he just hadn't known about it.

The girl had turned her face towards his hiding place, blinked her eyes, and looked around hopefully, then closed her eyes again. Did she sense him coming for her? Daggett's knees began to shake. There's no hurry, he cautioned himself, she is no different than any small animal. He waited for his trembling to subside.

The rabbit suddenly sprang straight up as if its paw had been hurt, and bounced away rapidly, until the leash tightened midair. The rabbit's forward momentum jerked sharply at the girl's shoe, yanking it off her foot, and the animal began lurching forward, dragging the shoe behind him. The girl leaped up and dashed unevenly after him, one shoe on and the other off. "Stop! Bijou! Come back!" she yelled.

His Daphne-girl was running directly towards him, Daggett realized, and his knees went weak.

Ben had to pass by Daggett's underground home to reach the spot where he thought the pond was, and had promised himself to keep going. For safety, he was going to do a basic mapping of Daggett's territory, so he'd know his way around in case he ever had to get out fast.

But first he had to take another look through that glass porthole, just to see what was inside.

It didn't take him long to reach the place where the water rushed from a fissure in the cliff down the hollowed cedar log. Did it *really* flow into Daggett's home as running water? He wanted the answer to that one question, and then he'd move on.

Creeping silently and slowly, he headed for the spot where the porthole had been. But before he reached it, he nearly stepped into another porthole. And then he saw a third one. He was so excited he could have shrieked. The place was covered with portholes. Ben felt as if he'd discovered a buried spaceship, unknown to the rest of the world. And he bent down to peer through the nearest opening.

What he saw inside made him gasp. There was a charred pit in the center, set with a little pyramid of sticks ready to light. And he'd been right about the water. A cedar trough poked right through a gray carpet that seemed to cover all the surfaces, carrying a stream of water downhill along the wall for about ten feet, then disappeared into the floor. And there were shelves around the walls, mostly out of Ben's view, but he glimpsed strange contraptions, jars filled with mysterious substances, rows of beeswax candles, a quiver full of arrows hanging from a shelf, and leaning against the wall, a roll of animal hide. What must be the bed curved with the round wall, and was covered in lush pelts. Ben could imagine curling up there, like a hibernating animal, how his spine would curve against the wall as he fell asleep wrapped in all that fur.

Strips of meat hung above the fire pit, turning to jerky. Ben's mouth watered. Two stacked fruit crates held books, most of them with white bands on the spine, like library books. Daggett with a library card? No, he must have stolen them. Ben shivered. And then he remembered his destination, the pond, and forced himself to move on.

As he moved stealthily through the woods, thoughts ran through Ben like a torrent. If only he could make friends with the old hermit, it would be so much easier to learn about him. Probably no one had ever tried to be his friend. And what if Ben could build himself a house like Daggett's, hidden on their side? It would be the best hideout in the world. Where was Daggett's entrance? How had this mysterious man survived for over fifty years without doing any of the things adults had to do, like work, or pay bills, or well, be responsible? How had he managed to take possession of so much land without joining the adult race? How, Ben wondered, could he make Daggett want to be his friend? If he finds me here, grimaced Ben, he won't be happy to see me, but if I tell him that he's my hero, then maybe he'll listen. I'll bet no one has ever told him that. And maybe I can think of something to bring him as a gift.

A few minutes later Ben stood on the steep bank of Daggett's pond, its green-black surface rippling in the breeze, circled by forest. Cattails ringed the far shore, and a meadow of yellow-flowered pond lilies, their enormous leaves spreading like plates on the water, floated near where he stood. He held onto a branch and peered out over the water to see the fat lily stems disappearing like green rope into the bottom where they rooted and grew, the giant trees of the underwater landscape. The forest inside the pond. Ben smiled to himself.

The lily pads were littered with the bleached, wingless husks of damselflies. Fat dragonflies buzzed and darted over the pond, snatching small insects in flight. Ben felt like an explorer discovering a whole new world. Surely there was treasure in the bottom of this pond! He could almost see the dark-haired girl in his story slowly wading into the water and disappearing beneath the surface to search for the treasure. The treasure that Ben's thundering heart told him he would find here, in the intensely alive, forbidden side of the forest.

The cry of an osprey overhead seemed to call out "Welcome!" to Ben. The raptor hovered above the pond, its mighty wings rigid, its head tilting side to side as it watched the water below. Only its head moved, the taut wings and body vibrating slightly over the currents streaming beneath it. Ben's breathing slowed, and the river of thoughts that had been rushing through him vanished into the immensity of space that held him and the bird, as if they were one being.

Suddenly the osprey plummeted so swiftly that Ben gasped, unable to turn his head fast enough to follow. As the bird arced up from the pond's broken surface with a squirming fish in its beak, Ben's mouth filled with a fishy taste and sensation of struggle. He spit, and looked back at the pond. Wavelets from the disturbance lapped against the shore, and with each lap they softened, until they were no more.

The mighty hawk had sought a treasure for himself: food. He had spotted his treasure and retrieved it masterfully. But he *had* disturbed the water. Ben's breathing quickened in frustration. In the vastness of feeling one with the bird, in that glory, Ben knew in his gut that he had tasted the answer to his riddle, but it made no sense. It was elusive, slipping away from him like a little fish darting out of his hands. It was as if he had tasted the answer, and then lost it.

How many times had Daggett watched this very osprey catch a fish? How many millions of magical moments had his hero experienced out here? Did he have the answer that Ben had tasted and lost? Deep inside, Ben knew he had to find Daggett to find the answer. And without further ado, he sat down, closed his eyes, and tried to visualize Daggett taking him on as an apprentice and a friend.

Sara frantically chased after Bijou, who was springing forward on three paws, crying out in little high-pitched shrieks, and disappeared into a spray of stiff, thorny blackberry vines. Sara had to run around the thicket, desperately hoping he would stop so she could catch him. Tripping over a cedar root, she picked herself back up, dashed after her pet, and stopped in astonishment.

"Is this your rabbit?"

"Yes." Sara stared at the tall gray-haired man cradling Bijou in his arms. "Who are you?"

"I am your Raven-Boy," he whispered, and Bijou gave a whimper. "Your rabbit is hurt," he added, gently turning the small animal on its back. He held out the paw with the black mark that looked like a single cloverleaf and stem to show Sara that it was already swelling. "I can help him, Daphne."

"I'm not Daphne!" gasped Sara. "Give me back my rabbit!"

"He needs help," said Daggett. He showed her Bijou's paw again. "It's swelling. He must have stepped on a hornet. I know how to heal him, Daphne."

"You're Daggett, aren't you?" asked Sara, backing away from him. "Give me my rabbit back. And my name is Sara, not Daphne. And this is our side of the forest and you're not supposed to be here!"

"The whole forest is mine now," replied Daggett, his lip curling. Why was she arguing with him? Why had she changed her name? "The whole forest can be *ours* now."

"Give me my rabbit!" cried Sara, reaching for Bijou, who had closed his eyes and gone limp. Daggett put Bijou into her arms, but she did not turn to go. "What's happening to him?" she whispered, and began to cry.

"He needs help," repeated Daggett softly. "Here, put on your shoe," he said, holding it out to her, "and follow me if you want my help. I am a friend to all animals." He watched her tie her shoe, then slowly turned and began walking down the hill towards the swamp, without looking behind. He untied the raft. Only then did he turn around. Sara stood behind him, tears streaming down her face, Bijou wrapped in her arms. Daggett gestured to Sara to climb aboard, and without a word they crossed the swamp together. On the other shore, Daggett took Bijou from her and told her to step lightly so she wouldn't sink in the mud beneath the reeds, and she hurried after him as he trotted into the trees. It seemed darker here than in Grandma Daphne's forest, and all of a sudden she longed for her grandmother more than anything in the world. What had happened in the past didn't matter anymore.

You Could Die Trying

The trees seem taller here, Sara thought, running her eyes up the threads of white light, fine as spider-silk, shooting straight and clean down through the shadowy treetops. She held out one hand and pulled it slowly through a twinkling line of pure light, watching it curve and ripple over her fingers like water, then stand straight and still again, as if nothing had ever happened. A pale jungle of ostrich ferns brushed her chin as she passed, but reached only to the waist of the man she was following into his mysterious woods.

As they neared the base of Mount Portal, it grew clammier and colder. Suddenly Daggett bent down and vanished inside a thicket of salal leaves. Sara followed.

The leathery greens sheltered a hollow beneath their frame of twisted brown branches. Sara left the sepia light of the sanctuary and hurried to keep up with Daggett as he vanished underground into a dark hole. He scrabbled through the tunnel on two legs and one arm, like a big insect, crooking his second arm around Bijou. Sara was able to walk hunched over, and let her fingers bump along the dirt walls. Why, it was like the tunnel beneath Great Aunt Eva's root cellar, in the story Grandma Daphne had left her! The passageway turned and twisted, and grew completely dark, so Sara had to follow the sound of the man in front of her and use her hands to guide her. In the pitch black she suddenly remembered the goblin dream that had scared her nine-year-old grandmother in Great Aunt Eva's tunnel, and shivered.

The man halted to listen. "Hush," he murmured, and went on. A moment later Sara was unable to touch both sides of the tunnel at once, and then the walls narrowed again. They must be passing an intersection,

where another tunnel connected to this one. A moment later, it happened
again, and then twice more. Where were they going in this maze?

Then there was the comforting sound of a stream, and a light appeared at the end of the tunnel. They emerged into a large circular chamber, where the sound of running water grew louder, and the earthy
fragrance of the tunnel was replaced by the smell of wood smoke, herbs,
and beeswax. She stared at the tiny pale fingers reaching out of a wooly
wall, then realized that they were roots, just like in Great-Aunt Eva's
garden beneath. "This is wonderful!" she gasped. Daggett beamed at her.

Everything she saw thrilled her: cooking pots hanging from a root,
the fur-covered bed, and a real bow and arrows. On a table made of
rough planks, wood shavings surrounded a half-finished raven carving,
and a silver dagger stood at attention, its gleaming tip stuck in the
wood. Three eggs sat in a basket, and a cracked pottery bowl held a
chunk of honeycomb, which oozed with amber syrup swimming with
the tiny bodies of bees. By the entrance, the wall was lined with neatly
stacked firewood. And a long shelf curved from the woodpile more than
halfway around the round room. It held jars of mysterious dried plants,
coils of sinew, and complicated-looking devices, traps perhaps. But best
of all, there was a stream running right through this cozy home, flowing right down the hollow center of a beautiful cedar log. Sara stood in
front of it, let the water run over her fingers, and sighed with pleasure.

"Bijou!" she cried suddenly, wiping her hands on her jeans and remembering why she was here. "Is he going to be alright?" She reached
for him, but Daggett motioned her away.

"I'll fix him," he said, and chose a small jar from a shelf. "Take the
lid off," he told her.

The lid was rusty and made a strange powdery noise as she pried it
open. Inside was a greasy-looking yellow goop with a peppery smell.
Sara held the jar while Daggett scooped out a bit and spread it gently
on Bijou's puffy red paw. "Give him to me," begged Sara, reaching for
her pet. "Please!"

"Wait," said Daggett. "I'm not done." He pointed to the jar of
seeds, honey, and water he'd prepared earlier that day. "Shake it up
good and open it."

Sara did as he said, and sniffed the contents. It smelled sweet and good, like the sticky buns her grandmother made at Easter. Daggett took the jar from her hands, propped Bijou's head up, and held the jar to the unconscious rabbit's mouth.

"Open his mouth," Daggett ordered.

Sara obeyed. She could feel Bijou's heart thumping, and Daggett's breath smelled unfamiliar and strange.

He poured a few drops of liquid into Bijou's mouth, but most of it dribbled out. "He needs this," Daggett muttered.

"Please let me hold him!" cried Sara. Daggett stared into her eyes as if he had forgotten the rabbit in his arms. She stared back, pleading, and tried to take Bijou from him. "Give him to me!"

"There is another way," Daggett said slowly. "You love your rabbit, don't you?"

"Yes!" bleated Sara.

"If you drink this, and then you hold your rabbit, some medicine will go through you into him."

Sara reached for Bijou. Daggett shook his head. "I think if you drink the whole jar, it will be enough to work."

Sara picked up the jar and drank it down. "Do I need to drink the stuff at the bottom?" she asked, her teeth splattered with dark seeds.

"Yes. Chew it and swallow it," replied Daggett. "That's the medicine."

When she had finished the brew, Daggett put Bijou into her arms and she cradled him close, rocking him like a baby, crooning to him, feeling his heart beating against hers, and sank to the felted floor to curl herself around him so the medicine would pass through better.

They had been lying there for a few minutes when Bijou gave a twitch and opened his eyes, then closed them again. He squirmed, and Sara sat up drowsily and smiled at Daggett. "I think it's working!"

Daggett petted Bijou, and nodded. When he pulled his hand away, Sara yawned and looked gratefully into his black eyes. There was something so strangely familiar in them, something pulling her in. She could see her own reflection in them, then she thought she saw Grandma Daphne's face, but that flickered out and was replaced by an image of the grandfather she'd only seen in photos; then her grandfather blurred and sharpened to become her mother's worried face, then her father's, then Ben's, and finally, back to Daggett's. His beautiful eyes were pools of radiance, very close to hers, and she felt as if she and Bijou were being lifted in someone's arms—or on the wings of her raven with his wand of light.

✳ Surrounded by the fresh beauty of Daggett's pond, Ben found it both easy and thrilling to imagine the hermit as his friend. In fact, he realized with a shiver, this was his innermost wish: to be adopted by this lonely chieftain of the forest. I've got to be careful not to make him mad before we become friends, he told himself, and tried very hard to think of something he could bring as an offering, something that might be of value to a wild man. Maybe a knife.

Ben had been still for so long that a deer and fawn had come to drink and graze not more than twenty feet from him, and although they frequently looked around cautiously, had not taken notice of him. A blue and yellow striped garter snake had slid right up and over his leg and into the pond, where it glided across the water like a rippling S, sending quivering undulations out across the silken surface. He heard a raven's curious "Craawk!" and waited for the bird to come into his field of vision. He knew that if he moved at all, he would suddenly be visible to the wildlife that seemed to be ignoring him, and would lose the wondrous opportunity of witnessing their true life. A second raven replied, and Ben listened to their conversation, wondering what it meant. Then suddenly one of the huge black birds dropped to the ground and began to hop and flutter towards Ben, as if trying to provoke him. He forced himself to remain immobile, not even blinking his eyes. Then abruptly the bird flew at his face, and before Ben could stop himself, he ducked and threw up his hands in self-defense. The raven instantly flew up and began screaming bloody murder, or the equivalent in Ravenese. His friend joined him, and together the raven security guards skated back and forth above Ben, screaming nasty things, flying faster and faster. There was no doubt that they were warning him to get out of their territory. Daggett's territory. And he had better hurry, before Daggett himself came along and decided his future apprentice was a hated trespasser. So Ben rushed, carefully retracing his route back to the ravine without taking care to move quietly, while the incensed, screaming ravens flew back and forth in the air above him like ferocious ice hockey players defending their turf. Their victim began to run.

Peter and Lily were eating lunch outside, rocking in the porch swing. "Listen to those birds squawking way off in the distance!" Peter said, his mouth full of tuna salad sandwich.

"Do birds have fights?" wondered Lily.

"Sure," replied Peter. "All animals fight." He listened for a while. "Sounds like it's coming from Daggett's side." He chuckled. "Guess you'd expect that sort of thing from over there."

"Lots of little apples are already growing on Michael's tree," said Lily. "They'll be ripe in a few months."

"What kind are they again?"

"All different kinds," replied Lily. "Every year, on the anniversary of Michael's death, Daddy grafted a new kind onto a branch, until he ran out of places to graft."

"Don't you think you should tell the kids about what happened with your brother someday?" asked Peter. "We're here now, after all."

"Maybe," said Lily. "But not yet."

At first Daggett did not register that the noise coming through his smoke hole was from his ravens. In fact, at first he didn't even hear the shrieks, because he was so overcome by his good fortune. But the urgency of their cries finally drilled a hole through his trance and he stood bolt upright. He dared not ignore their warnings a second time. His Daphne-girl was now asleep. She would not escape. He pulled his dagger out of the tabletop, slid it into the sheath on his belt, and dashed out the tunnel.

Soon after Daggett left, Bijou struggled out of Sara's arms and began hopping around the room, favoring his injured paw only slightly, and leaving little black pellets behind him.

Ben could not believe how relentless the birds were. Every now and then one swooped down as if to peck at him, so he tried to stay out of open spaces and run through the cover of hazelnut copses and salmonberry thickets. This slowed him down, but helped protect him from the birds. It did not protect him from being scraped and scratched by thorns, and whipped by stinging nettles, but he scarcely had time to notice any of that. However, his panic cost him dearly: he was soon lost.

When he realized he had no idea where he was, he wrapped his arms around a tree, trying to catch his breath and think. The ravens continued their wild hockey match in the air above him, screeching and darting towards him as if he were the hockey puck. No matter how lost he was, he had to keep going.

Suddenly the birds' screams altered, and they backed off, as if the referee had blown a whistle. The hullabaloo was replaced by what sounded almost like a conversation, as if the frenzied players were reviewing strategy. This is not a hockey game, Ben told himself, this is me trying to get out of here, and I've got to keep going. He leaped over a rotten log and noted that the ground was getting rockier. Good. He must be getting closer to the ravine. Hurry, he urged himself, scanning the ground to avoid tripping over the jutting rocks. Those crazy birds might be back.

But when he looked up again, Daggett stood before him, a dark tower of a man, arms folded across his chest, his face tight and bony, and his black eyes molten with rage. The ravens fluttered above him making gurgling sounds, servants awaiting orders. "Get out!!" the man roared in a voice that sounded like boiling gravel.

"I—I want to be your friend," Ben attempted, his knees shaking.

Daggett lunged towards him, and Ben bolted. He plunged through nettles, dove between saplings, and flew past the splintery bark of cedar trees. Daggett chased after him noisily, herding his prey as skillfully as a sheepdog, aiming him towards the biggest trap of all, the swamp.

❋ "The kids will back in an hour," Lily told Peter, and held up the yellow sock to admire it. "It's so good to be knitting again," she said. "See the tree design? Sara picked it out."

"That's our Sara," said Peter. "selecting a pattern from the forest. I'm going to go change the oil in the lawn mower."

❋ The trees had thinned out and the forest floor was becoming sunnier when Ben realized that he could no longer hear his pursuer behind him. But when he turned around, to his astonishment, there was Daggett bounding towards him, not fifteen feet away, silent and deadly. Like a rocket launched by terror, Ben burst forward.

Now there were alders among the firs, and then just an obstacle course of gray alder trunks escaping into the sky. Ben thought of the rope he'd foolishly believed would let him escape into a tree. But there was no time to even complete that thought, because suddenly the ground turned spongy and then soggy and then there were no more trees at all, and his feet plunged into a marsh of reeds and cattails.

He dared not look behind, but slogged awkwardly through the muck. This had to be the swamp, and as soon as he reached the open water, he could swim to safety. Through the reeds he spied a raft, like the one he had taken just a few days ago. He ran for it and launched into a flying leap off its solid surface.

His flight planted him firmly in thigh-high water and mud. He tried to run, but couldn't pull his feet out easily, so he tried to push against the mucky bottom while pulling his arms through the water in his best racing form, hoping Daggett wasn't a good swimmer. But he was having trouble kicking his legs. In fact, they were stuck fast in the mud. Why oh why hadn't he dived instead of jumping? He wrestled desperately to free himself, and to his astonishment, felt himself sink deeper. He could scarcely even bend his knees any longer. Filled with horror, he turned his head around to see if Daggett was stuck too.

His pursuer stood on the raft with an expressionless face, apparently no longer chasing him. Ben gratefully turned away and tried again to free himself, pulling one leg at a time, paddling vigorously with his arms. A brown cloud of water swelled and roiled around him as he struggled, darkening the waters.

"Learn, or die trying."

Daggett's voice rumbled towards Ben like a clap of thunder, but he was too frightened to turn around. *Die?* Now the mud had swallowed him up to the top of his legs, and the muddy water was lapping at his armpits. He'd never been in mud like this before, ever. It couldn't be quicksand, not here! "Help me!" he cried, and whirled his head back around to plead for mercy. But nobody was there.

The Light of Home

A trail of small dark pellets fell behind Bijou as he hopped about Daggett's home while Sara lay sleeping. He nibbled at the sinew binding on a moccasin, stood on his hind legs to try to reach the water running down the cedar trough, and managed to climb the stack of firewood and from there hop onto the shelf that circled the room. He knocked down a small carved acorn and a few jars, which bounced on the soft floor and rolled to a stop, but Sara did not awaken. Finally he burrowed behind the row of jars and ran back between them and the wall, sending a dozen to the floor, where several collided and shattered, spraying shards of broken glass, dried roots, and little wrinkled berries across the felt. On his way down the stack of firewood, Bijou started a small avalanche of sticks, and frightened by the clatter and chaos, sprang away into the dark tunnel.

The boy would learn the secret of surrender in the quicksand, just as he himself had learned it so many years ago, thought Daggett, as he hurried home to his Daphne-girl. Or he wouldn't. If the brat survived, he'd never admit to what had happened, and if he died, well, there was no way to trace it back to Daggett.

He took a different entrance to his maze, as was his custom, to avoid leaving a beaten path, and scattered leaves behind him before disappearing into a hazelnut copse and plunging into the earth. A moment later a coyote trotted up to the entrance, and lay down to wait.

The arms that had first lifted Sara as if she were weightless had gone blurry, leaving her with a floating sensation. She heard the cry of her raven and saw him waving his wand of light as he flew above her. Then the arms, soft as feathers, lifted her again. Were they arms or wcre thcy wings? Am I flying? was Sara's last thought before she fell fast asleep.

❈ As Daggett entered the main tunnel, something soft ran against his foot. He grabbed for it, and caught a bundle of whiskers. It was the rabbit. He laughed softly, cradling the panicked creature, calming it, and feeling its feet in the dark. The swelling was gone. The salve had worked for the rabbit, and the seed and honey brew had worked for his Daphne-girl. And with the rabbit under one arm, he hurried towards his beloved.

Strangely, a billow of warm air blew past him, or through him, lifting the hairs on his neck and making him tremble, as he neared the light of home. It felt as if his beloved were washing through him, gathering him into her heart. Where could such warmth be coming from? He felt a nearly overwhelming impulse to turn and join the eerie radiance, but fought it aside. He knew what he wanted. In a few seconds he would be home with his Daphne-girl, and thc story of his life would finally turn out the way it was supposed to.

❈ Lily finished knitting the heel of Sara's sock and got up to stretch. She'd forgotten just how satisfying it was to watch the shape take form like magic in her hands. And it gave her a good feeling of being in control.

Peter came in whistling, letting the kitchen door bang behind him. "Mower's ready to go!" he yelled. "When are the kids getting home?"

"Soon," said Lily.

❈ It was a sea, but a sea of trees that Sara saw when she opened her eyes. She seemed to be moving through the forest, or was the forest moving past her? Am I a bird? Sara wondered, as she felt her legs trailing limply out behind her like a duck's feet when it flies. And she was holding someone's hand. No, birds didn't do that. Esther, it was Esther's hand she was holding.

Below all she could see were tree tops, their branches swirling like waves, a stormy sea in shades of green. One lone fir loomed above them all, like a ship's mast above the sea, as Sara and Esther glided towards the mountainside. Something near the top of the lone fir glinted and caught Sara's eye. She whirled her head around for a better look and spied a nest with something shiny in it, and then it was gone.

"Where are we going?" she asked Esther, turning to look at her companion.

The sun must have broken through the sky then, and blinded Sara, for all she could see was brilliant light. "Home," came Esther's response. "Home."

"Home?" thought Sara, confused. "My home?" she asked, suddenly very anxious.

"True home," answered Esther.

Then daylight was swallowed up and all light vanished. The air turned chilly, and Sara's toes suddenly bumped a solid surface, unyielding as rock, and her feet came to a rest on an uneven, cold floor. "Did you say this was—home?" she asked in a small voice.

"Yes. You'll recognize it soon enough," answered Esther. "I'll start the fire."

One of Sara's hands was released, and a moment later a mysterious blue and silver glow appeared. It grew brighter and began to shoot off tiny little sparkles that arced and fell back into the center. The air grew warm, and so did the floor, and Sara began to be able to see a bit. Rock walls curved around her like a cave, and there were passageways leading out in several directions. "Where are we?" she asked.

"Here," said Esther. "Here."

Struggle and Surrender

Daggett must have gone for help, Ben told himself frantically. He wouldn't leave me here to die, would he? He's looking for something to help me get out. He wouldn't leave me here to die!

But his hero did not reappear. What was that thing Daggett had said before he disappeared? Something like learn or die trying? *Die*? Ben die?

The forest and swamp were silent except for the incessant buzzing of insects and abrupt twitter of birds. Ben held very still, listening hopefully. Of course, he had no choice but to stand still, because the quicksand was gripping him up to his waist now, and the murky water was at his shoulders. Defiantly, he jerked himself around to watch the trees for Daggett. Any moment now he would return, carrying a long pole to pull him out.

But there was nothing. Nobody. Daggett could have paddled his raft out to help me, thought Ben. Instead he just stood there, watching me sink. Leaving me to die!

Ben burst into tears and sobbed helplessly until it dawned on him that the mud's monstrous grip had gentled. Freedom! he pleaded silently, and mustered all his strength to wrench himself loose. But when he tried to fling his weight forward, the quicksand seized him fiercely again, like an enraged prison guard, and swallowed him more deeply, until the water licked at his neck.

His backpack had ballooned above his shoulders, as if it were trying to pull him up by the straps. He could hear a little rushing sound and knew it was water flowing through the zippers. His climbing rope was coiled inside, the rope that was going to protect him. The rope that Rupert had told him he might need today. If only he were here to tell him what to do now! Ben pictured the wily old man sitting in his wheelchair, zipping around his house in spite of his pain, and bitterly envied his freedom. Because Rupert was safe, and he, Ben, was going to die.

Then he felt something bobbing against his chest inside his shirt pocket. Was a fish trying to eat him even before he died? In the same moment that the nibbling sensation left his pocket, his acorn popped up out of the water, and began floating away. He grabbed it and clung to it like a tiny life ring. Would it call his Grandpa Henry and Grandma Daphne to come help him from wherever they were? They wouldn't abandon him like Daggett, would they? With tears streaming down his face, he blew into one of the holes in the little carving.

Water spurted out the other hole like a tiny fountain. He gulped for air, and blew again. Instead of sound, it was as if something invisible poured from the acorn to silence all of nature: the buzzing insects, the twittering birds, and Ben's heaving breath. For a timeless moment he experienced a pure floating weightlessness, as if he were not imprisoned in mud and water, but was supported by something so soft and light, so infinite, that air seemed heavy in comparison. He relaxed, scarcely breathing, free and safe, his impending death no longer alarming.

A water strider skated past him, its hair-thin legs gliding over the water's invisible skin, until a dragonfly swooped down to carry it off in its hooked mouth, leaving nothing but a ring of disappearing circles on the brown water. The birds and insects seemed not in the least frightened by the boy in their midst. He was just one more drowning insect in this underwater forest of swaying strands of algae.

The crooked branches and finger-like leaves of a willow growing on the hump of land in the middle of the swamp seemed to stretch towards Ben, offering to help. If only he could reach it to pull himself forward!

Again he remembered Rupert telling him he might need the rope today. And suddenly he knew why! With the extra ropes freed from their drawstring bags, his entire rope was nearly fifty feet long. He'd have to throw the rock-weighted bag just right so it would wrap around a branch several times and hold tight, but it was his only hope.

He had to balance the coil of rope on top of his head, so the rope wouldn't drag against the water when he threw it. But when he hurled the weighted end with all his might, the quicksand responded to his escape attempt to seizing him more tightly, sucking farther down its tight and evil throat. After three futile tries, Ben's chin was in the water and he dared not try again.

"Nature is never spent; there lives the dearest freshness deep down in things," sang Grandma Daphne's voice somewhere in his consciousness. She had often sung these words as the sun went down, while he and Sara leaned against her soft, warm bulk while they rocked on the porch swing on long summer nights. And now his sun really was going down; his life was about to be over. The dearest freshness deep down in Ben that Grandma Daphne had always loved so much was about to die out, be spent, be over.

"No, I won't die without a fight!" he steeled himself with a final surge of determination and terror, and attempted to dive forward and swim with all his might. With the lower half of his body anchored in the mud, pulling himself forward meant his whole head went underwater. When he came up for air, he had to stretch his neck to keep his nose free. His resistance had only pulled him deeper. The monster who was slowly swallowing him took a gulp every time he fought. And if he fought once more, it would be all over.

"When you cannot escape something, turn around and face it," came his grandmother's voice again, "Surrender to the way it *is*."

Ben trembled. What did that mean?

"*Now*, Ben, no need to think it over," his grandmother warned. "It's your only hope. There is another face to this monster you have disturbed. Surrender to the treasure."

The treasure? At the bottom of this swamp? Where he was about to become fish food?

"Move towards what you are trying to escape, Ben, just for this moment." Grandma Daphne's familiar voice was so comforting and peaceful, that Ben gave in. Just for this moment. He took a deep breath and lowered his face into the water, letting his arms float free, like a dead man. He held his breath, but otherwise let go entirely, as if he were already dead, swaying in the warm water, like a pond lily with its green ropy legs rooted deep in the mud. That was who he was now, a pond lily, not a boy. It was so quiet down here, the only sound the beating of his heart, the world above him all gone now. This was so much easier than struggling. The mud seemed to agree; it held him close, more and more gently, with a tenderness that was almost wonderful.

And then he began to run out of air, and slowly raised his head, praying that he would be able to reach the surface again. He swept his arms very slowly downward to help his body right itself, and felt his head bob up and break the surface. Then his nose was above the water, and he filled his lungs again, and went back down. He hadn't known he would do this; he had only been going to try this surrender business for a moment, but there was something enchanting about it, and the way the mud had begun to breathe with him was mesmerizing. He *liked* the mud. Once again he let his arms float free and his head hang down, once again he let himself be a pond lily rooted in the fertile mud, and he felt as if the whole swampy pond was swaying with him. It was so peaceful down here, where he was not separate from anything, but a part of it all.

Then he had to come up for air again, and this time his whole face broke the surface easily, and he opened his mouth wide to take a breath, then became a lily pad again, feeling the mud relaxing around his leg-roots, and some creature, a frog, or a little fish, swimming through his fingers. It was like sitting silently in the forest, when all the animals resumed their lives as if he was not there, like the deer and fawn that morning at Daggett's pond, and the snake that had slithered right over his leg as if it were just another log. And now he recognized that this was the very same peace. A peace that billowed and swayed like the swamp water that cradled him, leaving him weightless, embracing him perfectly, calming him so that he could watch life in motion around him without reacting. It was heavenly.

Once again he surfaced for air, and this time his shoulders rose out of the water as well, surprising him. Had the mud let him go? Did he even want to be let go? He filled his lungs slowly and sank into the water to become a lily pad again, but this time the air that filled his chest buoyed him up and he was unable to sink deeply like before. I'm an uprooted lily pad, he thought, and was filled with such immeasurable sadness that he felt like weeping. A longing for the security of the mud's embrace as well as a feeling of rapture and release overcame him, and then he realized that his feet were actually drifting free.

By now Ben had begun to float almost completely on the surface of the swamp. Now that no one was struggling, the water had begun to clear, so he tried opening his eyes as he floated face down, longing to see the gentle creature the mud monster had become. I understand you now, he voiced silently as he peered through the water, we fought, and I lost. And when I stopped fighting, you became my friend, and gave me everything.

He wanted to play the game all over again, this thrilling game of capture and release, now that he knew the rules. But as he rose for air, he noticed that the sun had passed the midpoint in the sky. That meant it was already between one and two in the afternoon, and he'd better hightail it home. The house, his family, their petty problems—they seemed almost unreal to him now that he had discovered this treasure. He poked his feet a little ways into the quicksand until it gripped him again, and then let himself hang weightless one last time to feel the bliss of being released.

Ben swam to the other side and climbed into the warm limbs of an overhanging madrona tree to look back at the scene of his awakening. There was Daggett's raft, still in the reeds. And buried like a treasure at the bottom of the swamp's surface was his friend: the mud. As he dumped what seemed like bucketfuls of water out of his backpack, he wondered if he had only imagined the quicksand. No, he hadn't. And it would stay his secret. This would be his special place. He would enter the mud again, wrestle with it, and then surrender and feel the gentleness surround him. Daggett's last words, so terrifying a short while ago, came back to him: "Learn, or die trying."

He *had* nearly died trying. It was the trying that had endangered his life, the struggling. He literally could have died trying, but instead, he had learned the monster's secret. The monster who had become a treasure. Had Daggett known he would discover the swamp's secret before he died? There was no way of knowing that, yet Ben was filled with a profound gratitude to Daggett for abandoning him.

And now, he told himself, looking at the sun's position, I'd better go find Sara and hurry home before Mom and Dad start worrying.

·24·

Skunk Cabbage

Sara pinched herself. That was what you were supposed to do to find out if you were dreaming. Esther laughed softly. "Well, are you dreaming, Sara?"

"I'm not sure," she answered. "Where are we?"

"Here," answered Esther, "Home. Now, don't ask again. You'll just get the same answer. Instead, find out for yourself."

The floor was littered with jars, some of them broken. His bed, where he had laid his Daphne-girl, was empty. The frightened rabbit was the only sign that she had really been here, that he had not imagined it. But where had she gone? Daggett held Bijou in both hands and stared into his small pink eyes. "Where is she, rabbit? She wouldn't have left without you!" Bijou struggled to get free, but when his captor's grip tightened, he went limp.

Daggett dumped the books out of his fruit crates and put Bijou inside one with the other on top. "She's going to want you when she gets back," he muttered, and skirting the broken glass, rushed back out the tunnel.

The coyote was waiting for him when he emerged into the light. Daggett laid his trembling hand on the animal's knobby spine and raised his face to the sky, screaming in Ravenese for help. Off in the distance Friend and Wife answered, and according to their master's instructions, separated and began to fly in widening circles.

The distant cries began after Ben had begun to climb the bank above the swamp on his way to find his sister in the clearing. It sounded like the ravens again, getting ready for another attack, hopefully not on him. And Sara had better be waiting for him in the clearing so they could get home on time.

How was he going to explain his wet clothes? No way could he tell the truth, so he had to think of a good story. He couldn't say he'd fallen in the pond, because he and Sara were forbidden to go there. So it had to be a creek. But why would he fall in a creek? Just the mention of falling might alarm his mother. Ahh! He had it! He could say he'd rubbed skunk cabbage leaves all over himself to disguise his human scent, but that the stink had finally gotten to him so badly that he'd had to try to wash it off in the creek. When he crossed the creek, where the skunk cabbage grew along the bank, he'd pick one of the waist-high leaves and rub it all over himself just to give his story the smell of truth. With that problem solved, Ben glanced up at the sun and hastened towards the clearing. The ravens were still calling to each other, but had flown towards the mountain. He was very much alive, and would soon be home free.

"I'm going to run into town to fill the gas can," Peter told Lily. "Be right back."

"Where are the kids?" she asked nervously. "It's a few minutes after two already!"

"Don't be such a worrywart," sighed Peter. "They've been real good about being on time. And they'll need something to eat before we start with the yard work, anyway. I ought to be back by the time they're ready." He walked out the door, leaving Lily alone to sulk and wait. And then suddenly it struck her: she was home all alone, in this house that she feared, for the first time. Where, oh, where were her children? She arranged and rearranged warm oatmeal raisin cookies on a plate and set them on the table to wait.

"Sara!" groaned Ben as he looked around the empty clearing. "Where are you, you idiot? We're late!" His watch said 1:11, but had stopped while he was underwater. Judging by the sun, it had to be past two by now. If she didn't show up soon, he'd have to go home without her, and so far, every time they'd gone in together they'd also come out together. Well, maybe not today.

He sat himself down in Grandma Daphne's throne for a few minutes. His clothes were clammy and reeked of skunk cabbage mixed with the compost smell of swamp mud. He let his arms and legs dangle and his head flop forward, trying to recapture the sensation of surrender and weightlessness. For the briefest of moments he was there again, and in that underwater space he heard his sister whisper, "I'm Home, Ben." She was already home? Ignoring her, he tried to return to the blissful floating sensation. But it was no use here. His mind was racing, wondering where Sara was, and the uneven surface of the cedar throne pressed hard against him, an annoying sensation after the weightlessness of the swamp's buoyant embrace.

Where was his dumb sister? Ben's heart sank. What if it was actually a lot later than two, and she'd already given up on him and gone home? He had no idea really, how long he'd been in the swamp. He sprang off the throne and began loping homeward.

Lily added ice cubes to the pitcher of lemonade and stirred it while gazing out the kitchen window towards the trees. When Ben appeared, she drew back from the window so her children wouldn't know she'd been watching and worrying. It was already a quarter after two. She put the pitcher back in the refrigerator and hurried into the living room to sit at the spinning wheel, her mind full of poison arrows. The yellow wool flew through her jittery fingers unevenly, making lumpy yarn, as she tried to calm herself. Slow down, she pleaded with herself, give your attention to the fiber. The monster didn't get Ben and Sara. And Daggett's out there, watching them, protecting them.

She heard the front door open and slam, and footsteps clatter into the kitchen. "Mom! Dad!" came Ben's voice. "I'm home!"

He appeared in the doorway with a cookie in his mouth and another in his hand. "Where's Sara?" he mumbled, his mouth full. "These are good!"

"Sara?" repeated Lily. The cloud of yellow fiber slid from her hand and stopped the spinning wheel, snapping the lumpy yarn in two. "Aren't you together?"

.   .   .

It made no sense what the birds were doing. Daggett shouted to them in Ravenese to spread out over the forest, and help him find his Daphne-girl. But Friend and Wife remained together, hovering halfway up the rock face of Mount Portal, and seemed not to hear him. They've probably discovered a falcon's nest, he told himself, and are going to attack it before the chicks grow up to prey on raven eggs. Again he shouted in Ravenese for them to resume the search. But instead of responding to his command, the birds seemed to have disappeared inside the mountain.

"I thought she was ahead of me—" Ben attempted. "My watch stopped, you see, when it got wet, so I didn't meet her in time—" He unstrapped his watch and handed it to his mother.

"Wet? You went swimming?"

"No! Mom, you're so suspicious! I've been scientifically observing animals from my blind, and yesterday a fox got really close but then the wind shifted and blew my scent in his direction and he took off. So I remembered I needed to camouflage my human scent and I rubbed myself with skunk cabbage—"

"So that's what that smell is." Lily wrinkled her nose.

"And it worked, Mom, the fox came back today and I got to see him drink from the stream and dig under a log and eat grubs and mark his territory and everything, but then on the way home the smell got to me so bad that I tried to wash it off in the stream and well, that's how—"

"Well, I don't like this one bit!" cried Lily. "You stink, and you lost your sister! And do you have any idea what time it is, young man?"

Ben grimaced. "Sorry, Mom, but my watch got soaked. It's not my fault." He looked around. "So you mean Sara isn't home yet?" He brightened. "She'd better have a good excuse, huh? Want me to go find her?"

"She has her whistle, right?' asked Lily.

"Uh, I suppose," replied Ben.

"You do carry yours with you at all times, don't you?" Lily asked sharply.

Ben pulled his whistle out, realizing with astonishment that while he thought he was dying, it had never occurred to him to blow it. Thank God he hadn't, because he never would've fallen into surrender if help had arrived. Not to speak of all the trouble he'd have been in for going near the swamp to begin with. What luck that he'd forgotten about the whistle. In the gap between that thought and his mother's next words, he fell into a weightless space, floating free, buoyed up by nothing, yet buoyed nonetheless. Pure liquid peace.

"Here," Lily interrupted him, "take my watch. You have fifteen minutes to find your sister. If you're not both standing in front of me by 2:35, I'm going to ground both of you for a week."

Ben looked curiously at his mother as the weightless feeling faded. Then his curiosity stiffened into anger. "That's not fair!" he shouted.

"Go," commanded Lily. "Fifteen minutes."

· 2 5 ·

The Lie Takes Root

Ben's whistle sawed through the forest like a serrated knife, once, twice, then a third time in quick succession. "Sara!" his angry screams shot through the trees. "Sara!"

"What's going on?" Peter asked, glancing at his wife's tight face, as she stood gripping the porch railing. He popped the trunk open, heaved out the gas can, and listened to Ben's shouts. "Why aren't they home?"

"Sara's—lost!" whimpered Lily. "B-B-Ben came home without her. I sent him back to find her."

"Well, then, they'll be back in a few minutes, won't they?" said Peter, and began to carry the gas can to the tool shed. "I'll just fill up the lawn mower."

"No one ever takes me seriously," muttered Lily. "Peter! Listen!" she suddenly cried. A lone coyote's mournful howl broke through the vastness of the forest. Again, and again, its voice spiraled up and fell away. "What if it's after Sara? Coyotes never howl during the day!"

"Yes they do," Peter said comfortingly. "They howl when there's something to howl at."

"No they don't," said Lily. "Go answer the phone, will you?"

"That was Archie," said Peter when he came back outside and stood beside his wife, gingerly putting an arm around her. "He wants to take the kids to a movie."

"Well, tell him they can't go!" Lily spit out. "We're grounding them!"

"Let's not get carried away here," said Peter. "I'm going to go help Ben."

✳ By the time Ben and Peter returned, it was nearly 4:00, and Lily stood on the porch furiously tapping her foot.

"Mom, it's not my fault," began Ben, "you can't ground me—"

"I'm going out with you," she cried. "I'll wait for Sara in the clearing while you two keep searching. I've called the police and they're on the way."

Ben groaned and rolled his eyes. "Mom, Sara's fine. She probably fell asleep somewhere. The forest's safe—"

"Don't you get started with me!" screamed Lily, and plowed ahead of her son and husband into the forest.

✳ The first thing Joe Finney heard when he slammed the door of his police cruiser was "Sara! Sara!" echoing through the surrounding forest. "Durn fools," he muttered to himself. "We'll have a whole lost family here at this rate." He bent through the car's open window to get his clipboard and pen.

No one answered the knock on the door. "Durn fools!" he muttered again. "How am I supposed to ask them questions when they're not here?" He knocked again, then opened the door and called out, "Anybody here? Deputy Finney at your service!" His voice bounced off the wooden walls, returning to him with a hollow feeling. Shaking his head and frowning, he began to walk through the house, opening closets, cupboards, the freezer, the dryer, anything big enough for a child to hide in. "I hope this turns out to be an easy one," he said to himself out loud, "find her right around the home. Hiding maybe, afraid of something maybe, got in trouble maybe, being a little rascal maybe."

The deputy finished searching the house and went outside. The cries still rang through the forest, punctuated by loud whistles. Joe checked the woodshed, looked under bushes, and went back to his car to get his binoculars. He scanned the trees near the house just in case she was in one. Nope. Then a glint of light near the base of the house caught his eye. When he investigated, he found a window behind the shrubbery. So there's a basement, he thought, and hurried back into the house. There was no door he hadn't already tried. How could that be? He went back outside to search for an outside door. None there either. What in tarnation? He got a flashlight from his car and aimed it through the window. Instead of the spider webs he expected, he saw a neatly arranged, clean workshop of some kind, with broad tables, shelves full of supplies, barrels, basins—kind of scientific-looking. He thoroughly scanned the room with his flashlight, looking for any signs of a child.

The sound of a vehicle arriving made him stand up sharply and turn around. "Archie! Glad to see you!" Joe shook hands with the older man.

"Lily told me Sara was missing," said Archie, "so I came over to help out."

"Where's the girl's family? I need to interview them. No sign of the child around here." He indicated the house and surrounding land. "Unless she's holed up in there," he added, pointing to the window, "but I can't figure out how in tarnation to get in there. D'you know where the door is?"

Archie looked startled at his question. He bent down to peer in the window. "Oh, there," he said. "The—the basement. Sure, I know how to get in there. Helped Henry dig it out years ago." He paused, as if he was unsure if he ought to have said that. "Follow me," he added. He led the way into the house and pulled open the hall closet, pushing the jackets to the side and revealing a door. Joe looked at it and then back at the hall and realized that the stairs he'd been up and down a few minutes ago formed a triangular space he shouldn't have missed. Archie unlatched the door and they descended another set of stairs into the basement.

"Why'd he put the door in the closet?' Joe wondered aloud.

Archie chuckled. "Henry was like that," he said. Then he turned serious. "I sure hope she's down here. Sara, honey, you here?" he called in a pleading voice. The air was utterly still, with no sign of life. They looked beneath the tables, and opened the barrels, which were full of some kind of liquid.

"Just a single room down here?" asked Joe, not wanting to miss anything again.

Archie's back was to him. The old man raised his head and stared at the wall before him. The serious look on his face took on a mysterious quality and he answered, "Just the one."

There was a clatter of steps through the ceiling, and Peter appeared halfway down the basement stairs. "What're you doing down here?" he asked. "Oh. Of course. You've got to start with the house. I came back to get a compass. Did you find her?" he added desperately.

"No, son," said Archie softly. "Not yet, but we will. Joe here wants to ask you some questions, and any minute now Thea and Matthias ought to be arriving. Joe, this is Peter Maclennon, the girl's father."

"Thea and Matthias?" asked Peter.

"Rupert's niece Thea, with his bloodhound Matthias. I phoned Rupert, and he's sending them over," explained Archie.

"So they're coming, are they?" asked Joe, nodding thoughtfully. "Oh, oh. I hope we haven't ruined the scent trail already." He looked at Peter. "I want you and your wife and son to stay in the house and let me ask you questions. We'll find your daughter, but we've got to go at this proper like. If her trail is out there, the dog will follow it. We'll have her home so you can tuck her into bed tonight, don't you worry. But I need information, and you need to let me do my job. Which means we do the searching, not you."

Peter looked from Joe to Archie. "He's trained for this," said Archie.

"I've used Matthias on cases before," said Joe. "Rupert's had bloodhounds all his life. Only right now he's laid up, can't walk, old guy, broken hip. Used to work search and rescue with his dogs. Thea's not Rupert, but she can work the dog good enough. She used to help him train his dogs summers when she was younger."

Peter looked relieved.

"Now where's your wife and other kid?" asked Joe. "Archie, go find my bullhorn and yell for them to come back to I can start asking questions."

The Search Begins

⬚ "Now I'm going to ask you a lot of things," started Joe, tapping his ballpoint pen on the kitchen table where he sat with the Maclennons. "Don't take any offense. These are standard questions." He studied the photo Peter had given him. "Cute kid." At the sudden sound of Lily sniffling he looked up with sad eyes. "Hey, don't worry. We'll find your little girl."

"Shouldn't you be out looking for her right now?" cried Lily.

"Best to wait for the bloodhound," said Joe. "He's the expert, not me."

"Matthias is coming?' cried Ben excitedly. "Oh boy!"

Joe's first question drew only helpless looks. "Okay, so you don't remember what she was wearing." He tapped the pencil. "When did you say she was last seen?"

"We headed into the forest this morning," offered Ben, "and were supposed to meet back in the clearing a little before two."

"You kids spend a lot of time in the forest?"

"That's all they do," said Peter.

"Would Sara know what to do when she's lost? Hug a tree?' asked Joe.

"She'd hug a tree even if she wasn't lost," said Ben.

"But does she know about staying put when she's lost, and was she carrying water, a knife, matches, a compass, extra clothes, a map, anything like that?" asked Joe.

"She probably had water in her backpack," said Ben. "But I don't know about all the rest."

"What was her mood like this morning?" Joe asked. "Was she mad about something?"

"No," said Lily and Peter in unison.

Joe turned to Ben. "Well?"

"She was fine," he replied, looking annoyed. "She was playing with her rabbit."

"A rabbit." Joe made a note. "She had this rabbit with her?" he asked. "In the forest?"

"Yeah," sighed Ben. "She thinks he's a dog sometimes, takes him out on a leash."

"Hmm," said Joe. "Might've had to chase the rabbit and gotten lost. Happens all the time."

"She's never taking Bijou out again!" cried Lily.

Joe turned to look at Lily and smiled weakly at her, then turned back to Ben. "Which way'd she go when you two separated?"

"I don't know. Towards the mountain, I guess."

"Where's that bloodhound?" muttered Joe, glancing at his watch. "You and your sister got any secret hiding places out there?"

"I don't know about Sara," said Ben hesitantly. "We usually go our own ways."

"You don't know anything about where she goes?"

"Well, I could make some pretty good guesses, I suppose."

"You'd better do just that, Ben," said his father. "Your sister's missing."

"Tell you what, Ben. I'm going to have you draw me a little map—" At the sound of a vehicle on the gravel driveway, they all jumped up and headed for the door.

A tall, sturdy woman climbed out of a faded red pick-up truck with a camper shell on the back, carrying a couple of plastic bags in one hand. "Archie, Joe," she greeted the two men, and reached her empty hand out to shake Peter's hand, then Lily's. She smiled at Ben. "I'm Thea Harkins. My Uncle Rupert's laid up, or he'd have been here himself. But I know how to use a bloodhound, and Matthias is one of the best."

She turned to Joe. "You have a scent article?"

"Not yet," he stammered. The deputy turned to Lily. "We need something she's worn close to her skin, like pajamas, underwear, a pillowcase. Something no one else has touched."

Lily lit up, as if having something to do gave her hope. "Oh! I'll go upstairs to get something!"

"Whoa," said Thea immediately. "Remember, you can't touch it. I'll come with you and make the collection myself." The two women vanished into the house.

"Where's Matthias?' asked Ben, looking in the cab.

"He'd be in the back," said Joe. "Bloodhounds, you can't just let them loose or you'll never see them again. This is not a dog like you're used to. And we're not going to mess with the dog. He's here to work. Come on back in and let's get started on that map."

A few minutes later the women came downstairs with a sock sealed in one bag and a pair of pajama bottoms in the other. Lily stared at the sight of her missing daughter's clothing encased in plastic, and began to weep.

Thea patted Lily's shoulder once and then ignored her tears. Pulling up a chair, Thea began. "Okay. I need to know where you last saw the girl. Her scent will be all over the house and all over your yard. Matthias will follow the strongest trail, which will probably be the most recent." She looked out the window. "Nearly ideal conditions," she said. "Overcast, not too breezy, so the scent won't have traveled too much."

Ben pointed out the window towards the meadow. "There's a path into the forest at the end of the meadow," he explained. "You follow it to a clearing. I can show you the way. That's where we were supposed to meet, and it's where I last saw her." He looked downcast. "But we might have already messed things up too much. We've all been out there looking for her."

Thea laughed. "A good bloodhound can pick one scent out of a mess of others. Once they know what you want, it's like if I were to drop a pile of colored sticks and ask you to pick out the yellow ones. You'd never confuse yellow with the other colors." She looked out the window towards her truck and smiled fondly. "And Matthias is good. But I can't take you with me, because I don't want any distractions.

The fewer people tramping through the woods the better. And now I'm going to go set up." She rose and headed for the door.

Everyone followed her outside. She hoisted the back of the camper shell and opened an oversize steel cage and reached in to clip on the leash. A moment later a huge tan and black dog loped out and bounded to the ground. He immediately lowered his nose and began loudly snuffling, whiffling, and vacuuming the ground as he pulled against the taut leash. "Not yet, buddy," said Thea, and she knotted his leash to the trailer hitch.

While she went to the car to get his harness, Ben kneeled in front of Matthias. Once at the zoo Ben had been very close to a lion when the great cat had padded to the edge of his enclosure where Ben was leaning on the railing, watching him. A similar sensation flooded him now, of being in the presence of a regal being who quietly owned the world, cage or no cage. The majestic dog lifted his snout from the ground to vacuum the boy from foot to head, covering every square inch as he snuffled and whiffled, guzzling in big draughts of air. When Ben reached out to pet Matthias, he found his hands buried in thick, luxurious folds of furry skin that hung from the dog's face and neck, like an elegant version of a lion's mane. Ben grabbed silken handfuls and let them flow heavily through his fingers. He was running one of the dog's long ears between his palms, having forgotten everything else around him, when Thea's hand suddenly appeared between him and Matthias, holding a leather harness. "Making friends, eh?' she asked in a kind voice. "Never seen a bloodhound before?"

"No," answered Ben. "He's the most beautiful dog I've ever seen. And he's got so much extra fur it's like he's—like he's wearing a bigger dog's clothes." He reluctantly removed his hands from the luxurious softness so the woman could buckle the dog up. "I already met your uncle," he added.

"So I hear," replied Thea, as she expertly fitted Matthias into the harness that went around his back, chest, and legs. "See how the ends of his ears are kind of ragged? That's from being dragged along the ground all the time while he follows scents. His ears rock back and forth and push the scent towards his nose. And all that loose skin falls down over his eyes so he can hardly see where he's going. But he doesn't need to see much. His nose is his eyes. Bloodhounds can smell ten thousand times better than the average dog. That's why he's going to find Sara." Thea stood up, "Now that he's got his harness on, he knows he's about to start working. He only wears it for working." She snapped a lead onto the harness and put on a backpack. "I always carry enough water and food for both of us for a few days, if we need it, along with medical supplies and other things," she explained, "just in case."

Lily reached out to pet Matthias with a trembling hand. "You *will* find Sara?" she asked weakly.

"Unless she's disappeared into thin air, Matthias ought to be able to take me to her. Now if all of you'll go back to the house I can get him started. We need to concentrate here."

They watched from the door as Thea opened one of the sealed bags, and presented it to Matthias. He immediately pushed his snout in and seemed to almost suck up Sara's sock. "Find!" commanded Thea. She unclipped him from the truck bumper while his nose was in the bag, and the moment she pulled the bag away, Matthias dropped his snout to the ground, and began swinging his head, body following, in a zigging and zagging path, nearly pulling Thea off her feet, as he threw and pushed his weight forward with a rotation of feet in perfect, powerful motion, whiffling and snuffling as he sought Sara's scent. His oversized fur coat swung gracefully side-to-side across his back with every lope.

"Dad," whispered Ben in a confused voice.

"What?"

"Matthias—he's only got one back leg!"

"I noticed that," said Peter. "Doesn't seem to slow him down, does it?"

"He's an amazing dog," said Joe. "Got bone cancer when he was about two. Day after he had his leg amputated, jumped right up on Rupert's bed. He ought to find your girl right away."

"Look! He's heading right towards Bijou's tunnels in the grass!" Ben cried. "She and Bijou were playing there before I caught up with her this morning! Dad, d'you think they'll find her?"

Peter was standing behind Ben, intently watching the woman and dog. He drew his son to him and wrapped his arms around the boy's chest, hugging him close. "They've got to, Ben. They've got to find her soon. Come on, let's go inside and see what we can do to help."

"Dad?" Ben asked in a small voice. "Is Mom going to sell the house now?"

"I don't know," replied Peter. "It's the last thing on my mind. I just want Sara back."

In the kitchen Joe was on the phone, tapping his foot as he spoke. "Twelve years old, strawberry blond hair, well, kind of reddish blond, four-eleven, about eighty-five pounds, no. Yes, it's that three-legged hound, the one who identified that liquor store burglar last year. No, Rupert can't. Broken hip. It's his niece. Thea. She used to help him train the dogs. Seems to know what she's doing. Okay. Yes. I'll phone as soon as we hear something. And you'll put an SAR unit on alert in case we need them? Thanks. Yeah, yeah. Bye."

"That was my commanding officer, Sheriff Barrett. He expects Matthias will find your daughter, but just in case, he's notifying a search and rescue unit to be on call."

Lily's teeth began chattering as if she were freezing. Peter pulled her up from her chair to hold her close, and shouted for Ben to go get her a sweater. Archie wandered outside and began circling helplessly until Joe came after him and together they searched the area around the house once more. When they came to the basement window, Joe stopped to shine his flashlight through the dim room again, while Archie heaved a great sigh and stared at the ground as if it might open up to reveal something that could help him find Sara. "Henry," he whispered to himself, as if pleading for help, so softly that Joe did not hear him.

The First Lesson

"How do I get back to my other home?" asked Sara, suddenly feeling very afraid.

"That will happen when you are ready, child," Esther said.

"I want to go now," Sara begged.

"Not really," said Esther, "you don't. Now, wait," she cautioned, and held out her hand to halt Sara, who looked ready to run, except that she didn't know in which direction to go, "don't you remember what you came for?"

Sara felt fear rise in her and begin to bubble.

"Here, read this again," said Esther, and handed Sara the white envelope her grandmother had left her. The sight of her grandmother's familiar handwriting made Sara's heart leap up.

"Which one is this?" cried Sara. Turning away for privacy, she opened the crisp white envelope with trembling fingers. It held just one thin folded page. This was not the same letter that Archie had given her on the day they read the will, or the second one she had found in her jar that time with Esther.

She unfolded the page and began to read. After a moment, a tear rolled down her cheek and she turned back around and then continued to read. Finally she offered the letter to Esther. "Would you like to see what she wrote?"

"I can guess," answered Esther. "Come here and sit beside me. You've had quite a sudden journey, haven't you? I can answer your questions now, for you are ready to hear."

·   ·   ·

The blue and silver fire danced in bits of quartz in the walls of the cave, while the two women talked and listened. Grandma Daphne's letter lay beside Sara, and she turned to touch it now and again, as if it were her grandmother's hand. The deep blue ink of Daphne's words twinkled on the page:

My dear Sara:

Welcome, dear. You are here now. Is it familiar? In a strange, long-forgotten, yet oh-so-well-known way?

Esther was my teacher as well, some years ago. This cave is the schoolroom where I learned the ways of the very heart of nature. It was this which I attempted to pass on to you and Ben.

Esther was my teacher; she is now yours. She would have been your mother's teacher had Lily wished to learn. Who knows, through you and Ben your parents may eventually be drawn into the same blessed space. Or not.

Let your heart rest here, dear granddaughter. Time will stand still for you, while outside this sanctuary, the world charges relentlessly forward. Certain people and a dog will come forth to help Ben and your parents while you seem to be missing. Once you "graduate" and return home, the world will pause in its relentless charging forward, to open its arms in stillness and welcome you back, and you will resume your life as Sara Maclennon. But inside you will be changed . . . always.

So, dear girl, turn your heart and soul to Esther now. She is our Grandmother—a true Grand Mother. You are completely safe here.

And—welcome Home!

Your Loving Grandma Daphne

Esther watched the sleeping girl. Here, deep inside Mount Portal, the cycles of night and day did not exist. The child would probably sleep for some time. Esther snuggled the quilt around Sara, and gazed at the face that rose and rested with each breath. It wasn't Daphne's face. And it wasn't Eva's face. It wasn't Thea's face. Neither was it Daggett's face, Archie's, or Rupert's. Each face was different. Yet glowing in each face Esther saw the same essence. The individuals seemed to be born out of this essence, to take on solid form by some miracle, before dissolving back into essence.

As the woman watched her apprentice sleeping, the girl's form became transparent, and the quilt too, until there was only a pool of pale blue fire leaping and dancing lightly, almost as if it too were not quite there. Esther's eyes closed, and she swayed slightly as she sat. She was fully alert, though, her eyes turned inward, breathing in the very essence of herself and her apprentice. The blue flames danced towards the seated woman, danced around her, caressed her, purified her. Then Esther fell asleep, and toppled over. Before she landed, the blue flames flowed beneath and over her to make a soft, warm bed, and for untold hours she slept without moving, while Sara slept on as well.

A blue flame flickered out from near Esther's head, and others followed, like ducklings on parade. They spiraled around and around and then up in a loop. Their movements slowed and the flames shifted texture until they appeared to be woven like a basket, and indeed, the spirals had formed a basket shape and the loop had become its handle. Another blue flame flickered out from the other side of Esther's head, and with its followers began to dance in formation to make a rippling, flowing square. When the movements slowed, tiny flowing lines appeared, leaning this way and that, in an intricate pattern, as if they were some mysterious writing. The blue shifted to a million colors of green, darting in tiny straight trails that suddenly zigged or zagged, like small scurrying creatures, alive as the thickest greenest forest. The cloth, for that is what it appeared to be, lifted into the air and settled into the basket. Then one more blue flame flickered out from the very top of Esther's head, and with its loyal followers flowed directly into the basket, beneath the cloth. The cloth rose as if a balloon were being blown up beneath it. For a moment there was such a bright light beneath the fabric that every thread and every color became distinct. Then the light blurred, and slowly the basket with its cloth and mysterious contents fell into a slumber, like the other two inhabitants of the cave on mount Portal.

Sara's first lesson was complete, taught by the hush of the blue fire.

·28·

A Treasure Found and Lost

Ben watched restlessly as Deputy Joe spoke in hushed tones on the phone, while his father and Archie were in the living room trying to comfort his mother. Seeing that nobody was paying much attention to him, Ben slipped outside and sprinted into the forest. He wasn't going to go very far, but he needed to find a quiet place to collect himself, where his mind could stop racing, where he could try to tune into his stupid sister before she messed up their entire year here. If he could tune into her, maybe he could find her even before Matthias did, and bring her home, and then his Mom wouldn't sell the house.

He longed for some message from Grandma Daphne. She would know not only where Sara was, but what to do. All this was racing through Ben's mind when he dropped breathless beneath a tree. His heart was hammering and the anxious words others had uttered in the last hours kept stampeding through his head. He knew that the chaos of thoughts would just intensify if he tried to fight it, and he knew that his heart would slow down if he waited. Sort of like quicksand, he smiled to himself. So he dropped into the comfortable feeling of the tree and ground cradling him, and waited.

When he felt his pulse surging against the tree and the earth, he relaxed into the widening pools of sensation until they filled his body like liquid. His heart began to slow and the anxious voices in his head faded. The tree's heartbeat kept perfect rhythm with his, until their separateness washed away, and then Ben and the tree seemed to merge with the forest, until they were one vast still pool if life. Somewhere in the treetops two limbs leaning against each other creaked and groaned.

A cricket leapt into the air, whirring and then clicking as it sprang again.

"Ben." Smaller than a cricket's chirp, the sound arose. "Ben." He heard the word, but did not register it, for he had ceased to be the curious Ben, and was the pool of forest essence itself. When "Ben" sounded a third time, some part of himself finally funneled towards it, alert and motionless.

"Ben. Listen. What you feel and hear now is real. The wellness you feel, your oneness with the forest, the infinity of this moment. *This is the still treasure at the bottom of the pond.*"

The voice became silent again, and Ben felt suspended in a sea of shimmering heartbeats.

"The treasure is infinite, as you are now experiencing. If you disturb the treasure by trying to possess it, or attempt to use it for any purpose, it will become temporarily hidden, like the sun behind a cloud.

"Soon you will return to your house, and once you are there, this treasure of perfect peace will become slippery. The doorway to your house, to your family, will seem so small, so cramped, that you may become confused, and try to pull the infinite into a limited space. You'll find yourself caged inside the house without the treasure. You'll look outside, and won't see it there either. You'll be certain it's still nearby, and believe you're on the verge of recapturing it. You will repeatedly make the mistake of struggling to grasp that which cannot be held. You will foolishly seek *that which you already are*, as if it is something you can earn or acquire or deserve."

Ben continued to absorb every word, floating in the vast space between the words. The foolish seeking the voice described, and the odd picture of him trying to pull the infinite through his doorway, seemed to drift like lost bits of transparent stuff in the sea, without importance or substance.

"Sara is safe. She is with me," the voice continued.

Me? Thought Ben. It was the first time he had questioned whose voice he was listening to, and then he drifted back into not needing to know.

"I am teaching you and your sister the same simple thing in different ways. I cannot give these lessons to your parents because they do not believe in them. Their minds do not have a gap where the treasure can seep in. But they are here, surrounded by the forest, and the forest itself may lull them into a state where they will learn in spite of themselves.

"You've already begun to trust Archie. Good." The voice paused, its warmth spreading like steam. Ben became lost in the warmth, and twitched awake when the voice continued. "Archie is unlike the others. Once he was with me, here where Sara is now, but he has forgotten. He too encountered the treasure at the bottom of the still pond. His training was interrupted, and will resume as soon as he is ready. In the meantime, you are refreshing his memory, helping him to remember what he knew long ago, and to believe in it wholeheartedly again. Like you and Sara, he is permanently saturated with the presence of the forest.

"You can trust Thea, and of course, Matthias, whose path is always true."

A bee zoomed past Ben, made a U-turn, and circled him several times before darting away. The hair rose on his scalp, then settled down, leaving him with a shivery spine and a sudden realization: this was the voice of the stranger he'd met near Watchful One, the strange woman who had known his name and called herself Esther. Her voice continued.

"Now you will return to the house. It'll be crazy there, especially when they can't find Sara anywhere. You'll see your parents suffering, and your heart will break for them. You'll find it impossible to tell them what you know about Sara being safe. Your love for them will swell and grow, and you will feel an urgency to get back to the forest in order to help them. They may not let you go. No matter where you are, remember to be still sometimes, and give the treasure a chance to flood you. Find a place to be alone, in the bathroom with the door shut if that is all that you can find."

Esther paused, and the forest was so silent it seemed to have vanished. She chuckled softly. "You will forget what I am telling you, until you remember. If you are forbidden to enter the forest, accept that. You do not need the forest to have the forest. You *are* the forest."

Raindrops splatting on Ben's face and arms jarred him out of his reverie. He opened his eyes and felt warmth oscillating through his body, his back and bottom continuing to pulse with the tree and the earth. Ben felt the rush of his own familiar energy, and sprang to his feet and sprinted back to the edge of the meadow, then slowed to meander through the tall grass, as if he were searching for clues about Sara, just in case anyone was watching from the house.

Organized Chaos, and Comfort

Daggett impatiently watched the towering face of the mountain, waiting for his birds to reappear, but they didn't. Again he shouted to them in Ravenese, and then again, but they had vanished, as if the mountain had swallowed them up. Couldn't they hear his desperate pleas for help? Meanwhile, the coyote remained patiently at his side, watching him with loyal yellow eyes. A whimper caught in Daggett's throat and the coyote's ears twitched at the sound. And then Daggett curled his head back to howl, to cry, and yip in Coyotese. His companion joined in the chorus, calling the rest of his pack to help search for his master's missing prey.

Before Ben could climb the porch steps, the door opened and his parents rushed out. "Where were you?" his mother cried when she saw him, then stumbled and caught herself on the railing, tears cascading down her cheeks. A black truck pulled up, and a tall bearded man wearing a baseball cap embroidered with "SAR" climbed out, smiled grimly at Ben's parents, and then straightened up when he saw Deputy Joe and Archie walk out from the back of the house.

"Ralph Delgado, Search and Rescue Unit Commander," the tall man introduced himself in a deep voice. "I'll be taking charge now."

"Oh," said Joe, looking surprised. "You're here already? I'll have to check with the sheriff. We already have a dog out there."

"Hmmph," snorted Ralph. "A dog?"

"Bloodhound. Rupert Fox's dog. Maybe you've heard of him—Matthias. He's real good."

"That three-legged critter?"

"That's the one."

Ralph looked doubtful. "I'll get my people started as soon as we can grid out the area." He beckoned to a woman who had arrived with him and together they unfolded a topographical map on the porch floor and began talking rapidly and penciling in lines.

At that moment Matthias emerged from the edge of the woods, noisily pulling Thea behind him, his nose still sweeping the ground as he traced Sara's path back through the now trampled tunnels in the tall meadow grass. Everyone fell silent to watch the dog and handler swiftly approaching.

Thea clipped Matthias to her truck's bumper hitch and knelt down. "Good boy, good Matthias," she crooned, petting him, and offered the panting dog a biscuit from her pocket and a bowl of water.

"What'd you find?" demanded Peter. He and Lily had pushed through the crowd to Thea. "Where is she?" He looked wildly all around as if expecting Sara to step out of the throng of people.

"My baby?" gasped Lily, clinging to her husband's arm.

Thea gazed at them compassionately, then turned to Joe. "We need an inflatable boat. The girl's trail goes into the swamp. I spotted a log raft in the reeds on the other side—maybe a hundred yards away." Archie gulped and rushed into the house.

"The swamp?" gasped Lily.

"Isn't that the boundary between our side and Daggett's?" asked Peter, his eyes big and scared.

Ralph shook his head incredulously. "You allow your kids in that lunatic's territory?"

"Of course not!" shouted Lily, and she turned to Thea. "Why didn't you find her?"

"I had no way to get across. That swamp's not safe to walk through," explained Thea. "Not for me, not for Matthias. There's so much underground water seeping out of Mount Portal that the mud beneath the surface is unstable, like quicksand."

Ben had to clamp his hand over his mouth to stop from saying something, and quickly coughed into his hand in case anyone had noticed.

"Quicksand?" gasped Peter. "But—Sara—"

"She's not in the swamp, she's on the other side," said Thea. "My guess is she crossed on that raft. If your daughter had been caught in the quicksand, she'd either still be struggling, or if she'd drowned, she would have floated back to the surface. It only holds you if you fight back."

"So where is she then?" screamed Lily. "Go back!"

"I will," said Thea calmly, "once we get something for Matthias and me to cross over with. You boys have anything?" she asked Joe and Ralph.

The porch door banged and Archie hurried back to the group. "I phoned Hank at the hardware store and he's sent someone out with an inflatable."

"Thanks, Archie," smiled Thea.

"Do you think our Sara could have paddled a raft across the swamp?" Lily asked Peter in a daze. "Why would she have done that?"

"Do you know anything about a raft, Ben?" his father confronted him. "You kids been playing near the swamp? Been building a raft, have you?"

"No!" cried Ben. "We haven't."

Archie put his arm around Ben's shoulder. "It's okay, son," he said. "But if there's anything you know that might help, you've got to tell us."

"You don't think Daggett would harm a child, would he?" Joe asked Archie.

"I don't know," replied Archie. "How would I know?"

Ben stood very still.

"But Daggett will help us find Sara," Lily suddenly exclaimed. "He has to! I hired him to protect them."

"You *what*??" cried Peter.

"I hired Daggett to protect Ben and Sara so they'd be safe in the forest," muttered Lily.

Joe craned his neck towards Lily. "You hired Daggett?"

"Yes." Lily stood up straighter. "I happen to have had personal knowledge that he could do the job."

Joe took off his hat, scratched his head, and replaced it. "So your kids have got to know him, have they?"

"No!" cried Lily. "He was just on the lookout, secretly watching them. He might know where Sara is right now. We need his help."

"You and him got walkie-talkies, or what?" asked Joe.

"No," muttered Lily.

"Smoke signals? Carrier pigeons?" he asked.

"No!" cried Lily. "I didn't discuss the arrangement with him. We didn't even talk. I had a go-between."

"And who was that?" asked Joe. "Maybe your go-between had better go-between right now."

Lily turned away. "It's a private matter. I'll go make a phone call, if you'll excuse me please." Peter watched her go, his face full of confusion, and then hurried after her, while Thea, Joe, and Ralph huddled together to talk in hushed tones.

Matthias still lay on the ground beside Thea's truck, his great jowls swaying as he continued to pant with his head held high. When Ben looked at him, Matthias slowly laid his massive head down on his paws without taking his eyes from Ben's. The dog's dark liquid eyes, set deep in sagging, richly veined sockets, poured right through Ben and into his soul, soothing him like gentle waves washing a shore.

"Matthias," crooned Ben, dropping to the ground beside him, and burying his hands again in the dog's heavy layers of velvet fur. "Matthias." Ben closed his eyes and breathed in the dog's unusual bittersweet fragrance. It smelled like the juice of an alder branch. He smiled and buried his face more deeply into the plush folds of fur.

When Ben came up for air, he saw that the SAR man, the deputy, and Thea were still in their huddle, their voices throbbing with urgency. The door to the house stood open, creaking to and fro in the light breeze. No one was paying him any attention. "Matthias," he whispered, "I'm glad you didn't jump in the quicksand."

The dog swung his great head around to study the boy who was blanketed in his furry folds. For a long moment they just stared into one another's eyes. Then Matthias sighed a long dog sigh and sank his head back down upon his paws.

"If you ever get stuck in quicksand, the secret is to surrender," Ben told him softly. "Just let go. Remember that." Matthias swung his eyes, but not his head, to meet Ben's gaze. "Did Mom really hire Daggett to watch us?" Matthias blinked slowly. "Why would she hire *him*? He's what she's so afraid of, isn't he?" Ben sat up and reached into the velvet on either side of Matthias's face, pulling furry handfuls towards him so that their noses were nearly touching.

The dog just stared into Ben's eyes without wavering, and then released another long sigh and rolled over on his back, stretched out like a huge cat, and lay sprawled out in luxurious peace.

"I wish you were my dog," Ben sighed, and as his words echoed inside his head, his heart sank. This lion-like creature belonged heart and soul to Rupert, not him. And his parents probably wouldn't ever let him or Sara even go into the woods again. Plus, now his mom was sure to sell the house. Just as that thought pierced Ben like a needle, Matthias stood up with a great groan and shook his head wildly. Long spurtles of saliva went flying through the air like small cream-colored snakes. He snorted noisily and his ears and jowls repeatedly smacked each other, making a sound like a beaver's slapping tail.

"Gross!" Ben cried, as the dog lay back down. He scraped his jacket sleeve on the ground to get rid of a string of saliva that had landed there. "I love you," he murmured.

The sound of heavy footsteps on the porch made Ben look up, and he saw the SAR man disappear into the house. The woman who'd arrived with him wandered over and leaned down to pet Matthias. "Don't worry," she told Ben, "we'll find your sister. You just stay out of the way and we'll find her."

Ben glared at her with offended eyes.

"We're professionals," explained the woman. "The family always stays at home while we find the missing person."

Ben was silent, and slowly Grandma Daphne's—or was it Esther's?—image arose in the pool of his mind. He looked down to avoid the woman's eyes, and caught sight of a string of saliva wobbling on the backpack that Ralph had dropped nearby. He grinned and tried to make his mouth relax. After the inappropriate smile had faded, he looked up. "Okay," he replied, and sank back down into the comfort of Matthias's plush curves, somehow feeling reassured, as if the sea of infinity he'd felt a little while ago had taken the form of Matthias's lush body, and he floated on the rising and falling of the dog's breath. I think I could fit this feeling through the porch door, he thought dreamily to himself. Especially if I could take Matthias in with me.

A faded van marked *Cedarwood Lumber and Hardware* spit gravel as it jerked to a stop in the driveway, causing Ben to sit up. Immediately his parents and Archie rushed out of the house and everyone gathered around to see the inflatable boat, which Ben knew was not going to take anyone to Sara. They weren't going to find her anywhere. Not until the lessons she and Ben were learning were complete, at least. I wonder what the lessons are? he wondered. Deep inside him the stillness purred, like a silent smile, while on the surface he felt energized, curious, and eager to participate in the adventure of searching. I can live in both worlds, he told himself, and for that moment he did.

"I'll help carry the boat," he offered.

Ralph turned and looked down at Ben, then shook his head. "You're not going anywhere," he warned, and turned to Peter. "Don't let this boy out of your sight. Kids like to be heroes in situations like this, and then we end up with two missing persons."

As Ben gaped in outrage at the tall man who had just made him feel so small, the infinite, wondrous world inside him shriveled. And then his father clamped a hand around Ben's arm, like he was a prisoner attempting to escape. The forest loomed dark and tall at the edge of the meadow, and he wanted to jerk free and run back to its wild freedom. Instead he stood rigidly, enraged, and vowed not to help his parents or the searchers at all. He'd wait until nightfall, and then sneak out and somehow warn Daggett not to help either. They weren't going to find her anyway.

Daggett's Maze Is Discovered

Daggett's ravens had not returned to help him find his Daphne-girl, so with the help of his coyotes, he'd been searching the green jungles of forest undergrowth around the many mouths of his maze of tunnels. Strangely, when the birds did return, they did not call out to him, but instead soared silently in a rising spiral, oblivious to their master's desperation. When Daggett spotted Friend and Wife, he cried to them to meet him on the ground, and the birds slowly unwound their spiral and a few minutes later swooped down, arching their great black wings in a rush of air to brake and land before him. In a frenzy of Ravenese, Daggett again described his Daphne-girl and the urgency of finding her, and ordered them back into the sky to fly a search pattern.

Instead, to Daggett's dismay, they flew back up to the same spot on the mountain's great rock face and disappeared a second time. Like before, he called to them and they did not respond. Cursing the birds, Daggett led his coyotes through the underground maze to the last entrance he had yet to check.

This tunnel opened into a mossy glade that faced the towering mountain, where water burbled out of cracks and bounced down the rutted cliffs, filling the air with fine mist. It was an entrance Daggett rarely used, because it was awkward to reach, for the ground fell away into a deep pool of water that hugged the mountain.

The coyote he trusted most, the father of the pups and the one who led the pack when Daggett was not with them, had sniffed the bed where he had laid Sara, and was seeking her scent now. The coyote had hurried through the tunnel to the opening, where he sniffed the air eagerly, then tried to leap up towards the high cliffs, yipping excitedly and wagging his tail. It was the same area where the ravens had twice disappeared. Daggett stared at the pool of water and the towering gray cliffs. In all the years he had lived here, he had dreamed of climbing the rock face. It was the one part of his territory he had never been able to conquer. So his Daphne-girl could not be up there, in spite of what his ravens and coyote seemed to think.

Trembling, he cut an alder sapling and poked it into the pool, feeling for something soft, hoping not to find it. He exhaled in relief, and flung the sapling away into the bushes like a spear. There was nothing. Wherever she was, she was safe. She had to be! Overcome by sadness, Daggett grunted to the coyote to go home, and turned back into his black maze to go home and clean up the broken jars, and think. How far could his Daphne-girl have gotten, anyway?

✳ Ralph tied the inflatable boat to a pack frame and hoisted it to his back, while Thea got Matthias ready to go again. Ben angrily shook himself free of his father's grip, and sat on the porch steps to watch them leave. He could've been their guide!

Thea turned to gaze at Ben, and winked, then smiled and nodded at him and turned back to her work. He started to rise from the steps, because it felt almost like an invitation, but she looked back again and shook her head, and a moment later Matthias was pulling her into the forest with Ralph struggling to keep up, as the bulky boat bumped against branches.

✳ Sara opened her eyes to see if her raven was still here with her. It was sleeping, curled up in its nest of twigs and mosses deep in the cave's alcove. Esther was still gone, but she had promised Sara that the raven would stay until she returned. Two other ravens had also come to visit, hopping and fluttering down the long passageway to peer at her and warble to one another, while her raven stood beside the blue fire and watched silently. Sara had tried to warble a greeting to the visitors, but they had just looked at her quizzically and after a while turned and hopped back out.

·   ·   ·

⁂ At the edge of the swamp Ralph pumped up the boat and held it while Thea climbed in and then beckoned to Matthias. "Give me the paddle," she told Ralph.

"Let me get in first," he said.

"You're not coming with us," she replied. "Give me the paddle."

"I most certainly am!"

"Don't be a fool," Thea said. "We'd never get off this sandbar with your weight, and besides, Matthias needs to concentrate." She reached up, yanked the paddle out of his hand, and pushed off.

⁂ Thea tied the boat to the raft and a moment later she and Matthias were plowing through the reeds and muck into the alder glade and then into the cool darkness of the tall fir trees. We'll find the girl in no time now, she told herself.

They'd been traveling for ten or fifteen minutes when suddenly Matthias plunged into a thicket of salal, yanking Thea after him. The springy branches whapped her in the face so that she had to cover her eyes for protection, and before she could get her bearings, they had descended into the earth and it was too dark to see where they were going.

Did the kids dig a tunnel hideout? she wondered in amazement, as she stumbled and fell in the cramped passageway, and shouted at Matthias to stop dragging her. "You're going to have to walk, boy," she told him, brushing the grit out of her palms, "*slowly*."

⁂ Daggett was sitting on his empty bed, cursing his bad luck, when from somewhere deep in the tunnel he heard a faint shout. A smile lit up his stormy face and he rushed towards the cry. It was his Daphne-girl, trying to find her way back to him.

⁂ "Slow down, buddy," Thea repeated. "I can't keep up with you in here."

Matthias pulled her around a curve, scraping her against the wall. "The kids couldn't have dug this," muttered Thea. "Slow down!"

A root caught her sleeve and ripped it as she jerked herself free.

"This is Daggett's work," she whispered.

Matthias suddenly stopped and Thea fell over him so they both collapsed in a heap.

"Sara?" called Thea into the blackness over the hiss of Matthias's nonstop snuffling. "Sara? You in here?"

Thea untangled herself from Matthias, but he did not lunge forward. Instead he ferociously vacuumed to the left, then to the right, back and forth, and finally whined.

"What is it, buddy?" asked Thea. "Let me get my flashlight."

But before she could fumble for the zipper, Matthias had plunged forward again and she had no choice but to follow, like a captive insect on a chain.

The blackness grew lighter, until Thea could make out the rocks and roots in the walls as they rushed past, and then abruptly she and Matthias crossed the threshold of the underground dwelling.

There was a scratching, scraping sound and a pair of fruit crates crashed over. Thea whirled towards the noise. A white rabbit hopped out, spotted Matthias, and instantly darted beneath the pelts of fur hanging over the side of the bed. Matthias lunged at the bed, ignoring the frightened rabbit, and began wildly vacuuming the surface for Sara's scent, as if he had suddenly found a concentration of it. Thea watched him, her heart beating rapidly. Clearly the girl had been there, and for more than a minute or two. But where was she now? That had to be her rabbit. Thea tried to reach under the bed for Bijou, but the space was a thicket of branches, and the rabbit had wedged itself deep inside, staring out at her in the dim light with its little pink eyes.

Within seconds of entering the black tunnel to greet his returning Daphne-girl, Daggett had realized that the snorting beast rushing towards him was not his beloved, but the unthinkable, an enemy invader. He didn't dare end up cornered in his home, so he darted down a side tunnel just before the creature collided with a second invader in the intersection and began calling for someone named Sara. Daggett did not pause to investigate. Instead, like a rabbit whose burrow is being raided by a deadly predator, he dashed through his maze and out into the forest to safety.

✳️ "Where's the girl?" Ralph asked Thea when she and Matthias paddled back across the swamp alone.

"Sara's vanished," said Thea, as she pulled the boat up on the bank. "But she was in Daggett's house—"

"His house?" Ralph exclaimed. "You found his house?"

"It's underground, next to the base of the mountain," she muttered. "You wouldn't believe the place this guy's built. Matthias took me straight to the hidden entrance."

"Oh," muttered Ralph, looking at Matthias with admiration.

"Nobody was there, but Sara's scent had pooled on his bed." Thea looked at Ralph somberly. "Which means she'd probably been there for a while. And there was a white rabbit inside a couple of fruit crates. Had to be hers."

"Oh God," muttered Ralph, shaking his head. "But you kept following her trail, didn't you? What happened?"

"That's just it. Matthias followed her trail back out the tunnel, but when we hit daylight, we weren't in the same place we'd started. Daggett's got a maze down there, like some insane gopher."

"But where did her trail lead then?"

"That's just it," Thea sighed. "Nowhere."

"I don't get it," complained Ralph.

Thea sighed and poked at the ground with her toe. "We came out right next to the mountain, and Matthias got strangely excited. He kept trying to jump up in the air, which"—she gazed at his missing hind leg—"isn't too easy for him, and trying to suck down the updraft. Like her scent had floated up, drifted way up into the trees instead of settling along the ground. He sniffed the ground too, but clearly, he would've followed her scent up if he'd had wings. Which would've come in real handy, because I could not get him to trail her beyond that spot on the ground."

Thea fell silent, and looked uncomfortable. "There's a little pond there, where water runs out of the mountain. Kind of place a child could fall into. I cut an alder sapling to check the bottom, just to be sure. She's not in there, thank God."

"Glad to hear it," replied Ralph. "But how do you interpret your dog's behavior?"

"I'm still thinking on that. Times like this, I wish a dog could talk. But I know what we need to do next, and we need reinforcements, because things could get dangerous. I'm going to track Daggett. He must've led the child to his home. It's virtually impossible she found it herself. I collected a scent article already." She held up a plastic bag containing a grimy wool hat. "I reckon if we find him," she sighed miserably, "we'll find her too."

Ralph stared at her grimly. "We've got more than just a lost kid here. Let's get this show on the road."

Loyalty and Lies

✳ "What do you mean, Sara's trail just disappeared?" cried Lily, her eyes wild.

"We'll find her, Ma'am," said Thea.

"You've got to find Daggett," shouted Lily. "She must have gotten hurt and he must've found her and helped her. Your dog probably got confused. You've got to find Daggett. He's the only one who knows that part of the forest. You've got to find him!"

Thea studied Lily. "I hope you're right." She turned to Ben. "Come here," she said softly, and beckoned him to follow her.

Peter stared at his wife. "Why in the world would our little girl have gone over there?"

"I don't know," uttered Lily, and broke into sobs. "She wasn't supposed to."

Around the side of the house, where no one else could listen, Thea asked Ben, "What do you know about Daggett and Sara?"

Ben's mouth dropped, and he looked indignant. "Nothing!" he cried. "She'd never go near him."

"What about you?"

Ben tried to keep his eyes steady. "I've never met the man," he said, and took a deep breath.

"Been over there?"

Ben's eyes darted side to side in spite of his effort to keep them steady. "A little. You're not going to tell my parents, are you?"

"I will if it will help us find your sister," she said.

"Ask me anything!" cried Ben.

"Take a couple of minutes to think, Ben," Thea said. "If I find out you're withholding information, I'll have your parents ground you for the next five years. I don't have time for games." She turned to leave.

"Wait!" cried Ben. "I know Daggett lurks around our house in the middle of the night, and you can't hear him when he moves. He's like a native. And he stole my rope from the ravine. I found his house, but not how to get inside, because it's hidden in the earth, and I know where his pond is, and I've used his raft to get across the swamp, and this afternoon he left me to die in the quicksand." He paused. "But as you can see, I'm here." Ben let his head sink.

"What time was that?" Thea asked.

"About 1:11," said Ben. "My watch stopped when it happened." He sighed, and quickly told her the story of being chased by ravens and then by Daggett himself, and how furious his hero had been, and how he'd gotten mired in the quicksand and when he'd turned around to plead for help, there was no one there. "You don't think Daggett caught Sara somehow, do you?" He stared at Thea. "She never would've snuck into his territory. He only chased me because I was an invader."

"Well, Matthias is never wrong," muttered Thea. "One way or another, your sister ended up in his home today, in one tunnel and out another, and vanished into the air. But she's got to be somewhere, and we're going to find her." She put a hand on Ben's shoulder. "When did you last see him lurking around the house?"

"Weeks ago. I was sitting in that big maple tree late one night and suddenly out of nowhere he appeared and climbed up the other trunk. We were both in the same tree. Scared me half to death." Thea raised her eyebrows. "He went up the trunk that leans against my window, and looked inside." Ben chuckled. "That time I was the silent one, watching him. He never knew." He grinned proudly.

"There a tree under Sara's window?"

"No, just mine," replied Ben.

"You know any other hiding places Daggett might have over there?" Thea gestured towards the distant forest.

"Haven't found any yet," Ben said, then grimaced. "You're going to find my sister, aren't you?"

"Yes," said Thea. "We've got to find Daggett. He's got to know where she is, or be with her." She pointed a finger at Ben. "You stay here. I've got to go."

※ When Sara woke up again, she wasn't sure if she was really awake, or had fallen into a peaceful dream. The blue fire still danced in the circle of stones, bathing the curves of the cave in blue flutters of light. It was impossible to tell where the floor became walls or the walls became ceiling, because they flowed into one another, like a great circle.

Esther appeared in the mouth of a passageway coming from the heart of the mountain. The raven looked at her and stretched its wings. Blue fire flickered through the space where its feather was missing.

"Awake, are you?" Esther asked, smiling at Sara. "Good. Then we can begin."

※ Daggett crept back through his black tunnel, spreading his feet smoothly and slowly on the ground as silently as soft butter on bread. Never before had he needed to enter his own home silently, cautiously. Never had his sanctuary been breached! Had that boy been here, too? In the final intersection he waited and listened for several minutes, then slunk closer to his ravaged home. Where oh where had his Daphne-girl gone? Had he only imagined her? His stomach was chewing on itself, and the pain was so intense that when he finally crept over his threshold, he was unable to straighten up. Like a grief-stricken hunchback, he stared at the home that had once been his alone, safe from mankind.

The fur on his bed had been tossed aside, revealing the springy mattress of branches. There was a sudden scrabbling sound. Was his girl hiding in there? His eyes suddenly afire with hope, he bent down and called softly, "Daphne?"

※ By the time Ralph returned to the swamp with four armed deputies, Thea had rigged a rope between their shore and the other side, so the inflatable boat could be pulled back and forth to ferry everyone across. She'd given Matthias water, and a biscuit to reward him for his good work, and made him lie down to rest, so he'd be ready for whatever came next.

"I'm going to give Matthias Daggett's scent article, and he'll follow his trail," Thea explained to the group when they had all assembled on the other side. She pointed to the guns in the deputies' holsters. "I hope we won't be needing those. But if Daggett's kidnapped Sara, he may be dangerous. But regardless of danger, I need for all of you to stay behind me. Matthias needs to be out front with no distractions so he can do his job. Stay at least as far behind me as I am behind Matthias. Got it?" Everyone nodded.

Matthias sucked in a deep draught of Daggett's grimy woolen hat. "Find!" commanded Thea, and an instant later the train of searchers rushed into Daggett's deep, dark forest.

"Is there anything I can do to help?" Archie asked Peter and Lily. Peter shrugged his shoulders and looked away, tears welling up in his eyes, and Lily just shook her head and wept. "Daggett's nobody's friend," said Archie. "I knew him when we were teenagers. He was in school with us for a few months. He's scared a lot of people, but as far as I know he hasn't ever actually hurt anybody." Archie tried to get Lily and Peter to look at him, but they wouldn't, although they were listening, so he went on.

"He's like a Native American, like that guy Ishi they found near Mount Lassen in California way back? Maybe you never read the book. A survivor, a loner. I do think he'd be kind to Sara if he found her hurt. And he might even know how to help her. He's taken care of himself for over fifty years now, without any help from anyone." Still neither Lily nor Peter looked up. "Confound it, I wish I could go help them search!" Archie cried, pounding his fist into his palm.

"Daggett was always sweet on your mother," Archie continued softly. "A goner. So he'd likely be real sweet to her granddaughter, even if she invaded his territory."

"I know all that," muttered Lily, wiping her nose with her sleeve. "Why do you think I paid him to be our protector?" Nobody said anything. "But if he isn't protecting her now, I'm not going to give him the diary or the money!"

"Why don't I know about any of this?" shouted Peter. "Why didn't you talk to me?"

"I couldn't!" cried Lily. "There're some things I just can't talk about!" And she hurried up the porch steps and into the living room, where she sank down onto the spinning stool, and grabbed a handful of the yellow fiber she had been spinning for Sara's socks. Her hands were shaking so hard she couldn't get started. Finally she dropped the wool and went to curl up on the couch and cry.

Thea's face grew grim as Matthias followed the same route that he had when trailing Sara. How long had Daggett been on the Maclennon's side of the forest, spying on the kids? Let whatever is happening now be innocent, Thea prayed.

Two ravens zoomed through the sky towards the search party and like black demons, began screeching and dive-bombing them, pulling up in fancy acrobatics a few feet above their heads. One of the deputies pulled his gun from his holster and tried to take aim at the whirling dervishes. Ralph grabbed his arm and pressed it down. "We're not out here to shoot birds," he growled, "just keep going." And to everyone's surprise, a moment later they plunged one after another into the earth, leaving the screaming ravens behind.

This was still another new entrance. That makes three so far, Thea thought, and yelled to Ralph and the deputies as she vanished underground. "You're going to have to crawl!"

Behind Thea, someone pulled out a flashlight and she caught glimpses of how well worn the ground was beneath her feet, and how many branches the tunnel took. As if he had a map, Matthias didn't hesitate, but dragged Thea onward, directly into Daggett's home. The men tumbled across the threshold and straightened up, rubbing their backs, stiff from being so bent over.

"Nicodemus!" shouted a deputy. "What a set-up!"

Matthias made a fast pass around the room and zipped right back out the tunnel, pulling Thea behind him. "Hold it!" cried Deputy Joe. "Shouldn't we take a look around?

It was no use. Thea and Matthias had already disappeared, and they had to follow, or be lost here in the center of the maze.

There was no way of telling the difference between the trip in and the trip out, except that at the end they found themselves outside again, but in yet another mouth of the maze, this one camouflaged beneath the low branches of a huge cedar tree. Matthias trotted directly to a creek a few feet away and drank and drank.

The rest of the search part staggered out of the tunnel and looked around in bewilderment.

"This is insane!" cried Ralph. "Where are we?" He pulled a compass out of his pocket and stared at it. "We're all turned around. Hey, what's your dog doing, anyway? Lost the trail again, I suppose? That's what happens when he gets out of the maze, isn't it?"

But before Thea could answer, Matthias squatted sideways against a tree and peed. "He's finally got that figured out," she said. "About the only problem he's had since losing his leg is when he forgets it's gone, and lifts the wrong leg to pee." She shook her head and chuckled. "But he's a better trailing dog than ever." She stared at Ralph. "Just sometimes we humans aren't smart enough to follow him." She nodded at Matthias and he plunged forward again, dragging Thea while the others charged after her, through bristly brush and waist-high ferns and over rocks and fallen limbs.

Not far away Daggett cowered in another hideout, trying to bury himself beneath the dismembered skeletons, dusty hair, and trampled leaves. This tunnel was a dead end, so he wasn't going to be able to escape if they found him here. But he wouldn't have to. *No one* would dare enter this place.

The Coyotes

❈ Rupert wheeled his wheelchair rapidly away from the old woman chasing after him. "I don't need you, Mabel!" he cried. "Go home!"

"You don't know when your niece will be back, sir," Mabel replied. "You know you can't get in and out of that chair by yourself. You've got to have someone here."

"Out!" screamed Rupert. "I don't want you!"

"I will not leave you alone in your helpless state, sir," said Mabel. "It would be wrong."

❈ Bijou waited until the noisy search party stormed back out the tunnel, then crawled out of the thicket of springy branches beneath Daggett's bed. He'd found a few roots to nibble on, where they grew through the floor, but now he was thirsty and hungry for something green. And there was nothing green in sight. The lanolin scent of the felt beneath his paws was unpleasant to the rabbit's senses, and so he hopped towards the dark richness of the open tunnel. Somewhere deep in his instinctual brain it was familiar, like a rabbit's burrow, and so he eagerly sprang forward, seeking comfort and food.

❈ The search party trampled through the forest after Matthias, huffing and puffing, cursing at the stinging nettles and springy branches that whipped them in the face. Worst of all, the air force squadron of two ravens had discovered them again, and resumed their attack.

"They're more scared of us than we are of them," Deputy Joe muttered, "Right?"

Nobody answered.

Matthias suddenly gave a single loud bark, and lunged forward with renewed enthusiasm, nearly yanking Thea off her feet. The ravens suddenly swooped up into the air and flew off.

"What is it, buddy?" called Thea.

Matthias heaved himself forward, baying at the top of his lungs, lunging towards three yipping, barking, growling, slavering coyotes who had suddenly appeared. Thea leaned her entire weight back on the leash, but it was no use. The wild dogs, screaming bloody murder, surrounded the bloodhound, rushing him from all sides, nipping at him. A gunshot rang out and a male coyote fell to the ground. Instantly the other two vanished into the bushes, and Matthias, blood dripping from one flank, tried to lunge after them.

❋ "Oh God!" cried Lily, jerking upright on the couch where she had been curled up, weeping. She ran outside where Archie and Peter were sitting immobile in the porch swing. "They shot someone!"

❋ Ralph grabbed Matthias's lead to steady him, and turned to stare at Thea. "He still following Daggett's trail?" Ralph asked.

"Yes!" Thea replied in a shaking voice. "Hold the leash while I check him, okay?" A thin stream of crimson blood was bubbling out of a small gash on his hind leg. "You're okay, boy," she said, as Matthias ignored her ministrations to vacuum the ground in front of him. "Let me give him Daggett's scent article one more time."

She pulled the bag out of her pack and opened it under his nose. Once again he nearly sucked the hat right into his nostrils before pulling his face out of the bag. "Find!" Thea commanded, taking the leash out of Ralph's hands, and the bloodhound instantly vacuumed a path in the exact direction the coyotes had vanished.

"He's after those coyotes again!" groaned Ralph.

"He's after Daggett," said Thea angrily. "Don't distract us."

A second later they were deep in the underbrush and Matthias's front half disappeared into the mouth of yet another tunnel. Out of the opening came a nightmare cacophony of shrieks and barks and screams and yells.

"Pull your dog out and I'll kill 'em all!" screamed a deputy. "I'll empty my gun in that hole!"

Daggett trembled beneath his cover of deer, rabbit, and bird skeletons, matted leaves and moss. Only his bony fingers stuck out, and that was because he had twined the soft little legs of the five coyote pups in between his fingers, to keep them above him as another layer of camouflage in case the enemy managed to enter the burrow. He was having trouble getting enough air. Let this be over soon, he prayed.

Ralph yanked the leash from Thea, and with brute strength, dragged Matthias from the hole. A deputy took aim and shot once into the darkness, before Thea threw a karate chop at his arm and knocked the gun into the underbrush. "You idiot!" she screamed. "Daggett's in there, and maybe Sara!"

Peter held his wife close in his arms, and they both shivered. "There's another shot," he whispered into the thickening air, as the sun vanished behind the mountain.

One pup had ceased to struggle in Daggett's grip, and a moment later the others freed themselves. The bullet that had gone straight through the little animal had also entered Daggett.

"They couldn't be in there!" shouted the deputy, rubbing his arm. "I think you sprained my wrist."

"He's right, lady," snorted Ralph. "This is a coyote den. You and your dog gone mad?"

"Matthias doesn't make mistakes," muttered Thea. "You fools." She took a few breaths and faced the others. "Daggett went down here. And by now he's probably vanished into his maze again, maybe with Sara. That is, if you didn't shoot one or both of them."

The others looked back sheepishly. The deputy who had shot into the tunnel took a deep breath. "I've got to find my gun," he said. "I'm responsible for it."

"You may be responsible for a lot more than that," snapped Thea.

"Give me your flashlights, all of you!" The men darted looks at each other, but handed them over. "Ralph, hold onto Matthias. I'm going in."

"You can't!" shouted Ralph.

"I can," replied Thea calmly. "Slow and easy, I can take a look."

※ Ben had hunkered down alone on the back steps outside the open kitchen door. What was going on? Not that many hours ago he had thought *he* was going to die. Instead he had survived and had the most wondrous experience of his life, of exquisite surrender and the transformation of fear to joy and freedom. Now it seemed like death was stalking his sister, or maybe she was already dead. What had those shots been about? And the coyotes screaming and fighting? Had they killed the coyotes? Was Sara really somewhere with Esther, or had it been his imagination? Whatever had happened to his peace and joy, to the floating sensation he'd had only hours ago? All he knew now was that he was never going to be allowed out of his parents' sight again, never would set foot in the forest again, and for all he knew, maybe he'd never see his little sister again either. Ben's head sank onto his knees and he closed his eyes and fell into despair. How could things change this fast?

Ben didn't hear Archie approach, and when the man touched his arm, he jerked up.

"You okay?" Archie asked.

Ben didn't look at him, just shrugged his shoulders.

"You heard the shots?"

"Yeah," replied Ben. "Obviously."

"Your parents were wondering where you were," said Archie softly. "Shall we walk around to the front?"

"No," said Ben.

"Will you walk out to the apple tree with me then? We can sit on the bench there, and at least your parents will be able to see you," Archie suggested.

"I hate this," said Ben. "I hate everything." But he got up and followed Archie through the meadow and plopped down on the bench facing the forest, his back pressing into the rutted trunk. Archie sat beside him, and turned to wave at Lily and Peter on the porch.

Thea spoke softly and gently as she moved slowly towards the mouth of the den. "I'm not going to hurt you," she whispered. "I just want to take a look."

A harmony of low growls greeted her as she came closer. "Shh," she murmured, "I'm not going to hurt you little doggies." The growls continued.

With two flashlights in one hand and three in the other, Thea shone the beams into the tunnel. More bright yellow eyes than she could count shone back at her. Maybe it wasn't another entrance to Daggett's maze after all, just a coyote den. The two remaining adults defended a litter of pups, every animal's fur standing erect along the spine, their teeth bared. Except for one. A little pup lay sprawled out, blood-stained. Tears welled up in Thea's eyes. "Poor baby," she said. "I'm sorry." For a moment she just breathed. The growling subsided. "Anybody in there with you?" she whispered. "Daggett? Sara? I'm here to help." But she asked the question with crumbling faith. She ran the flashlight beams over the frightened animals again, noting with relief that the mother of the pups, her teats swollen with milk, had survived. Thea studied the nesting materials of leaves, moss, and twigs, as well as the bony remains of the family's meals. For a split second she thought she saw something else twitch, a twig, or perhaps a bone. It had looked like a finger, really. But when she steadied the light and searched for it again, she could not pick it out, and all was still. "I'm stumped," she told herself. "I need Uncle Rupert." And she backed out, murmuring her sorrow for the two deaths to the family of coyotes, and returned to the men and Matthias.

33

A Tree in the Sea

A small, sharp crack sounded, and a few minutes later there was another. From deep inside the mountain Esther and Sara heard the shots. "Listen," whispered Esther after the first one. "A life-form is passing. Only this Presence we feel is left." Sara listened, aware of her heart pulsing softly against her ribs, like a small bird sleeping against the bars of its cage. The surfaces of the cave vibrated as if they were not solid, and truly, Sara no longer knew if they were. As solid as the mountain had always seemed, like a monolithic rock rising out of the forest, now it seemed to be vibration alone, molecules floating in space. "There lives the dearest freshness deep down in things," Grandma Daphne had always said. Yet now it was deeper than things, beyond things, through things, everywhere. The sweetness Sara had tasted all her life, the essence of all the love she had ever felt and received, had become an endless ocean of unidirectional love.

When the second shot was fired, Esther murmured, "Another life-form is evaporating. Can you feel how Presence increases in intensity as it gathers Itself unto Itself?"

And indeed, the dissolving walls seemed to radiate a warmth that grew again, filling Sara and dissolving her at the same time, washing, washing, washing. The solid sensation of the floor beneath her had vanished, as if she were resting in warm air.

Then out of the billowing radiance a tiny particle tightened and seized another particle to itself, and in a nanosecond the particles burst into the form of a taproot shooting down into the fertile warmth, and sprouted an infinity of microscopic root hairs that reached for particles to shoot back up into an explosion of green leaves, and still in that nanosecond, the leaves hungered for more and the roots branched out to seize particles and bind them into root hairs and send their nutrients up to the leaves, where branches had begun to form, now shooting into a small tree that needed more nourishment, and the never-ending cycle of need and fulfillment spun at a dizzying rate, until the first particle that became a taproot had become a towering tree. All in the same nanosecond.

"Bijou," cried Sara. "Bijou! Is he okay?" And she stared at Esther with pleading eyes.

"A thought sprouted," replied Esther, "and became a tree in the sea. Pay it no mind."

"Is he alright?" begged Sara.

"What matters most?" asked Esther, "The dearest freshness deep down inside Bijou, or Bijou's rabbit appearance?"

"I love them both," said Sara.

"Which one is truly here, now?"

Sara smiled. "His dearest freshness."

"This is the only lesson I have to teach you, my dear," said Esther. "That which this lesson points to is all there is."

"Oh," murmured Sara. Her eyes closed and she sank into the sea again, Bijou's dearest freshness the sea itself.

The coyote mother licked her lifeless pup, then cradled his limp body against her belly, trying to get him to nurse. Behind them, their master pushed his face through the pile of bleached bones, gasping for air. The dead pup's uncle crawled to Daggett, his snout pressed against the bones, and without raising his head, turned his eyes up to his master, begging for permission. When the man gazed into his eyes and nodded, the coyote began to clean him, licking his ears and hair, and finally, the salty tears running down his face.

"The dog was all messed up," Ralph explained to Lily, Peter, Archie, and Ben. "Took us on a wild goose chase that ended in a coyote den. Matthias got in a fight with the beasts and we had to kill a couple of them. That's the shots you heard."

"You shot the coyotes?" cried Ben.

"Had to defend ourselves, son," Ralph replied. "And the dog. Anyway, I've called in a complete search and rescue team. They'll be here before dawn. We'll start a proper, thorough search, grid out the whole area and cover it square by square."

Ben stared at the tall man as if he couldn't believe what he was hearing, and walked away. He had to find Thea and Matthias and learn what had really happened.

"But how long will that take?" cried Peter. "Our little girl's out there somewhere, and it's going to get cold!"

"I'm taking the deputies back out with me until it's too dark to see," replied Ralph. "With luck, we'll find her before the team even arrives. But if we don't, we'll be ready to go back out at first light."

"She could be hurt!" cried Lily. "Bleeding to death, unconscious—" she tried to continue, but her speech was lost in the choking sounds that came from her throat.

"I've asked for an infra-red flyover tonight as well," said Ralph. "That's a plane with equipment that senses anything warm, like a little girl. If we don't find her before dark, that may help us pinpoint her location so we can get to her first thing in the morning."

"I want to go out with you now." Peter's voice croaked and broke.

"Sorry, Mr. Maclennon," said Ralph. "We always require the family to stay home. This is where Sara will return, and you've got to be here. In a way, the family anchors the magnetic field that draws the missing person back. I know that sounds weird, but well, it's what I know."

"Ben! Where's Ben?" Lily cried.

"He's gone over to talk to Thea," murmured Archie, pointing to Thea's truck. "I'll go make sure he knows to stay right here."

Bijou began to run when he saw the light at the end of the tunnel, and the green foliage that draped the opening. He popped through a curtain of honeysuckle vines and scampered towards a patch of grass, where he began to munch happily.

"How you doing, Ben?" Thea asked when he walked up.

Instead of answering, Ben sank down and put his arms around

Matthias, burying his face in the soft fur. "Matthias didn't get hurt, did he?"

"Just a little," sighed Thea. She showed Ben the gash on his leg. "I've got to get him home and clean the wound." She unclipped Matthias's leash and gestured for him to jump up into the truck bed and through the door of his travel cage.

"You're leaving?" asked Ben in a dismayed voice.

"I've got to," explained Thea. "Matthias needs attention, and Rupert can't do a thing for himself in that hip cast. The lady next door comes over to help when I'm gone, but she's kind of intimidated by my uncle." Archie walked up, but she waved him away, then closed the door of Matthias's cage and crouched before Ben. "Worried about your sister?"

He nodded glumly, and tried to fight back the tears that welled up.

"Let's go talk," she said. "Privately," she added, darting her eyes towards the group on the porch watching them. Thea put her hand on Ben's shoulder and walked him around the back of the house, where the grass still needed mowing. Bending down so that she and Ben were at the same level, she looked at him with so much gladness, familiarity, and such a sister-like smile that Ben melted. Then he blinked his eyes and felt confused. What was happening? There before him was Thea, glowing with tranquility. It was as though the world was entirely at peace here, as if there were no desperate people trembling inside the house or thronging the driveway ready to search for an endangered child. A fat red-breasted robin dropped from a low branch and hopped about the grass, searching for bugs. The bird also seemed to be living in a harmonious world, as if Sara were not missing.

"What do you know about Sara?" Thea asked Ben gently.

"Wh—what do you mean?" stammered Ben. He felt his hands in Thea's, but did not know when she had taken them. Peace flowed through his veins, and he asked, "You mean—do I know where she is?"

Thea smiled and nodded.

Ben peered into this woman's warm hazel eyes, and saw all the colors of the forest flicker through them. Dare he tell her? He attempted to part his lips to speak, to say something to protect himself, but he couldn't quite begin. Thea blinked, and when her eyelids opened, Ben saw a tiny flash of white in one pupil appear and vanish. It made him think of Bijou.

"Well—" he began. "I'm not sure anyone would understand," he said and paused.

Thea just kept listening and gazing gently at Ben.

"I—well, I know something, but it's a feeling, not a fact like cops want." He watched Thea closely to see how she responded to his vague answer.

Thea's kind eyes held Ben's for a minute, and then she let go of his hands, which shivered when her warmth was withdrawn. "Let's sit for a bit," she suggested, and they sat side-by-side. "If you think I might understand, you can try me," she said quietly, and then stretched out her legs and ran her fingers contentedly through the grass. The robin continued to dig for bugs.

Ben picked up a twig and began bending it back and forth, careful not to snap it. The bumpy bark was moist and dark and felt good in his hands. "Sara and I know a lot about the woods," he began. "We're not scared of anything out there." He laughed. "Mom and Dad are scaredy-cats, so we've had it to ourselves since we arrived." He sighed. "It used to always be the three of us here—me, Sara, and Grandma Daphne. Grandma Daphne died last spring. She was the best grandma in the whole world."

His tears welled up again, and he let them fall. "If Grandma Daphne were here, she could go right to Sara, I know it." When he caught his voice again, he added, "As good as Matthias."

They were silent. Ralph's bass voice thumped through the walls of the house, unintelligible and insistent. Joe's anxious voice sounded weak in comparison, and then Ben heard his father's familiar tones, squeezed crooked by fear.

The twig snapped in Ben's fingers, startling him, and releasing that Matthias-like fragrance. He looked up at Thea, who gazed back with a face that seemed here for him alone. "I don't know where Sara is," he began, "but I might know—how she is, that is, sort of where she is and why." He'd said too much, way too much. "It's all just a feeling," he muttered. "I don't really know anything. Nothing." He snapped one of the broken pieces of the twig in half again and sniffed it.

Thea leaned back and looked up at the sky. Her hand found Ben's and she gently cupped his hand in hers. Ben felt strangely like a small wild creature being tamed. "Think your sister is okay?"

"Yeah," whispered Ben.

"Why?" asked Thea.

"Just do," said Ben. He bent forward to reach an unbroken twig. "She's not lost." He immediately knew he shouldn't have said that.

"She's safe?" asked Thea.

Ben gathered more twigs. He lined them up and began rotating them so their tips met in the center and they fanned out like the rays of the sun. He pushed his fingertip into the center of the sun and twisted it back and forth, digging into the dark moist earth. "Yes," he whispered.

"You're sure?"

"Yes," he whispered once more. He pulled his finger from the earth and smeared the dirt on his jeans.

"It's pretty interesting, you know, that Matthias lost Sara's scent at the mouth of the tunnel, and that he wanted to follow it up into the air, as if he was after a bird," Thea said. "I didn't want to say too much back there, but the truth is that everything I saw Matthias do tells me she went *up* from that spot."

Ben pressed his palm on the radiating twigs. "You mean—" and he studied her quizzically.

"I don't have an explanation. Got any ideas?"

Ben lifted his hands in an "I-don't-know" gesture. "Sara can't fly," he muttered.

"If she's where you think she is"—Thea turned to look directly at Ben, holding his eyes in her knowing ones—"she needs space." Both were silent for a while. Then Thea asked, "Would you agree?"

Ben nodded.

Thea stood up. "I've got to get back to Rupert," she laughed. "He's a crotchety old man when his supper's late."

Ben grabbed her hand, unwilling to end their conversation. "But—" he stammered.

"Come on," said Thea, and started back around the house. "I'll be back tomorrow, even if they think Matthias took us on a wild goose chase." She shook her head. "What nincompoops."

When she reached her truck, she waited for Ben to say goodbye to Matthias before closing the camper door, then winked at him and drove away.

34

Aloft

◈ When the woods around the coyote den grew completely silent again, and the scent of the killers began to drift away, the remaining adult male crept outside to lie beside his fallen brother, and then the mother coyote crept out, carrying her dead baby by the nape of his neck. She nuzzled him into place between her paws, stretched out beside her dead husband, and began to howl a spiral of grief that swirled through the woods and made every leaf on both sides of the forest tremble.

◈ Ben sat alone on the porch steps, feeling the coyotes' symphony of loss reverberating in his hollow chest, weeping with them. Framed in the amber glow behind the glass of the living room window, his father stood watching the sky darken around his missing daughter and his shuddering son.

◈ The pups tried to burrow under their mother's belly to nurse, but she refused to roll over for them. Finally the little dogs nestled against her side, pointed their faces to the sky, and added their puppy voices to the chorus of lament.

Still buried up to his neck in old dinner bones, Daggett forced himself to ignore the throbbing, burning pain where the bullet had lodged in his foot, and dragged himself out of the rubble to reach his family and the fresh air. Neither adult paused to look at their master, who at any rate was not behaving as a master, but crawling towards them like a subservient creature. Daggett reached out to touch the fallen adult, who was already growing stiff and cold, and his head sank to the ground and his chest heaved with grief. When his breathing had returned to normal, he too threw back his head and keened his anger and desolation with the others.

"Come inside soon, okay, Ben?" his father called to him from the open door.

"I will," replied Ben. How could he leave the wide-open world that stretched endlessly into sky and forest, or the caress of the cool night air, and enter that narrow cage again? It was like Esther had said, a narrow door, too narrow to pull this vastness through. And Ben could not bear to strangle his freedom by going inside. The coyotes were probably going to cry all night long, and Ben's heart sang in chorus with them. He did not want to stop.

"Ben." A whisper drifted up from inside him, as gentle as a waft of warm air.

He cocked his head and listened with closed eyes, holding still except for his beating heart. Was it Sara?

"Ben," it continued, "I'm up here." And with the voice came an image of Sara sweeping her arm to show him what seemed to be a cave, with blue light streaming across the walls like a school of tiny tropical fish. "I'm with Esther," she explained. "Grandma Daphne sent her to help us. I'll be back when I learn—"There was a silence again, with only the beating of Ben's heart. He heard his sister laugh. "I just realized it has no name, what I'm learning. When I learn this treasure of no name, I'll come home."

"You're safe, right?" Ben heard himself whisper.

The image of his sister brightened and sparkled, full of blue light, as if tiny tropical fish were swarming circles around her. "Absolutely," she answered. "Yes."

Then her voice became somber. "Sorry to leave you with the mess. Don't try to explain what you know to Mom and Dad. They're supposed to discover it themselves."

"Where are you?" Ben whispered. He'd feel much better if he knew.

"Up here, Ben, but I have no idea if it's a place. Up here is the best I can describe it. Sorry I can't tell you more."

Ben waited, but there were no more words rising inside himself, and outside, the night prickled with tiny rustlings and scratchings of nocturnal creatures. An owl hooted softly in the distance, and the coyotes' sorrowful song reverberated through the dark velvet blanket that veiled the landscape. Finally, Ben began to shiver in the chilly air, so he reluctantly rose and opened the narrow door to go inside, willing the beautiful universe of haunting night songs and mysterious voices and images to enter with him.

They would be back, of that Daggett was certain. He did not dare hide again in the coyotes' den. And he could not go home; his sanctuary had been exposed forever. *I am homeless*, he told himself. There was only one place he might be safe. How he would get there he did not know, but he had to try now, while it was dark, while he had a chance of hiding himself again before daylight, when they were sure to return.

His Daphne-girl, where might she be? In the morning his ravens would hopefully heed his orders and find her. How would he ever provide for her without his home, his nest? His sorrow was too heavy to think. The tree, he told himself, the tree. Get to the tree, and climb.

He crawled to the creek on two hands and one foot, quenched his thirst, and then rubbed his entire body with skunk cabbage, to confuse the dog if it came back. He couldn't bear to touch his swollen foot, but undid the rawhide laces to release the pressure. And then he set off again, like some great insect with a damaged limb, creeping noisily towards the raven roost.

Ben awoke very early the next morning, before dawn, at first disoriented and confused by the hubbub of voices outside. Then he remembered everything that had happened and lay very still, suspended in mystery and anxiety. It had been very late indeed before anyone had gone to bed last night. Finally, long past midnight, his father had insisted Ben go to sleep even though Sara had not been found.

The house was strangely quiet. Maybe Sara was already back home? Ben pushed his covers aside and hurried into his sister's room. Her bed was carefully made, with the covers folded back invitingly, the way his mom used to do when they were younger, so they could come all warm and cozy from a bath and climb into bed. The door of Bijou's cage stood ajar, the cage as empty as the bed.

Ben sighed deeply. He dreaded going downstairs to face his parents, or anyone else, until he could digest the mysterious information Sara had given him last night. He sank down on his bed while echoes of her voice swam through his head. Had he listened carefully enough? What if he just had an overactive imagination, and Sara was really and truly lost, maybe even hurt? He tried to make himself believe that his sister was really in trouble, like one of those kids on a milk carton, but he couldn't. The forest was as safe and loving as Grandma Daphne's arms had been. He didn't have to make himself believe that. He knew it. Especially after surrendering to the quicksand. Would he ever get to go back to the quicksand again? "Sara," he whispered desperately, "you've got to come home!"

Back in his room Ben picked the acorn bird-flute up absentmindedly and went to look out his window. The driveway was now jammed with vehicles. A large motor home with an elaborate radio antenna was in their midst. In the meadow half a dozen tents were set up, and the grass looked trampled. Ben shook his head and felt tears falling. What if Sara—? But no, it couldn't be true. She had told him, Esther had told him, and Thea—Ben couldn't figure Thea out, but he liked her and hoped she'd come back today. It was odd how, when he'd told her he might know something, she hadn't tried to make him give her details. Instead she seemed to agree with him that Sara was safe—and that she needed space. Thea had seemed to kind of know what he knew, or at least it had seemed that way. Ben sighed again. Maybe he should ask her questions. What was he supposed to do next? And when she'd said that Sara must have gone *up* from the tunnel—could that really be true? Could Matthias be that good at trailing? And if so, what in the world did it really mean? If only Thea were here so he could ask her.

He knew the minute he went downstairs, he'd lose his freedom to sort things out peacefully. Well, maybe peacefully wasn't quite accurate, since he definitely felt worried about Sara, in case he was wrong. But once he stepped into the madhouse of everyone else's fears, it would be hard to hold on to the things he thought he knew. Let everyone else search for Sara in the usual ways, with their eyes wide open, while he kept his faith in the world he entered with closed eyes. They weren't letting him help search for her anyway, so he might as well do what he was best at. Maybe his faith would help his sister complete her mysterious lessons, and then she'd come back home, somehow, wouldn't she? And if Grandma Daphne had really sent Esther to them, like Sara had told him, everything must be okay.

He grimaced as he recalled his terrified parents' outbursts the night before. "Don't you dare leave our sight!" his dad had bellowed once, when Ben had started out the door.

"We don't want you lost, too," begged his mother, weeping and reaching for him. His parents were in such obvious pain that he dared not argue, and he had let his mother cling to him and blubber onto his neck.

Then Deputy Joe had taken him into the kitchen and spent an hour questioning him, taking notes in left-slanting script, and making Ben mark locations on a map. Every few minutes the phone rang and Joe had to talk to someone from headquarters or the media. Ben marked the places he and Sara had shared with Grandma Daphne, but he was pretty sure that Sara, like him, had discovered her own special places, so he couldn't help Joe with any of those.

The sound of his mother's weeping filtered up the stairs, fracturing the house's silence. Ben's throat tightened and without thinking, still in his pajamas, he hurried down the stairs towards her. She was in the kitchen, wearing yesterday's rumpled clothes, standing before the sink and looking out the window at the meadow. The dishpan was full of coffee cups and plates from the night before, but she wasn't washing them. She stood there, shoulders trembling, pressing her hands to her cheeks, and when Ben put his arms around her from behind she cried out in fear, then saw it was her son, and clung to him and wept on his shoulder like she had the night before.

"I wish I could go help look for Sara," said Ben after a while. Lily looked at him with red eyes and shook her head in a frightened manner. "I know," muttered Ben, "I won't go anywhere. Where's Dad?"

His mother shrugged her shoulders.

"Did they search all night?" asked Ben.

Lily burst into fresh tears. "They had to give up. Ralph sent out his search parties a little while ago. They're talking about getting a helicopter now," she managed to say. "And more searchers. The Red Cross is coming out to help feed everyone." She looked at the sink, wrung her hands, and wept harder.

"No one expects you to cook, Mom," Ben tried to comfort her. "We'll find Sara today, don't worry. How far can she have gone?"

"But she's got to be hurt, or unconscious!" blurted out his mother. "Otherwise she'd have answered when she heard them calling her name. Or—or she's gone, kidnapped!" And again she burst into tears, only this time uncontrollably, and Ben guided her to a chair and made her sit.

"Isn't there something I can do to help?" he pleaded. "What can I do?" Lily looked up at him and tried to smile. "I really think the searchers ought to take me with them since I know the woods and they don't," he added. "I might be able to help."

Lily stared into his eyes. "You could, couldn't you? But it's against their rules."

"I really want to help," insisted Ben. "Will you at least ask them if I can?" Lily shrugged and nodded. Ben looked out the window to see who had just driven up, hoping for Thea and Matthias. "It's Archie," he said. "Can I go out to talk to him?"

"Yes, but don't go anywhere," answered his mom.

Ben was out of the house so fast that he opened Archie's door for him. The older man slowly swung his feet to the ground and bent to ease himself out and straighten up. He coughed and reached for his handkerchief. "Lousy time to be sick," he muttered, then looked up at Ben hopefully. "Well?"

Ben shook his head. "They're still looking. A helicopter's coming I guess."

Archie groaned and looked away. "Good," he said. "She's got to be somewhere close by. You going to get dressed?"

Ben looked down and realized he still had his pajamas on. As he put his hands on his chest in surprise, he felt something in his pocket. He pulled out the acorn bird-flute and stared at it for a moment, for he hadn't been aware of putting it there.

Archie leaned over and peered at the carved acorn in Ben's hand. "Say," he whispered, and looked at the boy in awe, "you've got one of Henry's marvels!"

"My Grandpa Henry made this?" asked Ben, bewildered.

Archie tipped Ben's palm to roll the acorn back and forth, and a look of boyish joy brightened the old man's face. "Yup. Haven't seen one of these for years! Mind if I try it?"

"Sure, go ahead." Ben said, his eyes wide.

But Archie suddenly sneezed and fumbled again for his handkerchief. "Got so excited I forgot I had a cold," he sighed. "Don't want you to get it. I'd be much obliged if you'd play the little flute a bit. Haven't heard one in years now."

As Ben lifted the acorn to his mouth, he was flooded with the memory of the first time he and Sara had tried it, back in the city, before they had moved here, the night they'd met Archie, the first night the three of them had been together. He pursed his lips and blew into the hole, but only a dull *fftttt* came out. "Oh, yeah," he remembered, and blew through the other hole. As if he had touched a magic button, he felt instantly swept deep into the forest. Archie's mouth hung open and he sighed a long, contented "Ahh—," his arms hanging limply as he stood gazing dreamily up at the sky.

Both were still for a long time, listening to the echoes of the forest's music and feeling a rush of gold shimmer through their veins.

Finally Archie spoke. "It's like I remember," he said reverently. "Thank you." He looked around cautiously as if he were about to say something secretive. "If you'll go get dressed, I'll show you something. I think it's time."

Ben stared at him curiously. "Okay!" He trotted up the porch stairs and disappeared inside.

Archie walked back around to the side of the house with the basement window. He didn't look towards the window. Instead, he bounced gently on his heels a few times on the grass about ten feet away from the wall, looking thoughtful. Then he went to the tool shed behind the woodshed, and climbed up on an old chair so he could grope around the hidden top surface of a crossbeam. A smile spread across his face as he grasped several objects and dropped them into his jacket pocket. They made a single clunking sound, like metal. Then he went into the woodshed and unscrewed the cap from the top of a large pipe. He set the cap on top of a beam and leaned a shovel against the open pipe to hide it.

As he headed to the house, one side of his jacket swayed and hung lower, but there was no more clunking sound. Before he stepped through the door, he put his hand in his pocket to touch the heavy, quiet objects again, and paused to feel the rush of happy memories that came through them.

35

Dragonflies, Mountain Goats,
and Cow Magnets

Archie stepped into the kitchen from the back door, took one look around, then brewed a pot of coffee and rolled up his sleeves to begin washing the dishes. "It makes me feel better to do something," he replied when Lily looked at him helplessly. "Do you want to dry?"

She accepted the towel he handed her, but stood beside him, leaned her head on his shoulder, and began to sob. Archie put an arm around her, kissed her forehead, and handed her a dish to rinse. "We'll find Sara today, little one. That we will."

After their endless night of grief, the coyotes had fallen asleep exhausted outside their den, gathered around their cold beloved. Their sleep was so profound that none of them noticed the small rabbit who munched a zigzag path through the dew-laden greenery to within four feet of the furry sleepers before it stood on its hind legs, sniffed the air, and frantically darted away.

The bright gaiety of birds singing morning songs around the Maclennon's house was drowned out by the throbbing clatter of an approaching helicopter. A pair of large neon blue dragonflies zigzagged above the driveway, expertly snatching tiny gnats out of the air. The man-made metal dragonfly high above flew around the edge of the forest, beginning its search for Sara.

Ralph stepped out of the motor home holding a walkie-talkie to one ear and talking rapidly while he watched the helicopter. "Come on back. With the chopper up there the girl won't be able to hear a thing.

Yes. Once we get information from them I'll assign everyone new territory." He contacted the next pair of searchers and repeated the same orders. The dragonflies, oblivious to the human activity, continued darting above Ralph, seeking and finding their prey.

On the other side of the forest, the coyotes jerked awake at the sound of the helicopter. Ignoring the hungry puppies, the two adult coyotes tugged their dead back into the den.

It had taken nearly all night, and he had fallen once and knocked the wind out of himself, but Daggett had managed to struggle up the fir tree by using his arms, thighs, and his one good foot. Finally he clambered into his roost beneath the ravens, gasping for breath, his heart like a rock someone was pounding against his ribs. His foot had swollen so much it seemed on the verge of bursting through his boot. Collapsed in the roost, he picked the rawhide laces out to ease the pressure, every touch a shot of agony.

"Craa-aaak?" inquired Friend from their nest above, leaning over to look down at Daggett.

"Croa-aak," grunted the man, "crrrtzzzz," as his teeth ground together. "Don't leave me," he begged in Ravenese, "Don't leave me."

Archie, Lily, and Peter clustered on the porch, staring up hopefully, Peter following the helicopter's path with binoculars. Just as Ben ran out to join them, the helicopter tilted and made a tight turn, moved closer to the trees, and hovered in place. "Oh!" cried Lily. "Maybe they found her!" But a few moments later the chopper slowly turned and resumed its lazy curve around the edge of the forest.

Ralph strolled over. "Morning," he said, and tipped his cap. "The chopper's doing a careful pattern search. They'll identify the best areas for us to search, places your girl might have gotten trapped or fallen, any clues to help us pinpoint her whereabouts. If we don't find her by tonight—"

Lily's face went rigid, and Peter gripped the porch railing so tightly the bones of his hand showed white.

"—they'll use a heat-seeking camera to find her. Can't do it during daytime, because stones absorb too much heat and the camera can't tell the difference between stones and people."

"Why didn't they do this last night?" demanded Peter, his teeth clenched.

Ralph looked sheepish. "We were sure we'd find her. We don't actually know she's out there for sure, either. Someone could have taken her in a car. If we don't find any sign of her today or tonight, we're going to have to expand our search."

"I can't believe this," muttered Peter.

Lily snapped, "Why aren't *you* out there looking for Sara?"

"I'm sorry, Ma'am," answered Ralph, "I'm in charge of the command post. I keep in touch with all the searchers by radio, and make decisions. All the information comes back to me for analysis. I'm trained to sniff out the clues and send people to follow them. I'm doing my best, Ma'am."

"Mom," interrupted Ben, "you were going to ask about me helping."

Peter turned to look at his son, his eyes worried. "What do you mean?"

"I know the forest," Ben pointed out. "I know how Sara thinks. I could go out with a search party and help them, maybe." He looked up hopefully at Ralph, who studied him carefully.

"We'll see," the man finally said, "in the meantime, if there's anything you haven't told us, start talking."

Ben looked unwaveringly into the man's eyes. "No sir," he said, "there isn't."

The chopper continued its lazy journey above the forest, making a circle five or six miles in diameter, and then flew back and forth across the area as if it were writing notes on lined paper. Many times it paused to hover over a certain spot, and each time it did so, Ben's parents rose on their toes and gasped hopefully, as if they could almost see Sara.

Pairs of searchers began to come out of the forest and climb into the motor home, where Ralph was debriefing them. The family remained standing on the porch, too frightened to talk, watching the sky and the faces of the searchers, desperately seeking some sigh of hope.

It was becoming a hot day, and when Ben borrowed his dad's

binoculars and trained them on the stone face of Mt. Portal, he saw the air beginning to undulate along the baking surface. Suddenly a bearded white face appeared at the edge of his field of view. It vanished behind a rock outcropping and a moment later a mountain goat clambered sure-footedly across the side of the cliff, nipping at tufts of grass growing in cracks. Ben had never seen a mountain goat through binoculars before. The animal's utter lack of fear of heights was obvious. The cliff fell away for over a thousand feet to the forest below, yet the goat seemed not to notice. Ben felt a certain gust of air rise up within him, swelling his chest with courage. He glanced sideways at his fear-stricken parents, and let their grief flow through him and pass on. He listened to argumentative voices coming from the motor home, and suddenly, as if he could bear the world of the adults no longer, looked back through the lenses. The goat had stopped browsing, for it had already eaten all there was of the sparse grass. It stood with its head held high, its great curved horns spiraling backward, seeming to pose in the golden sunshine and blue sky with its four hooves rooted firmly in the massive granite mountain. There was no way this magnificent creature could fall off the mountain it was so much a part of. And there was no way Sara could be in danger in the forest she and Ben were so much a part of either, was there? The goat wandered over the top of the cliff and out of sight.

The helicopter finished scrolling back and forth across the forest and then rose, tipped forward, and flew away. Deputy Joe walked up to the family, and reassured them. "I'm sure the chopper will have some clues for us to follow. They'll relay the information to us as soon as they land, and Ralph will assign searchers to comb those areas thoroughly. We'll find Sara."

Archie put his hand on Ben's shoulder, and Ben remembered that Archie had been going to show him something. He looked up at the old man and saw a twinkle in his eyes. He thought fast, and said to his parents, "I know you don't want me out of your sight, but is it okay if I stick close to Archie for a while?"

Peter sighed helplessly. "You're not going anywhere, are you?" he asked Archie, with despair in his voice.

"No," said Archie, "I'll keep a close eye on Ben."

.   .   .

▓ Peter and Lily went to talk to the searchers beside Ralph's motor home and did not watch Ben and Archie return to the house. Archie shut the porch door behind them and opened the hall closet. "We're going down there?" asked Ben, curious.

"Yup. Hurry up now. We can't let anyone see us." He picked up a flashlight from the closet shelf and followed Ben down the steep stairs.

Daylight from the single window showed Peter's workroom was neat and tidy. "No, don't switch on the light," warned Archie. "This isn't where we're going." Ben looked at him like he was crazy. Where else was there to go down here?

"I helped your Grandpa Henry build this," whispered Archie, "a long time ago. You're about to be the only other living person who knows about it." Ben's eyes grew wide.

A few feet beneath the window, at about shoulder height, a shelf ran the length of the wall. Peter had arranged cans of adhesive, boxes of chemicals, and tools on it. All four walls of the basement were paneled in plywood.

"I'm sure glad your dad didn't put up another shelf right here," chuckled Archie. "I offered to help him set up his workshop, but he didn't want my help." He laughed again. "I was going to make sure he didn't put anything right here. Guess we got lucky." And he pulled a cigar-shaped smooth metal object from his pocket and placed it horizontally across the vertical seam between the plywood panels. He let go, but instead of falling, the metal cigar rolled down, snapped an inch towards the left, and miraculously stayed put, like the mountain goat on the cliff.

"What???" cried Ben.

"Shh!" Archie hushed him, laughing softly. "This was one of your grandpa's inventions," he said proudly. "I'll explain in a minute." He took a second metal cigar out of his pocket and held it a foot lower against the plywood seam. Once he let go, it too rolled down, then snapped smartly to the left and waited obediently in place. Ben reached out to touch it, but Archie motioned him away. "Wait to see how it works," Archie cautioned him. "I'm passing this knowledge on to you now." He handed Ben the flashlight. "We'll be needing this," he

explained. Then he took hold of one metal cigar in each hand and carefully pulled them to the right and rotated the left ends up half an inch.
When he let go again, the metal cigars stood in place once more, at the
angle he'd left them, as if held by invisible glue. They no longer crossed
the seam of the plywood panel, but waited just to the side.

Archie let out a deep, satisfied sigh. "It's been such a long time," he
said. "The air may be foul." He spread both hands on the plywood
panel and pushed. It swung evenly inwards, apparently hinged at the
other seam. Archie pocketed the metal cigars and then leaned forward
and sniffed. "A little stale, but not too bad," he grinned. "Come on in,
and bring that flashlight."

Ben followed Archie through the door and down five wooden
steps. Light from the workroom behind them revealed a cozy chamber
of shelves and boxes and small tables crowded with tantalizingly mysterious objects. "Don't turn on the flashlight just yet," warned Archie
quietly. "Just in case someone's looking through the basement window.
Here, stand behind me while I close the door and when I say, turn on
the light."

Ben held onto Archie's belt loop as the door closed with two loud
snaps, and the room was plunged into pitch black. "Light!" whispered
Archie.

The inside of the door appeared in the flashlight's beam. "See
here," said Archie, "inside these compartments"—and he indicated
two horizontal wooden boxes that crossed the seam of the plywood,
where the door had opened—"are metal bars the same size as the cow
magnets—"

"Cow magnets?" asked Ben in confusion.

Archie pulled the metal cigars out of his pocket. "That's what these
are. You get a cow to swallow one of these and it stays in her stomach
all her life, so when she swallows nails and bits of barbed wire, it all
collects on the magnet and doesn't tear her up."

Ben held the three-inch long magnet in his hand and shook his
head in amazement. "You gotta be kidding."

"No, I'm not," said Archie, and turned back to the door. "Henry
got 'em from a local rancher. See, there's a little spot right here where
the bar can be tipped up and wedged"—he pointed to the edge of the

door—"and the bar is spring-loaded, so when we leave, we can dis-
lodge it and it will spring right back into the box on the other side and
hold the door tight." He ran his hand over a metal plate on the door
between the two spring-loaded compartments. "This here is how we
shut the door. I put one cow magnet against this spot from the outside,
like a handle, and pull, then use the second cow magnet to tip the first
bar closed, and then the second. Works like a charm."

Ben was speechless. He'd almost forgotten his first glimpse of the
mysterious shelves. "Can I look around?" he begged.

"One more thing," said Archie, taking the flashlight from him, and
shining it on a capped pipe like the one he'd uncovered in the woodshed. "Let's get us some air in here!" he exclaimed, and unscrewed the
cap and set it aside. "This ventilation pipe runs underground to the
woodshed," he explained.

36

The Golden Thread

Sara had ceased to wonder if she was dreaming. In fact, she had ceased to wonder if she was awake or asleep, for these ordinary states seemed to have vanished along with the world she had known before. She sat on a quilt with her legs crossed, her hands resting on her knees, her spine straight and supple, her neck graceful and long. She had become quite used to the blue fire, in fact, she could not take her eyes from it.

Esther had gone somewhere. Perhaps down one of those passageways Sara had glimpsed when she first arrived.

It seemed like forever since she'd met Daggett in the forest. It was a comfort to know he'd be taking expert care of Bijou while she was here. The mysterious man's voice and face were almost present, as if he might suddenly appear like the blue fire had, or vanish like Esther seemed to have.

Sara wasn't hungry, although she couldn't remember eating since she'd arrived here. Her very breath seemed to sweeten each cell in her body with moisture and warmth, and then draw back, to resupply with nectar to fill her again. The blue fire began to flicker and fade, until the last sparkle dimmed to black. Sara continued to breathe in and out, the nectar of her breath making the inky darkness delicious.

Esther was still not back.

Where the blue fire had been, a pale gray fog began to take form. Sara gazed at it, her mind as peaceful and smooth as a still pool of water. Handful-sized clouds of the gray mist slowly swirled and spiraled, crowding against each other as if they needed more room. In one spot the clouds began to thin until a ragged opening grew, and Sara could see inside.

It was Ben. Ben, and Archie. Their voices were a low murmur and she could not distinguish words, but their warm tones made her close her eyes and smile deeply. They were becoming true friends, Ben and Archie. Now there were two of them to bring home. Esther would be glad.

The opening did not close, but the vision inside seemed to dissolve, and for a moment there was nothing but the swirling gray fog. When Sara looked again she saw her parents. Their shoulders were sagging. Her mother's eyes were swollen, her face streaked with salty trails of dried tears, and her fingers were in constant motion, gnashing and clutching. Her father's fingernails had left red marks in his palms, like bite marks. He was breathing heavily, and his shoulders rose and fell with anger. They were standing beside three strangers who sat on car bumpers drinking coffee and eating handfuls of trail mix. Sara's father glowered at the strangers, seething with frustration. Her mother occasionally tugged at the rear pocket of his pants, as if begging for something, but he did not notice.

Sara could not distinguish the blurred words, but the quality of the sound was unmistakably raw, gritty, and red. Sara's breath quickened and she gasped for breath. Her parents were in such agony! As her own emotions ballooned, the scene in the gray mist expanded until the figures were life size, and their words became more distinct. Sara unbent her legs and was just about to stand up and move towards her parents when they vanished. She was surrounded by blackness once more, but this time it did not feel lovely. She shivered and pulled the quilt around herself. Esther! Where was she?

A few sparks fountained upwards and arced away, vanishing. Then a few more, and still more. Slowly the blue fire pooled again beneath the sparks, and a moment later it was as Esther had first made it. But no longer was Sara entranced by the fire. She looked around distractedly and pulled the quilt around her neck, then over her head, so that just her face showed. She tried to watch the fire, but something made her twitch. Her breath went unnoticed. She began to weep.

The fire seemed to hear her weeping. It spread out like a soft blue ether, growing wider and wider, and flowed all around her, breathing its radiance through her as if she were empty space, and filling this space completely. The vision of her parents faded, and the nectar of breathing returned. When Esther sat down in front of her, Sara was once more sitting serenely, her shoulders relaxed, her head rising from her neck like a lily on its stem.

"So," Esther said. "What did you learn?"

The two ageless women gazed into each other's eyes and felt the ever-present warmth of life flow through them.

"Ben and Archie will be home soon," she told Esther.

"Perhaps," said Esther.

"My parents—" Sara hesitated. "I could not—"

"You could not stop them from being in pain." Esther finished her sentence for her. "Right?"

"Well," Sara struggled. "I didn't get a chance—" She cast her eyes inward, reviewing her experience. "It was awful to see them in such agony!"

Esther let her weep. "And Ben?"

Sara looked up and wiped her eyes. "Oh, he's fine. He understands enough to know I'm safe. And—"

"So there are two versions of reality out there. Is that right?"

Sara nodded, unsure where Esther was taking her.

"Ben's version of reality, and your parents' version."

Sara nodded, clasping her hands and waiting for Esther to make it clear to her.

"Which version is right?"

"Ben's, of course," exclaimed Sara. "I'm safe."

Esther chuckled. "You are, are you?"

Sara nodded apprehensively.

"Not if you think like that!" declared Esther, shaking her head.

"What do you mean?" pleaded Sara.

"Neither one is right, not Ben, not your parents."

Sara's eyes begged Esther for an explanation.

"Ben believes you're safe because we've given him some information. That plus his kinship with nature are enough to keep him from worrying."

Sara nodded. She understood that much. But didn't it mean he was right?

"Your parents, on the other hand, haven't yet begun to trust nature. Without that trust, we haven't been able to give them any information. So they're terrified that you've been hurt or kidnapped or even killed."

"That's right," said Sara, and began to cry. "What can I do?"

"Nothing," said Esther firmly. "Nothing. Not for Ben, not for your parents."

"But why?" begged Sara.

"Because they both believe something is so, which isn't."

Sara looked hopelessly confused.

"What happened when you first saw your parents in the gray mist?"

"I noticed how upset they were and I—I felt desperate to comfort them," she said.

"What changed in the gray mist when you became desperate?"

"Mom and Dad got bigger—until they were life-size—and I could almost make out their words—and then they vanished and everything went black. And I felt so scared, then." Sara shivered.

"And when you saw Ben and Archie?"

"Oh," cried Sara. "That was so wonderful! They were glowing with happiness, in some wonderful little cave—"

"And how did you feel when you saw them?"

"So happy," said Sara. She pondered a minute. "Not at all like I felt when I saw my parents."

Esther smiled. "What is safety?" she asked.

"Not what I think it is," ventured Sara.

Esther laughed. "Wise answer," she said, "but I want more. What is safety?"

"Well, I feel safe here—" Sara began. "I didn't at first, I was frightened, but then I read the letter and we talked and—oh, I love it here." She felt fear rising in her again. "But when I saw my parents—" Tears welled up in her eyes, but she lost interest in them and they retreated. "When I saw my parents, it was like I became them"—she reflected—"it was like suddenly walking on broken glass, when a minute before I was floating on air. Kind of like my feet were safe and then they weren't." She looked up at Esther with excitement. "Is that it?"

"You're getting very close," encouraged Esther.

"B-but, how else can I help them if I don't feel what they feel?"

Esther laughed. "Does that help?"

"Yes!" insisted Sara. "I know it does. If I skin my knee and my mom looks at me with hurt eyes and tells me she knows how much it stings, I always feel better."

"You do?" asked Esther.

"Yes," said Sara.

"You do?" repeated Esther as if Sara had not heard her question.

Sara sighed in frustration. "Well, a little anyway. My knee would still hurt."

Esther reached out and slapped Sara hard on her arm. Sara was speechless. Immediately Esther reached towards her with obvious tenderness, and touched her softly. "It stings, doesn't it?" she asked compassionately.

"Yes!" cried Sara angrily, covering the burning spot with her hand.

Esther drew back and then bent towards Sara again with fresh eyes. "Are you remembering when your arm hurt?" she asked innocently.

Sara looked up and lifted her hand from her arm. It tingled with sensation, and so did the rest of her body. The tingle was more intense in her arm, as if there was more energy there. She remembered when it had hurt. And now—this was not pain, but—an unnamed sensation. "Yeah, I kind of remember," she grinned, "but I like this better."

"Yes," smiled Esther. "It was right here waiting for you." She picked up her basket and beckoned Sara to follow her down one of the passageways. Blue light surrounded them as they moved along, lighting their way. "So," Esther began, "tell me again what you've learned."

"When I tell myself my arm hurts, it keeps hurting, almost like I'm encouraging myself with a story about my arm hurting," said Sara carefully. "When I stop saying that, there's something else, something—curious, something almost magical."

"And you're not safe when you—" Esther prompted Sara.

"When I trick myself with a story that keeps me upset about something that's already changed?"

"Very good. And what else?" prompted Esther.

"When I tell myself a story about somebody else's pain?" asked Sara.

"When you tell yourself a story about somebody else's *imaginary* pain," corrected Esther. "Mostly, pain comes from stories, from imagination."

"Is my parents' pain really imaginary?" questioned Sara. She paused to follow the river of her breathing through a few loops, and to absorb the shimmering stream of blessedness that flowed through Esther's hand into hers. Her entire body tingled with intense light, like the light she saw behind her eyelids if she looked away from the sun and closed her eyes. Only this light wasn't just behind her eyelids, it filled her whole body. "I think I'm safe here," she declared, looking at Esther, "as long as I don't walk on broken glass. When you asked me if my arm stung, you were walking on my broken glass with me, weren't you?"

Esther nodded, and added, "I was walking on your *imaginary* broken glass with you."

"And it really stung then."

Esther listened patiently, waiting.

"But a second later, when you asked if I remembered when it had hurt, it was like the scene changing in a movie or something where the whole mood shifts and the music changes and you see things differently."

Esther nodded again, inviting her to continue.

"My story changed," ventured Sara. "And when my story changed, so did my experience. All that awful broken glass went away." She was quiet for a moment. "What I liked most was how it was when I noticed what my arm actually felt like. It felt so interesting, all tingly and fresh. I liked it." She looked at Esther, who smiled at her and squeezed her hand.

"Stories have a life of their own, child, and they steal you away from this lovely, endless moment that is all we actually have," said Esther softly. "Enough for one lesson. If I give you too much, you'll arrange it into a tidy package and we'd just have to undo it. Now come along, there's something I want to show you."

The passageway ended in a spacious chamber in a warm amber hue, smooth and glowing, almost like a beach lit with gold at the end of a day. A spinning wheel with a crescent moon-shaped stool waited in the room, near a little mountain of sun-colored fiber.

"Sit down, dear," Esther invited Sara.

"I already know how to spin a little," Sara smiled. "Mom taught me."

"I know, dear," responded Esther kindly. "Thank goodness. The connection is already made, and this will be simple." She presented a handful of golden fiber to Sara. "Spin," Esther whispered. "Spin."

Sara did as she was told. The fiber rose and spiraled for her hand to become a thin golden thread, which swirled into the orifice and wrapped around the bobbin. The wheel hummed softly like a purring cat as she treadled. After a while, Sara remembered that her mother had taught her to check the bobbin to see that it was filling evenly. When she slowed her treadling to look, to her surprise there were only a few wraps of thread on it, when by now there should have been hundreds. Then she saw that the thread somehow passed out the back of the bobbin, away from the wheel, and was disappearing down a passageway, like a long tail. She looked up at Esther.

"Keep spinning, dear, and I will explain," said Esther. "The golden thread you are spinning goes to your mother."

"Oh!" cried Sara with a quick gasp of happiness.

"She won't see it," continued Esther thoughtfully, "but it will tug at her as surely as if it were attached to her breastbone, tug her deep inside, away from the broken glass of her mind, into the still pool of peace that is her home. It is a thin thread, but cannot be broken. It is already connected to your mother."

Esther motioned for Sara to stop treadling, and the wheel slowed. Esther felt beneath the vibrant green cloth in her basket as if to get something, but there was nothing in her hand when she withdrew it, although she held her fingers cupped as if they sheltered something precious. She held the precious nothing beneath the thread that ran down the passageway, and a moment later the strand drifted apart, and the two ends floated lazily to the floor. Esther planted each frayed end in the mountain of fiber. Immediately the end that ran down the passageway to Sarah's mother began quivering like a glowing violin string. Then Esther gave Sara a new handful of the golden fiber, and nodded for her to begin spinning again.

Sara watched the new thread travel around the bobbin, and saw the end rise where it had been planted in the golden mountain of fiber, and flow down the passageway. When she knew she had spun enough, she stopped. "This one goes to Dad," she said simply.

"Yes," whispered Esther. "It is all they need."

37

Grandpa Henry's House of Marvels

"Shh!" Archie hissed softly, putting his hand on Ben's arm. Footsteps were moving through the house above the basement. Although Ben and Archie were in the secret room dug into the earth off to the side of the house, they heard the sounds and froze.

There was the scraping of a chair, silence, and a moment later a low rhythmic hum vibrated into the secret room. Ben listened carefully. "It's Mom," he finally whispered. "That's her spinning wheel. It sounds like a beehive."

"We'd better get out of here while we can," said Archie. "Take a quick look around while I put this cap back on." And he carefully screwed the cap back onto the pipe, grimacing when it made a sudden loud squeak.

Ben shone the flashlight around the small oval room. It was a treasure house! The wooden shelves lining the walls were ornately sculpted with leaves and tendrils that seemed almost to be growing. Carved, amazingly lifelike animals were arranged in family groups on the intricate surfaces. There were five foxes, a father and a mother and their three cubs, all rolling and tumbling and wrestling. There was a family of bears, and another of deer. Rabbits stood on hind legs, or scratched an ear with a foot, slept, scampered down a hole in the shelf, or sat on their haunches, looking curious. Wait till Sara sees this! thought Ben. His flashlight beam paused on a shelf of dogs. Basset hounds, golden retrievers, and—bloodhounds, like Matthias! Two floppy-eared puppies nestled beside their parents, while a third adult bloodhound lay sprawled behind the others. Ben reached out and stroked the animal's satiny wood. On the next shelf there were birds of all kinds, some in flight, others curled asleep in carved nests that fit right into the leafy branches sculpted into the shelf.

On the next wall were no animals at all. In fact, there was nothing he could identify. Tarnished metal thingamajigs, festooned top and bottom with sagging tarnished roundish lumps, were stacked in a jumble along several shelves, as if Grandpa Henry had been experimenting with something that never quite worked out.

"Let me have that a minute," whispered Archie, taking the flashlight. A throaty murmur of pleasure came from him. "They're still here!" The flashlight beam revealed three acorns similar to Ben's in a corner among the animals. They appeared to be still attached to the carved oak leaves sprouting from the branch that wound across the shelf, but when Ben reached out to touch one, it wobbled and rolled into his hand. Then he noticed a piece of white paper, folded small, tucked behind a cluster of spiny oak leaves. Without asking, Ben replaced the acorn and put the paper in his pocket. "Okay," whispered Archie. "See anything else you need today?"

"Can I come back again?" asked Ben.

"I can't keep you out," whispered Archie, "but this has to last you and Sara for a long time. It's for both of you, you know. Your grandmother left it to me to tell you about it at the right time. You are not to let anyone else know about it."

This was a lot to take in. Questions popped up in Ben's head, but he just nodded. He took the flashlight from Archie and shone it on the wall with the dogs, looking for the extra bloodhound. The dog's family wouldn't miss him, he hoped. He put the small animal in his pocket.

Footsteps sounded again from above. Archie handed Ben one cow magnet and silently demonstrated with the other one how to rotate the steel bars up so they could open the door, watching while Ben copied his movements. Then Archie moved his magnet towards the metal plate to pull the door towards them. The metal plate instantly rushed towards the magnet and rang with a piercing *clink*! They froze, listening. Footsteps hurried in the direction of the hall closet. Archie quickly pushed the door closed and secured the steel bars back in place. "Turn off the flashlight," he hissed.

There was a loud clatter of feet rushing down the basement stairs. "Sara?" called Lily's hopeful voice, "Sara baby?" They listened to her walking about the room, calling Sara's name, and then weeping and climbing slowly back upstairs.

"I wish it was Sara here and not us," muttered Ben in the dark.

Archie put his arm around Ben and they waited in silence. Finally he whispered, "You'll be showing her this place sometime. Soon, I hope. Now let's try and get out of here."

Archie moved the metal bars again and then wrapped the magnet in his shirttail and held the door shut while he slowly moved the padded magnet towards the metal plate. It connected with a faint thud, and a moment later they were on the other side. "Now we're in an even bigger fix!" Archie whispered. "Your mom knows there was no one down here, so we can't just climb out like we were in here looking for clues."

"I'll go up first," offered Ben. "I can wait in the closet for a chance to slip out. I'll—" He paused to think. "I'll run the water in the kitchen if it's safe for you to come up. I know you can hear it because the pipe runs right up there." He pointed to the ceiling. "It makes a gurgling noise."

"Okay," answered Archie hesitantly. "Go."

Ben tiptoed up the stairs, leaving the basement door ajar for Archie. But no sooner had he put his hand on the closet door than he heard voices, and then the front door, only a few feet away from the closet, opened. He heard the voices of Joe, Ralph, several strangers, and his father as they walked past him towards the kitchen. Ben shrank into the corner behind the coats and jackets that hung from the rack, and pulled shoes and an umbrella against his feet and legs. His movements made rustling noises against the slick surface of the jackets, and he tried to breathe without moving so there would be no more sound.

He could hear loud conversation from the kitchen, and murmurs from the porch. Footsteps came down the hall towards him, but stopped and turned off into the hall bathroom. The toilet flushed and water ran in the sink, and Ben prayed Archie didn't mistake that for their signal.

The footsteps returned to the kitchen. Somebody on the porch went down the steps. Ben wriggled free from his coverings and reached for the doorknob again. He had opened the door and slipped halfway out when Ralph, still wearing his SAR cap, leaned out the kitchen door, facing him. "Hi, kid," he waved, and walked down to meet him. He looked in the closet. "What're you doing in there?" he asked.

Ben thought very fast. "Me and Archie were checking for clues," he said, and pulled the basement door open. "Archie, you coming up?" he yelled.

Ralph reached for the basement door. "What's down there?" he asked curiously.

"Oh, just the basement," said Ben glibly. "My dad's work room."

"Mind if I take a look?" asked Ralph.

"Oh, sure," said Ben. "I'll show it to you." He followed the large man down the stairs, flashing Archie a wide-eyed look from behind Ralph.

Ralph nodded to Archie, and began to hunt around the room, tapping on walls, looking on top of shelves, and peering out the single window. Archie remained planted in front of the secret door, casually guarding it. "She couldn't be down here," Ralph finally said.

"Obviously," answered Ben, "but we thought we might see something that would give us some kind of clue—"

"You've been watching too much TV, kid," said Ralph. "But we'll find her, don't worry." And he headed back up the steep stairs.

"Whew!" said Ben, looking up at Archie, "That was close!"

Archie had a troubled look on his face. He nodded distractedly.

"I'm worried about Sara," he said, and his voice choked. "She's—" and he quickly shook his head. Ben followed him outside, and watched him close the pipe in the woodshed and replace the cow magnets on the cross beam of the tool shed. Ben longed to reassure the older man somehow. Archie had trusted him to know about the hidden room. Was he to repay that trust by telling him what he knew? Would Archie even understand?

"I'm not feel well," Archie interrupted Ben's thoughts. "Mind if I go home for a while?"

"Oh," said Ben. "You going to take a nap?"

"Yeah," sighed Archie. "You'll phone me as soon as they find your sister?" Ben nodded, anxiously searching Archie's eyes for some sign that he could tell him more. But before he could decide, Archie had turned and shuffled off towards his car. He turned around once and waved Ben towards the house. "Go on now," he called, "stay with your parents."

Ben watched him weave through the crooked mass of strangers' vehicles to his car, parked at the far edge. A lump rose in Ben's throat, and he felt like part of his own self was leaving. "I'll phone you," he yelled, "And, thanks!" He had to stop himself from running after the old man.

38

Rupert Fox, the Trickster

Matthias lay sprawled across the slip covered sofa, watching Thea and Rupert arguing. The dog's deep-set eyes shifted from side to side in his motionless face as he followed their conversation.

"You're *not* going to do that!" declared Rupert, struggling to hoist himself out of the wheelchair on his scrawny arms. The long, tangled hairs of his eyebrows twitched, and his breath came in quick puffs.

"You're not there, and I am, Uncle Rupert," countered Thea calmly, and she bent over him to examine his teacup. "Want another spot of tea?"

"Quit changing the subject!" snapped Rupert. "Ouch!" he screamed.

"You've got to sit still," scolded Thea, as she cleared their break-fast plates. "Doc Sanders told you that broken hip won't mend if you keep jostling around like that. I'll be back with more tea." And she got up and left the room.

While his niece was in the kitchen, the old man wheeled himself down the dimly lit hall and stopped beside a bookcase. It was haphazardly stuffed with books, papers, and magazines, and badly needed dusting. He poked about until he found an old mustard-colored volume with a worn binding, and carefully extracted the book with his bony fingers. "Heh heh heh," he chuckled to himself quietly. "I'll show her."

Thea returned with a teapot and a small pitcher of warm milk to find her uncle dozing where she'd left him. She put the tea things down on a small table and tugged an afghan out from under Matthias's paws on the couch. Just as she was about to drape it over Rupert, he opened his eyes and shook his head wildly, nearly choking on his own laughter.

"Stop that!" protested Thea, smiling affectionately at her uncle. She noticed the worn book wedged between his body and the side of the wheelchair, and pulled it out. "*The Dain Curse*, first edition, 1929," she murmured approvingly, looking inside. "Wow. I've never seen one. Dashiell Hammet collectors come into our store to buy, not sell. Didn't know you had one." She looked at her uncle with arched eyebrows.

"Lots of things I've got you don't know about," muttered Rupert, eying her sideways. "And you ain't going to know about them either, if you don't listen to me."

Thea set the book down and picked up the teapot. After she had handed her uncle a full cup of milky tea and refilled her own, she sank back into the sofa beside Matthias and tipped her head to one side, studying Rupert curiously. "I'm listening."

"Are you now," muttered Rupert. "Are you now." His eyelids drooped and shut, and slowly the teacup and saucer in his hands began to tremble and rattle. He opened one eye. "You're no fun," he complained. "You're supposed to think I fell asleep."

Thea grinned. "You'll have to do better than that. I'm still listening, Uncle Rupert."

Rupert drained his teacup and thrust it at his niece. "Here, take away this danged little old lady cup. Ain't no good for a man like me. No more'n a sip. Okay. Let's see. Where were we?" He waited a moment and then peered at Thea with one eye again. "Like I said, you ain't no fun. I gotta do all the talking around here."

Thea handed him his refilled teacup and waited. "I'm listening, Uncle Rupert," she said patiently, and stroked Matthias's long ears as she waited.

Rupert took a sip and handed his cup back to Thea. "All righty." He looked lovingly at Matthias, whose large head now rested on Thea's lap. Matthias gazed back at his wheelchair-bound companion with shining eyes. "Matthias knows," Rupert began. "You can count on him. I want you to tell me again exactly what he did, and I'll tell you what it means."

Thea described, for the third time, how Matthias had tracked Sara directly to the end of the tunnel and seemed to follow her scent up into the air.

"Remember when you were a kid and we went to Flaherty's lake, where they had that rope swing out over the water?" asked Rupert. "Had Thunder then. He'd be Matthias's—let's see." Rupert counted back on his fingers. "Thunder'd be Matthias's quadruple-great-grand-father."

"I do remember," said Thea quietly. "In fact, that's what it reminded me of too."

"Course, you didn't really disappear up into the air. Your scent dispersed because you dropped into the water, way out into the lake. It would've been much tougher for Thunder to follow the trail when you swam all the way across and climbed out on the other side."

"I always wished I could've seen Thunder at Flaherty's searching for my scent," said Thea. "Remember how I used to beg you over and over again to describe it to me, like we'd finally gotten the best of old Thunder?" Thea smiled at the memory, and added thoughtfully, "Truth is, Matthias acted the same way at the end of Sara's trail. But there was no lake to disappear into."

"Yup," agreed Rupert. "It matches. So little Sara had to have gone up. Like the sky was a lake. And you're sure, now, she wasn't up in a tree?"

"She wasn't in a tree," said Thea.

Rupert rubbed his bristly chin and stared at the floor, pondering. "She's Daphne's grandchild, you know." He looked up through the salt and pepper thicket of his eyebrows at Thea. "Daphne loved to talk about those kids. How they trusted the forest—just like her. She used to tell me"—Rupert looked cautiously at Thea—"that they were in line for—"

After a long silence the old man pulled at his bristly chin, and muttered, "Hiding down the coyote's hole, that's a good one alright. But he doesn't have the girl with him. Poor coyotes."

He paused, and the grandfather clock by the stairs tick-tocked loudly in the long silence that followed. Finally the clock chimed nine times.

When it stopped, Thea stood up and collected the teacups. "I told Ben I'd be back today. I'll fix you some lunch and leave it in the refrigerator, and be back in time to make supper. I'll check with Mabel to be sure she's right next door if you need her."

"Sit yourself back down," commanded Rupert. Thea sat. "There's a thing you might be needing to know." The clock tick-tocked. "No point in looking for the girl. She'll be fine, sure as gold. There's something else more important than finding someone who isn't ready to be found." He stole a look at Thea, and was pleased to see she was staring at him with rapt attention. "And that's the trick of pulling together those people who can't see what's right in front of them."

Thea looked puzzled.

"The girl's parents, for one. Why'd you think the girl disappeared? She's pulling her parents into the forest. Daphne would've seen to that. They moved out here because of what Daphne wrote in her will, right?"

Thea nodded. "That's what I heard."

"She made it seem as though it was for the sake of the kids, and not the parents, right?" Rupert waited to see agreement in Thea's eyes. "Daphne talked to me about it. Really it was for all of them. Right now those parents are falling into a whirlpool that's going to suck them right into the forest, where they'll find something they lost long ago. Sara'll stay away until they catch a whiff of it, and then she'll be back."

"How do you know all this?" Thea inquired curiously.

"Hmmph!" snorted Rupert, clearly pleased to have the upper hand. "Been around a lot longer than you. Don't you forget that. And my name ain't Fox for nothing." He seized the wheels of his chair and swiftly pivoted and disappeared down the hall. "You get over there now and see to that Ben!" he called from the distance. "Bring that boy by for a visit if you get a chance." The toilet flushed. "And tell that old bat Mabel to stay away from me!"

39

The Homing Device

When Ben entered the kitchen, the conversation suddenly died. "Archie went home," Ben told his uneasy-looking parents, "He's sick. I figure you want to keep track of me, so here I am." Lily and Peter were sitting at the table with Joe and Ralph. Lonely-looking cups of cold coffee had been pushed to the center of the table and abandoned. Ben's mom reached out for him and he stood beside her while she wrapped her arms around him. Ben stroked her hair softly and kissed the top of her head. "I'm sorry all this is happening, Mom," he said in a gravelly voice.

"It's not your fault, son," muttered Peter, and when Ben could pull away from his mom, he went to his dad and they silently wrapped their arms around each other.

Ralph began drumming his fingers on the table, and shot Joe a sideways look, as if to say, "We need to get on with this!"

"I'll be in my room," Ben said. Ralph looked relieved.

At the top of the stairs he pulled the folded paper from his pocket and started towards his bedroom. Suddenly there was a small tug on the inside of Ben's breastbone, as if Sara were pulling, or as if he were pulling her, both at the same time. "I'll read it in her room," he thought, "if she were here that's what we might do." He closed the bedroom door and squatted in front of Bijou's cage to show him the letter before he remembered that the rabbit was missing as well. The carved blood-hound in his pocket poked his leg, so he pulled it out, and set it on the floor as his audience.

My dear Henry, began the letter. So it was to his grandfather. He'd kind of hoped it would be to him from his grandfather.

Have you made the homing devices yet? I hope my instructions were adequate. It's just that no one has ever made one before, and I wasn't sure if I'd left anything out. Just in case it's ever needed, I'm writing down the directions for using them. I advise you to keep this note with the seven acorns.

Ben reached in his pocket to pull out his acorn-flute. Seven? He had one, and he'd seen three on the shelf in the secret room. Where were the other three? His was radiant and warm from resting in his pocket, and now Ben examined it with fresh curiosity. A homing device? He thought of homing pigeons, and spy movies. He spread the paper out flat and eagerly continued reading.

As you know, the acorn may be played like a flute. One hole makes a dull sound only. This is the hole you must use if you want to find somebody. The other sound gives rise to a chorus of birds, crickets, rustling breezes, along with fragrances and such from our forest. This is the hole you use if you want to find yourself.

Really? Ben stared at the little flute. Would he be able to use it to find his sister?

I am confident that you have made the little acorn flutes properly. You and Daphne are natural students, and now fathom the secret of the treasure in a still pond. It is, of course, this secret that you have embedded in each little acorn.

Ben's heart galloped. The still pond? It's secret was embedded in his acorn? It had been this close all along?

To use the acorn to find yourself is easy. It works for anyone who loves the forest. But to find someone else, you must first find yourself. So the first step is to blow in the musical hole, and lose yourself in the beauty and beingness that flood you. To lose yourself here is to find yourself, to discover that you are that infinite beauty which the forest displays so perfectly.

You have done the first step particularly well if you forget you are looking for something. This is actually a shortcut, to forget. But if you do remember, here is the second step: To find someone else, blow softly into the other opening. Feel the path the sound takes. As you know, this hole goes to a round chamber within the flute. Here your warm breath will spin around the smooth walls, filling with essence. When your breath has become whole, it will reenter your mouth. For this reason, you must keep your lips to the hole until you feel your breath return. There is also a tiny passageway from the round chamber that winds out the stem of the acorn. A little bit of your breath flows out this passageway to connect with the person you are seeking. This connection, once made, is alive and cannot be broken, and in fact need not be made because it already exists.

Should one of the acorns fall into the wrong hands, it will seem a pretty but useless plaything, unable to make music or connections. By the time you, Henry, read this, you or Daphne will have given one of the seven to the wrong person. The others will go to their rightful owners.

Ben felt a shiver travel up his spine. He quickly checked the end of the letter for a signature, but there was none. Who could have written it? And he couldn't be the wrong person, could he? No, he told himself, Grandma Daphne would never have made a mistake.

What happens after your breath has circled the chamber and flowed out the stem to the person you seek, and returned to you, like an invisible thread, is always a surprise. There are no instructions at this point. Either you are capable of following the thread by forgetting it exists, or not.

Keep the acorns together if possible. They like each others' company, when they are not in use. But there is nothing they like more than to be given to the person they are meant for, and you will know who those people are, except for the one who will deceive you.

That is all, Henry. May you always dwell in the living stillness of a silken pond.

The letter ended here. Dwell in the living stillness of a silken pond? Ben scratched his head in puzzlement. He wasn't sure just what that meant, and he wanted to understand so badly. He was disappointed the letter hadn't given him more information. And who in the world could have written it? What about that woman who'd told his grandparents the story the day Ben was being born? How else would this writer know about the treasure in the bottom of a still pond?

Ben thought about his story. The middle brother who loved the mysterious girl, how he'd carried her into the forest and then lost her when he couldn't retrieve her lost treasure at the bottom of the still pond without disturbing the water. Of course, the girl hadn't been able to, either. And how the boy had returned home without the girl, determined to discover the secret of finding the treasure and bringing it back up without disturbing the still water, because only then would the girl return to him. But the story had ended without solving the problem, with the girl still hidden in the forest. Grandpa Henry had said this was his very own story, offered at his birth, and had challenged him to discover the answer to its mystery, as if he were the middle brother. As if he was to finish the story himself, by finding a way to retrieve a treasure without disturbing the water it lay hidden in.

Nothing made sense, really, yet Ben felt a surge of confidence and an undeniable sense of moving forward. It was as if this letter and the little carved acorn were homing devices. Like a newly released homing pigeon lifting its wings to follow an invisible path through unfamiliar territory back to its home roost, Ben felt his pulse quicken around the acorn in his hand, and the drumbeat of his awakened pulse streamed through his whole body like liquid light. In that moment his sister swam towards him in the endless pool of light, and floated before him. They swam and played together in the same easy shimmer of golden warmth that they had shared in their house in the city, the night they had first played the brand new acorn-bird-flute and had been astonished at how it transported them into the forest, right there in the city.

Ben knew that when he opened his eyes, probably Sara would not actually be sitting with him. But it was her essence, and his essence, and the forest's essence, and the sun's essence, all flowing together through him like warm breath in the round chamber inside the acorn flute, that mattered. This was the real Sara, this was the real Ben, this was the real—Ben sighed deeply—Mom and Dad. If only they knew the dearest freshness that lives deep down inside all things. If only they knew how simple and immediate it all was.

When Ben opened his eyes, only the carved bloodhound was there, watching him. He still felt Sara's presence, and the presence of the liquid light, which seemed to rise like steam from the wooden dog, as well.

Although he hadn't even tried the acorn flute yet, now that he had instructions for using it, he seemed to have already succeeded. He had found himself, and forgotten that he was seeking Sara, which the letter had said was a shortcut. He hadn't understood that then, but now it made sense. He and Sara were more connected right now than if she sat beside him. Curious, he picked up the acorn anyway and blew into the musical opening. The faint sound of voices drifting through the floorboards faded completely. Shafts of sunlight shot through the windows, and multi-colored birdcalls danced through the liquid air surrounding Ben. It was like sitting in the bottom of a swimming pool looking up through the water at the sun shimmering in a trillion little bouncing orbs of light, but now the music of the forest had joined the light, and there was an intense fragrance of wild raspberries, warm cedar bark, and swamp mist. The myriad stream of life was in infinite motion, yet a sense of stillness penetrated everything.

He'd already found himself, and Sara, but he wanted to blow into the connection opening anyway. The letter writer was right: it was very easy to forget there was a second step. Remembering to blow very softly, he sent this breath into the acorn. There was no *fftttt* sound this time. He felt the sound more than heard it, as if his spinning breath was a small curled furry creature rotating in its underground chamber, finding just the right position for a long, contented slumber. Then the movement ceased, followed by a moment of perfect, empty balance. Ben sensed a tiny tail, no thicker than a hair, flow out the acorn's stem and swiftly onward while the center breathed itself back into his mouth. The connection was made. He held the acorn in his lap and sat beside Bijou's cage, his eyes closed, taking in deep, satisfying breaths and releasing long flows of warm air, cycling in and out, in and out, as if his lungs were the chamber of contentment inside the acorn.

Knitting a Tree House

"Did you really hire Daggett to watch our kids?" Peter asked Lily.

She looked back at him with strangely distant eyes. "Yes. When I was about ten, my mother took me to pick pears in that old orchard over on the far side of town. She'd gone back to the car to get another basket, and I began wandering through the rows of trees, following a mysterious humming sound. It grew louder and louder, almost like music. Suddenly a bee buzzed out of nowhere and circled me, and then another, and before I knew it I was surrounded by so many bees that it was like a horror film. I froze, paralyzed and terrified. Too terrified to scream for my mother, because I knew if I screamed, hundreds of bees would sting me, maybe enough to kill me. In that moment I believed that my mother was going to lose not one, but two children in the trees." Lily began to shiver uncontrollably. "Then I felt hands touch my shoulders, and heard a man's voice. 'Trust me,' the stranger said.

"The hands guided me slowly forward, through the swarm of bees, and not a single one stung me. Very gently the hands kept pushing me, until there were no more bees. 'Keep going,' said the man, and the hands pulled away.

"I obeyed my rescuer. But after a moment, I had to turn around to see who it was. And to my astonishment, it was Daggett, the monster every child in town had been warned never to even look at."

Peter gaped at his wife. "Daggett?"

"Back then he used to walk into town in broad daylight once in a while, with a wicked look on his face, just to scare people."

"It could've been anyone," argued Peter.

"No," replied Lily. "It was him."

"And this is why you hired him?" prodded Peter, looking bewildered.

"Obviously," said Lily calmly. "He practically *is* the forest, but he's the good part. He saved my life. I'm counting on him now to help find Sara."

Peter shook his head. "Unbelievable," he muttered. "What a long shot."

There was a loud knock on the door, and without waiting for an answer, Ralph and Joe came in, trailed by Thea.

"I've got sixty people out there looking for Sara," said Ralph. "We've gone through all the data from the heat seeking camera we flew last night, but every warm spot they identified must've been sleeping wildlife, because we've combed through every area and there's nothing there." He glanced at his watch. "It's nearly ten o'clock now. Just to cover our bases, I want to get the TV news out here so we can ask the public to watch out for your daughter. Just in case," he murmured.

Thea gazed compassionately at the parents, who sat side by side clutching each other's hands, their faces strained and tight. "I'm sorry," she said softly, "for the agony you're in."

Ralph glanced at Thea and shrugged. "Thing is, we don't have any new leads for you to follow with your dog. That girl's spent weeks playing in the forest, and her scent would be scattered all over the place."

"I'm sure it is," agreed Thea. "But you forget that my dog can pick out her most recent scent."

"I'd like to have you around just in case," Joe urged Thea. "Seems like Matthias gave us the only clues we've come up with so far. Maybe he could sniff out something else."

"I left Matthias home with Rupert," said Thea. "I'll be glad to bring him back any time you want." She turned to Peter and Lily. "In the meantime, I thought maybe Ben and I could spend some time together. Thought I'd take him home with me, let him have a chat with Rupert, if it's okay with you folks. And give Ben some time with Matthias. Sometimes a good dog will get a boy to talking, and Ben might just need somebody to talk to."

Lily looked weakly at Thea and nodded agreement, and Peter said gruffly, "Sure, if he wants to go."

Ben's bedroom was empty, so Thea tapped on the other door. "What?" responded Ben.

"Hey, Ben, it's me, Thea. Can I come in?"

"Yeah!" He threw open the door and greeted her with an eager smile.

"This is Sara's room—?" asked Thea, as her eyes grazed the letter on the floor.

Ben bent down to retrieve the letter, folded it, and put it in his pocket. "Yeah. I was just—well, you see, it's like—there was something I wanted to show her so I came in here to find her." He gritted his teeth, sighed, and looked out the window to avoid Thea's eyes. What he'd blurted out probably sounded ridiculous, and he felt embarrassed.

"You're very wise," said Thea. She bent down and put her fingers between the wires of Bijou's cage. "So her rabbit's out there somewhere, too?"

"Yeah. Sara's going to be pretty upset if we don't find him, too. No one's even thinking about Bijou. What if something eats him? He doesn't know a thing about coyotes, or eagles."

"Maybe we'll get lucky and find both of them," murmured Thea. "Come on, I'm going to take you home to Rupert and Matthias for a while."

The yard was enclosed with high chain link fencing and it was obvious why. Matthias stood over six feet tall on his one muscular hind leg, leaning heavily against the fence, drooling and trying to suck in their scent as they approached. Thea unlocked the gate and pushed Matthias back as they went in. "It's Ben, sweetie," she told him. "You know him." Matthias immediately vacuumed both of them noisily and thoroughly and then loped off and came swinging back to play with Ben. Thea watched as the two raced around the yard, wrestling and playing tag. There was a scrabbling noise at the sliding glass door behind her and a moment later Rupert wheeled himself onto the deck. Rupert and Thea watched the boy and the dog in silence for several minutes. Ben seemed to have entirely forgotten about everything but Matthias, and didn't even glance their way. "He's a good one," muttered Rupert.

"He is," said Thea.

"Let me talk to him alone," ordered Rupert. "You go see if Mabel has any of those molasses cookies for the boy. Bring the cookies, but not her," he growled.

Rupert continued watching Ben for several more minutes. Matthias finally dropped to the ground at Rupert's feet to catch his breath. Ben was chasing the dog at such a speed that they nearly collided, but he managed to screech to a halt and collapse on the steps beside him. He stretched and settled himself against Matthias's heaving belly, but when he lolled his head back, he was startled to see Rupert peering down at him.

"Howdy."

"I didn't see you there!" cried Ben.

"I've been here," said Rupert slowly, drawing out the words and chuckling. "Like my dog, do you?"

"I love him," said Ben, hugging Matthias's huge head.

"Well, so do I," said Rupert. "No other dog like them in the world."

"I guess not," said Ben.

"We ain't got much time here, boy," said Rupert. "My meddling niece Thea'll be back any minute with cookies. And I want to talk to you. I'm going to ask you some questions right direct, and you'd best answer me right direct."

Ben stared at the old man with wide eyes.

"I know where your sister is," Rupert said.

Ben's mouth dropped open.

"I've been there myself," he added.

Ben's eyes grew wider.

"You worried about her?" Rupert asked. When Ben paused, he barked, "Just answer me!"

"Uh—no—" mumbled Ben anxiously.

"Good! That's all I need to know." The old man wheeled himself abruptly in a reverse U-turn and yanked the door open. "Thea!!" he roared. "Cookies!!" He slammed the door and wheeled back to face the astonished Ben. "Like to keep her on her toes," he grinned conspiratorially.

Thea did not appear.

"Durn girl!" griped Rupert. A big grin suddenly replaced his grumpy expression. "She's my favorite niece," he said tenderly. "A right good girl."

"Can I ask you a question?" asked Ben in a voice that sounded rather small to him.

Rupert gave him a toothy smile and nodded.

"Where *is* Sara?" Ben asked.

Rupert grinned. "Now there's a right direct question. We'll get to that later. First I'm going to teach you how to make a tree house, 'cause you'll be needing one."

Ben turned to look at Matthias, hoping the dog would give him some kind of clue or encouragement. Matthias just sighed contentedly. "Okay," said Ben. "I was planning on building one this summer anyway."

"Good!" declared Rupert. He flung the door open again and hollered, "Thea!! Cookies!!" then slammed it shut and cackled happily.

Thea appeared with a grease-stained paper bag of huge round molasses cookies, their edges and surfaces cracked and sprinkled with sugar. "'Bout time!" declared Rupert, and snatched the bag from her. "Here, boy," he said, handing one to Ben, "best cookies you'll ever have, made by an old witch." He cackled again.

Thea stood shaking her head, gazing fondly at her uncle. "Takes one to know one," she said, and took the bag away from him.

"Not so fast, Missie," warned Rupert. "Get some money out of my drawer and go buy us three hundred yards of good strong rope at the hardware store. And hurry!"

An hour and a half later, Ben lay comfortably gazing at the sky, stretched out on a rope floor he had made between two limbs of the oak tree that leaned over the deck. It had been amazingly simple. Rupert had instructed him step by step. First Ben had wrapped the rope around one branch in a long spiral, for about six feet, and tied it securely at the end. Then he'd taken the rest of the rope, which was hanging from where he'd begun the spiral, and pulled a loop through each of the coils on the branch so that they hung down like a long row of floppy rabbit ears. Rupert had pointed to the garden hose and told him to run it through the loops to hold them in place.

Then Rupert told him to pull a row of loops through the loops on the hose, and run a second hose through the new loops to hold them in place. He'd pulled out the first hose, and kept pulling rows of loops through rows of loops, back and forth, until the net-like fabric was wide enough to stretch to the other branch. Then he'd looped rope around the branch and through loops until he had a sturdy rope fabric stretching between the two branches. Rupert showed him how to tie the end securely, and then, rubbing his hands together with excitement, invited Ben to climb into his tree house.

It was easy for Ben to hoist himself up because he could grab the net-like fabric anywhere and swing his legs over the branch and flop onto the floor. "I'll show you later how to build a roof and walls if you want them," called Rupert gleefully from below.

When Ben lay down, the fabric snugged around him with perfect ease. His fingers played in the spaces between the taut loops while he gazed at the blue sky through the notched green leaves of the great oak tree.

"Know what you've just learned, boy?" Rupert asked. He didn't wait for Ben's answer. "You, my boy, have learned how to knit a tree house."

Ben sat up in astonishment. An image of his mom knitting swam before him, and another of Grandma Daphne. "This was knitting?"

"Yup," smiled Rupert broadly. "Pulling loops through loops with one long thread, that's all knitting is. But ain't too many who've thought to knit a tree house, now, is there?"

Ben stood in his knitted tree house, holding onto higher branches for support, and studied the rows of loops. He supposed it did look like magnified sweater fabric.

"Now undo it, boy, 'cause you're going to be needing it elsewhere."

"How?" asked Ben. He hated the thought of undoing this amazing structure. "Do I have to?"

"Yes. Get down first. I'll time you. Okay, undo that knot." He pointed at the final knot. Ben reluctantly untied it and stood unhappily with the end in his hand. Rupert stared at his wristwatch. "Ready, set, go!"

Not knowing what to do, Ben simply pulled. To his astonishment, as he pulled, the tree house unraveled before his eyes, and what looked like a heap of gigantic spaghetti noodles rose on the deck.

"Forty-seven seconds!" cried Rupert. "Quick, untie the last knot! Hurry! Okay, now you're up to one minute thirteen seconds." And he slapped his knee and cackled merrily. "I ain't had this much fun since—since that last time I had this much fun. It's been a while," he added wistfully.

"As you can see," he cautioned Ben with a very serious look, "a knitted tree house comes undone rather rapidly. Wouldn't want that to happen while you're in it. You've got to run a chain stitch—that's a loop through a loop all in one long line—up and down all the edges to make it really safe. You remember that."

Ben listened to his mentor with utter enthrallment. He'd completely forgotten about Sara, even about Matthias, who now lay snoring beside Rupert's feet. He was overcome with love and appreciation for the old man, and every bit of his hesitation about trusting him was gone. Then he remembered that Rupert had said he knew where Sara was. "Rupert—" he began to ask, feeling certain he'd get an answer now.

"Just a minute, son," Rupert interrupted him. "A good climber always oils his rope right away. I'll teach you how to do it up in a butterfly coil." Ten minutes later the massive heap of spaghetti was neatly coiled and tied. "There's a book I want you to have," continued Rupert. "Go tell Thea to find you *Mountaineering*. It's got a green cover and it's in my room."

Ben went inside, but Thea seemed to be gone. He ventured into one bedroom for a look. At the window, a sheer curtain floated inwards on sunlight and a warm breeze. There was a bookcase along one wall, and he bent down to search for a green binding. A red book with a picture of a bloodhound on the spine caught his eye, but the green book wasn't there.

He found another bedroom, which had to be Rupert's, because it smelled like him. Kind of peppery and warm. Behind the bed a single long bookshelf was built into the wall. It held books, rocks, dried leaves, acorns, and framed photos. Ben scanned the bindings and there it was. *Mountaineering—The Freedom of the Hills*, in a tattered green cover with white letters. He pulled it out and then studied Rupert's rock collection. One was a geode, one of those bumpy rocks with a side sliced off and polished like glass. But this one didn't have any exposed crystals in the middle like all the others he'd seen before. But he could see crystals faintly beneath the dim glassy surface, and a pale milky white blob. When he picked up the rock, the blob wobbled and swam about as if it were in a pool of fluid. As he moved the rock, the blob traveled around what he realized was a crystal ball inside the rock, with space around it. Puzzled, he turned it over to see if it had an opening for filling it with water. But it appeared to be just a rock. The blob acted like a bubble of air, moving in water. How in the world could air and water have gotten inside a rock? He hurried back to Rupert with the book and the rock, not stopping to wonder if he should have even been touching Rupert's things.

"Rupert!" he cried. "This rock!"

Rupert did not respond immediately. There was a faraway look in his eyes when he turned to Ben, and he didn't seem to have heard what Ben said, or to notice the rock or the book. Instead he motioned Ben to come closer and gazed directly into the boy's eyes. As Ben looked back into Rupert's green eyes, the green part seemed to suddenly turn molten and sink back into itself like an inhaled breath, and then return. Ben felt a deep molten mass in himself surrender and plummet, and then rise to fill his body. All this happened in moments.

Rupert's eyes twinkled and he asked, "Show me what you found."

Ben held up the mysterious rock.

"You like that, do you?" smiled Rupert. His face was serene, every trace of gruff old man gone, as if it had never been.

Ben felt tears rising and falling from his eyes, and streaming down his cheeks, as if the water inside the rock was in him too, and overflowing. He couldn't make words come out of his mouth.

"It's yours," whispered Rupert. His craggy eyebrows arched high and settled back down, and he closed Ben's hands around the rock. "On one condition. You must never disturb the water or the air inside, no matter how curious you are about them. It's an enhydrous geode agate, very rare, and the water and air inside are millions of years old. The rock in your hands holds air, water, earth, and sunlight."

Tears continued to stream down Ben's face. His lungs filled with air and his face was awash in water, like the rock.

Rupert patted him on the shoulder. "I can see how glad you are. You're very welcome."

Ben smiled.

"And this book"—Rupert patted the green book—"it'll teach you more about using a rope, and a lot of other useful things as well. You're a mountain boy, and you need a good mountain book."

They sat in silence for a long time, and Ben's tears made the glassy surface of his rock glisten. Rupert showed him how to hold the geode up to the sun, so that the fiery light shone through it and illuminated the crystals and water and air.

When Thea opened the gate and walked into the backyard with a bag of groceries, she found Ben sitting peacefully at Rupert's feet, leaning against his legs, while Rupert's hand rested on the boy's shoulder. Matthias looked up from Ben's lap and gave a long contented groan.

"I'll put these things away and then I'd better take you on home," said Thea.

Rupert waved his hand at the rope, the book, and the rock, which was still clasped in Ben's hand. "Don't forget any of your stuff," he said. "And come back soon."

Namasté

High on Mount Portal, a blue light peeked out from an opening in the steep rock face. Twenty feet above, the mountain goat and her two youngsters were grazing on oat grass and sedges. They grasped the tough greenery between their teeth to yank a mouthful free, then chewed and chewed. *Rip, munch, rip, munch, rip, munch.* The sky was clear and blue and bright up high on the gray cliffs, and little waves of heat curled upwards, ruffling the white hairs on the goats' legs as they chewed. A current of warm air streamed up the face of the mountain, carrying with it small sounds from below, which arrived as distinct and clear as if they had not traveled from a thousand feet away. The bright splashing gurgle of the stream that ran along the forest floor into the pond rose up the mountain, and made the goats thirsty. The voices of two searchers examining the ground near the mountain's base drifted up to the goats too, but the animals paid them no attention.

We've been through here before," said one searcher.

"She's not in these woods," said the other. "We would've found her by now. Hate to say it, but I'd drag that pond if I was in charge. Poor kid."

One of the young goats looked out across the sea of treetops to follow a raven's flight. The black bird landed in the top of a fir tree that rose so high above the others that it appeared to be growing from the surface of an evergreen sea. As the raven folded its wings, a shaft of sunlight glinted through an empty space between two wing feathers. The mother goat bleated and trotted over the rounded tops of the cliffs into the stubby trees that grew along the mountaintop, to lead her children to the stream that fell away on the other side.

.   .   .

Just inside the mouth of the cave in the mountain, where blue light seeped out over the forest, Sara and Esther stood viewing the world. When the faint *rip, munch, rip, munch, rip, munch* from above stopped, Esther took Sara's hand and led her back into the cave.

"You heard the voices?" asked Esther.

Sara nodded. "They're looking in all the wrong places."

Esther's face curved in a wry smile. "Curious, isn't it?" and handed her basket to Sara.

The girl ran her fingers over the soft cloth that billowed up from inside. "Ben isn't looking for me at all, though. He knows what we know."

"Yes, he does," smiled Esther. "He's had some interesting teachers down there. When you go home, ask him about the quicksand." They drifted into silence for a long time, and then Esther spoke again. "Can you think of something you really want?"

Sara searched inside herself for an answer, but couldn't find one. "Not really," she murmured.

"Good," replied Esther. "Can you remember wanting something in the past?"

"Sure," said Sara. "Bijou. I saved my allowance to buy him."

"Would you like to see him now?"

"Yes!"

"Well, look inside the basket then," suggested Esther.

Eagerly Sara pulled aside the green cloth, but before she could reach in with her other hand, both the basket and the cloth vanished. Sara looked at Esther suspiciously. "Where's Bijou?"

Instead of answering, Esther asked, "What do you love most about Bijou?"

"His furriness," said Sara. "Not just his outside fur, but the warm furriness of his invisible self."

"If I told you to look inside the basket for Bijou's invisible self, would you?"

Sara looked at the basket that had reappeared in her lap as if it had never vanished. "No," she said slowly. "It doesn't fit in places like that. It's—it's sort of everywhere." She paused. "In fact, Bijou's invisible self feels just like the invisible self of a flower, or you, or my parents—"

"And if I were to tell you that you could open the basket and find your Bijou in there, but with his invisible self missing, what would you do?"

Sara gaped at Esther in horror. "I wouldn't want him."

"Oh," said Esther. "And which Sara are you parents looking for?"

Sara stopped breathing. "My invisible self," she whispered, and tears began to stream down her face. "But they're trying to track my body self. They've got it all backwards."

"Have they lost your invisible self?"

"No," whispered Sara. "They've never been this close to my invisible self before. It's hard to tell," she added, "where my invisible self ends and theirs begins. I don't think there's a difference."

The basket grew heavy and toppled over in Sara's lap, and Bijou's invisible self hopped out, wearing his rabbit costume.

"When you looked for Bijou in the basket the first time, you pictured his body, didn't you?" Esther asked.

Sara watched her pet hopping about the cave and nodded.

"And the basket vanished. Why?"

When Sara looked at Esther, a smile shone from inside her. "Because I was looking for the part of Bijou that isn't *real*."

Esther nodded and waited for her to continue.

"Bijou's body goes lots of places, but only one place at a time. His invisible self is everywhere, always. It's the only part of him that doesn't change. I knew his invisible self in me already before I got him. It's what my Grandma Daphne calls 'the dearest freshness deep down in things.'"

"Yes," replied Esther. "Yes."

"But my parents," said Sara, "shouldn't they try to find me?"

Esther chuckled. "Absolutely! But what causes them to suffer so much is that they think they need to find you," and Esther pointed at Sara's body, "in order to have the invisible you they love."

"Isn't that strange?" murmured Sara.

"Look at your rabbit for a minute," said Esther. Bijou hopped towards Sara and she picked him up and rocked him in her arms like a baby, pressing her cheek against his silky fur. "Now look at me," Esther ordered.

Sara looked up, suddenly aware that the sensation of Bijou's body in her arms had vanished. In its place an upwelling glory streamed in all directions.

"Do you miss him?" asked Esther.

"No," Sara smiled at her empty arms. "He's here."

"Namasté," whispered Esther. Stars pulsed and sparkled in the black sky outside the mouth of the cave. "That is an ancient Sanskrit word which matches what you're feeling."

The Tree of Many Apples

❋ Thea and Ben peered up to watch a news helicopter churning through the sky as she drove Ben home. "Probably getting aerial shots for the evening news," Thea commented.

The crowd of vehicles in the Maclennon's driveway had spilled out into the road, and now included two wide, windowless motor homes, each brightly painted with a different TV news station's logo. The sun was low in the sky, shading Mount Portal's face, and the trees at the edge of the forest pierced the trampled meadow with long pointed shadows.

Thea turned off the engine but made no move to get out. Neither did Ben. The geode still rested in his hand, and the heavy coil of rope lay on the floor at his feet. The bag of cookies sat on top of the green book on the seat between them. Thea lifted the bag and chuckled at a large grease stain the cookies had left on the book's cloth cover. "I own a used bookstore with a friend," she told Ben. "That's what I do for a living when I'm not taking care of my uncle. If I were in the store, I'd shake my head and think what a pity it is for a first edition book to get stained and drop in value. But here, now, it means something entirely different. It's a mark of the wonderful time you had today, so it's a *good* stain."

Ben grinned at her, and then looked back out at the crowd of vehicles and TV news station motor homes with their towering antennas. They seemed so out of place. A few days ago it had been just he and Sara with the forest all to themselves. He'd scarcely set foot in the forest since then, and yet here he was full to overflowing with the familiar bliss he normally sought there. Maybe it was everywhere.

What a contrast there was between the anxious world of frantic thinking and the vast, wondrous universe he knew as his true home, and that Thea and Rupert also seemed to inhabit. "Well," he turned to Thea, suddenly curious to see what was happening in the world of fear, "shall we go in?"

As they opened the door to the house, Ben had a fleeting recollection of Esther's earlier warning. Would he disturb his inner peace when he stepped through this narrow door? The question dissolved as he moved fluidly into the house, with Thea behind him. The hall seemed dim and narrow, and the painted wood that framed the kitchen door glowed yellow from within.

"Ben!" cried his mother when he appeared. A dozen serious-looking strangers, including several cameramen, heavily loaded with equipment, suddenly stared at him. He recognized a reporter from the evening news. "You're back just in time to help us," whispered his mother.

"They say people respond best when they see the whole family," explained his father in a thick voice.

Joe put his arm around Ben's shoulder. "I know this can't be easy for you, Ben," he said. "I—I've got a boy at home myself." His voice caught and he cleared his throat. "At this point we think your sister was probably taken somewhere, and we need the public to help us find her."

Ben shuddered, and looked around at all the people watching him. Some looked away in embarrassment, and a woman rapidly scribbled something on a note pad. Their eyes were tight with fear and the bleak conclusion that Sara had been forcibly carried away by some awful person. Was there a way to communicate to these people what he knew? Each pair of eyes he looked at for an answer was shuttered and dark with gloomy belief. "What do you want me to do?" he asked his parents.

"Just stand with us," his father answered, "Just stand with us while we talk. You don't have to say anything unless you want to."

"Let's get started while there's still enough light," encouraged one cameraman. "I'd like to get the mountain in the background." The news crew guided the family outside and into the meadow, where Ben stood in front of his parents, who pressed their arms across his chest, as if to protect him from whatever had taken Sara.

A reporter took a position beside the family, and raised the microphone. "As this Wednesday evening draws to a close, the Maclennon family awaits word of their twelve-year-old daughter, Sara, whose picture you see here." The reporter held up a photo of a grinning Sara, her reddish blond hair in braids, sitting in a swing. "Young Sara Maclennon was last seen Monday by her thirteen-year-old brother, Ben, when they went exploring in the forest." He gestured towards the trees. "Search and rescue volunteers have combed the area since then, but without success. A bloodhound and a helicopter also failed to locate her, and authorities believe that the girl has been abducted." The reporter paused for effect. "And now her parents want to talk to you."

Ben's parents tightened their hold on him and their out-of-sync, rapid heartbeats drummed chaotically into his back. His mother spoke first.

"Help us find Sara," she whispered into the microphone. "Please."

"She's about this high," added Peter, holding his palm near Ben's ears. "Sara's friendly and trusting and—" he couldn't continue. No one spoke for a moment.

The reporter turned to Ben. "Ben," he asked, "could you tell us how your sister disappeared?"

Ben looked up at his father, whose face seemed to indicate that he could do whatever he wanted. "I really don't know." He shrugged his shoulders. "I still think we'll find her, safe and sound."

"Well, we certainly hope you're right. No secret forts out there?" asked the reporter.

"Not yet," answered Ben.

"What's the next step?" another reporter asked Ralph, who had put on a jacket with "Search and Rescue" emblazoned across the front before the camera turned to him.

"We'll keep looking through the immediate area and beyond," Ralph replied, shaking his head sadly, "but I suspect we won't find her here. The search has got to move out across the state. The girl could be anywhere. I'm sending my exhausted searches home and bringing in a new crew tomorrow, though, just in case we've missed something."

"Sounds like the best hope right now is for all you viewers to keep a sharp eye out for any sign of this girl." The reporter held up Sara's picture again and stared solemnly into the camera, speaking to the audience in their cozy homes. "Call your local law enforcement agency right away if you spot her, or have any helpful information. We'll be updating this story as news breaks."

Friend and Wife peered over the edge of their nest at their master in his roost a few feet below. His eyes were closed, and he was curled up with one very swollen foot propped up high.

"Quorrrk?" asked Friend, but there was no answer.

"Rmblrmblrmblrmble," Wife warbled to their master, but he gave no sign of hearing her affectionate greeting. She looked at her mate, and a moment later he flew off.

The crowd dispersed and Ben followed his parents into the house, thankful that Thea followed too. The searchers were lining up in front of a large Red Cross motor home, and Ben thought he smelled meat loaf. Normally his mom would have dinner on the table by now, but instead she sank into a chair and laid her head on the table and sobbed. Thea opened the refrigerator door and rummaged around, pulling out containers of leftover food, and an onion. Ben showed her where the pots and pans were, and soon she had the onion sautéing. "Got a can of tomatoes?" she asked.

"Sara'll be home soon." Ben tried to comfort his mom, patting her heaving shoulders. "I know she will." He was pretty sure of that, but as he tried to communicate it to his mother, the words withered and narrowed, until by the time they reached her, they had no substance left.

"You're my good boy," sobbed Lily.

"Are you going to finish Sara's socks before she gets back?" he asked his mom. Lily looked up at him. "Knitting for Sara might help you feel better."

Lily dragged herself out of the chair and followed Ben into the living room. She looked around in confusion. "I don't know where I left them," she finally said listlessly.

"Sit down, Mom," insisted Ben, and he rushed out to find the socks. A minute later he handed them to her. "Can I watch you?" he asked, eager to see another kind of knitting. She nodded and picked up the needles. Her fingers picked up speed as she pulled loops through loops across one half of the sock, then let that needle dangle on its cable while she pulled loops through loops with the other needle. The yellow sock was growing upwards, with a branching fir tree design that grew from the foot up the leg. "Sara wanted a tree," Lily told him. "She likes trees."

Ben was itching to try knitting this way too. It seemed so tiny after the tree house, where the yarn was rope and the needles were hoses. "Could I try?" he asked.

"Wait until I get to a plain spot," his mom responded. She handed the sock and needles to him and watched him curiously. It was a little awkward at first, but he knew what he was after—loops through loops—and he knit along to the end of the plain spot and handed it back to his astonished mom.

"You figured it out so fast!" she marveled.

"It's easy," said Ben. "Loops through loops, all with one long thread that never ends, right?"

"I guess so," said his mom, her needles clicking away, "I never thought of it that way." At the end of that needle she held the straw-colored sock at arm's length to admire it. "Sara's going to love these, don't you think? I can almost see her pulling them on her feet."

Thea appeared in the doorway with a wooden spoon in her hand. "How about some supper?" she asked.

"Come on, Mom," urged Ben, taking the knitting out of her hands and pulling her up. "You can knit more later. If you know enough you might even have them done by the time Sara comes home, or maybe— I'll have to help you."

"It's called 'Leftover Soup,'" Thea explained as they all sat down. "My mom used to make it every Friday and it was never the same twice, except it was always good."

"You'll have to stay in touch after we get Sara back," said Lily. "I know she'd like you." Then she put her head down and wept.

"I will," answered Thea. "I've enjoyed getting to know your son. He's a fine boy." She smiled at Ben. "Rupert thinks so too."

"I wish you'd bring your bloodhound back. Couldn't he try one more time to find Sara?" Lily asked in a timid voice.

"I'll bring him back tomorrow morning," Thea said. "It's worth a try. I've still got the scent articles sealed up." She looked at Ben. "You an early riser?"

"Yeah!" he replied. "Real early."

"Tell you what. I'll be by with Matthias a little before dawn. If you're up you can come with me. He knows you now, and if you stay behind me it ought to be fine." She turned to Lily and Peter. "Okay with you if I take him along?"

They looked at one another and nodded. Thea looked at her watch and started to get up, but Lily motioned her to sit back down, and took a deep breath. "Wait. I want to explain something." She turned to her son. "Ben, I once had a baby brother."

"You did?"

"His name was Michael. Baby Michael," said Lily. "He's buried out under the apple tree in the meadow. That tree is thirty-four years old, same age as Michael would have been if he'd lived." She wiped away a tear.

"He died?" Ben asked.

"My parents were still building this house when it happened," Lily continued. "I was five years old. I was sitting on the plywood floor while the frame was going up around me, playing solitaire jacks," she smiled sadly. "I've never played since. It was a sunny day and Archie and Dad were working, hammering and sawing away. Mom had gone for a walk in the forest without me. For some reason I hadn't wanted to go with her that time. I've always wondered if that's why it happened—" Lily gazed off into the distance.

"Going for walks in the forest with Mom was my favorite thing back then." She smiled at Ben. "Just like you and Sara. Until that day." Again she looked into the distance, and fresh tears streamed down her cheeks. "The ravens were squawking like crazy and maybe that's why we didn't hear her at first. There I was, playing my solitaire jacks, dreaming of the baby brother or sister I'd soon have who could play with me so it wouldn't be solitaire anymore, when suddenly my mother with her swollen belly appeared at the edge of the trees, screaming, holding onto her belly like it would fall off if she didn't hold it there. Dad and Archie ran to her. I chased after them and then I saw what had happened. A monster had attacked her. There was blood all over her legs, and she had a look in her eyes I'd never seen before, and she seemed to look right through me. They wrapped her in towels so I couldn't see where she'd been bit, and in seconds we were all in the car driving like crazy to the doctor. When we got there, Archie's wife, Martha, came and got me and took me home with her. I was too scared to talk. I thought my mommy was dead."

Peter handed his wife a box of tissues. She blew her nose and went on. "Three days later my parents came home from the hospital. They told me my baby brother Michael had died before he could be born. Archie and Martha helped us bury him in the meadow, and they planted the apple tree over his grave so we would always have him." She broke down and sobbed and sobbed. "But we don't have him. We never had him. We lost him."

"Dad grafted a new variety of apple on Baby Michael's tree every year on his birthday. None of us could ever bear to eat a single one of the apples. It would've been like eating Baby Michael." She shuddered, and Peter laid his hand over hers.

"I guess I'd been a happy little girl up until then," Lily said. "My parents adored me, or at least I thought they did. But after that they seemed to turn hollow, like walking shells, like their insides had emptied out. Archie and Martha helped them finish the house and we moved in, even though I was terrified. I was afraid that the monster that ate my baby brother and tried to kill my mommy would get me, too. I couldn't trust my parents after that, or anyone else. By the time my parents recovered and turned their attention back to me, it was too late. I hated this house, and most of all, I hated the forest."

Everyone looked out the window towards the forest.

"And now the monster has Sara," Lily's voice stuck in her throat. "My baby Sara."

"What kind of animal did it, Mom?" asked Ben.

"I never found out!" she cried. "Mom had a miscarriage. But no one thought to explain that to me. No one talked about what had happened. We hardly ever talked about Michael except when Dad grafted new apples. So to me there's always been a monster in the forest, who eats babies. Since I never knew what it looked like, I imagined the worst."

"So Grandma Daphne didn't get bit?" asked Ben, looking worried.

"No, honey," murmured Lily. "I guess not. But I didn't figure that out until I was a lot older, and by then the damage had been done."

"Oh, Mom." Ben began to tremble. "That's horrible."

"Sometimes I talk to Baby Michael," Lily whispered. "I have ever since he died. It feels like he's there, like a warm thing you can't see, but you can feel. I've been asking him to bring Sara home."

"Why didn't you ever tell us about this?" Ben asked. "We could've helped you."

"I don't know," muttered Lily. "I knew I'd tell you someday."

The Yellow Socks

"Let me do the dishes, Mom," insisted Ben. "You go knit." When she started to argue, he shepherded her back to the couch and handed her the growing sock. As she resumed pulling loops through loops again, she relaxed visibly.

"You're right, honey," she admitted. "This makes me feel better. It feels like Sara's with me, and loves her socks. Do you really think she'll be home soon to wear them?" Lily's face shattered with her question, and she sobbed into the wool.

"You have to finish them before she gets home," urged Ben. "Imagining the worst doesn't get you anywhere, but knitting the socks so you feel Sara close by helps you a lot. And who knows, maybe it even helps Sara." He handed her a box of tissues. "I'm sure Baby Michael would agree, right?"

Lily sniffled and blew her nose, then accepted the sock from Ben. He waited until she resumed knitting, and left to do the dishes.

Friend landed on the edge of their nest with a piece of meat from one of the food caches he and Wife had stashed in the trees. He fluttered down to Daggett's roost and began to prod his master's mouth open so he could feed him the strip of rotten deer meat. Above, Wife fluttered approvingly as the immobile man twitched and suddenly jerked his eyes open.

Daggett stared wildly for a moment into the eyes of the heavy raven standing on his chest with a stinking strip of carrion hanging from his powerful beak, before he realized he was awake. Hot sharp pain was hammering through his swollen foot and up his leg, and he gasped for breath.

At the sight of his hungry master's open mouth, Friend bent forward and stuffed the rotten meat down his throat. Wife hummed a happy sound from above.

Daggett gagged and vomited over the side of the nest, nearly choking on the slimy mess. Friend cocked his head to study him sadly, and flew up to join his wife. Together they leaned over the side of their nest to watch their uncooperative master.

"Water!" croaked Daggett in Ravenese. "Water!" This time Wife flew away.

While the sink was filling with hot sudsy water, Ben pushed the window open to gaze out at Mount Portal and the forest, taking in deep draughts of evergreen-scented air. Poor Grandma Daphne! And Grandpa Henry, and Mom. Why hadn't anyone ever told them about Baby Michael before, not even Grandma Daphne? Memories of standing here beside his grandmother returned, of her sending the heavenly smell of her freshly baked bread to the mountain to remind it that it wasn't really missing its front end. Had she been thinking of Baby Michael when she did that? He wiped away a tear. No freshly baked bread, he thought, looking around the kitchen, but there are a few biscuits left. He broke one open and set it on the windowsill, then blew on it to send its fragrance to the mountain. Small crumbs scattered from its soft surface and bounced through the window.

The sun had set and the mountain's face was darkening, although there were no stars showing yet. Ben's hands moved through the warm slippery water and he was scrubbing the inside of a mug when a small blue light winked at him from high on the mountain face. He stopped scrubbing and remained still, waiting and watching. There it was again, in the same spot. And a moment later, a third time.

There were no more flashes of blue light after that. Ben continued washing the dishes and listening to the faint clicking of his mother's knitting needles. He couldn't understand how doing dishes had ever seemed a burden. His hands swam through the silky warm water, rubbing the dishrag against the smooth, curved surfaces of plates and glasses, up and down the even tines of forks, the strong handles of knives, and over the billowing backs of spoons. In that moment, the dishes had become as wonderful as the forest.

When he finished he went and sat beside his mother. "Can I do some more?" he asked, and added, "I'm glad you told me about Baby Michael. You can talk to me about him anytime you want."

Lily smiled gratefully at her son, tears streaming down her face again. She reached a plain spot and handed him the sock. He knit across the needle and handed it back. For the next hour they took turns knitting Sara's sock. Peter came in from outside where he'd been talking with the searchers, sat down and watched them, then went back outside.

"Rupert taught me to knit today," Ben told his mother after a while, as he expertly knit across the plain spot.

"Really?" she asked.

"Yeah," laughed Ben. "We knit a tree house."

"I see," replied Lily doubtfully.

"If you ever want to come out in the forest with me, I'll show you how," Ben offered. "Really. You'd be good at it. It's the sort of thing you and Baby Michael would have done together."

"I'd like to do that with you and Sara," she answered, and dropped the knitting in her lap. "I'm so scared," she cried, and began to moan quietly while rocking back and forth, clutching herself.

Ben picked up the sock and began knitting the tree section. "We'll knit a tree house together, Mom," he said. "The three of us. You'd better give me some help with this part."

There were no searchers pressing through the forest that night. When darkness fell, the original crew had gone home exhausted, to be replaced in the morning by new volunteers. Everyone hoped that fresh eyes might spot something the others had missed, but no one held much hope. Ralph, also exhausted, had already gone to sleep in his motor home.

"We'd better get some sleep," Peter suggested. "There's not much anyone can do in the dark. They'll phone us if any leads turn up from the evening news."

·   ·   ·

✳ Ben lay in bed beside his open window, sniffing the spicy night air and listening to the delicate rustle of mice and other small nocturnal creatures outside. To his mom, after Baby Michael died, these night sounds must have sounded huge and terrifying. But to Ben, it meant that the forest surrounded him, which gave him indescribable joy. He heard footsteps on the stairs and his father crept in and sat on the edge of his son's bed.

"You're not asleep yet?" Peter asked.

"No," said Ben. He could tell his father was struggling for words, so he reached out for him. Then Peter made a choking noise, and put his head down on Ben's chest and began to weep. Ben patted his father gently, and held him. When Peter sat up, he tried to apologize. "It's okay, Dad," Ben said comfortingly. "I'm glad Mom told us why she's been so afraid."

"Yeah," sighed Peter heavily. "Maybe tomorrow will be a better day. I'd give anything to have Sara back."

"She'll come back, Dad," whispered Ben. "She will. You're not going to be out there grafting apples."

✳ When the moon rose after midnight, all three Maclennons were asleep. Seven miles away in Cedarwood, Rupert lay in his bed snoring almost as loudly as a lawn mower, while down the hall Thea somehow slept through it. Matthias dozed upside down on the couch, his soft belly rising and falling, his three legs sticking out in three directions, and one long ear flowing over the cushion so that its soft fur spread out on the carpet.

A few blocks away, Deputy Joe lay awake and troubled. He rolled carefully out of bed so he wouldn't disturb his wife, and tiptoed down the hall to look in on his four-year-old son, anxious his child might also be missing. A night-light illuminated the sleeping boy, and his white pillow seemed to cradle his face like reverent hands. Joe kneeled beside the bed, ran his fingertips along the boy's glowing cheek, and wept.

✳ When the round moon moved silently out from behind the trunk of the maple tree outside Ben's window, it shone full in his face and woke him up. He opened his eyes and closed them again, but did not fall back to sleep right away. The blue light he'd seen on the mountain while washing the dishes reappeared behind his eyelids. Instead of winking, the light held steady, and grew larger.

When Ben awoke a second time, the light was gone, and the moon had moved out of sight. He felt deeply rested, and lay still for a moment, enjoying the feeling. Then, with nothing in mind, he pushed his covers aside, swung his feet to the floor, and dressed in the dark. Downstairs, he filled a glass of water as quietly as he could at the kitchen sink. As he stood there drinking, the blue light on the mountain face winked at him. He waited, and it winked a second, and then a third time, and then no more.

Thea and Matthias will be here by dawn, thought Ben. I'll tell her about the blue light and we can go find it. He glanced at the clock on the wall. It was only a little after two. There were hours to wait.

Ben crept down the hall to the open door of his parents' bedroom and listened to their even breathing. Could he? Yes.

He began to write a note to Thea to hang on the door where she'd be sure to find it if he wasn't back by the time she arrived. *Stay on the main trai —*, he began, and stopped in the middle of a word, filled with sudden excitement. She didn't need directions to find him! Matthias could lead her directly to him, if Ben left them a scent article. He crept back upstairs and rubbed a dirty T-shirt between his hands and over his face just to be sure it had plenty of his scent. He stuffed it into a plastic bag like he'd seen Thea use, sealed it, and sat down to write a new note.

Dear Thea,
I'm gone already. I'll explain when I see you. Have Matthias
bring you to me. My shirt is in the bag for him to smell. Thanks.
Your friend, Ben

Ben put the note and the shirt in a grocery bag and wrote *Thea* on it in big block letters, then hung it on the porch doorknob. He put on his shoes, got his jacket, and backpack, then slipped noiselessly out the door to the tool shed to get his rope. There was an old hose coiled in one corner, and he used a pair of garden loppers to cut two pieces. With an awl, he poked a hole in the end of each length and threaded a piece of strong garden twine through for a handle, so he wouldn't drop them once he got up high.

Only Ralph's motor home was left in the driveway now, and its windows were dark. Ben tiptoed through the meadow, past the flattened spots where tents had been, and into the welcoming trees, moving as surely and gracefully as a stream of water.

When Lily first stirred from her slumber to the sound of her son moving around the house, she'd smiled contentedly. She drifted in and out of sleep, savoring the sweetness of following him with her heart. Maybe today she'd finish spinning the yellow wool for Sara's socks— or had she already finished? Sara's socks—something puzzling tugged at her. She and Ben had been knitting them together, that's what it was! Had it been a dream? For a split second her heart grew warm with the cozy memory, and then a lightning bolt of pain shattered her warm heart into shards of ice. Sara—was she still missing? Lily sprang out of bed and hurried upstairs to see if by some miracle her daughter had come home and was asleep in bed.

Peter awoke to the sound of footsteps pounding upstairs, and then listened to the sobs that came from Sara's room. Lily's raw pain invaded his already bleeding heart and he pulled the blankets over his head and shivered with grief.

"You'll wake Ben," Peter told his wife a few minutes later, pulling her to him on Sara's bed. "Shh."

Lily sadly shook her head. "He's already up."

"Where is he?" asked Peter.

"Let him go," said Lily. "I think he's going into the forest."

Peter studied Lily's face for a long time. "I'm going downstairs," he finally said. "Will you come with me?"

They stood together in the dark kitchen window, looking out at the meadow and the forest, and at the silhouette of the mountain against the moonlit sky. A moment later Ben passed beneath the window. In the silvery light his parents saw his glowing face and how he gazed expectantly at the forest. He was wearing his backpack, and carrying some things as well—a large coil of rope and two curved sticks over his shoulder.

"He has to go, doesn't he?" murmured Peter.

Lily nodded, trembling.

They watched their son disappear into the trees.

"He's our bloodhound," whispered Lily. "We've had all the experts looking for Sara, but they don't know what Ben knows."

"And we don't know what Ben knows," whispered Peter. "Let's trust him."

✳ Shortly before dawn Thea found the bag with her name on it and carried it to her truck. She smiled as she read the note. It was what she had expected. Ben knew his sister and could follow her instinctively better than any bloodhound, if she was ready to be found.

"Come on, Matthias," she told the eager dog pressing against the door of his traveling cage. "Let's go see what Ben finds."

✳ Archie had hardly slept all night. His cold was getting worse. It was too early to phone and check on Sara. He got up and made himself a cup of tea and stirred a big glob of honey into it the way Martha used to do for him when she was still alive.

✳ In a few hours the fresh search crew would arrive, and Ralph would give directions again.

✳ The forest was just as Ben had left it. The scores of people trampling through the underbrush and up and down the trails, calling Sara's name, had not disturbed its infinite life force. The birds were still asleep, but the leaves rustled in the breeze, sounding almost like a feathery rainfall, blending with Ben's footsteps and his steady breathing. Beneath the small sounds lay a vast sea of silence.

He turned off the main path and headed directly for the tall tree he'd climbed the summer before. In the pale moonlight he had to move more slowly now. If only I had a nose like Matthias, he thought, then I could follow my own trail. His thought dissolved in a pool near his breastbone and he began moving more swiftly, pulled forward by some inner thread.

At the foot of the massive fir tree, Ben untied and splayed out the rope as Rupert had showed him, so it wouldn't tangle. He secured one end of the rope and the two hoses to his backpack, and hoisted himself into the tree.

Halfway up he paused to rest and catch his breath. He was still beneath the surface of the sea of trees, but soon, he knew, he would rise above them, able to see in every direction.

He kept climbing. The cut ends of the hoses jammed against branches and had to be knocked free, but the rope rose up with him like a graceful candle flame.

His hands and legs were sticky with sap now, so that he had to pluck them free from the bark every time he moved. The resin smelled like the very essence of the forest, and flooded Ben's senses like concentrated, pure fuel. The last stars of the night began to twinkle above him as the nearby trees fell away, and the sight of dawn over a sea of trees spreading out in all directions below renewed him so that he felt as fresh as if he had just begun to climb. The face of Mount Portal leaned towards him, as if it were curious about this creature rising out of the evergreen sea just as the moon was silently sinking beneath it.

Lily had made a pot of coffee and taken her cup into the living room. She finished Sara's first sock and wove the end of yarn into the cuff. When she cradled the golden foot in her arms, it felt so alive, as if Sara's very being shimmered in the warm wool. She laid the first sock in her lap and began the second. As the sock grew upwards, it gathered the same shimmering Sara-like energy, or was it Baby Michael-energy? And Lily felt a longing for Ben, her son who calmed her and knit with her. She wept with gratitude, and when her mind snuck in and attempted to lure her with terrifying thoughts about Sara, she remembered what Ben had told her and just pulled loops through loops, watching the new sock take shape around her invisible daughter's foot.

Peter came inside, rubbing his hands together to warm them. "I wish I knew more about the forest. I want to go in myself, but I'm afraid I'd get lost." Lily smiled at him through her tears. "We need to learn more," he added, and went to get a cup of coffee and then sat beside her, quietly watching the yellow sock grow. The steady rhythm of Lily's hands soothed him, and the yellow sock seemed to somehow contain Sara. He could not take his eyes away from it.

Silver to Gold

※ Ben discovered that it was a lot easier to knit a tree house standing on a deck than it was perched hundreds of feet up in a fir tree in moonlight. But once he got going, he flew through the rows of loops. Attaching the knitted fabric to the second branch was tricky, but he succeeded, and heeded Rupert's solemn warning about securing the fabric with a chain of stitches up and down the sides. By the time he tied off the last chain, there was only about twenty feet of rope left. He secured the hoses and his backpack with it, and then hoisted himself up and over onto the strong surface.

His sudden move shifted his weight away from the center of the tree, and instantly the trunk leaned to one side and rocked wildly back and forth, like a ship in high waves. Ben clung to the rope net with his fingers and dug his feet into the loops. Then he realized that the ends of the two branches were leaning closer together so that the fabric cupped him almost like a sling, and unless the whole thing unraveled, he was as safe here as he was on the ground. He lay secure and euphoric in his cradle at the top of the world, as the birds in the forest awoke and began to color the dawn with their merry morning songs, and the dewdrops on a spider web in the branch above him shone silver in the moon's glow.

※ Matthias had sucked up Ben's scent from the plastic bag and instantly pulled Thea nearly off her feet and into the forest before she could give the command, "Find!" Finally she managed to halt him and they proceeded forward at a more reasonable speed. Matthias loped along with his nose to the ground, making a continuous sloppy

vacuuming sound, while Thea followed, watching the path and looking up at the slowly lightening sky as if expecting something.

※ "Can I come back again?" Sara asked Esther, as they stood at the
mouth of the cave together.

"Yes." Esther smiled. "The real learning is not in here, though, but
out there."

"Look," cried Sara, "that's our kitchen light! Someone's awake in
my house. I wonder who?"

Closer to the mountainside, the top of the tallest tree was slightly
bowed, and swaying. Sara had begun to peer curiously at it, and
opened her mouth to comment, when Esther took her hand and pulled
her back into the cave. "Come," she murmured, "There's a little more
spinning to do before you go home."

When they arrived in the spacious chamber at the end of the passageway, two spinning wheels awaited them. Beside each was a heap of
golden fiber. One spinning wheel was already revolving, drawing a
golden thread from the heap of fiber beside it, and the thread flowed
from behind the wheel down a passageway that Sara didn't remember
seeing before. Before she could ask a question, Esther guided her to
the stool beside the other wheel and indicated that she was to begin
spinning.

When Sara sat upon the stool, she felt strangely thick and stiff, and
when she tried to raise her arm to reach for a handful of fiber, she
could barely budge. She managed to turn her head to look up at Esther,
who was studying her closely as if trying to determine something. She
did not look in the girl's eyes or respond to her inquiring look.

Sara closed her eyes then, and followed her own breathing, which
seemed to be flowing naturally in spite of her rigid body, patiently
carving out a passageway like an underground river inside a cavern.
The river became warmer, as if sunlit, and the shores felt softer, like
warm sifting sand, and slowly her senses revived and the warmth
spread to every cell of her body, so that she shimmered with light. Then
her hand rose without her intending it to, and gathered a cloud of
golden fiber and she opened her eyes and began to spin. Or rather,
spinning began.

Esther sat at the other wheel now, and both wheels hummed and whirred like giant bumblebees. A strand of golden thread flowed from each wheel down the new passageway.

The music of the spinning wheels slowed and ceased. The heaps of fiber were nearly gone, but the twitching and pulsing in the thread flowing down the passageway continued, although more gently now. Esther rose and took one handful of fiber from each heap and let them fall and drift together on the floor. Immediately the little pile grew tall and wide, and a third spinning wheel appeared beside it.

"Where do our two threads go?" Esther asked her apprentice.

Sara did not know, so she waited. "Oh!" she said. "One goes to the city, where we used to live. And the other goes to Grandma Daphne's house, where we live now."

"Yes." Esther nodded. "I don't know where this thread is going to go," she explained, touching the third spinning wheel. "But you will spin, and it will go where you go." She nodded. "You may begin."

Sara began to spin. Or more accurately, spinning began. Before Sara could take a handful of fiber, or set her feet on the treadles, there was fiber in her hand and the wheel was spinning and pulling a thread from her hand, and then her feet joined the treadles, pushing and releasing, pushing and releasing. She leaned forward to see where the thread was going, and forgot to pay attention to the fiber in her hand, but it didn't seem to matter. The golden thread flowed from behind the wheel and disappeared into a whirlpool-shaped hole in the floor. She got up and peered down into the hole, while the wheel continued to spin without her.

※ Matthias arrived at the foot of Ben's tree and leaped up against its trunk and vacuumed it excitedly. He stretched as high as he could to taste more of that wonderful Ben scent. "Another one went up, eh?" remarked Thea. Matthias finally gave up and lay down panting, and Thea took off her backpack and poured water into a bowl for him, then took a long drink from the bottle herself. "Good job, Matthias!" she praised him, and handed him a biscuit. Matthias snurfled the treat from her palm, rubbed his head against the tree, and sighed a deep rumbling purr.

.   .   .

※ "I'm going out into the forest," Peter told his wife. "I promise to stay on the path so I won't get lost."

"Are you going after Ben?" asked Lily. She was working her way up the leg of the second sock now.

"No," insisted Peter. "I trust him. I'm going after—after myself." He shook his head in confusion. "All I know is that I just have to go into the forest. I can't believe how little time we spent there with our kids when we had the chance." Lily looked pained. "We just didn't realize," explained Peter. "We had no idea how important it was."

"When will you be back?" Lily called after him as he hurried down the hall.

"I don't know!" he cried. "I'll come back when I find what I'm looking for." Lily stood at the kitchen window to watch her husband disappear through the half-light into the woods. She threw the window open and almost called out to him to be careful, but stopped herself. Instead she listened to the first birds singing tentatively in the silence-washed dawn, and let the chilly air blow across her face, refreshing her skin like cold water. She refilled her coffee cup and carried it back into the living room, and continued to knit the final, highest branches of the tree on Sara's second sock.

※ Ralph rinsed his toothbrush and checked his watch. The new crew ought to arrive any minute.

※ Even in the delirium of his fever, Daggett knew he would die if he didn't get water. Wife had brought him a second helping of carrion, but he'd been alert enough to keep her from shoving it down his throat. He'd hoped they would somehow understand his request for water and come back with their mouths full of the precious liquid, but it hadn't worked out that way. His whole leg felt like it was on fire, and the pains were shooting into his chest now as well, but he had to somehow climb down this tree unless he wanted to perish here. Or he might fall and die that way. What did it matter anyway? He was homeless now, and finding and losing his Daphne-girl seemed to have been the torture of a cruel dream.

Seizing a branch with each hand, he lowered himself, one-legged, onto the broken stump of a branch below, and his foot slipped, smashing his bad leg so hard against the trunk so that he nearly lost his grip. Quicksand, he told himself, relax or die. Finally he managed to work his good foot onto the stump and rest before venturing again towards the ground, which looked incredibly far away.

Ben found he could sit up very comfortably in his tree house. In fact, no matter what position he took, the rope net seemed to shape itself around him and support him, so he adjusted himself to face Mount Portal. He'd discovered it was best to move slowly, so the tree only swayed lazily when he shifted his weight. It was probably already too late to see the blue light, if it flashed again. Then something dark moved on the face of the mountain. Ben wished he'd brought his dad's binoculars. He stared hard at the dark shape, which stretched wider and arched against the gray rock. It was a bird, a large black bird, who must have been perched on the side of the mountain. It flew towards Ben.

Matthias stood up against the tree on his one hind leg again and threw his head back. A long warbling howl curled out from his throat and spiraled into the trees and the sky, long and lonesome, hollow and full at the same time, as if he were calling home a long-lost love. A mile away, Peter heard it and stopped. Shivers coursed up and down his spine. He hurried towards the sound.

"There's one last thing," said Esther, standing beside Sara and looking down into the whirlpool-shaped hole beside the spinning wheel. "No matter what happens, return to the shimmering sensation. Rest into stillness. It will communicate with others, when you cannot."

Sara nodded.

"If you should forget, this golden thread will always remind you with a little tug right here." She laid one fingertip lightly on Sara's breastbone. "Here," she invited Sara, "take a hold of the thread and try to break it."

The golden thread was still flowing swiftly from the wheel, but when Sara touched it, it stopped. She held it in both hands, then gave it a fierce yank. It didn't even stretch.

"So you're all set now, right?" questioned Esther.

"I think so," whispered Sara.

"Then off you go!" cried Esther, and as she embraced her apprentice, the girl vanished in her arms, leaving only a fading blue light.

Ben heard Matthias's call from below and trembled. "Not now, boy," he murmured softly, "wait." The raven continued to soar straight towards him. It carried something in its beak, something that glinted gold in the first bright rays rising from the sun beneath the horizon. The raven's shining treasure seemed to trail out behind him all the way to the mountain like a thread.

Peter was lost, and he knew it. When he'd heard the dog howl he'd forgotten to watch where he was going, and now the trail was nowhere in sight. He hugged a tree.

Ralph stood on the Maclennon's empty porch, drinking lukewarm coffee from his thermos. The family must still be mercifully asleep. But where was the next crew? He frowned at his watch. Every daylight minute was valuable.

The raven glided directly towards Ben, as if sliding down from the mountain on an invisible string, and at the last minute swooped up and landed on the branch above him, where the dewdrops had been glistening silver on the silken threads of the spider web. As the raven came close, Ben saw that it had a missing wing feather, and in that very moment the sun's great circle lifted above the horizon and flooded the silvery spider web with golden light.

The raven cocked its head to peer at Ben with one beady black eye. Its stout beak was empty. What had happened to the treasure the bird had carried? Ben crept to the edge of his rope floor and twined his fingers through the net to secure himself, then leaned far forward to see if it had fallen and caught on the branches below. The tree-top bent with him at an alarming angle, like a ship about to take on water.

Suddenly the treetop righted itself, and steadied. Ben felt the rope net tighten beneath him and pull up and back as if something heavy were making the other end sink towards the trunk. He turned to see what it could be, and beheld a grinning Sara sitting cross-legged, holding tightly to the rope net with both hands to steady herself. The raven had perched on her shoulder, and after having nipped her lightly on the cheek, it flew off.

"This is awesome," said Sara. "Did you make it?"

"Yeah," replied Ben. He stared at his sister. Finally he added, "Nice view, huh?"

"Beautiful," agreed Sara as she looked around. "I had a good one, too."

Matthias leaped up on the tree trunk again with renewed vigor, snarfling and snurfling the delicious scents that were drifting down. Thea pulled out the plastic bag that held Sara's scent article and put it under Matthias's nose. He lifted his head towards the sky to suck at the air, and howled again.

"Guess we'd better climb down," suggested Ben. He untied his backpack and strapped it on. "I'll go first," he offered. "Be careful. We're probably not supposed to be up here."

A few minutes later Ben dropped from the lowest branch to the ground and reached up to help his sister. Thea stood to the side, watching them, smiling widely, keeping a tight hold on Matthias's leash. When both kids had landed safely, she released the dog and he eagerly vacuumed them, hungrily going from one to the other until he was satisfied. "Matthias is a real bloodhound!" Ben told Sara proudly, and showed her how to gather lush handfuls of his silken fur and let them run through her fingers like water.

"Let's get you guys home," said Thea, and she reached out her hand to Sara. "Hi. I'm Thea, and I'm real happy to see you."

"Is Matthias yours?" asked Sara.

"Nope," answered Thea. "Belongs to my Uncle Rupert. You'll get to meet him, I'm sure."

Peter thought he heard his daughter's chattering voice coming through the trees. *I must be dreaming,* he told himself. And there was Ben's voice too, and Thea's, and that strange sucking sound the dog made wherever he went. He must be imagining Sara's voice. At least they could show him how to find the way home.

Trembling, Lily held up the sock. Only a few more rounds remained. Would Sara—?

Ralph had the new searchers lined up and as attentive as students on the first day of school, while he explained his procedures and expectations. He finished and began pairing people off. "You in the blue shirt, work with the guy in the horn-rimmed glasses. Get a couple radios from the box. Lady in the ponytail, you're with yellow-cap over there. Green windbreaker—"

Everyone froze at the sound of someone hollering in the forest. A man's voice. Who in tarnation had gone in early? wondered Ralph. "Saraaaa!" cried the voice. It wasn't a searcher's cry, but a shout of jubilation and astonishment.

"Everyone stay put and study the map," ordered Ralph, pointing to a roll of paper. "I'll be back in a few minutes." And he sprinted towards the sound.

Lily wove the last bit of yarn into the cuff and balanced the yellow socks upright on the palms of her hands. Sara seemed to stand in them and fill them with her invisible self. In the kitchen Lily set them upright on the windowsill looking out upon the forest, the mountain, and the new crowd of searchers milling around.

Then Lily heard the shout. It was Peter's voice, and he was crying their child's name with such joy. Could it be? She rushed out of the house in her robe and slippers, past the bewildered searchers, and disappeared into the trees.

.   .   .

◼ Esther stood in the mouth of the cave listening to the cries of celebration below. The raven swooped down at her feet, and she accepted
the acorn from his beak. "Thank you," she said, and smoothed the
feathers on the top of his blue-black head. She lifted it to her mouth
and blew softly into one hole. No sound could be heard, only felt.

◼ Ralph dismissed his new crew and notified the authorities that the
missing girl had been found. He had trouble explaining how, though,
and finally, in exasperation, told the officer on the other end of the line
to ask the family himself, and hung up. On his way out he met Archie
on the gravel road and rolled down his window to tell him the good
news. Archie thanked him profusely and accelerated towards the house.
On the final curve, he almost collided with Thea, who confirmed that
yes, Sara was really home, and explained that she had to get back to
Rupert because a very frustrated Mabel had phoned to say her uncle
was being a jackass, and wouldn't even let her through the door.

◼ Fifteen feet above the ground Daggett fainted, lost his hold, and fell.

◼ In Grandma Daphne's living room, Peter looked at his beautiful
daughter nestled next to her mother on the couch, and asked her for
the tenth time, "You were in a tree?"

"Mmm-hmm," she responded, pointing her yellow toes and waving them in the air. "I love them, Mom," she gushed for the tenth time.

"How'd you—are you sure you were in a tree?" he repeated.

"Ask Ben." She smiled.

"She was in the tree," Ben agreed. "I'm not sure how she got there,
but she was in the tree, and we came down together."

"What about Daggett?" Peter asked. "Matthias trailed you through
a tunnel and into an underground house on his side of the forest."

"Daggett saved Bijou's life," said Sara. "He was wonderful."

"But how'd you get from Daggett's house to the tree, darling?"
Lily asked.

"I have no idea," laughed Sara. "There are passageways every-where."

❋ "She'll tell us more tomorrow, don't you think?" Peter asked his wife that night as they lay beneath their comforter, filled with the simple joy of knowing both their children were safely asleep upstairs. "How in the world could she have been in a tree for almost three days?"

"She'll explain it later," answered Lily. "I think she's just so happy to be home."

"She hasn't noticed that Bijou's missing yet," groaned Peter.

"I know," sighed Lily. "Let's not bring it up, okay?"

"Remember that book about the woman who lived in an old-growth redwood tree in California, to protect it from loggers?" Peter continued.

"Julia Butterfly," offered Lily.

"Yeah. She was in that tree for a whole year."

"I might have read some of it to the kids," suggested Lily. "I don't remember. You think it gave them ideas?"

"Who knows? I don't think Sara has a clue what she put us through. Do you think we should thank Daggett?"

"Probably," Lily murmured sleepily. "Good night."

❋ "So, Sara," began Joe the next afternoon. He'd courteously waited until later in the day so the family could have their time together first. "Can you tell me how you got lost?"

"Was I lost?" said Sara.

Joe hung his head and gave her a look that begged her to be serious.

"To me it was a journey," she said, "not being lost."

"A journey?" asked Joe.

"Mmm-hmm," Sara nodded happily. "Daggett helped me in the beginning and then I went on."

"Where did you go?"

"Up," Sara answered thoughtfully, looking off into the distance as she spoke. "It's really hard to explain."

Joe sighed heavily. This wasn't going to be easy. He stared at the blank space on his report form, imagining what would happen if he wrote down Sara's vague words. "So you climbed a tree?" he tried prompting her.

"I'm not sure," replied Sara thoughtfully.

Joe turned his frustrated face towards Peter and Lily, who sat nearby. "Is she always like this?" he asked.

"Sara," demanded Peter, "tell Deputy Joe exactly what happened. We had a huge team of people and all kinds of expensive equipment out here looking for you and they have to know where you were, so they can learn from it."

"You just didn't look high enough," Sara murmured.

"Where were you exactly?" demanded Peter again.

"On the mountain, and in the tree," answered Sara.

"On the mountain?" exclaimed Joe. "How in the world could you have gotten up those cliffs?"

"I don't know," replied Sara. "It was easy." She smiled.

"Where'd you sleep? What'd you eat and drink?" Peter pushed.

"I slept a lot," explained Sara. "Even when I was awake, it was like sleeping, like a dream. I don't remember eating or drinking."

"She's always been a very dreamy child," offered Lily.

Joe was chewing on his pencil. He took it out of his mouth and asked, "Has she ever sleep walked?"

Peter and Lily looked at one another. "No."

Joe just shook his head and turned to look pleadingly at Sara. "Sweetheart," he tried, "I'm so happy you're home safe. That's the main thing. But my God, following a stranger home like that, out of sight of anyone who might help you, was incredibly dangerous and you must never, ever do anything like that again. You and your parents have had a long talk about that, right?"

Sara nodded.

"Good," sighed Joe. "But now I have to fill out this report and my boss is a very serious man. I've got to write something that makes sense. Please, can you tell me more?"

There was a soft tug at Sara's breastbone and she felt the familiar current of shimmering light purr and swirl through the vast space within her. She reached out to touch Joe's hand lightly, her eyes warm with innocence, and instantly he felt an overwhelming blossoming of presence, like standing in a shaft of sunlight in a cathedral of tall trees in the forest, and it blocked out everything else in that moment. When he blinked, Sara was still looking at him and he blinked again. The presence remained, and he took a deep breath. "Oh," he said.

Sara reached out to lightly touch her mother's and father's hands, and Ben's, then sat back with her hands in her lap, smiling at everyone radiantly.

The only sounds were the whispers of breathing and the ticking of the clock on the wall.

"That's where I was," said Sara quietly. "It's hard to explain, as I think you can see. But it's right here."

"Go!" Rupert told his niece. "Find him. Don't even bother looking in his underground home. He'll never trust that place again."

"I'll just follow Matthias," replied Thea, showing her uncle the plastic bag containing Daggett's woolen hat.

"Hurry now," urged Rupert. "If he was shot, he could be in bad shape. We shouldn't have waited this long."

· 4 5 ·

A Riddle Unraveled

✳ "Do you hear that?" Lily whispered to her husband. She poked him in the ribs. "Peter! Wake up! I hear the kids!"

"Mmmm," protested Peter. "Stop that."

"Shh! Listen!" Lily demanded. The stairs were creaking. "They're sneaking out in the middle of the night!"

"No they're not," murmured Peter, and rolled over and resumed snoring lightly.

Lily thought she heard the hall closet open and close. "Peter!" she pleaded in a louder voice. "They're going out!"

"They wouldn't dare," murmured Peter. "Go back to sleep."

Lily listened suspiciously, then got up and checked the shoes beneath the hallway bench. They were all there. She started up the stairs, but the house was so still that she sighed and returned to bed, where she poked her husband again. "I guess you're right," she said.

"Mmm," muttered Peter.

"Wasn't that weird what Sara said about Bijou yesterday? 'He's not in his cage anymore, but he's here.' Should we have her talk to a psychiatrist?"

"Not unless you go to one too," said Peter.

"I can't help worrying," Lily replied, and snuggled up behind her husband.

✳ Daggett groaned and tried to roll over, but couldn't get his body to respond to his commands. A dull pain flooded him as he tried to remember what had happened. The tree, he'd fallen out of the tree. How long ago had that been? The hard ground he'd smashed into had gone soft, like quicksand after a long struggle. He had a vague memory of a dog and a woman, and then he fell back to sleep.

Ben had retrieved the cow magnets and uncovered the pipe in the tool shed the day before. Since they couldn't risk going into the secret room during daytime, he and his sister had agreed to wake up in the middle of the night to visit Grandpa Henry's House of Marvels.

Sara held the flashlight as her brother wrapped the magnets in his T-shirt to silence them, and slid them down the plywood seam until they clung to the metal bars on the other side. A moment later he pushed the door gently open and took the flashlight from his sister. "You go first," he offered, lighting the wooden steps for her.

Sara stood speechless, gaping at the leafy shelves of animals. The foliage and creatures seemed to be holding their breath, as if any moment they might resume moving. "It's like Aunt Eva's underground garden," she whispered.

"What?" asked Ben.

"Grandma Daphne's great-great-aunt," explained Sara.

"I never heard about her," replied Ben. "Underground garden?"

"It's in my letter from Grandma Daphne. Look, Ben, look at this rabbit's eyes, how they connect with you, just like Bij." Then she carefully lifted a plump robin from its nest, and found three small eggs set among sculpted twigs and leaves. The eggs wobbled in place when she touched them with her fingertip. "This must be Grandpa Henry's Forest Inside," she whispered, staring at a raven, all its feathers intact.

"I want to find out what's over here," murmured Ben, shining the flashlight on the wall of tarnished metal thingamajigs.

Sara followed the light. Something stirred in her the moment she saw the jumble of metal forms. Her right hand clenched around the memory of the small paper-wrapped object that had come with Grandma Daphne's letter. She felt tender young leaves growing around it, and the stiff shape in her clenched fist softened, to be replaced by the tickling sensation of tiny roots darting every which way as they sought nourishment for their green tendrils above. And then her fingers fell limp again, and empty. "I'm not supposed to see this wall yet," she told Ben slowly. "You can, but don't tell me about it." And she sat on a stool in the middle of the small room, with her back to her brother. "Take all the time you want," she added.

"Okay," muttered Ben with disappointment. How could he not tell her what he had just now discovered? Which one should he put in his pocket? He held one in each hand, weighing them against each other, then held them side by side. Finally he put back the one with three sliding metal balls, and lowered the other one into his pocket, where it clinked.

"There might be more letters hidden somewhere in here, you know," he suggested to Sara before they got ready to leave, trying to tempt her to look around a bit more.

"I know," she replied simply. "They'll wait."

A light appeared, like the light that was so familiar at the end of his tunnels. Daggett smiled and leaned towards it. But what were those voices?

"Since we're all here, your mother and I would like to know what you want to study next year for home-schooling," announced Peter at breakfast the next morning. "We'll follow the school calendar of 180 days." He glanced at his wife for confirmation.

"Yes," continued Lily, "this will be new for all of us, won't it? It's important you keep up with your peers for when you resume regular school a year from now. You'll need to be ready for eighth and ninth grade then."

"You mean you're not going to sell the house?" Ben burst out.

"I don't know," replied Lily. "Not for now, anyway. I'm—not as afraid as before. My baby came back." She smiled at Sara.

"Well, I know what I'm interested in," said Ben. "I want to learn more about bloodhounds, and I have a book on mountaineering that Rupert gave me, full of science, like geology, and physics, and botany. Math, too, I think. I want to read it and learn everything in it. I think Rupert has some books on bloodhounds he'd let me borrow, too. And I want to learn more about rope, like I want to know how to make rope, and more about knitting, net-making, things like that. And I want to learn to carve."

Peter nodded approvingly. "Well, there's a good start. Glad to see you're including some recognizable school subjects. We'll make a checklist to be sure we cover them all. And how about you, Sara?" He looked happily at his daughter. Ever since she'd returned, every time he laid eyes on her he was flooded with relief and joy.

Sara toyed with her scrambled eggs and dripped a bit of raspberry jam on the point of her toast triangle, then watched it hang, swell, and drop onto her plate. She looked up at her parents with an expression so fresh and innocent that they waited expectantly for her words. "I have no idea," she surprised them, and bit the end off the toast. "I like everything," she explained as she chewed. "Could I just choose day by day?"

Her parents sighed. "I don't think so," replied Lily. "You're going to have to choose topics, like Ben. You both need a complete curriculum."

"Okay," agreed Sara, "I'll try."

"And maybe I can help Rupert take care of Mathias when Thea leaves," continued Ben. "He's going to need someone to walk him, and I could ride my bike over—"

"Or we could drive you," offered Lily.

"And Rupert has a lot to teach me too," Ben muttered. "He's had a very interesting life."

"I'd like to learn stuff from him too, and Thea, if she's around," said Sara. "They remind me of someone."

He must be back in the coyotes' den now. His bizarre nightmare of bright lights and mechanical sounds and being trapped inside a room full of grim strangers wearing masks seemed to have passed. And his leg didn't hurt anymore. In fact, there was a strange transparent quality to it, as if it had become ghostly, like the mist that feathered his pond summer mornings. Daggett wrapped his arms gratefully around the warm furry coyote who had curled up next to him and drifted back to sleep.

"I think we should get Mom and Dad to come with us once a week or so," Ben said as he and Sara left to spend the day in the forest. "They can be our students. This home-schooling thing ought to apply to them, too, don't you think?"

"Yeah. They have more to learn than we do," replied Sara.

When they stopped beneath Watchful One, the great oak tree, Ben pulled Grandpa Henry's acorn flute from his pocket and held it beside a cluster of acorns growing on the tree. It was hard to tell the difference, except that his had holes.

At the pond they stopped to crouch down and watch the movement of life. Turquoise dragonflies darted here and there over the glossy water, snatching tiny insects from the air. Fish surfaced to swallow insects and the occasional dragonfly with a splash, and the damp, soft fragrance of the pond and its teeming life filled Ben and Sara.

Ben watched the tiny movements on the surface of the pond, movements he was powerless to stop long enough to reach for a mysterious treasure beneath. The pond *was* movement itself, it seemed. Maybe after Sara read his letter, she could help him find a way through his riddle. "Let's go," he urged her, and they picked their way around the edge of the pond to the sloping bank, and passed through the cleft in the boulder and came out into the small meadow on the other side.

"We'll see if it's here," said Sara, kneeling beside a stone and taking the trowel out of her backpack. "I've found that things appear and disappear quite a bit." Ben knelt beside her, eager to trade letters at last.

"Not yet," murmured Esther.

Sara looked up with a bright face and flew into her teacher's arms.

Ben's mouth hung open. Esther lifted her arms from Sara and opened them to Ben. He moved into her embrace, and felt himself disappear and then reappear.

Esther pulled the trowel from the ground. "Let's leave the letter here to grow," she smiled, and eyed Ben's pocket, where his letter was waiting. "It's not time to share them yet."

The three sat in silence for a while, and the movement of life sang and twittered and buzzed around them. Finally Esther asked, "Do you have any questions?"

My riddle, thought Ben. But before he could speak, Esther had drawn his eyes into the liquid of her own. "You already I know the answer," she assured him. "It has nothing to do with the pond. Where is the treasure, really?" And then she smiled and touched his hand.

In that instant Ben felt as if his body had no boundaries, as if he was teeming with infinite life just like the pond, or the swamp, flooded with the exquisite joy and beauty of each molecule shimmering within him. Was this the treasure? If so, he had it already, had been enjoying it all along, and it wasn't hidden in the pond at all.

"Yes," nodded Esther, and as Ben looked at her he saw no point where he ended and she began. The treasure was everywhere, always moving in stillness, and nothing was disturbed.

"Sara, how about you?" Esther asked, turning to her. "Any questions?"

Sara shook her head. "We already have it all."

"You do. You both know how to return Home," agreed Esther. "But you will lose it now and again, I assure you, sometimes for so long that you'll think Home is far, far away, unreachable, instead of right here where you are. You'll think the Forest Inside is outside, and you'll look there. It is the way of the world. And when you do run astray, feel in here"—she touched her breastbone—"for the small tug of golden thread. Let the forest breathe its infinite self inside you. Let the pond shimmer inside you. Let the quicksand release you. Move from here out into the world." Then she lifted a stone from the grass, uncovering flattened white roots and white blades of grass, all streaming towards the light at the edges. There, where the blades had grown out of the stone's dark embrace, they were a sudden brilliant green. "Know this," Esther told them, "There is *always* the dearest freshness deep down in things."

"We're going to be home-schooling this year," blurted Ben. "Will you—"

"—be one of your teachers?" laughed Esther.

Ben and Sara both nodded vigorously.

"You two are your parents' teachers now," responded Esther, smiling. "You may read each others' letters from Grandma Daphne when *your* students have learned how to return Home." Her eyes twinkled. "Nature will help," she promised. "Hand me my basket, will you, Ben?"

He hadn't noticed it before, but there it was, beside him. The green cloth rose and fell lightly as if it covered a sleeping animal's belly. Yet the basket felt light as dandelion fluff. He passed it to Esther.

"You'll need this," she told Ben as she took something from be-neath the cloth, and handed him a small, very heavy bundle wrapped in the same green cloth. "You'll know when. And Sara, this is for you." She handed Sara another small green bundle, which moved within its wrapping. And then Esther stood up, shaking her head firmly. "No," when her students tried to follow, and glided backwards until the trees swallowed her up.

Matthias sneezed and gave his great big head a wild shake, flinging long elastic strands of saliva across the room. Daggett curled against his side and dug his fingers into the dog's silken fur. Strange, how ghostly his hurt leg had become, almost like a dream rather than a leg. He slowly opened his eyes at the sound of a woodpecker, or was it a knock?

"Lily's here to say thank you," Rupert informed him. "You and Matthias make a marching pair now," Rupert chuckled. "Two wild creatures who lost a leg." He wheeled his chair to the door and called out, "He's awake now."

Acknowledgments

I wish to thank my publisher, Connie Kellough, whose constant support and presence helped birth *Treasure Forest*; Eckhart Tolle, author of *The Power of Now*, for encouraging me to write this book and for meeting me in silence; my daughter Jenny and son-in-law, Fernando, for their loving faith in me and my forest; my parents, for delighting in my passions; Kim Norton, for uncovering jewels while pulling loops through loops; Ev Tuller, for weaving Esther's mysterious green cloth; Sheriff Bill Cumming, for taking my search for Sara seriously, and sending me after a bloodhound; Susan Paine, for welcoming me into the world of bloodhounds; Thunder, her magnificent three-legged bloodhound, for winning my heart and making Matthias real; Bruce and Jen Conway, for lending me Tom Brown's wilderness books and watching everything with shining eyes; my former student Steffan Iverson, for engineering a model of the secret door and asking me if I had to revise the novel because I got a "C" on it; his sister, Genevieve, for providing me with insider information about sibling quibbling, and wanting to be Daggett for Halloween; my sister, Diana, for her illuminating insights; Bijoux the Bichon, for appearing as Bijou the rabbit; my buddy Ethan, for being Ben in and out of trees; Howard Kellough, for his early and lasting enthusiasm; Mary Kellough, for opening my eyes in so many ways; Elaine Pretz, for wonderfully picayune proofing; and Quinn Gillespie, for capturing a thousand words in a single drawing, again and again.

I thank the hundreds of students I've had, each one utterly original, whose untamed nature and spontaneity have delighted me more than anything I can think of, and whose honesty rigorously trained me as a writer; I hope you'll accept my final revision and not make me redo my homework.

And to the one who slipped my mind as I wrote this, thank you for the moment we shared, when something passed from you into my heart and from there into the book. I hope you find it and know it is ours.

About the Author

Born in San Francisco in 1951, **Cat Bordhi** spent part of her early childhood in a small village on the edge of the Black Forest in Germany, where she became utterly enchanted with nature. Returning later to the United States, she continued to cherish, explore, and learn from her natural surroundings.

She was educated at the Universities of California, Santa Barbara, and Western Washington. Her life narrative, like her writing, is both intricate and compelling: extensive travel in her younger years, significant life and health challenges, deep personal and spiritual exploration, and dual careers as a textile artist and award-winning school teacher.

Cat currently resides in the Pacific Northwest, where she continues to live closely with nature while guarding her privacy.